Books by Matthew Lowes

Fiction

The End of All Things (2018)
Journey to Elara (2025)
Dark Mage of Midgard (Coming in 2026)
Crypt at Maleistria (Coming in 2027)

Spirituality

That Which is Before You (2020)
When You are Silent It Speaks (2021)
A Billion Fingers Point at the Moon (2022)
Lighting the Sacred Fire (2024)

Games

Elements of Chess (2012)
Dungeon Solitaire: Labyrinth of Souls (2016)
Dungeon Solitaire: Devil's Playground (2018)

Praise for *The End of All Things*

"Taking its own unique place among iconic SF quest stories like William F. Nolan's *Logan's Run* and Robert Silverberg's *Downward to the Earth*, *The End of All Things* is a well-written tale with a heart. The world building is deftly realized, and the lure of mystery so compelling that the book is hard to put down. Pulling off the magic trick that was a hallmark of Ray Bradbury's works, Lowes takes you through the darkest of human potentials without letting you lose your affection for humanity. A marvelous read."
     —Stephen T. Vessels, Author of *Fall of the Messengers*

"Took me right back to my early teens and late nights in Ohio watching old drive-in monster movies. I loved it!"
     —Eric Witchey, Author of *Beyond the Serpent's Heart*

"It kept me hooked from the beginning all the way through to the mind-bending end."
     —Mary E. Lowd, Editor of *Roar* magazine

Journey to Elara
Three Earths: Book 1
/ Matthew Lowes
ISBN 978-1-952073-08-3 (pbk.)

Empty Press

matthewlowes.com

JOURNEY TO
ELARA

Three Earths: Book 1

MATTHEW LOWES

Empty Press

JOURNEY TO
ELARA

1

FAEDYN

Near the small apartment in Chinatown where he lived, people always recognized Faedyn on the street. They called out to him from steaming street carts filled with noodle soup or from fish stalls where fresh catches were displayed under bright fluorescent lights. They smiled, waved, and bowed as he passed by. He smiled and bowed back, even as he walked.

The locals called him *Yi sheng*, which means "Doctor." He had many names though, in a variety of languages. Some of them he had even forgotten, and there were a few of them he wished he could forget. *Faedyn* was an old name he still used, known only to a few. There were older names, but those he had long kept secret.

He was just returning from a house call where he treated a young boy with the flu. A cup of thelis tea had brought the boy's fever down, and Faedyn expected him to be fine in a few days. Faedyn enjoyed this work. It was good work, but no amount of good he could do now would erase the things he had done in his distant past.

As he walked, Faedyn felt something strange in the margins of his senses, something at once familiar and abhorrent, like a foul odor that abides unwanted in memory. So many long years had passed that he didn't fully realize what it was, and yet he followed the scent, seeking its source with the kind of morbid curiosity that always leads to trouble.

Down a littered alley he went, where rickety fire escapes clung precariously to the brick like the skeletons of giant snakes, and where a cloud overhead suddenly cast a gloom over everything. Cockroaches and rats fled into hiding before his footsteps, and a terrible voice seemed to echo in the air, like the shadows of demons prophesizing evil deeds.

As he turned into the back alley, he saw two cloaked men hunched over a teenage girl lying motionless on the ground. The girl's clothes were half torn from her body, white cotton soiled by the filth of the street.

Faedyn recognized something about the men. He couldn't place it, but the sight stirred an anger that had slept for hundreds of years. His stomach turned. His hands clenched into fists.

The men were still obscured by shadows, but sensing Faedyn, they looked up. He saw their pale, unearthly faces, and their eyes, windows into fallen souls, and he knew. These two had come from Maleistria. They were assassins of the Black Guard, followers of the cult of Saziel.

Faedyn had no time to contemplate how this could be, how the Malar could have found a way into this world. The assassins attacked without the slightest hesitation. One dashed to the right to flank him, and the other sprang forward, drawing a long dagger as he charged.

The distance closed quickly. At the last moment Faedyn altered his step, drawing in the attack. The assassin thrust his knife toward Faedyn's face.

Faedyn moved aside, perfectly matching his opponent's speed, dodging the knife, striking the man, and breaking his neck with one swift movement. But even as he did, he knew he had been careless, for he'd lost track of the other one. He whirled about, sensing the threat, but it was too late.

Out of the darkness the other assassin came, stabbing his blade into Faedyn's side. Undaunted, Faedyn trapped the assassin's arm as it retreated and, all at once, doubled him over, broke his elbow, took his knife, and cut his throat. The entire encounter was over in seconds.

Faedyn glanced down at his wound, put a hand over the bleeding hole, and knelt down to check on the girl. She was dead. But he noticed her face had the look of the elar. She was human, but she had inherited some elaran blood from somewhere. Such things had happened, and the blood of the elar does not diminish. There was nothing he could do for her, though, and it would do no good for him to be found here. He couldn't explain what had happened, and few would believe his explanation, if he could.

2

Ken Ashbury

Ken Ashbury's cell phone vibrated against his chest, deep in the inside pocket of his St. Christopher's Academy uniform jacket. Cell phones were strictly forbidden in class. If he took the call where he was, right in the middle of a two-hour calculus class, he would get in a lot of trouble. Nevertheless, Ken had been instructed to carry this phone and answer it promptly. So, somehow, he had to create a ruse to get out of the classroom.

It was a simple matter of decisiveness. The quicker he got out, the less time for suspicion to be aroused. Ken closed his books and slid them into his backpack. While he did this, he conjured a feeling of grim discomfort and let it play about his face. Then he zipped the pack, got up, and walked to the front of the room, an urgent resolution in his step. He noted the eyes of his peers and Mr. Hildenbrand turning on him. Just when he knew he had their complete attention, but hopefully before they had any time to think about what was happening, he clutched his stomach, grimaced, mumbled "diarrhea," and exited stage left.

The door to the class room slowly and silently eased shut on its pneumatic arm. Ken straightened up. With any luck, class had resumed after a few distracting laughs from his classmates.

The hallowed halls of St. Christopher's Academy were floored in marble, lined with walnut panels, and hung overhead with elaborate light fixtures. The walls were punctuated by somber portraits with brass nameplates embedded in the bottoms of their heavy frames. These halls had fostered the education of many senators and congressmen, and even a few presidents, not to mention legions of doctors, lawyers, and businessmen.

Ken walked quickly down the hall, ducked into the nearest bathroom, and locked himself in a stall. The phone was still vibrating. He fetched it out of his pocket and glanced at the screen briefly before answering. It said "Smith," which was no surprise. Mr. Smith was the only person who had the number, and the phone was used for only one purpose.

Ken always answered in the same manner, the way that he had been instructed to, by saying his name, "Ken Ashbury." Then he waited a moment. Mr. Smith had a biometrics routine running to verify his identity.

Smith's voice was articulate and precise. On a connection such as this he would only say what was necessary and nothing more. "Report to the Citadel," he said.

Ken replied, "Yes, Master." Then the line went dead. What Smith had said was more than enough for Ken to know he wouldn't be going back to calculus. Instead, this brief phone call would send him from the halls of St. Christopher's, and from the pampered lawns on which its neo-gothic buildings rest, to the heart of the city for a meeting with one of the most powerful men on the planet.

†

When Ken was ten years old, his parents had sent him to St. Christopher's. He hadn't seen them much since. A year after his enrollment, he was gradually approached through a series of interviews and tests for recruitment into a powerful secretive organization. The fellowship of the Loremasters has, for millennia, dedicated themselves to the preservation of hidden knowledge, and to understanding the legacy and the destiny of mankind. Ken had little idea what was going on during the recruitment process, but when it was over he was the personal assistant and student of Loremaster #957, a man known to those few who knew him, simply as Mr. Smith.

Ken was never at the top of his class, but he was close, and presumably the Loremasters thought he was more capable than the knuckleheads ahead of him. Also, looking back on it, Ken suspected they must have seen he had a natural gift for viewing and interpretation, the method by which the Loremasters attained their psychic visions.

Nobody but Smith knew what Ken really did, not his parents, his teachers, or his peers. Smith arranged it all like some kind of political alchemy. His connections were unfathomable. Somehow Ken's secret was kept from the highest levels of the school board. He was still a student at St. Christopher's on paper, but he went only to official functions and whatever classes Mr. Smith deemed necessary, both to keep up appearances and to supplement Smith's instruction.

Although Smith had become more like a father to Ken than his own father, and he was impossibly rich, Ken had to take the train into town because Smith believed the luxury of an automobile would only distract Ken from his true purpose. Ken accepted this begrudgingly, although he never failed to think of it as he sat on the hour-long train ride between St. Christopher's and the Citadel. Never mind that it would probably take just as long in a car.

On the train, he watched as scattered rolling suburbs patched with the green of manicured lawns turned to urban sprawl, grey with concrete and tagged with graffiti. Before he entered the dense center of the city, the train passed underground and snaked through subterranean tunnels to its final destination. From Central Station, he walked.

The glass of the Citadel was a deep impenetrable blue. The building lofted so high that at times its apex rested in low-lying clouds. Its walls were like the sheer cliffs of Antarctic ice shelves.

The Citadel was not actually called the Citadel by anyone other than Ken and Mr. Smith. It was actually called Parkview Tower, and most of the building was filled with luxury apartments owned or rented by movie stars, politicians, investors, lawyers, and CEOs. *The Citadel* was a codename Smith used for the top two floors of Parkview Tower, where he lived and worked. There, overlooking the city, this place was a kind of fortress, marked more by remove and influence than by thick stone and ramparts.

The very top floor housed Smith's huge office, his bedroom, his library, and a giant supercomputer they nicknamed Pandora. Off the library was the viewing chamber, where the Loremasters would confer through their communications network, and where Smith would do his viewing and analysis. A few other rooms were always locked, and Ken had never been in them. On the floor below were various bedroom suites, including Ken's, as well as conference rooms, a gymnasium, a kitchen, and storage.

Ken took a private elevator that required a numeric keycode and a scan of his palm print. He slapped his hand down on a black screen and waited for approval. On the long ride to the top, after a while he didn't feel like he was moving, but he still had to yawn to release the pressure that built up in his ears. Finally, with a weightless floating feeling that always gave him a touch of nausea, the elevator came to a halt.

Ken's weight settled back into his feet and the doors opened. On the other side was a space that seemed too vast to be there. The floors were laid with large slabs of polished brown stone, the expanse of which was only interrupted by an enormous Persian carpet right in the middle of the room, unencumbered by any furniture. Near the four corners of the wide floor, ancient Egyptian columns rose up to the broad ceiling, whose black firmament was inlaid with silver in patterns representing the stars of the heavens. The side walls were adorned with a pair of Sumerian stone reliefs depicting lions as guardian figures of the gate. The far wall was entirely glass, from which one could look westward over the park or southward over the city. At the far end of the carpet, in front of the glass wall, was an enormous, modern mahogany desk. Behind the desk sat Smith, silhouetted by the afternoon light.

Smith's face did not look like a face of power. The skin was creased deeply with wrinkles around small dark eyes. The cheeks were pale and mottled from too much time spent indoors. The hairline receded, and what hair there was fell in wispy grey tufts about the back of the head, a bit long and unkempt. The lips were fat and purplish and around them were the coarse hairs of a grizzled beard.

Ken walked forward, across an expanse of stone, across the carpet, which felt like a cloud beneath his feet, and across more stone. Two chairs stood in front of Smith's desk, but Ken was always obliged to stand for these formal meetings. He looked at his master with a keen eye, attuned to his many moods and expressions, and saw about his stolid visage some trace of what in him passed for excitement.

Smith looked impassively into Ken's eyes for what amounted to a long moment of silence between them. Finally, his stony face broke into a slight smile. "I think I've found her," he said.

"Found who?" Ken said, his mind still unfocused, a few seconds in the past. He was so intent on figuring out what had Smith so excited that he overlooked the obvious answer.

Smith looked at him disapprovingly. "The keystone to our collective. The person I have been searching for all these years."

"Really?"

Smith's eyes gazed downward into the glow of a screen that angled toward him on the side of his desk. "Yes," he said. "The one from our vision, and from our old prophesy—the vanguard of our destiny will come as a human girl descended from the elar, a girl with the power to see through the darkness between worlds."

"You have been searching for years. How sure are you this time?"

"There is always a margin of error, as you know, and the other masters are not all in agreement. However, I have never felt so personally certain."

"Where is she?" Ken said, not quite sure how much he believed the old prophesies of the Loremasters. He was at the limits of his knowledge. He wasn't even sure he could fully believe there was a world called Elara, though Smith clearly had no doubts, and he imagined the other Loremasters, whoever they were, possessed an equally great faith.

"She's here in the city," Smith said triumphantly, and not without a touch of irony. "All this time we have been searching, and she's been right under our noses."

"Are you going to bring her in?"

Smith curled his fingers in the air and then stroked his beard, thinking. "We must be sure it's her before we do anything. And it's a delicate situation to bring an outsider into the fold. We must not be hasty. I'll give you all the pertinent information. Keep a close eye on her for the next couple weeks. Follow her carefully when you can, and mark precisely the time and location at distinct places throughout the day. Include what she may be doing and any apparent emotional states. We will use this information to confirm her identity."

"Yes, Master."

Smith touched the screen that he had been looking at earlier and swiveled it around so Ken could see it. He leaned back in his chair while Ken took a closer look.

On the screen was a picture of a girl, maybe fifteen or sixteen by the looks of her. She had dark hair and green eyes. She was smiling in the picture, a school photo probably. Ken studied her face. Her teeth were slightly crooked, but in a way that made her mouth seem even more attractive. Her eyes were wide-set, and very green—deep, brilliant pools of green. "That's her?" Ken said.

"Her name is Anna," Smith said. "Anna Karova."

3

Anna Karova

A murky shadow descended upon Anna's already troubled dream. A chill in the air rolled over her body like mist, and a low unearthly hum, a terrible resonance, enveloped her. Its visible form was an inky, featureless figure, but it was more feeling than shape, and that feeling was of palpable darkness. Anna was only half asleep now, gripped in terror as the thing took hold of her. Paralyzed and speechless, she was caught between the world of waking, which she could sense just beyond reach, and a horror beyond imagining. Desperately she tried to scream, but all that she managed was a twisted, suffocated moan of anguish.

She woke with a start, finally, as if she had thrown herself free with a sudden exertion of her will. She blinked her eyes in the gloom of night. The sheets were damp with sweat and the oppressive humidity of the city in summer.

For some time, she could still feel its presence, whatever *it* was, but even after the feeling subsided, she didn't dare sleep. She padded across the worn linoleum floor in her bare feet and flipped the light switch. A single bulb, dangling from a wire overhead, lit up the tiny room. Three months had passed since her mother had died.

From next door, through the thin walls, came the distinctive garbled speech and muffled sounds of a television that had been on continuously since Anna had moved into this wretched place. And from down the hall came the incessant bass thump that indicated the boys from BS-Click were shooting up heroin.

Anna didn't sleep again that night. She sat cross-legged on the bed and flipped through a book of old nature photographs, just trying to forget that awful feeling. *There's nothing there,* she told herself. *It was just a dream, and it's ridiculous to be afraid.* But no matter how hard she tried, she couldn't rid her mind of the very real feeling that something had been there, some dark force. Although she didn't know what it was, she felt sure she hadn't merely dreamt it, just as she knew she wasn't dreaming now. She flipped through the book for the third time, looking at pictures of far-off forests, fields of wildflowers, mountain lakes, and jeweled skies above pristine waters.

Toward dawn, it was finally quiet, except for the continual chatter from the TV next door. Anna went about her small room, watering and tending to a few house plants she had collected. They were a small token of that far-off world she saw in books, a world free of people and chaos, free of pollution, crimes, hatred, concrete, garbage, and that peculiar stench that inhabited the subway. And most of all, free from the pain of loss.

At last, Anna put on her headphones and read a paperback book she had picked up at the grocery store. Her eyes glazed over once or twice. The text became black blurs in a field of white, and the letters seemed to transform into some language she had never seen. But the night couldn't last forever, and soon the light of morning poured through the dirty window.

†

She made two breakfast sandwiches that morning, fried egg with cheese on toast. One of them she wrapped in a piece of tin foil and put in a brown paper bag. The other she ate with her coffee and a small glass of orange juice. Then she threw some books, her wallet, and a subway card in a backpack, grabbed the paper bag, and left.

The stairway reeked of alcohol, urine, and other things she tried not to identify. A flight or two down she discovered a man passed out or dead in the middle of the stairs. His hair and clothes were oily and foul. His face was pasty and sick looking. A small trail of what could only be described as slime oozed from his mouth and nose. Anna tried not to look at him. She held her nose and carefully stepped around.

The outside air seemed fresh by comparison. As polluted as the city air was, it was better than the stairwell. She walked to a back alley behind the building and looked around. There was nobody in sight. The noise of the street was a muffled sound, like wind in trees, only more monotonous and mechanical. If Anna listened carefully, she heard an occasional small rustle that might be taken for the scurrying of rats.

She picked out a dry spot near the wall that seemed relatively clean and set down the brown paper bag that contained the extra sandwich. Then she retreated around the corner and hid where she still had a view of the bag. After a few minutes, she heard a noise and saw something move in the shadows.

From behind the dumpster, a raggedy-looking creature emerged, looking more like a wild animal than a small person. But the long, tangled hair, dirty face, and ragged clothes couldn't hide what was clearly a young girl, much like Anna, perhaps, when she was seven or eight. The girl crouched down in a furtive step and moved toward the bag. Her eyes darted around as if looking for predators, and once or twice she stopped, stood perfectly still and listened, at any moment ready to dive back into whatever hole she had crawled out of. When she made it to the bag, she squatted down in front of it, looked around, and seemed to sniff the air. Then she picked up the bag, opened it with her little fingers and smelled inside. She looked around once more. Anna was almost afraid she'd been spotted. Then, apparently satisfied, the girl closed up the bag, scampered off and was gone so quickly that in a moment it didn't seem like she had even been there.

Residents called her Mouse. Anna thought she must have found a way into the basement and built a nest down there, but she could be spotted from time to time and was known to scrounge around in the back alley.

A month ago, Anna started leaving food for Mouse every morning. She didn't show up right away, but Anna would go out for the day and when she came back, the food was gone. After a few weeks, Anna had won a bit of trust, and now Mouse seemed to be waiting each morning. She barely hesitated to scurry out and collect her breakfast. Maybe she even knew Anna was watching her.

The city could be a cruel place, where even good people turned a blind eye on suffering. Anna was just one person and didn't have a whole lot going for her, but she thought if she could just make a small difference somehow, each day, there was hope. Maybe someday, if she really gained Mouse's trust, they could live together in Anna's apartment, and Anna could take care of her. They would be happy, and everything would be different.

4

Unhealed Wounds

Faedyn sighed. Maybe he was getting old, or maybe it had just been too long since he'd had to fight like that. Assassins of the Black Guard were vicious killers. He was lucky to have survived. But the fact of their presence he could not fathom. Why were they here? And how?

Faedyn sat in his small office, which was simply a room in the back of his apartment. The walls were covered with cabinets and shelves, everywhere filled with jars of herbs and roots, medicinal supplies and books. Everything was neat and orderly. On his desk was a gauze pad, a pair of scissors, some tape, and a small bowl containing a pungent ointment. Today he was his own patient.

After removing the old bandage, he examined the wound in his side. It was healing well, but was still quite tender. He smeared some of the ointment over the stitching, applied the gauze pad and taped it in place. If he moved around too much now, he risked tearing open the wound, but in a few days it should be healed.

The assassin's dagger lay on a table at the side of the room. Faedyn recognized the design. He was quite certain the weapon came from the forges of the Crypt itself. If his memory served, it resembled those carried by the Black Guard during the Elara-war. Faedyn longed to forget that fateful era, but now he suspected he would never have the chance to.

For a month now, or maybe more, in the twilight of his dreams, he had heard a calling from far away, from the old land or beyond, bidding him to *return … return.* He had ignored it at first, attributing the voice to some echoing pain of his past, but he knew now he couldn't ignore it any longer. Still, he had vowed never to return to his ancestral home. He had vowed never to return to Elara.

Faedyn closed his eyes and breathed deeply. The air was filled with the rich scents of many herbs and medicines. *Maleistria, the fallen realm, city of despair …* he had hoped that place had faded away, simply ceased to exist or, at the least, he would never have to hear or think of it again.

Had the assassins come all the way from Maleistria to kill that girl, a human girl in whose veins the blood of the elar flowed? The followers of Saziel had always sought to wipe out such humans, but they had never found a path into this world. He wondered if the spirit of Saziel still endured within the Crypt at Maleistria. Was that ancient evil now spreading across the darkness between worlds?

5

Candle Flames

Anna had walked past St. Michael's Cathedral twice already. After a morning in the park, she had gone down Fifth Avenue to Alberici's Pizzeria for lunch, then back up to Toy Bazaar, where she bought a small teddy bear for Mouse. There were plenty of other places she could have gone and other routes she could have taken. Nevertheless, she wandered back down Fifth Avenue, and when she passed the Cathedral a third time, she looked up at the hulking doors and paused.

Gothic spires towered above her. People brushed by her on their way up or down Fifth Avenue, while Anna stood there looking up at the doors, wondering vaguely if she might want to go in. Five minutes ago, this possibility hadn't even occurred to her.

Anna wasn't raised to be particularly religious, but her mother had been a spiritual person and sent Anna to a religious school when she was younger. She said Anna would get a better education there than in the public schools where they lived. Maybe she did get a better education, but regarding the subject of religion, it was confusing. Most of it didn't make sense to Anna, and seemed like a hodgepodge of earthly dogma and elaborate ritual. Some of what they said made sense though, and it was a comforting idea that there was something out there watching over things, someone who would always be there for her. Anna was pretty sure she didn't have faith in it, though—whatever that meant if it wasn't blind belief.

She walked in the great cathedral doors with a hesitating step. Inside, Anna craned her head back to marvel at the high vaults of the ceiling and the columns that supported it. The sheer sense of space was incredible. She had been there once before on a school trip and her sense of awe had been much the same as it was now.

Tourists mulled about near the entrance. Most just gawked at the architecture for a few minutes, snapped some photos, and left. There was a little shop to the right where some of them browsed around and purchased rosaries, crucifixes, and St. Michael's memorabilia. Others wandered down the nave or among the aisles, looking at things in greater detail. All the while, scattered throughout the pews and in the various ancillary chapels, a few people knelt in prayer or sat in silent meditation.

At the beginning of the nave, and by many of the chapels that lined the aisles and the apse, stood iron racks of small burning candles. There were fresh candles, thin sticks of wood to light them, and a drop box to make monetary donations. Not knowing what to do and feeling a bit conspicuous, Anna thought it would be nice to light a candle for her mother. She didn't want to do it right at the entrance, though, in front of all those people, so she wandered down the left aisle and found a quiet, empty chapel. She dug a quarter out of her pocket and put it in the box for the candle. She put the candle on the rack and lit it.

For a long time, she stared at the array of candle flames. They burned steadfast. Some jumped and twitched with imperceptible air currents. And some, reaching the end of their wax, flickered and died—leaving only a wisp of smoke and a glowing ember at the tip of the wick, all of which was soon gone too.

Her mom had always said everything was going to be fine, that when she died she was going to a better place, and she would always be with Anna. If there was a place like heaven, Anna knew her mom must be there, watching over her. She had thought a lot about it, but she just didn't know. Sometimes it seemed to her as if there was some benevolent force watching over her, and sometimes it seemed like there was nothing, just suffering, despair, and death.

Anna closed her eyes and tried to pray, but nothing came to her, no comforting words, no revelation. The picture of her mother she held in her mind faded, without hope of renewal, and all she felt was deep sadness and the pain of loss.

She opened her eyes and stifled her tears. There was something deeper in the coil of emotion that hadn't quite fully surfaced, a paroxysm of anger that she shook off with a scowl as she left.

6

Ken's Notes

Ken glanced over his notes. He had secretly followed Anna through most of the day, periodically writing detailed notes, just as Smith had instructed.

At 6:31am, Anna left the brown apartment building where she lived wearing blue jeans, a brown t-shirt, and tennis shoes. She carried a red backpack.

At 7:10am, she sat on the train and stared out the window. She looked sleepy.

At 10:20am, she sat on a park bench near the war memorial, reading a paperback book. Unfortunately, he couldn't read the title from where he watched. That would have been a good viewing detail.

At 12:37pm, she ate a slice of cheese pizza at Alberici's. Old movie posters lined the walls. The booths had red vinyl benches.

At 2:08pm, she bought a small teddy bear at Toy Bazaar.

At 2:46pm, she stood in front of St. Michael's Cathedral for a few minutes before going inside.

At this point, Ken had stopped following her. He was exhausted. The girl walked with a kind of frantic determination, as if constantly trying to get away from something. A few times he had wondered if she was trying to get away from him, but there was no indication she knew she was being followed, and he had been extremely careful. All day there had been something though. He could see it in her every move. Something troubled her deeply. He wished he knew what it was.

In any case, he had watched her disappear into St. Michael's with some hesitation. He wondered if this Anna Karova was really the one the Loremasters sought. In their visions, they had seen the person the ancient masters spoke of, a high-born child who could fulfill the destiny of the Loremasters, a girl with the abilities of a true seer and powers to match the great wizards of old.

Ken looked down at his notes. Perhaps he held the answer in his hands. Smith and the other Loremasters would target the unknown person they sought, the one from the prophesy, at these specific times in their viewing. If what they saw matched Ken's notes, then her identity would be confirmed. He slid the notebook into his bag and headed for the Citadel.

7

OLD ACQUAINTANCES

Faedyn had no great love for the Loremasters. He didn't approve of the direction they had taken long ago, into hiding and secrecy, so eager to control and manipulate. Nevertheless, he maintained a tenuous relationship with them, long after the others of his kind, who had advised them in the early days, had either returned to Elara or faded into obscurity.

He didn't visit them often, but from time to time, when he thought he might have some influence, he felt a duty to go. Perhaps it was loneliness, too. A part of him could never really let go of the past. Among the Loremasters, he could feel some small link to ages gone by, for they alone among the humans of Midgard knew of his race, and their long, sad history.

In the elevator, Faedyn touched the still-tender knife wound in his side, a reminder of the reason for his visit. How had Maleistrian assassins found their way to this world? And what were they doing here? Perhaps the Loremasters had some information of their own, but that was probably just wishful thinking. He could only hope they would understand the danger and use their powers to investigate. Even the Loremasters had the human tendency of being incredibly short-sighted.

†

Smith was already standing in front of his desk, at the far end of the carpet, his hair combed, his suit straightened, when the elevator door opened and Faedyn strode across the wide room. "We are honored by your visit," Smith said, and bowed deeply.

Faedyn stopped and stood before the Loremaster, towering over the small man. "You were a young apprentice when I saw you last," he said.

"Now I'm an old man," Smith said. "But you haven't changed at all. Even with what I know, it's amazing to see. You don't look a day older."

"There is a saying among the elar: 'With each passing year, with every fallen blossom, the depth of sorrow grows.' How is it for you, Loremaster? Do the years make you weary?"

Smith didn't know how to answer. This is what he remembered from Faedyn's last visit, the strange way he talked, the feeling of being tested, and of failing miserably. That had not changed either, even with all his power and knowledge.

And so a silence followed, and though he knew the elar were at ease with silence, Smith felt it crawl on his skin with discomfort. Faedyn was scrutinizing him. His cool eyes were like a weight upon him. Smith's chest felt heavy. What did he see? Did Faedyn see into his very soul?

Ken entered through a side door, drawing Faedyn's attention. *Finally.* Smith had summoned the boy when Faedyn was still on his way up. "Ah, this is my apprentice," he said, breaking the silence, "Ken Ashbury." Ken bowed, but not as low as he should have. Smith made a mental note to reprimand him later. "Please," Smith said, "let's sit down. Mr. Ashbury will bring tea."

They sat at a coffee table in a corner of the office, and as soon as they were settled, Faedyn wasted no time. "How do the Loremasters fare these days?"

"The mission continues," Smith said diplomatically. "We continue to teach the histories as your people taught them to us, and to pass down the knowledge of our forebears. And with the development of new technologies, we continue to develop our science of viewing and further our understanding of mankind's destiny."

"As always has been your goal," Faedyn acknowledged. "It's something concerning the future of mankind that I came here to talk about."

Could he know about Anna Karova? "I see," Smith said. "What is it?"

Ken Ashbury set the tea on the table and poured two cups. He stood by to see if anything else was needed, and also perhaps to get another look at Faedyn.

"The dark ones have come to this city," Faedyn said.

"You mean the Malar, those of you who inhabit the fallen realm?"

"Yes, those who in ancient times followed Saziel's rebellion, those who founded his dominion in the realm of Maleistria, who covered the earth in war and laid waste to the gleaming cities of my ancestors … and who always sought the destruction of all humanity."

"Is it possible for the Malar to reach this world?"

"It's true the Malar were barred from coming here. They lost the way when this realm slipped from their consciousness. But we both know evil still holds great sway in this world, so it is not hard to imagine they might find it again."

Smith's mind raced. "Are you sure? We've seen nothing of this."

"I ran into two of them the other night," Faedyn said. He drew the blade from his bag and held it up for Smith. "I took this knife from one of them. I've seen ones like it before. It's from the forges of the Crypt at Maleistria."

Smith looked at the long knife, its grey metal etched with strange runes. Here was an artifact from another world. "May I see it?" he said, his hands outstretched and his eyes widening.

Faedyn put the blade away. "It's better that you don't."

Smith withdrew his hand. "What does it mean?"

"I don't know. Perhaps it was an accident they found their way here. Such things have been known to happen, slipping between worlds by chance. We can only hope that's the case. If not, then their presence represents a danger beyond imagining."

Smith nodded. "Of course, we'll do everything we can. But we cannot see through the darkness between worlds. We cannot see into Maleistria itself."

"Focus your attention here in Midgard. Perhaps there are more of them. The two I found killed a young girl in Chinatown, a human girl with elaran blood."

My God, Smith thought, *could the Malar know about Anna?* "I'll inform the others and we'll begin at once to look into the matter." Just as soon as he brought Anna here to the Citadel. There was no time to waste if she was in danger.

"Good," Faedyn said. "I'll do what I can. If anything comes up, you can find me here." He handed Smith a business card. It was printed in Chinese and English—*Wing Chen Restaurant.* "Just ask for the Doctor."

8

STEEL PIPE

Anna remembered the stuffed bear just as she reached the front steps of the apartment building. Maybe if she could give the bear to Mouse, if she could see some trace of happiness on Mouse's face, she might feel better about the day.

Digging the teddy bear out of her backpack, Anna started around toward the back of the building. Before she reached the corner though, even before she heard voices, she knew something was terribly wrong. Deep inside her, she felt something bad was happening. She heard boys' voices, and slowed to a stealthy step.

"Bet you never thought we'd catch you. Did ya?" one of the boys said.

Anna peered around the corner.

It was three boys from BS-Click. Two had Mouse held from behind, and one stood in front of her, dangling a paper bag from his hand. "All we needed was some cheese," he said, and the other two laughed.

Mouse was utterly calm in the grip of the two boys. She stared into their eyes without fear, almost as if she was totally disconnected from what was happening. If anything, she looked annoyed, indignant.

The boy chucked the paper bag. It hit the wall with a dead thud, dropped into an oily puddle and lay there motionless, slowly wicking in water. Something about the boy's look Anna loathed, a malicious look, cold and inhuman, like the touch of the shadows that haunted her nights. Suddenly he lunged at Mouse, stopping just before her face.

Mouse didn't flinch.

The boy laughed and taunted her.

Something inside Anna stirred. It started like a cramp in her gut, a feeling of long-suppressed anger. She tried to think clearly, but her thoughts raced, tangled together, and finally were obscured totally by a kind of static. The cramp in her gut broke free and began to spread through her body in the form of a shaking chaotic vibration. Her pulse quickened. Her eyes dilated. The stuffed bear dropped unnoticed from her hand.

"Let's see," the boy said. "I thought you were a girl, but with all these rags on, I can't tell." The two boys holding Mouse chuckled and shook her a little. She was limp as a doll.

Anna reached for the nearest thing at hand, a two-foot length of black steel pipe, leaning against the building.

"Why don't we see what we have here?" the boy said.

"Do it," the others said. The boy reached for Mouse's shirt and tore it open with a violent tug.

Anna rushed in with a kind of berserk rage, the steel pipe raised above her head, screaming incoherently. The boys holding Mouse were startled and confused for a moment, until the steel pipe split the skull of their leader. It made an awful crack and a few drops of blood spattered across Anna's face. Then they were in a state of shock. They looked straight into Anna's green eyes, twin flames, burning in anger, and were terrified. Mouse slipped from their numb fingers and the two boys ran off as fast as they could.

When the boys were gone, Anna dropped the pipe, which fell to the ground with an ominous clang. Mouse hadn't moved. She stood expressionless, staring at the limp body of the boy at her feet. A puddle of blood pooled around his head. Anna took off her own shirt, leaving her in a tank top, and put it on Mouse. Then she took Mouse's hand. It felt small and weak in her own. "C'mon," Anna said. "We can't stay here."

She looked into Mouse's eyes, brilliant blue eyes set in a dirty face, sad, calm eyes, eyes that had seen too much too soon and were now seldom shocked by anything. "Do you know where we can go?" Anna said. "Someplace we can hide. Someplace away from here. They'll be after us."

Mouse looked blank for a moment, then nodded. She squeezed Anna's hand and led her off down the back alley. They went several blocks like this, neither saying anything. Mouse looked back once or twice to see how Anna was doing. She had begun to shake and stumble.

They turned a corner and Mouse led them down another alley. She paused for a moment to make sure the coast was clear before leading them out onto the crowded street. Anna collapsed to her knees in the stream of pedestrians, and Mouse had to practically drag her up to her feet.

They made straight for the subway. The cacophony of voices on the street was like a nightmare to Anna, a manifestation of the thousand and one thoughts and images in her mind, racing and battling against each other with the realization of what she had done. She had killed that boy.

They went down two flights of stairs. Mouse pulled a subway card from somewhere within her tattered garments, slipped it into the reader, and pushed Anna through the turnstile. Then she put the card through again and came after her.

This might have surprised Anna had she been anywhere near coherent enough to be surprised. Mouse led her by the hand, and she followed.

Luckily, the train downtown wasn't crowded, and there were no signs of BS-Click. Anna sat staring at the window, her eyes fixed in a near catatonic gaze. Mouse held her hand, squeezing it lightly and awkwardly.

Anna had no idea where they got off, only that Mouse led her through the station. They went down another flight of stairs and along several corridors, apparently on their way to another track. At some point they jumped a railing and descended into the track pit. It was a wide, dark space where several tracks came together in a bottleneck. The ground was littered with dirt and debris. Ancient concrete pillars breached the expanse, covered with the soot and filth of immeasurable time.

Every few minutes a train would roar by like some bioluminescent subterranean monster, a giant worm, a dragon, roaring in the darkness. In the flickering light of the windows only the shadows of human beings could be seen, silhouetted for a moment in the midst of a movement or gesture, and then gone, doppler shifting into the distance, and disappearing into some black tunnel in the earth.

Off to the right, a derelict tunnel had long fallen into disuse. Some rotting boards partially blocked the way, and the floor of the tunnel was half littered with rubble. Mouse led Anna into the abandoned tunnel. She produced a small keychain light with an LED that lit up when you squeezed it. The dim flashes from this light was all that lit their way.

At the time, Anna vaguely thought they passed other living things, some large, perhaps human, many small and definitely not human. She caught glimpses of odd shapes, and heard movement in the darkness. Foul odors invaded her senses with each breath. All was like a strange kaleidoscopic dream flashing before her in the blinking beam of Mouse's light—crumbled concrete, twisted rusting steel, heaps of garbage, out-of-place objects like an old shopping cart and a porcelain toilet, and numerous side tunnels, dark and seemingly infinite, burrowing into the earth ... or into other dimensions. Finally, they climbed up, through a doorway half blocked by rock and dirt, and into a tiny room.

Mouse pulled a thick, oily curtain over the hole they had climbed through. She began lighting candles scattered about the room, on the floor and a few rudimentary shelves. There was no other furniture.

In one corner, a pile of blankets and old clothes looked like a nest. On one shelf lay some books, pamphlets, and comics. The books were of the type various religious organizations hand out on the street. Here and there were propped a collection of old barbie dolls, which looked scavenged from dumpsters around the city. Most of them were naked, their soiled plastic skin smudged and stained, and many of them were missing limbs or heads, making their stiff poses seem even more awkward than usual.

Mouse led Anna over to the nest in the corner. Anna lay down in the pile of old blankets, curled into a ball and shut her eyes tight. The little girl knelt down and covered her with one of the blankets. It seemed like such a sweet gesture, like the loving hands of a mother tucking in her child. But Anna couldn't purge the image of that boy's crushed head from her mind. She just lay there, horrified by the inescapable reality of it, and was unable to think about anything else.

9

The Loremasters

Twelve black monoliths stood in a circle, looking vaguely like Stonehenge, only the stones were darker, smoother, and mathematically perfect. From Smith's point of view, only eleven of the black rectangular blocks could be seen, for the twelfth stone represented him in the virtual conference room. The blocks were really only bits of data streaming through the supercomputer they called Pandora, with each of the Loremasters represented as a holographic monolith.

Everything in the viewing chamber was a holographic projection, except the sleek chair supporting Smith's body in something approximating a neutral-gravity position. Here in this windowless room adjacent to library, high atop the Citadel, Smith entered the deep meditative states necessary for viewing. The Loremasters' limited ability to see remote events in time and space was achieved through the rigors of a technical methodology. The application of these techniques allowed them to access what could be conceptualized as an enormous database of nonlocal information embedded in the fabric of the universe.

Attached to the frame of Smith's chair were large touchscreens where he would make notes, sketches, and other records of his visions. When he conferred with the other Loremasters to correlate and analyze the data from their viewing, each of the Loremasters would appear in the chamber as a black monolith. A red number near the top of each monolith identified the Loremaster and glowed brightly when he spoke.

There were always twelve Loremasters, and all were present for this important meeting. Smith touched one of his screens and dragged the photo of Anna to the display window. Now, somewhere below the number on his monolith the other Loremasters could see the photo. It would appear also on their own viewing screens.

962: "All our visions matched the targets provided by your apprentice."

959: "Our analysis would seem complete on this matter."

"Then there should be no doubt," Smith said. "She is the one we've been looking for, the one from our prophesy."

955: "The margin of error is ... how shall I say ... unusually low."

953: "So low that it may be anomalous."

"She is the focal point of our futurity," Smith said. "I have never seen anything more clearly. Her destiny is among us."

953: "There is much about the future that is unclear."

958: "Whatever the case, darkness surrounds her now. We must watch her closely and consider this matter more deeply, before we act."

There was no further discussion. Smith didn't mention the assassins Faedyn had encountered. There was no proof they were after Anna, and he was worried how the others might react. There was time for that later, if needed. In the meantime, he had to find Anna Karova.

One by one the monoliths blinked out, disappeared without a sound, as if by magic, until Smith was alone. He took a deep, contemplative breath, stroked his beard, and dialed Ken

Ashbury with the touch of an icon that resided on one of his screens.

10

LOST AND FOUND

Three days passed in hiding before Anna thought about anything other than what had happened. She only left their room occasionally, venturing down the tunnel to the place they used as a bathroom. Mouse took care of everything, leaving with trash, lighting candles, and returning with food. The fare was not luxurious by any means. Most of it was scavenged, half eaten or half empty. Occasionally she would come back with a burger or a piece of pizza that seemed half fresh and half warm. She brought back more candles, wrinkled magazines, and another doll. Every so often she curled up next to Anna to sleep. The only thing she didn't do was speak. The entire time Anna was with her, Mouse never said a word.

They couldn't just stay here, Anna thought at last. She had to pull herself together. Regardless of what she had done, and everything that had happened, she couldn't just give up. She wolfed down the hamburger Mouse had brought for her. Afterwards, she washed it down with a cup of lukewarm coffee and took a deep breath. "Thank you," she said.

Mouse looked pleased. It was barely noticeable, but the hint of a smile played about the corners of her eyes in the candlelight.

"I'm sorry about the last couple of days," Anna said. "I haven't been myself."

Mouse didn't say anything.

"I'm feeling better now though, and we can't just stay here forever. What do you think we should do?"

Mouse was silent.

"Maybe we can go someplace and start over," Anna said.

Mouse was still silent. Candlelight flickered across her face. She clearly understood everything Anna was saying.

"I guess you don't talk much," Anna said, "but that's okay. We're going to get along just fine."

Mouse almost nodded.

Anna smiled. The language was subtle, but she was beginning to understand Mouse already. "Anyway," she said, "before anything, I have to go back to my apartment."

Mouse looked suddenly worried and glanced down at the ground.

"I know it doesn't sound like a good idea, but I have to go back, just to pick up a few things."

Mouse didn't look encouraged. She twitched her head sideways as if shaking her head once to say no.

Anna sighed. She had to go. How could she make Mouse understand? "It's like this," she said. "A while ago my mom died. In my apartment, I have a picture of her. Sometimes I feel like the image of her in my mind is fading, and I have to look at that picture to remember. I need to get that picture. I need to look at it now."

Mouse didn't look happy but she seemed to understand. She was right to have her doubts. If the police weren't looking for them, she was sure the boys from BS-Click were, and they probably didn't have anything nice planned if they found her.

"It'll be dangerous," Anna said. "I should go alone and meet you someplace afterward."

Mouse sprang to a half-crouched position, as if to block Anna's path to the exit. It was clear that she wasn't going to let Anna go alone.

"Okay, we'll go together. They might be watching the front door anyway, so we'll need a back way in. Do you know one?"

With a look and a nod Mouse seemed to speak. *Leave it all up to me,* she said.

†

Anna and Mouse approached the building from the rear, through a maze of side streets and alleyways. They had talked it over, or rather, Anna had talked it over while Mouse either nodded or shook her head. If she shook her head, Anna would talk some more, changing the details until she nodded.

They would go in and out through a secret way that Mouse knew. Then they would use the back staircase to get up to Anna's apartment and get the picture. They hadn't thought much beyond that, but for now, it was enough.

In the back of the building was an unlocked basement window. In the dark, Anna could barely see it—a small dirty pane of glass right down by the ground. Mouse pushed the glass inward and slid though with an ease and grace indicative of much experience.

For Anna, sliding through was slightly more arduous. At first, she wasn't even sure she would fit, but Mouse was already down there, so she had no choice. She got down on the ground and stuck her feet through the opening. She thought for a moment, trying to figure out the best way to proceed. Then she turned over to lie face down on the pavement and began to inch backward.

For a while, her legs and feet were suspended in a disturbingly empty space. She couldn't see the space in her present position, but it had looked pitch black through the window. For a moment, she felt her legs dangled over a pit of such terrible depth that the darkness itself had a gravity that pulled her downward. Her legs shook, and only a matter of rational faith reassured her that Mouse was just below, on a solid floor, waiting for her, and not some horrible creature rising up from the abyss.

Nevertheless, she felt the panic of fear welling up in her. Finally she slid back far enough that her hips cleared the ledge. Her legs were now able to flop down and make contact with the wall at least, though the floor was still some unknown distance below her. Her whole body was shaking. A hand grabbed hold of her leg and she nearly screamed before realizing it was just Mouse trying to help.

When she hung only by her arms, she tucked her head, tried to grip the wall with the toes of her sneakers, and went into a semi-controlled fall until she landed safely, although a bit scraped up, on what felt like cement. It was dark. After a few moments, Anna could make out Mouse's face, and other vague shapes that were apparently the kind of things you find in the basements of rundown apartment buildings.

Mouse flashed her little light and nearly blinded her. For a moment she could see. In the corner of what appeared to be an old storeroom, under a kitchen table piled high with broken chairs, was a nest of bedding. Scattered around the nest were brown paper bags, the remnants of the meals Anna had made.

With the light out again, Anna couldn't see a thing. Mouse took her hand and led her through the inky darkness. Finally they reached a door that Mouse pushed open, revealing a staircase flooded with fluorescent light. This was the back stairwell. They took it straight up to the fourth floor where Anna's apartment was.

The only problem with this plan was in order to get to Anna's apartment, which was on the far end of the hall from this side, they would have to walk straight past the apartment where the boys from BS-Click hang out. They could hear the bass beat even before they reached the fourth floor. They could feel it deep in their chests as they hesitated at the door to the hallway.

Anna pulled on the door, whose heavy pneumatic arm was reluctant to budge. She opened it far enough to stick her head through and peer down the hall. "It looks clear," she whispered. Hopefully everybody in that apartment was in such a stupor from drugs and alcohol that they were passed out or otherwise incapacitated. "Let's go," Anna said.

The two girls held hands and stepped into the hall, feeling dangerously exposed. They began their long walk down to Anna's apartment door. The hallway seemed longer and brighter and narrower than Anna had ever remembered. She felt like turning around and running back down to the basement. But she kept going, step after step, with Mouse in tow, closer and closer to the dreaded door.

Within a few steps of BS-Click's apartment door, Anna and Mouse stopped and stood still like rabbits trying to hide in mowed grass. Anna didn't know why they stopped. They just did. Maybe they were listening, but over the din of the bass and some yelling that accompanied it, she couldn't hear anything. She pulled at Mouse and they dashed past the door, running the rest of the way down the hall.

Only when Anna was safe inside her apartment and had taken a good look around at the mess—stuff strewn about the room, half of it smashed or gone, spray paint on the walls and rotting food spilled out of the open fridge—did she realize just why her door had been unlocked. BS-Click had trashed the place. That meant there was no doubt now they knew who she was.

Mouse stayed at the door, listening for any sign of movement in the hall, while Anna rummaged about the remains of her things, looking for the small photograph of her mother. Her search became increasingly desperate, and she started to cry, before she finally found the picture beneath a pile of ripped up clothes that reeked of urine. The wooden frame was crushed, and shards of broken glass obscured her mother's smiling face.

Anna knelt on the floor and gazed down at the picture. Her eyes glazed over, as if falling into a beatific vision. Slowly, she reached out and carefully picked the fragile looking photograph from the shattered pieces of its frame. Looking deeply into the image of her mother's eyes, she searched for a feeling of her presence. She kept searching until Mouse looked up from where she was positioned and indicated with an urgent glance that she heard something outside.

Anna put the picture in her pocket and crawled over to the door by Mouse. With her ear gently pressed to the door, she heard the sound of clunky offbeat footsteps in the hall. For a moment they seemed to pause—Anna couldn't tell where—and then they continued onward, receding toward the door at the front stairwell. She shut her eyes and focused her whole consciousness on the minute sensory inputs entering her ear. She thought she heard a door open and shut.

Then all was quiet, aside from the droning thump of the bass and the muffled chatter of television next door. Every second they waited contained greater risk. It seemed certain BS-Click would be looking for them, and Anna thought she had a pretty good idea what would happen if they were found. She took a breath. "Let's go," she said, as much to herself as to Mouse.

Outside in the hall, though still trying to tread lightly, they rushed toward the back stairwell, feeling with each step a growing sense of imminent relief. All they had to do was make it past BS-Click's door and into the stairwell and they should be safe. But halfway to their goal, the dreaded door opened and somebody stumbled out.

Anna and Mouse froze, like deer caught in the headlights of impending doom, a freight truck barreling down the highway at a hundred miles per hour. It took a second for the guy to recover from his exit, and another second for him to even notice Anna and Mouse. Those seconds lasted an eternity, and for a moment it seemed he wouldn't even recognize them. But then, almost unbelievably, a glimmer of cognition dawned upon his pallid face like a post-apocalyptic sunrise—a look of confusion, then surprise. Mouse took hold of Anna's hand. They still hadn't moved.

"Hey," the guy shouted dumbly. "Hey," he shouted again, his vocal center still playing catch-up with the rest of his drug-addled brain. It was unclear whether he was shouting at Anna and Mouse or back into the apartment. Then he shouted, "Hey guys! It's that girl. Hey, it's the girl!" He was shouting now directly through the apartment door. "It's the girl who killed Raphael."

"We'll have to go out the front," Anna said, with Mouse already pulling her in that direction. "Run!"

†

At the behest of Mr. Smith, Ken had temporarily taken up residence in an empty room across the street from Anna's apartment building. Smith had outfitted him with a whole mess of high-tech surveillance gear, like a digital camera with a huge zoom lens, image-stabilization binoculars, and a night-vision scope. With the amount of money Smith must have dropped on all the equipment, Ken figured he could just as easily have bought him a car.

Anna had disappeared a couple of days ago and Smith was eager to find her. "Imperative," he said. The Loremasters had been unable to establish an identifiable location through viewing. All they got were dark and troubling images, unsuitable for analysis. So they put Ken up there with a box full of toys and told him to watch the building twenty-four hours a day, which he was, however impossible after a day or two, dutifully trying to do. He would have gladly driven around the city looking for her, but apparently they thought this was a better idea.

Ken yawned. He had to admit he was a little worried about Anna. After following her around, he felt like he knew her, and he had a weird feeling something bad had happened.

So he felt a sense of relief, beyond the possibility of just getting off his ass, when he was startled from his half-sleeping watch at three-something in the morning by two girls busting out of the front door across the street. A glance through the binocs revealed one of the girls was Anna. Something was wrong though, because they ran down the street and disappeared into an alley as if somebody was chasing them.

Sure enough, a group of young gangsters cascaded out of the front door looking right and left, desperately trying to figure out which way to go. They finally sent a squad out in both directions. Ken should have been going after the girls by now, but something kept him at the window a moment longer.

He looked through the nightscope and scanned the street below. In the shadow of the alleyway beside the building he saw a man standing in the darkness. After the gang passed him by, chasing the girls in the wrong direction, this man emerged onto the street and walked swiftly in the direction the girls had gone. There was something about him, a stealthy undeterable purpose to his movement, that worried Ken a great deal more than any gang.

†

For several blocks, Anna and Mouse ran, not caring which direction they went, as long as it was away. Through alley after alley they ran, mindless, as if into the dark heart of a labyrinth. The cracks in the pavement were like gaping maws and the brick walls like great slabs from collapsing towers.

Finally, as if coming to terms with the surge of adrenaline that coursed through their veins, they stopped for a moment in the middle of an alley-way intersection. Over the sound of their heavy breathing, they could hear faintly the boys from BS-Click in the distance, shouting at each other as they searched. Anna thought she heard a whisper too, that carried on the still air and put a chill in her spine. But that must have been in her mind, or it was the rustling of sewer rats, or the settling of garbage heaps. "Which way?" she said to Mouse.

Mouse turned as if to point, saw something, and clung to Anna, stiff as a board. Anna looked and stifled a scream. There was a man at the end of the alley, a tall figure who emerged from the shadows. Something about him terrified Anna, a kind of dark radiance that struck her like a physical force. She knew at once this person was no member of BS-Click. This was something worse. As if to prove this fact, one of the boys suddenly came out of a cross alley between them. He looked at Anna and Mouse, then looked at the man. "Man, who the hell are you?" the boy said.

Although this man was human in form, Anna could only see him as some malevolent creature, a monster, like the nightmares that haunted her sleep. His eyes were cold and empty, like twin moons, expressionless in the black of space.

He walked toward the boy, and the boy puffed up a little, indignant-like. "I said, who the hell are you?" the boy said.

The man kept coming, silent and horrible. Anna could barely watch, though she could not turn her gaze, either. At once she knew what was about to happen, and had to see it.

The boy pulled a gun from his jacket and thrust it straight out in front of him. "I'm gonna shoot your ass," he said, but the barrel of the gun had already begun to shake. He didn't know how much trouble he was in until the last second, when he looked right into those eyes and faltered. His whole body started to shake, and the gun dropped from his hand.

Anna and Mouse watched as the man grabbed the boy by the neck and lifted him up off the ground with one arm. A crack, like breaking ice, echoed through the alley. Then he threw the boy through the air. The limp body impacted against the wall, where it hit with a dreadful thud and crumpled to the ground like garbage. Anna and Mouse ran.

Three frantic blocks later they rounded a blind corner and crashed into somebody so hard that not only did they knock him over, but the two of them tumbled right on top of him. Anna wound up more or less straddling a boy, who she could see, as soon as she propped herself up on her hands and got a good look at him, clearly wasn't from BS-Click, either. He was just some dopey guy with a stupefied look on his face. These back alleys were starting to seem awfully crowded for the middle of the night. She and Mouse scrambled to their feet.

"You better get out of here," Anna said. "There's a killer back there."

"I know," the guy said, getting to his feet. "I can help you."

"You know?"

"My name is Ken Ashbury. You're Anna Karova. I came to help you. There's no time to explain. We'd better go now or I'll never have the chance to. Follow me."

"And just why should I trust you?" What she really wanted to know was who this guy was and how he knew her name.

"Because I'm not them. Anyway, you better make up your mind." Off in the distance they heard a scream cut short, and the only thing worse than that scream was the silence that followed it.

Anna and Ken's eyes met for the briefest moment. "Okay," Anna said. "Let's get out of here."

11

The Three Earths

Deep within the caress of a warm, soft, all-encompassing embrace, Anna woke over the course of several minutes. From the mist-like shroud of a dream she rose, at first slowly, taking a step back for each two she took forward. Then all of a sudden, as if her ascent was accelerated by some external force, she was awake, staring up at the rich velvety canopy of an enormous four-post bed.

She floated on an ocean of bedclothes, the surface of which spread out in every direction, gentle rolling waves of fine starched linens and goose-down comforter. At the four corners of this vast ocean, the posts rose up like the carved trunks of giant trees, up into a sky where celestial branches supported the dark blue velvet of the heavens.

Mouse was curled up by her side, still fast asleep. For a moment Anna just lay there, blinking, replaying the night in her mind and reminding herself how she came to be here. Ken, the boy they had met on the street, brought them to this place and left them in this room. He seemed to know a surprising amount about her, which was weird. But he seemed harmless enough, the place was nice, and they had nowhere else to go.

Anna slid out of bed. This took quite a bit of sliding actually, but she finally made it to the edge and stepped down onto the plush fibers of an elaborately patterned rug. Beneath this rug, and a few others spread throughout the room, the floor was tiled with marble.

Anna had never seen such a large room, not a room for living in anyway. It was enormous, and very clean. The effect was a space that seemed almost disturbingly unreal.

The giant bed they had slept in was not up against a wall, but rather, as if in direct opposition to any principle in the economy of space, was positioned at an angle in the middle of an area that represented only one corner of the entire room. And there it would surely stay, for it looked so massive and heavy that it would take industrial machinery to move it. Perhaps the four posts had even grown roots into the marble floor.

The rest of what really amounted to an apartment was outfitted with an eclectic array of furniture that looked like it belonged in a museum. In the bedroom area, which was the starting point in Anna's exploration, there was a dresser, armoire, and long table. Next was a sitting area where a few over-stuffed chairs surrounded an ornate coffee table. Then an open door led to an all-marble bathroom that was as big as Anna's old apartment.

The door to the hallway was closed, and Anna left it alone for now. The middle of the apartment was taken up by a living room area, complete with leather sofas, chairs, and tables on an immense patterned carpet. The area was roughly delineated by lengths of low, freestanding bookshelves. The shelves were packed with books on both sides, the tops accented with Greek vases and other priceless-looking artifacts.

The far side of the apartment had a sitting area with a television in one corner and a workspace in the other corner. The desk was sleek and modern, the leather chair outfitted with all the latest ergonomic accoutrements. The interior walls were decorated with a collection of old maps in matching frames. The long, outside wall was completely made up of floor to ceiling windows. They were adorned at regular intervals with heavy silk drapes that hung down and billowed up on the floor, presumably concealing the steel support beams that were holding up all the glass.

Anna approached the windows, where a polished brass telescope was pointing outward, like a sentient eye, beckoning her to look. The sense of vertigo was immediate and overwhelming. As she drew near the window her feet began to drag. Finally, they just stuck to the floor involuntarily, leaving her more or less paralyzed with fear. All her body heat seemed to drain right out of her soles into the cold marble, and yet simultaneously she broke out in a sweat.

Slowly, Anna crouched down until she was on all fours, trying to get her breathing under control. She crawled forward until she was almost at the edge. She remembered getting into the elevator last night, but she had no idea how far up they had gone. They must be at least eighty floors above the concrete of the sidewalk. After a minute, her heart rate slowed a little, and although she could still feel the odd, drifting pull of vertigo, she didn't feel like she was going to altogether fall off the face of the earth.

Mouse stirred in the bed. Anna dropped down to her belly and looked out. It was a real bird's eye view. She could almost imagine herself as a falcon, gliding between the skyscraper canyons, riding endlessly on the subtlest currents of air. She had lived in this city her whole life, but she had never seen a sight like this. She could at once look west across the park, south to the tower-lined boulevards of Midtown, and up toward the Northland sprawl. Suddenly, everything came into perspective, her whole life up until this point was laid out before her like a three-dimensional map.

A knock at the door startled Anna. She turned her head just in time to see Ken Ashbury enter with a large breakfast tray. "Ah, you're awake," he said. He looked at Anna curiously. "Enjoying the view?"

"Um ... yes," Anna said, scooting back from the window and getting to her feet. "It's nice."

Ken strode across the room toward the sitting area by the bed, holding the large tray steady with apparent ease. "I brought breakfast for you and ... Mouse. Is that right?"

Anna nodded. "Thank you, but what I'd really like is to know who you are, how you know me, and why I'm here."

Ken seemed to ignore her. He darted into the bathroom for a moment and then reappeared. "I've programmed a bath for you. It'll be ready in half an hour. It's all electronically controlled so you don't have to do anything but get in when the water turns off. I hope a hundred and one degrees sounds good."

"Um ... yes, but ..."

"And if you'll just wait one moment." He went out the front door again and came back ten seconds later carrying a stack of clothes, with two pairs of new shoes perched on top. "I took the liberty of getting you and your friend some new clothes." He said this on his way over to the long table by the armoire, where he divided the clothes into two neatly-folded piles and placed the shoes on the floor.

By this time, Mouse was sitting up in bed and the two of them exchanged a look of amusement and confusion. "'That's um … very nice of you," Anna said. "But I'd really like to know what exactly is going on."

Ken looked at Anna and their eyes met again, just as they had the night before. "Everything will be made clear in time. In two hours, my master will see you. He will explain everything. We're here to help. Please trust me."

Anna sighed. All she wanted was some answers. Was it so difficult? But she supposed she would go along with things for a while. They were a hell of a lot better off here than they were on the streets right now, and a bath sure sounded good. So without saying anything more, she nodded her head. Ken smiled and left them alone again.

†

They spent twenty minutes gorging themselves on scrambled eggs, toast, juice, and coffee. Then on to the bath, which was ready and waiting, just as Ken had said. They sat together in the oversized tub and washed each other in the hot water. After the last couple of days Anna was almost as dirty as Mouse, and it took some work to get them both clean.

As she wiped Mouse's face, Anna felt like she was seeing it for the first time. Under who knows how many months or years of grime, her skin was soft and radiant, but her pink lips still wore a near-permanent pout. It took some time to comb the tangles out of Mouse's hair, but when Anna had finished, she turned Mouse around and admired her. She looked prettier and younger than she had before, but there was still the same sadness in her eyes. "Everything's going to be okay," Anna said.

The clothes Ken had brought fit perfectly. Anna cringed a little at putting on clothes that he had gotten her, especially the underwear, but at least they were nice simple clothes. Mouse just cringed at having to put on a skirt, but she looked adorable and Anna dragged her in front of the mirror to prove it. "Look," she said, "we look like sisters." Mouse looked at the mirror, and then up at Anna, and the pout on her face broke for the briefest moment.

Before long, Ken came to get them. Anna cocked her head playfully. "Well, how do we look?" she said.

Ken looked away, blushing. "You look nice," he said flatly.

"Is it time to see your master now?" She put a special mocking effort into the word *master*.

Ken scratched the back of his head. "Yes," he said. "Follow me."

Anna and Mouse were ushered into Smith's colossal office. Anna gazed first at the broad ceiling, then at the giant columns, down to the huge stone lions that flanked the room, and finally across the wide expanse of space to where a bearded man rose from a massive desk to greet them. "Please," the man said, "feel at ease," which was just about the most ridiculous suggestion Anna had ever heard.

Mouse took hold of her hand and they walked across the room together. It seemed to take a long time to cover the distance, but as they did, Anna noticed that the man was a little pudgy, slouched, and smiling. All this was disarming enough that Anna did feel a little more at ease.

The man offered his hand to Anna and to Mouse. Anna reached out and shook it politely, but Mouse just stood there unmoving, looking into the man's face with a steady gaze. The man finally withdrew his hand, without taking any apparent offense, and simply bowed precisely to Mouse as if apologizing for his own ignorance in etiquette.

"Well," the man said as if summing things up. "My name is Smith, and I must say it's a pleasure to meet you, Anna, and your devoted companion. Mr. Ashbury tells me the two of you are quite inseparable."

Anna didn't say anything.

"Well, please sit down." Smith gestured invitingly at two chairs in front of the desk. Anna and Mouse sat. "Can I get either of you a glass of water or something?" Smith said.

Anna had the feeling that if she said yes, Ken Ashbury, who was dutifully standing by, would have to run and get it. For a moment she thought of saying yes just to see that, but in the end she shook her head.

Smith walked around his desk and sat down. "Normally, with guests," he said, "now is the time I would ask if you're enjoying your stay and if the accommodations are satisfactory." A silence followed in which he seemed to let this sink in before proceeding. "But under these unusual circumstances, perhaps we should dispense with the pleasantries. I imagine you're more interested in knowing who exactly we are, why we seem to know you, and why you are here."

Anna nodded. "Finally."

Smith folded his hands together on his desk. "I know you're an intelligent girl, so I'll be very straight forward with my answers," he said. "I am part of a very old organization dedicated to preserving certain knowledge about the past, and to understanding the legacy and destiny of mankind. Mr. Ashbury is my apprentice.

"We brought you here because you may be in grave danger." At this point, he took a breath and searched Anna's face to see if he'd lost her. She was still with him, more or less, so he continued. "You see, Anna, this is not the only world. There are many worlds, maybe an infinite number, and some of them are intricately connected. These worlds are shaped not only by matter and energy, but by consciousness. Through consciousness the boundaries of worlds are defined, and the pathways between them are created or preserved. There are several worlds we know of, and perhaps some we don't, that are closely linked to the world we live in. We even know how they came to be.

"Long ago, at the dawn of humanity, the earth was a single world. On the earth at that time was an ancient race of people. They were older than us, unimaginably more advanced and knowledgeable than human beings. These people played a role in the birth of our first civilizations. Under the guise of many names, the knowledge of these people has survived in myth and legend. In some cultures they were known as gods, and in others angels, or even elves. In our long tradition they are known by the name they give themselves. They are called the elar.

"In what to us is ancient pre-history, more than ten-thousand years ago, there was a dispute among them over the role of humanity in the future of the earth. One of the elar, Lord Saziel, rebelled against the decisions of the high council. He began a terrible war against the elar and the tribes of humanity alike, plunging the world into the darkest age that has ever been. It was an age of such chaos and violence that the conscious boundaries of the world were broken.

"From the ashes of this one earth, three worlds were born. Midgard is the world we live in. Elara is the home of what's left of the elar. And Maleistria is the home of the Malar, where the followers of Saziel continue to wage their endless wars. These three worlds share a common origin. They are all earth, and they are linked together like three interlocking spheres."

Smith breathed a troubled sigh. "All night, I have been in consultation with the other masters of my order. We have reason to believe the man you saw last night is an assassin from Maleistria. Why they are after you we cannot say yet, but without a doubt you're in terrible danger."

"So these guys," Anna said, "are out to get me?" She was still trying to wrap her head around so much of Smith's speech, but one thing she could picture were the empty eyes of that man she saw in the alley last night, and how he broke that boy's neck and tossed him aside as if it were nothing.

"We believe so," Smith said.

"But why?"

"As I said, we don't know, exactly. But in life, how many of us truly know who we are, and the importance of the part we play?"

"So what am I supposed to do?"

"We fear that even here, we may not be able to protect you. Fortunately, I know someone who may be able to advise us further."

"And what if I decide I don't want your help? What if I decide to get up and walk out of here? What would you do?"

Smith paused and seemed to choose his words carefully. "That is your choice to make, of course. I won't stop you. But the assassin you saw last night will find you. And what do you think he will do when he does?"

Anna took a breath and sighed. What could she do? She might not have believed a word of this if she had not seen that man last night, like a horror from the depths of her own nightmares. It was just enough to think that everything Smith said was possible. Why should she be surprised? She always felt there was something more to the world.

She looked at Ken, who was still standing by like a vigilant servant. He nodded once, as if to reassure her that everything the old man said was true. She looked at Mouse, whose expression was unreadable and of no help whatsoever. Finally, she fixed her eyes back on Smith and let out a nervous laugh. "All right," she said.

12

HEIR OF ELGARD

The next thing Anna knew, they were all down in a garage, piling into Smith's Land Rover, as if preparing for some bizarre dysfunctional family outing. They headed downtown, toward Chinatown, where they were going to see a man named Faedyn. Anna and Mouse sat in the back, breathing the arctic blast of the air conditioning on high, and sliding around a little on the firm leather seats while the Land Rover tackled the city streets with ease.

Smith parked the Land Rover on a street that was barely wide enough to admit it in the first place. Below the second story, the walls of the buildings looked as if they were wallpapered with Chinese characters in a variety of styles, sizes, and colors. Anna couldn't tell what half the places were. They were just dirty glass fronts plastered with signs and posters. There were a few identifiable shops, selling everything from backpacks to personal computers, and from fruit to seafood. There were also a few restaurants, which Anna picked out mainly by noting the ducks hanging in the windows.

Smith led them into a small restaurant called Wing Chen. The smell of food made Anna hungry, but they weren't there to eat. An old woman behind the counter eyed them suspiciously. Smith stepped forward. "I am looking for the Doctor," he said. "Can you help me?"

The woman just stared at them for a moment, and then turned toward the kitchen behind her and yelled something in Chinese. Then she just stood there. A moment later a young man came out, lightly gripping a meat cleaver. "How can I help you?" the man said.

Without even glancing at the cleaver, Smith repeated his question. "I am looking for the Doctor. He told me I could reach him here?"

"Are you a patient?"

"I'm a friend. I have some business to discuss with him."

The man looked Smith up and down, then looked at Ken and the two girls. He nodded his head and a smile broke across his face. "Next door down," he said, "up the stairs, number four."

"Thank you," Smith said with a slight bow, and led them back outside.

Back outside, they passed through an unmarked door, ascended a dingy staircase, and went part way down a windowless hall, bare bulbs burning overhead. Smith knocked at number four, and a moment later the door opened.

The man who appeared looked both youthful and old. The skin of his face was taught and lively, and his body was lean and muscular, but his head was crowned with short white hair, and around the eyes and in his general bearing was something that could be seen alternately as wisdom or weariness. Beyond that, there was an ineffable quality to his appearance, perhaps a kind of beauty or an unearthly calm, that gave his presence an air of the inhuman. She couldn't say exactly how, but Anna could tell immediately that he belonged to another race of beings, who although appearing human in many ways, were at least to her quite obviously not.

The man at the door was already looking past Smith and directly into Anna's eyes. A subtle change came across the guarded landscape of his face. Anna would have called it recognition, were she not absolutely sure she had never seen this guy in her life. So instead, she called it confusion, which she thought was just as weird. "I'm Faedyn," the man said, his eyes still on Anna. "I welcome your visit. All of you, please come inside."

They entered through a small foyer, which seemed to double as a waiting room. Although nobody was there now, chairs ran along the left-side wall. To the right, Anna caught a glimpse through an open door into what could have been a doctor's office, although not like the ones she was used to. Beyond the waiting room, they passed into what appeared to be a very small and simply furnished apartment.

Faedyn invited them to sit down in the living room. Ken, Anna, and Mouse crowded onto a small sofa, while Smith and Faedyn sat in chairs. It was clear from their body language that Smith and Faedyn knew each other in some way. Smith made formal introductions, gesturing to each of them on the sofa, "Ken Ashbury, Anna Karova, and ... Mouse."

Faedyn kept his eyes on Anna, but remained silent. Finally, he stood. "I'll make some tea," he said.

There was obviously some sort of unspoken social etiquette being followed here that Anna couldn't quite fathom. Faedyn was gone for some time. They could hear him preparing tea around the corner in the kitchen. Ken and Smith just sat there, waiting quietly. Once, Ken shifted his weight as if he would say something, but only silence followed. Finally, Anna couldn't stand it anymore. "Is this guy going to help us?" she whispered.

Smith smiled at her. "Be patient. For the elar everything happens in its own time."

Anna sighed a sigh of forced patience. Mouse didn't seem to mind the long silence. She looked happier than she had all day, which wasn't saying much, admittedly.

Eventually, Faedyn emerged. He carried a simple wooden tray, laden with a rough ceramic teapot, enough cups for everyone, and a plate of cookies. He set the tray on the table and began to pour the tea, which he did with graceful ease. Golden liquid splashed into the small bowl-like cups. "Please, help yourself," he said.

Anna reached forward and eagerly ate a cookie. Then she picked up her cup. In her grasp, the warm ceramic surface somehow felt rough and smooth all at once. The cups looked crudely made from a distance, but there was a surprising elegance just beneath their rustic form. They were really nice, and she had never seen anything quite like them. "Did you make these cups yourself?" she said.

Smith looked at her rather sharply, but Faedyn didn't seem to mind, and she'd be damned if she was going to let this guy Smith tell her how to behave.

"I did," Faedyn said. He looked into Anna's eyes again, searching there for something. For a moment he seemed lost, and then he remembered his other guests. "Please, everyone, try the tea."

Even Anna, who had acquired a taste for coffee, had to admit this tea was something special. "It's delicious," she said, almost involuntarily.

Faedyn nodded. "I'm glad you like it. It's missing a few ingredients, but it's still good." Almost with reluctance, Faedyn turned his attention to Smith. "So, what news do you have?"

He said this in such a way that it could mean several different things, and yet, as he glanced back at Anna, suggested that he already suspected at least part of the answer.

Smith cleared his throat. "We believe the assassins from Maleistria are looking for this girl."

"Why would you think that?"

"She ran into one of them last night. We have reviewed the data and the Loremasters are all in agreement. They must be here for this girl, but whether they wish to kill her or capture her we do not know."

"It's clear she has the blood of the elar in her," Faedyn said. Then he laughed a little, "much removed perhaps, but nevertheless." He paused for a moment of thought. "She's not the only one though. Since ancient times, even before the Dark Age, many elaran bloodlines have passed into humanity. The girl I saw killed the other night was also high born. Why would you think they're after this girl in particular? Do you know her lineage?"

The conversation had the feel of a guarded diplomatic exchange, each side unsure of what secrets the other might hold. Anna sat quietly and listened. It was strange to hear them talk about her like this.

Smith sipped his tea thoughtfully. "No, we don't. But we believe she may have some psychic potential. We thought to take her as a student. Now that she's under our care, we're bound to protect her."

"How noble of you," Faedyn said. "But even the Loremasters can't protect her from the Malar."

"What can we do then?"

"The answers to all these questions can only be found in Elara. There is someone there who can see through the veils between worlds. Princess Arisu must see this girl for herself. Only then will we truly know why the Malar are after her, and have a chance to save her from them." Faedyn looked at Anna. "How about it? Would you be willing to go on a journey?"

Anna looked at Faedyn. She seemed to trust him implicitly, and she nodded her head without really knowing why or what it meant.

Smith set his tea down abruptly and sighed. "Isn't there some way to keep her here?"

"While these assassins are after her, she will never be safe. If they cannot find her body, they will find her mind. In Elara she will have some sanctuary. But even that is difficult. Someone knowledgeable in the ancient paths must guide her, and there are few of us left in Midgard."

Smith stroked his beard. "We would rather she stay here, but her future must be safeguarded at all costs. Could you guide her?"

Faedyn looked at Anna. He stood up abruptly. "Please excuse me for a moment," he said. They watched, confused as he went down a short hallway and through a door.

†

Faedyn entered his tiny bedroom. There was only one way to know for sure. The resemblance in Anna's face seemed unmistakable, but he had to be certain. The Elara-stone of Elgard would glow in the presence of any descendent of that bloodline, and Faedyn happened to have this ancient treasure buried in his sock drawer.

He couldn't be sure what Smith knew or if he was hiding anything from him. It was clear the girl was important to them, and certainly she would have abilities, but did they suspect what he did? How could they?

He removed a small wooden box from within neatly folded socks. Holding the box in his hands, he hesitated to open it. He feared what it might reveal, that this girl, Anna Karova, was a living descendent of Lord Elgard. The very idea overwhelmed him with memory, and a mixture of deep emotion.

The voice he had been hearing became clearer to him now. *Return … return.* He wondered, was this why the Malar sought to destroy her? Had an heir to Rayaden been found?

The wooden box had darkened with age. The lid and corners were inlaid with tarnished silver. He held it up in the dim light of his room and thumbed the latch. Slowly, he lifted the lid. As the box cracked open, a pale-green glow broke through from within, and he knew.

Faedyn's eyes widened as he looked inside at a green, oval stone about an inch in length. The stone was set in a tarnished silver pendant. For thousands of years the surface of this stone had remained a flat, dark green, but now it emitted a pale light. Faedyn closed his eyes and took a deep breath.

†

Several minutes passed before Faedyn returned. Silence reigned again around the coffee table. Smith stroked his beard with a troubled, pensive expression. Ken kept glancing down the hall. Mouse ate cookies, and Anna fidgeted with her hands. The blood of the elar? What did it mean?

When Faedyn walked back into the room, he appeared changed somehow—perhaps stunned—as if a heavy fog had lifted, revealing many things both good and bad. His eyes fell on Anna with an expression she couldn't interpret. Then he spoke softly, as if to himself. "What once was passes from us, and yet we abide in stillness and sorrow."

"What is that?" Anna said.

"Lines from an old song," Faedyn said. "You are in danger, Anna. I can guide you to Elara if you wish. You will be safe there. It is your ancestral home. There you will have sanctuary at the Shrine of Andurin, at least for the time being, and hopefully we can find the answers we seek."

13

LAND ROVER

Early the next morning, Ken sat blissfully behind the wheel of the Land Rover, with Faedyn in the passenger seat and the two girls in back. Anna had insisted Mouse go with them, so the four of them headed north on the freeway, past seemingly endless suburbs and satellite cities, through the great urban sprawl that spread uninterrupted, up and down the coast.

Smith had handed Ken the Land Rover keys only after a long lecture about how important Anna was to the realization of their goals and the future of their order. Smith couldn't go himself because the Loremasters depended on the collective. Their powers were diminished without all of them working together, so Smith had charged Ken with seeing Anna safely to the Shrine of Andurin. He went on and on about how lucky Ken would be to see another world with his own eyes, and that he must take notes and return with reports on every detail. *Whatever.* Ken had more important things to think about, like driving one of the best off-road vehicles ever made. Finally, he felt like he had come into his own.

Every once in a while, Ken would glance into the rearview mirror and catch a glimpse of Anna staring out the window, watching the world go by with a half-blank and half-troubled expression on her face. Since they set off, she was as quiet as Mouse, who apparently never said anything.

Ken tried talking to Faedyn once or twice, but didn't find him very conversant. All he did was sit there and brood, occasionally rousing himself from silence to tell Ken to "turn right" or "exit here" to take some other highway. The old man was supposed to guide them to Elara, so Ken just went where he said, but he didn't see how it was getting them anywhere closer to another world or another dimension. The whole thing was beginning to seem ridiculous. Were they just going to drive the Land Rover right into some ancient elaran stronghold off exit 42A?

Of course, Smith had educated Ken about the elar and their history, but Faedyn was the first one he had ever met. This morning he had been excited, because Smith regarded the elar with awe, but by midday all he felt was a little disappointment. He only hoped the others they met in Elara—wherever it was—were more impressive than this guy.

"Turn right here," Faedyn said. He didn't even seem sure where they were going. But Ken turned anyway. At the moment, he was more than content just to be behind the wheel and on the open road. He liked the way the power of the V8 engine kicked in when passing.

Faedyn forbade them from stopping for more than a few minutes, so for lunch they passed out sandwiches and ate on the go. In the afternoon, they started heading west, eventually turning off onto a smaller, two-lane highway. They travelled this road for several hours before turning onto an even smaller road that snaked its way back into the woods. Every once in a while, they would see a logging truck or an RV, but traffic began to trickle away, until it seemed they were the only car on the road.

The air became thick with moisture, and the Land Rover filled with the smell of rich soil and pine. The trees grew larger and larger as they progressed deeper and deeper into an old forest. In some places, the branches arched overhead, defining a sinuous, narrow, green tunnel, through which they sped. The afternoon sun came into the woods at an angle, breaking through here and there with great beams of radiant light, and casting long shadows across the road. Alternating bands of light and dark disappeared under the hood of the Land Rover with a kind of hypnotic effect.

Soon Faedyn had Ken turn onto an unmarked dirt road. They had to slow down considerably, but they travelled this road for an hour or two, the Land Rover really coming into its own on badly eroded sections. Were it not for the Land Rover, Ken would have felt out of his element. This morning they had been downtown, at the epicenter of an urban explosion of steel, concrete, and glass radiating out in every direction, setting off secondary explosions along the way. Now they seemed about as far from all that as was humanly possible.

Then Faedyn told Ken to turn onto a barely recognizable track. It couldn't even really be called a road. It was just two old ruts, with long grass between them, overgrown with underbrush, and the forest encroaching from every direction. Ken nosed the Land Rover into the entrance and stopped, slamming the automatic transmission into park. "Are you sure about this?" he said.

Faedyn arched his eyebrows and looked at Ken. He didn't look sure at all. He looked more amused than anything. The whole day was beginning to look more and more like a big wild goose chase.

"You're not exactly sure where you're going, are you?" Ken said.

Faedyn opened his door abruptly, unbuckled his seatbelt, and got out. Ken watched as he walked out in front of the car and proceeded ten or fifteen feet down the track. There he stopped.

Anna unbuckled her seatbelt, leaned forward between the front seats, and looked out the windshield with Ken. Through a few green branches that hung over the hood, they could see Faedyn clearly. He just stood there, his back to them, and his head swaying slightly from side to side, as if he were listening to music. "What's he doing?" Anna said.

"I don't know," Ken said. "Maybe he's crazy."

"I don't think he's crazy," Anna said.

Faedyn crouched down, his hands in front of him, and bowed his head.

"Are you sure?" Ken said.

After a moment, Faedyn stood up, walked back, got into the car, buckled his seatbelt, and simply nodded resolutely. That was it.

Ken looked down the overgrown track and then at Faedyn. "Whatever you say." He jammed the Land Rover into drive and took his foot off the brake.

Progress was tediously slow. The track they travelled was twisted and clearly nobody had been down it in a very long time. For the first mile or so, Ken cringed as numerous over-hanging branches scraped against every surface of the Land Rover with paint-scratching intensity. It happened so continu-ously, however, that after a while he just put his faith in the protective clearcoat and pressed on.

Several times, they were forced to simply crash the Land Rover through a web of undergrowth that had almost completely obscured the track. At one point they all had to get out and move a fallen tree that blocked their way. Driving consumed most of Ken's concentration, and he relished the challenge of steering the Land Rover up the treacherous path.

They went up for a long time, climbing laterally up a hillside, making several switchbacks along the way. When at last they crested the hill and began to come down the other side, there were a few places where the hill dropped off steeply from the side of the road. From these vantage points, they caught glimpses of a vast forested valley that stretched on for miles, deeply shadowed in the setting sun. There was no sign of civilization—no buildings, no roads, nothing. That was where they were headed.

Of course, all they saw were the tops of trees, but already Ken sensed a strangeness about the place. An untouched feeling prevailed here, notably stronger than in the old forests they had already passed through. A sense of secrecy and mystery permeated the air, and through the windows of the Land Rover drifted a magical, almost primordial smell that made the earth seem young and alive.

"I've never seen a place like this," Anna said as she hung her head out the window and breathed the air deeply. "It's wonderful."

Ken had never seen a place like it either, but he couldn't spend too much time admiring the sights. They were, after all, still on a pretty treacherous track, and if he didn't keep an eye on things, they would tumble off a cliff to their deaths.

If anything, going down seemed even more dangerous than going up, and to make matters worse, it was getting dark.

Faedyn made no indication he had any intention of stopping. Ken switched on the Land Rover's multiple headlights, and for once they didn't seem like an overkill. The visibility was still low because of the trees and undergrowth, and beyond the headlights it was black as pitch, but the Land Rover lit up the way immediately ahead of them with a reassuring intensity.

For several hours after dark, they made their way slowly down into the valley until the track leveled off. Then they made a few random turns and came to an abrupt stop. This was not a matter of a log in the road or some simple under- brush. The track had dwindled and dimmed for a while, get- ting progressively less distinct, but then it just faded away to nothing, disappearing into a wall of dense, impassable forest. Not even the headlights of the Land Rover could penetrate those woods for anything more than a few feet.

Ken locked his foot on the brake. "What now?" he said. He glanced back and saw Mouse fast asleep, her head on Anna's lap, and Anna half asleep too.

"Turn off the engine," Faedyn said.

Ken was too tired to ask any more questions, so he put the transmission in park and shut off the engine. It was suddenly very quiet and very dark inside the Land Rover. And then it wasn't quiet at all, but from outside, from deep in the forest, the ghostly voices of nocturnal things began to fill his senses. The odd cries of woodland frogs, the shrieks and hoots of nightbirds, the trill of insects, and the howls of things unknown created a landscape of utterly unfamiliar sounds. Outside the Land Rover, the night was darker than Ken ever imagined possible. Not a thing could be seen, for neither starlight nor moonlight could filter through the dense forest canopy.

"We're in the twilight realm," Faedyn said. "Try to get some sleep. Tomorrow we'll continue on foot." That was all he said, and it haunted Ken all through the uncomfortable night.

14

Log Bridge

There was no way to describe the sound. On the surface, it was just a crack, but underneath it was like the calving of icebergs or the shifting of tectonic plates, a noise that seemed impossibly large, which overwhelmed the senses, a noise that came as much from within her, in her blind rage, as it did from the steel pipe breaking the boy's skull. The taste of blood filled her mouth—warm, thick, and metallic.

A thousand times, Anna had seen this scene in her mind's eye. A thousand times the boy fell, limp and senseless. His body cascaded to the ground in what now seemed like an infinite number of increments.

Through the buildings she ran and ran, down endless alleyways until she stood in a forest, with a mossy cliff face looming in front of her. She walked forward, feeling the moist ground beneath her bare feet. There was a crack in the rock, and as she approached, she realized it was the entrance to a cave.

She walked down a narrow corridor for what seemed like a long time. It became very dark, but somehow she could still see. Eventually she came into a large chamber deep in the earth. A few rudimentary torches were fixed to the walls. In the dark corners she saw what might have been stacks of bones. She couldn't tell for sure.

In the middle of the room, circled by loose stones on the rough floor, was a hole, about six feet in diameter. Already she had a bad feeling, increasingly bad, but she walked forward to look, compelled by something she could not fathom.

The water, if it was water in that dark pit, was black and smooth. Her own reflection stared back at her, only there was something wrong. She wondered why she didn't look like herself. What was it? Who was she?

Then, quite suddenly, her bad feeling became an unspeakable dread, magnified a hundred-fold in an instant. It wasn't just a creepy feeling. It wasn't simple trepidation or fear. There was something there, something all around her, something inside her, something horrible.

Whatever was at the bottom of the pit, which looked more like crude oil than water, began to move, distorting the reflection of Anna's face. It happened slowly at first—a ripple here, a wave there—but soon it bubbled ferociously. What troubled Anna was it didn't move randomly or mechanically, but somehow with an unmistakable sentience, and she knew that it was only the beginning. It was like a great drum beating inside her. It grew stronger and stronger, faster and faster until she could hardly breathe, until the beats collapsed into a single sickening vibration that spread throughout her body. Whatever it was, it was emerging. It was about to transform from this nascent state into something unimaginable. Anna didn't want to see it. She would give anything not to see it, but she couldn't turn away, and she couldn't shut her eyes.

Suddenly a hideous column of black ooze rose from the pit. It reached the ceiling and began to spread out across the vault of the chamber. Like a deafening storm, it drowned out everything with its maddening, impossible presence. Anna needed to scream. An overwhelming feeling brought her to the brink of insanity. Her mouth opened, terrified, but utterly silent.

†

Anna woke with a start, her head jerking painfully against the window of the Land Rover with a clunk. It took her a moment to remember where she was. In the dark, she could make out Mouse curled up and sleeping on the seat next to her, and she could hear the deep breaths of sleep emanating from the slumping shape of Ken's body. Somehow though, she knew right away that Faedyn was gone. The passenger seat was empty and the forest outside had grown deeply quiet.

Anna couldn't sleep again that night. For a long time, she still had the feeling of a malevolent presence, waiting to descend upon her if she let down her guard, if she only drifted off again. She waited nervously for the light of day to come and dispel the horror of her vision. She waited and wondered. Where was Faedyn? What was out there, beyond the mildly comforting walls of the Land Rover?

The sun had already broken the horizon when Faedyn finally returned. He emerged from the forest in the dawning light as if appearing out of a green mist. Suddenly he was just there. Anna got out of the Land Rover.

"Ah, you're awake," Faedyn said.

"Yeah, I was awake most of the night."

"Did something happen?"

She swung the car door shut, waking both Ken and Mouse simultaneously. "No, nothing happened." She couldn't tell him about the dream. She couldn't even begin to explain. It would sound like a child's nightmare, which she knew it wasn't. She was not a child, and it had not been merely a nightmare.

They ate a quick breakfast, and then each of them put on a backpack. In the morning light, a rough footpath was now visible in front of the Land Rover.

Anna, Mouse, and Ken followed Faedyn into the forest. After about a mile, Ken shouted up from the rear. "Hey Faedyn, how far is this place anyway?"

Faedyn ignored him.

"What about the car?" Ken said.

Faedyn turned his head. "Forget about the car." That was all he said until they reached the river.

Anna heard the water before she saw it, but the noise increased so slowly she didn't notice until they came to the edge of a small gorge. Some fifteen feet below, whitewater cut through the forest, flowing over exposed granite, worn smooth through the years.

Anna stopped in surprise. "Oh," she said, "a river," and took a step back from the edge. The canopy gave way to open sky above the water, and for a moment they looked up at small white clouds drifting overhead in the pale blue.

Ken looked down the length of the river. It was far too swift and treacherous to wade across. He screwed up his face as he thought about it. "Which way now?"

"We cross," Faedyn said, still gazing skyward.

"It's too fast to cross," Ken said.

"Mouse doesn't think so," Faedyn said, his eyes still fixed on the sky.

Anna suddenly realized Mouse wasn't next to her. Looking around, she spotted her twenty feet up river, where a large tree had fallen years ago, bridging the gorge. Out on the middle of the tree, high above the raging river, was Mouse, waving happily. "Mouse!" Anna yelled. "What are you doing? Get back here!"

"No," Faedyn said. "Follow her across."

Anna's fear of heights kicked in just looking at the tree. "I'm not sure this is a good idea. There has to be another way. Let's just walk along the river. There'll be another way. There has to be." Anna was talking a mile a minute now, but Mouse was already on the far bank, and Ken and Faedyn were on their way. The small gorge suddenly looked like the Grand Canyon to Anna, and the broad tree like a flimsy rope spanning its vast expanse.

"Ummm, this doesn't look very safe," Anna said. Ken and Faedyn were already halfway across the log. "Maybe I'll … go around … or … or something." But it was already clear that there was no way around.

"It's perfectly fine," Ken said, rather overconfident. "See," and he jumped up and down a few times before going the rest of the way across.

Showoff, Anna thought. Then she took a deep breath and looked around for some other course of action besides the obvious.

"Anna," Faedyn said.

She looked out across the log and caught Faedyn's eyes, his deep, harsh, kind, scary, and reassuring eyes. He stood there on the log almost at the other bank, with a statuesque solidity, a physicality unfettered by fear or doubt, looking at her with his beautiful eyes.

"Anna," he said. His voice had a calm, soothing resonance, even over the roar of the rapids. She had never heard her name said like that. She looked past Faedyn to where Ken and Mouse were standing on the far bank, each of them trying to look encouraging in their own way.

"Oh, hell," Anna said. Then she yelled across the river, "If I fall, it's your fault, Ken."

"Why my fault?" Ken said, but she couldn't hear him over the din of the current.

She stepped toward the log, and very slowly, step by step, made her way onto it, keeping her eyes fixed on Faedyn. Though it seemed narrow as a twig to Anna, the log was broad, so the surface was only gently curved. However, there were several branches, half broken and dead, that she would have to maneuver around. In places the wood was wet and slippery, and in places rotten. The river rushed beneath her. She could feel it like the thunderous, continuous passing of some giant terrifying serpent, but she dared not look.

Then, of course, she looked.

Every muscle in her body froze up in an instant, locking her eyes downward and halting her feet halfway across the river. She imagined the fall of her body, stopped only by its impact on the rocks below, and then, likely dead, she would be washed downstream in a torrent of water. She felt dizzy and weak, her legs like pieces of meat disconnected from her body. Slowly, she began to crouch down, shaking, until she was on all fours.

Without looking up, she managed to speak. "I ... uh ... did I mention I'm afraid of heights?"

"Really?" Ken said.

"Your sarcasm isn't appreciated. I'm in a bad situation here."

"The worst thing you can do is look down."

"Don't you think I know that!" Anna yelled.

"Look, you're already halfway, so there's no point in going back. Just get up and walk the rest of the way."

"I don't know if I can do it." Her whole body was trembling. She was afraid she would shake herself right off the log. "Can somebody come and help me … somebody … Faedyn?"

"Anna," Faedyn said. "You're okay. Take a deep breath."

Anna took a deep breath.

"Now look at me," Faedyn said.

She looked up to see Faedyn at the far end of the log, calm and patient. Normally she would despise anybody who put her weakness on display, like at this moment she despised Ken, but she didn't feel that with Faedyn. He didn't look at her like she was weak, and somehow that gave her strength.

"You must cross of your own accord," Faedyn said.

Anna blinked her eyes.

Faedyn stood, confident and resolute.

Slowly Anna got to her feet, keeping her eyes on Faedyn. The shaking in her legs abated. She took a step, and then another, and then another and another until she took a few quick steps to throw her arms around the solid ground of Faedyn's body, burying her head in his chest. She pressed against him, feeling the muscles that covered his stalwart frame. She stayed there for a moment, clinging to him, and it was the most wonderful thing in the world.

When she finally looked up, embarrassed, Faedyn was looking down at her. There was a slight smile on his face. Perhaps it was just amusement, but she would treasure it forever. She let go of him. He nodded, as if to conclude the matter, and continued down the path.

Anna scowled at Ken and followed. Mouse mimicked Anna's scowl, flawlessly.

"What?" Ken said as he brought up the rear, but he didn't get an answer from either of them.

†

They continued on into the woods on the other side of the river. The footpath began to look more and more like a track made by animals. Eventually, it disappeared altogether. They trampled through underbrush when they had to now, but much of the forest floor was surprisingly clear, due to the thick canopy overhead. Small ferns here and there, moss covered boulders, and fallen trees were their only obstacles.

Anna lost all sense of direction. Everything looked the same, but she just followed Faedyn, who seemed sure now they were on the right track. They paused to rest and drink occasionally, and once to eat the remainder of their food. They went up and over another ridgeline and down into a valley where the forest was even more dense. And the trees grew larger and larger with each mile they walked.

As afternoon waned on, Anna's feet began to ache. A dreary gloom fell over the woods, and their little group spread out more and more along the way. Faedyn showed no sign of fatigue and walked on, steadfast, occasionally pausing to let the rest of them catch up. After the river incident, Anna was anxious to show Faedyn that she had some backbone. No matter how tired she was or how much her feet hurt, she was determined to keep up and go on without complaint, and without any sign of wanting to stop, which she wanted very badly to do. If Ken slowed down, she picked up her step. If he mentioned resting, she said she was fine, why rest now? She took Mouse as her example, who marched onward in silence, keeping pace with Faedyn despite being half his size.

Finally, at dusk, they stopped. In truth, it was to everybody's great relief. Even Faedyn seemed glad. They stopped in a small clearing, unshouldered their packs, and sank to the ground, leaning their backs against the trunks of broad trees. They breathed the moist air, rich with the deep, organic scents of life in every stage of blossom and decay. They tasted the salt of their sweat and heard the sound of wind in the high branches and leaves.

To Anna, it was intoxicating. She found there was a fullness and a sweetness to nature unrivaled by anything she had ever experienced. Here, surrounded by the forest, her senses were satiated. She could feel the abundance of life around her and felt herself as a part of it, pulsing with energy.

Faedyn stood at the edge of the clearing as if he were listening to the same pulsing energy that filled Anna's awareness. He bowed, clapped his hands together as if in prayer, and mumbled something inaudible to Anna. Then he turned to the three of them. "This is a good place," he said. "We'll camp here," and without another word, he disappeared into the woods with the speed and stealth of a wild animal.

Ken surveyed the area. "Looks like we're roughing it tonight."

"It's not so bad," Anna said.

"I suppose I could sleep just about anywhere at this point. But what's for dinner? Bark? There's nothing in these bags but blankets and clothes."

"It'll be okay. Mouse looks happy."

Ken glanced over to where Mouse was completely sprawled out on the ground. Her eyes were closed and there was more of a smile on her face than he had ever seen. "Well, that's something, I guess. What do you think of Faedyn?"

"I'd say he knows exactly what he's doing."

"Don't you think it's strange that he's barely said a word since we left the city. And now he just disappears without saying a thing about where he's going or when he'll be back."

"That's just the way he is," Anna said.

"I don't like it."

"Well, it was your *master* who set us up with him."

Ken sighed and didn't say much after that. After a while, Faedyn returned quite as suddenly as he had gone. Over his shoulder, he carried a small cloth satchel. He set it down and in no time at all, while there was still some dusk light filtering through the trees, he had a fire going. Soon he was boiling up the various foraged foods from his satchel.

Anna, Ken, and Mouse were each, in turn, drawn from their resting places by the unmistakable smell of food wafting over from Faedyn's stew. They crouched down around the fire and peered into the pot. Faedyn added more ingredients. There were mushrooms, herbs and roots, as well as some strange potato things Faedyn cut up into chunks before adding to the mix. Some of the things were recognizable; others were a total mystery. As Faedyn added a bunch of what really did look like bark, Ken gave Anna a funny look. "What did I tell you?" he said.

"It smells good," Anna said.

And it was good.

Even Ken had to agree. "It's not half bad," he said, sounding surprised when he had downed his second helping. "These starchy things are really tasty."

With a full stomach and a warm fire, and blankets from their packs, it didn't take long for all except Faedyn to fall fast asleep.

†

In the middle of the night Anna stirred from her sleep, troubled by the prelude of her dreams and roused by some noise in the forest. From where she lay, she looked through her half-opened eyes. Faedyn sat on the ground near her head. He threw another log on the fire. Some of the older logs collapsed into coals and a cloud of sparks crackled and took flight from the flames.

The firelight cast a glow on Faedyn's face, and deep shadows were drawn along the lines of contemplation, distant and melancholy, whose paths were traced there. He noticed Anna was awake and looked down to meet her gaze. His eyes, which seemed weary and sad, showed a kind of spark when he looked upon her, and his face filled with a touching benevolence. "Anna," he said, "when I first saw you, I could hardly believe it … after all these years. Even now I can see your father in my memory … and the people of your bloodline."

Anna looked up at him, wide eyed, wondering if she had slipped back into a dream. She wanted to ask … but didn't know how … and she was so sleepy.

Faedyn reached out and gently touched her forehead. "Go back to sleep," he said. Then he shrugged his shoulders, wrapping his blanket tighter around him, and shut his eyes as if he would sleep, as well.

15

Flight of the Alates

A beam of radiant light broke through the thick canopy of the forest and fell on the sleeping face of Anna Karova. Her eyes flickered for a moment and then opened wide, scintillating with consciousness as they took in her surroundings. The warmth, as much as the light, roused her from her slumber. The others were already awake. She could hear them talking in low voices and packing up their stuff. Little blue butterflies flittered through the clearing, in and out of the light that cut through the dewy morning. They were buoyed up on microcurrents visible in the swirling mist that filled the air.

Anna stretched out lengthwise like a cat. "I slept so wonderfully," she said.

"So did I," Ken said, clearly amazed by the fact. "Never would have thought I could sleep like that in the middle of the woods, but I feel great."

"Good," Faedyn said. "We have another long walk today."

After breakfast they began walking, but somehow it wasn't quite as arduous as the day before. The walking was easier, and their legs moved with renewed vigor, as if imbued with new-found life. Much to Anna's relief, they traversed no log bridges. And the forest itself became of sudden and intense interest to her. No matter how much they walked, there were always new things to look at and marvel over.

She began to notice things. The trees really were getting bigger, and the plants were larger and lusher and greener. Everything began to take on a super-vivid quality. It came on so slowly that she might have missed it, but the world itself seemed crisper, brighter, and altogether more alive. In truth, she could not say exactly what it was, but things were different, and of that she was sure.

They came to a place where Anna was sure there were trees of a type they had not seen before—a remarkable-looking tree with smooth, silvery bark. It was a small tree, residing in the shade beneath the upper canopy. The spindly arms of the tree supported clusters of bright, shimmering, green leaves that seemed impossibly brilliant where any ray of light fell upon them. Along the outer edges of the tree, white blossoms shook gently in a rare breeze and dropped a shower of petals which drifted to the forest floor.

The trees were so startling that Anna stopped to look at one through the forest. She waited for Ken to catch up so she could point it out to him. "Look at that," she said, pointing through the stands of huge trunks to where the strange tree stood. "Have you ever seen a tree like that?"

"It's just a tree," Ken said.

"We've been in this forest for a day and a half now. We haven't seen a single tree like that. Look at it. Have you ever seen anything so beautiful?"

Ken considered the tree for a moment, at least entertaining the idea that he might have missed something. "I'm from the city, Anna. A tree is just a tree to me."

"I'm from the city too, but you'd have to be blind not to see that's an unusual tree."

Eventually, even Ken couldn't deny that the character of the landscape was changing. The strange, blossoming, silver trees that Anna had first noticed were soon all around, and they followed Faedyn through what seemed like a snowstorm of falling petals. The ground turned white with them, and the air was filled with them, drifting down in a slow, fluttering, dreamlike movement.

As they approached a small stream, a group of five or six animals lifted their heads in curious unison from where they were drinking. The animals resembled deer, but were only about two feet tall. A moment later, the creatures darted off into the woods with gazelle-like grace, leaping over fallen logs and disappearing into the nearby underbrush with barely a patter of their tiny hooves.

Faedyn stopped at the stream. "We'll rest here for a while."

"Where exactly is 'here?'" Ken said.

"We are in Elara," Faedyn said.

"Really?" Anna said.

Faedyn crossed his arms and nodded.

It was not hard for her to imagine this place represented an entirely different world. In fact, she knew it was true. Somehow, although the transition had been seamless, she had already known they had entered Elara. She could feel it in the earth. And although there was no reason for it, the place seemed strangely familiar and comforting.

"What about the car?" Ken said.

"If you turn around now," Faedyn said, "you won't find the car or your home or anything else familiar. You have crossed between worlds, and you cannot go back by simply turning around."

All afternoon they headed upstream, following the course of the water up into the hills. In places, the stream flowed over little cliffs, into rocky canyons, and over boulders slick with algae. The water cascaded down all this in a great staircase of shimmering waterfalls. At one point, they paused near a small niche cut into the rock beside the falls. Inside were some smooth river stones.

"What's that?" Anna said.

Faedyn looked. "Ah, it's an ancient shrine, built to honor the spirit of this place." Faedyn bowed toward the shrine and then clapped his hands together before leading them on.

They climbed a steep course along the banks of the stream, scrambling up rock and loose dirt, at times with only a pro-truding root or a flimsy sapling making the difference between another step and a nasty fall. They continued this ascent, until they reached at last the source of the stream, a tranquil lake nestled in the heavily wooded hills.

The lake was a jewel, hidden from sight until the very last moment, when its polished surface opened up before them like a dazzling mirror. All around, the limbs of ancient trees overhung its depths, and in its glassy surface, the reflection of the blue sky and green hills was so clear that Anna could see individual leaves on the trees as she perched upon a rock at the water's edge.

From the shores of this place, they turned west again into the forest and walked on until late afternoon. At last, they emerged from the woods and stood at the edge of a high bluff overlooking the land as far as the eye could see. Here they pitched camp and for a while did nothing more than rest their weary feet. They ate the food Faedyn had collected throughout the day, and as the sun went down in the west, they all sat and looked out over the far, wide land.

†

For miles upon miles, the great trees formed a canopy whose roof billowed up like layers of verdant clouds. An ocean of green stretched to the horizon. As dusk fell, they began to see tiny, green fluorescent lights rising up out of the forest below. At first the lights came in fleeting, intermittent bursts, like shooting stars—one here, another there—barely visible against the backdrop of growing darkness. Over the course of a few minutes though, the frequency of the lights increased dramatically.

Soon the green lights were raining upward out of the trees for miles and miles, forming great luminescent swarms that flowed across the treetops in waves. They rose, hovered, fell, and mixed together endlessly. Faedyn, Ken, Anna, and Mouse sat transfixed by this strange, hypnotic spectacle. "What is that?" Anna finally said, still gazing out at the swirling lights that drifted upward in the darkness.

Faedyn took a breath. "Those are the alates of the giant rot-wood termite. For years they remain in their nests, transforming deep in the rotting wood of fallen trees. Once a year, those that are ready take flight like this. Most of them will die, but a few will establish new colonies and another generation will begin." His voice was sad and distant, residing in a memory of long-lost things.

"Those are bugs?" Ken said.

"The insects help break down the dead parts of the forest," Faedyn said. "Without death and decay, there can be no new life, and with new life, the earth is reborn."

"It's beautiful," Anna said.

"Long ago," Faedyn said, "this was the land of Farhalin, and many elar lived in peace here. We shall see what we find now." Faedyn then got up and walked off, leaving Anna, Ken, and Mouse alone.

They looked out over the darkened world. The stars had come out and shone above in abundance with a radiance and intensity they had never seen before. Below them, and as far as they could see, great masses of bioluminescent insects were still emerging from the forest, one swarm seeming to set off another as they took to the air. Anna turned to Mouse, "Isn't it beautiful?"

Mouse didn't respond, but Anna could see the enchantment in her face. Mouse watched the flight of the alates with a hypnotic fascination too deep to be bothered with answering questions, and for a while, silence passed between them all.

At last, Anna spoke. "Ken?"

"Yeah?"

"What do you know about Faedyn?"

"So, you're interested in him, huh?"

"Aren't you interested … in the elar I mean?"

"I guess so. It's part of the knowledge that the Loremasters keep."

"If they live in this world, in Elara, what was Faedyn doing in the city?"

"There have always been a few, from time to time, who have lived among us in Midgard. I believe Faedyn was there for a very long time. Smith said he was a refugee of the Elara-war, but that was over a thousand years ago. Who knows who he really is."

"What was the Elara-war?" Anna said, becoming ever more curious about the new world unfolding before her.

Ken told Anna and Mouse the story of the Elara-war as he had learned it from Smith, and as Smith had learned it from his master, and so on until the time when the events the story spoke of first became known in Midgard.

In very ancient times, when the great elaran cities fell before Saziel's armies, much was lost, for the elar had made many wondrous and marvelous things in their Golden Age. Among them were eight magic swords, forged in a time when the elar were at the height of their powers, and had at their command a profound understanding of the relationships between matter, energy, and consciousness.

At this point, Anna interrupted. "Magic swords?"

"Not hocus-pocus magic," Ken said. "That's only a dim counterfeit of what was once a true science. This magic was essentially the most advanced technology the world has ever known, born out of an understanding of how consciousness interacts with matter and energy on the most fundamental levels of the universe. That's what they say, anyway. We Loremasters only barely understand the most rudimentary aspects of the field of consciousness alone. Anyway ..." And he continued to tell the story.

These swords and their wielders were once the protectors of great cities. Most of them were destroyed in the Great War or lost forever in the Dark Age that followed. Only three survived into the new age, when the earth was broken apart into the three worlds. The great swords were secreted away and hidden, like the elar themselves, deep in the forests of Elara. Steeped in powerful magic, the three remaining swords—named Rayaden, Saraden, and Elladen—were a bastion of strength and hope to the fugitive race for thousands of years.

The swords were passed on, but in time the wielders of these weapons no longer practiced the deep secrets of their art. Almost without notice, the power of these weapons waned and finally fell asleep, while the powers of darkness were once again joined together under the emperors of Maleistria.

A high-ranking official, a lord of Elara named Beyore, was seduced by an evil force, a demon they say. He betrayed the elar. He revealed the existence of the ancient swords to the Malar and opened the way into Elara. The armies of the Maleistrian emperor set sail, crossing between the two worlds.

They marched on Shoaelin first, in the South, where Gairen, the wielder of Saraden, went forth with an army to meet them on the field of battle. But in the battle, Gairen fell and Saraden was lost to the Malar. Then the dark army laid siege to the mountain-home of Kalla. Armandiel, the wielder of Elladen, and the elar of Kalla fought bravely, but Kalla could not stand against the Malar. When he saw the walls would be breached, Armandiel took Elladen deep into the caves of Kalla. Rather than let Elladen fall into the hands of the enemy, he destroyed it. A massive explosion shook the earth and collapsed the mountain on top of him. Thus, Kalla fell and the power of Elladen was removed from the world forever.

Lord Elgard, the wielder of Rayaden, took the last of the swords, and realizing there was but a single hope, he gave it to Miura, his most trusted warrior. He sent Miura on a quest to hide the sword where the Malar would never find it. Then he set a trap for the army that approached his forest home.

When Beyore learned that Elgard had hidden Rayaden and would not reveal where, he kidnapped Elgard's daughter, Yume, and went to warn the approaching army of the ambush that awaited them. Though his daughter was in the hands of the enemy, Elgard would not reveal where Rayaden was. He couldn't, for he deliberately told Miura not to say where he planned to go with it, nor in which direction he would leave.

Elgard and many elar fought to their deaths that day. Many fled too, or were sent into the deep forest to endure. The Malar killed Yume, and in time they returned to their dark realm. Rayaden was saved, but at a great cost, and to this day, nobody knows where Miura hid it.

16

WATCHERS IN THE WOOD

In the morning, Faedyn led them down into the vast and sprawling land of Farhalin. The path tracked wide around the sheer cliffs of the bluff and down a manageable slope. At the bottom, they again passed beneath the canopy of trees and into the cool, green world, where the shade wrapped Faedyn in a comfort that felt like home.

Many plants and animals revealed themselves to his keen senses. They were like old friends, and their voices were woven together in a tapestry as rich as any chorus. It was a feeling, a living remembrance he never thought he would return to. *Arhasun,* the organic totality of being, was felt everywhere, but nowhere did its manifestations please him more than here.

A curious sense of dread accompanied his nostalgic reverie, however, for in subtle signs he read that this land had come upon troubled times. Even yesterday he felt a certain tension in the air that infected his head with gloomy thoughts. Now, as they walked, it became clear. He could sense it in the soil and the trees. They whispered some dark secret to him. There was no doubt that even in the midst of this forest, the weight of evil lurked in the air about them, and in the ground beneath their feet. All was not well in this place.

Faedyn paused for a moment, just a half step, cocked his head and then continued. To the eye it seemed like nothing, but in that brief second, he knew they were being followed. Somewhere, out there, someone or something watched them through the arboreal veil. He walked on, casually and steadfast as was his way, showing no sign of this discovery. He said nothing to the others, but made a point to keep their presence and locations fixed in his perception.

Like a net, Faedyn spread out his awareness over the whole of the forest around them, and along the pathways of countless sensory inputs, information began to flow into him. In this limited and subtle way, he kept an eye on the hidden presence, tracking its movement, and trying to catch some glimpse of its form or intent.

That morning, as they descended from the bluff, Ken had questioned him. "How far to Andurin? When will we come to this sanctuary?"

He could not fault the boy for his attention to his duty, but he had that very human quality of wanting to know everything. Faedyn had tried to ignore him, but the boy was quite persistent. Finally, Faedyn stopped and said, "Andurin is still a long journey from here. As for sanctuary, we'll see what we find there. For now, we all go where fate leads us."

Ken didn't seem very satisfied with the answer, but for a while he at least fell quiet, a mask that covered the inner turmoil still quite obviously troubling his mind. Actually, Faedyn felt a little sorry for him. It's a state of suffering not to accept when a situation has passed from one's personal control.

When he reflected on it, Faedyn was not so sure he liked the answer himself. Things had not been this unclear for a very long time. His vision of the future was empty, a bowl waiting to be filled. It had been ages since the pathways of possibility had grown so broad and numerous. When he peered ahead, he saw only the next few steps and not a glimmer of anything beyond. The uncertainties became too vast to coalesce. Prescience was a dangerous game anyway, but he wondered, where was fate leading him? What path of destiny had they all set out upon?

He glanced back at Anna, who trudged resolutely some ten feet in his wake. The existence of this girl had taken him by surprise. He was still recovering from the memories this discovery had awakened. At times, he felt awe in her presence. She was so familiar, and yet so different … so human. And he had many questions. How had the Loremasters found Anna? And what vision did they have for her? Did they know who she really was? Did the Malar know? Did anyone know but him?

The voice he heard in his mind became stronger by the day. It beckoned him from afar, to *return … return.* And now he knew where it came from. It was from Andurin. Perhaps Princess Arisu had already foreseen this present course, or some fragment of it. She was the only one who could have the perception to learn of his existence in Midgard. He wondered, if she expected him, would she also be expecting the girl? Had her vision grown so vast that she could anticipate even this?

Whatever the case, it seemed that in Andurin—if they got there—some answers might await them. Too bad he didn't like the price he was almost sure he would have to pay. But the past held him in a debt of duty he could not escape, and he had already resolved upon this course. In a way, he had chosen this course over a thousand years ago. The matter was beyond his control. Though he knew not where it led, nor how far, there could be no doubt that he strode the path of his destiny.

These thoughts played across the background of his mind, while his attention was focused on the trickle of information regarding whoever was following them. He knew now, for instance, there was a group of them. They were very quiet and careful, keeping upwind and moving with remarkable stealth. But by the faintest traces, such as the sounds and patterns of birds and small animals, he tracked their movement.

Whoever they were, they had split up and moved into flanking positions, trailing only slightly behind now. Slowly, they were advancing. He sensed the possibility of an imminent threat. There was fear and confusion out there, and that was always a dangerous combination.

†

Anna thought it would be another uneventful day of walking. They had walked wide of the sheer cliffs where they had camped. She had worried about the descent, but the trail wasn't bad. As long as some semblance of earth was in front of her, she could fix her eyes on the ground and stay calm.

For her, acrophobia, the fear of heights, was not merely a function of altitude. Anything that simply dropped away caused vertigo when she approached the edge. It was a strange thing, because it wasn't necessarily falling she feared, although that was certainly a part of it. When she examined her feelings, it was clear what terrified her was, at least in part, the edge itself.

The edge was a place of marked significance, a place where the possibilities were laid out before you as plain and as undeniable as anything ever is. It was a symbol of the realities we are all bound up in. The edge cleaved through the future mercilessly, dividing paths, creating the dualities from which all action emerges. To stand or fall, to live or die. No, it was not falling that terrified her, not entirely. It was this manifest duality that required the conscious intervention of the will.

She feared these fundamental choices, from which the course of her destiny unfolded. As she neared the edge, she felt the pull of the abyss, and the path beyond became just as clear to her as the one she was on. It was as easy to fall as it was to stand. No, it was not death she feared, not entirely, but this moment of choice that was right at the edge, where only she could tip the balance of a divided future.

At the edge, a bubble of uncertainty formed and grew around her, and as the probability of each path approached a mean, she became paralyzed with terror, with this immense responsibility that she bore. She began to sweat and tremble, her knees buckled and her strength drained out of her. This was vertigo, a moment of indecision, drawn out toward eternity.

†

The character of the forest changed. Gone were the groves of strange silvery trees, the open ground covered in white blossoms, and the evergreens that towered above them, as straight and true as any skyscraper. The forest below the bluff, the place Faedyn called Farhalin, seemed to grow in every direction. Giant oaks dominated the forest here, along with maple and elm. Massive trunks gave way to huge branches that spread out and twisted together so much that one tree's limbs were indistinguishable from the next. The canopy was nearly unbroken, a thick roof rich with green foliage. Where the sun broke through, impenetrable thickets had formed, dense with brush.

The ground below became a treacherous tangle of gnarled roots that always seemed to protrude right as one was about to take a step. There were plenty of vines to trip you up, and hidden rocks to stub your toes, all of which elicited occasional grunts, groans, and cursing from Ken as he brought up the rear. But between the trunks of the trees and their network of exposed roots, mosses grew in great enormous patches, soft as the plushest of carpets and almost preternaturally green. Mouse moved among the trees, darting here and there as if she were a creature of the forest herself.

As they walked, again and again Anna's thoughts returned to Faedyn's words. "Even now, I can see your father." He had said this to her in the uncounted hours of the night, when the world of dreams held as much sway over her as the world around her. Now, her recollection colored those words with layer upon layer of thoughts, feelings, and images that had come to her in the sleep that preceded and followed them. Soon the words themselves, Faedyn's voice, and the distant, timeless look on his face when he spoke to her, all took on a dreamlike air in her memory. But how could Faedyn have known her father? It didn't make sense.

Anna picked up her pace to catch up with Faedyn. As she approached his broad back, without a look he made room for her to walk beside him. He said nothing. His attention was still out there in the forest, and perhaps beyond, in a perception of the world that Anna couldn't imagine.

Faedyn's stride was silent and powerful. And with his attention focused outward, everywhere at once, as if he were intent on encompassing the whole world with his consciousness, he didn't have a disposition that invited questions. Anna felt small and girlish beside him. She hesitated to speak.

"Sometimes," Faedyn said abruptly, as if reading her mind, "things are said before their time."

Anna looked up at him and did not hesitate now. "What did you mean when you said you remembered my father?"

Faedyn didn't answer right away, but gazed off into the trees in a way that made Anna wonder whether he would answer at all. When he finally spoke, it seemed to be in the most careful and circuitous manner. "The lineages of the elar are traced through millennia," he said. "And many different people may be considered the father of a single bloodline. In ancient times, when there was but a single earth, sometimes the two races, elar and human, intermarried and bore off-spring. In later times, the conscious spheres of these two races drifted apart and contact between them dwindled. The knowledge of the elar faded from all the tribes of humanity, except those who still dwell in Elara, and those doomed to dwell in the dark realm of Maleistria. But still, through the ages, it has occurred from time to time. To you, the father I spoke of may only be a distant relative, but once the blood of the elar passes into a line of humanity, it does not diminish. For many generations it may sleep, but eventually it awakens, and a child who bears traces of the elar is born among humans, someone like yourself."

"Then ... you didn't know my real father?"

"No, not your birth-father, just a distant relative from a time gone by."

Anna thought about this for a while as they walked. When she spoke again, her voice was faint. "I never knew my father. I think he died before I was born."

"I'm sorry," Faedyn said. "The other night when I spoke, I spoke as if from a dream."

Anna knew so little about her family that even the knowledge of a distant relative seemed like a treasure. She was about to ask about him, when Faedyn held out a hand and stopped her in her tracks. He cocked his head and held a cautioning finger to his lips.

Anna looked around, but whatever Faedyn sensed was lost on her. Without the sound of their own footsteps and voices, the forest became incredibly still.

Mouse came silently to Anna's side. She took hold of Anna's wrist and looked up at her with questioning, apprehensive eyes.

Ken approached. "Why are we stopping?" But Faedyn gave him a look that silenced him immediately. It was a serious look, perhaps the most serious look Ken had ever seen, and a look that sent a wave of fear down Anna's spine and into her increasingly numb legs. To her mind came the image of the assassin they had seen. Though they were on ground that was relatively flat in all directions, she began to have a feeling a lot like vertigo.

"What is it?" Ken whispered.

"We're surrounded," Faedyn said, speaking softly.

"Surrounded?" Ken said. "By who?"

"Stand still," Faedyn warned, "and be quiet. Life is sustained through the breath of peace." He gazed into Ken's eyes. "Right now, ours is held by the thinnest of threads."

17

Face to Face

Suddenly a person appeared in front of them. He emerged with an unearthly silence, almost apparition-like from the shadows of the wood ahead. The ice-blue eyes of another elar fell upon them with a steely gaze.

Anna's attention quickly went from the man's chiseled, angular face to the panoply of archaic weapons that seemed to hover about him in a state of perpetual readiness. In his left hand he held a bow, and at his shoulder the flights of arrows stuck up like the spines of a porcupine. He wore simple gray-green clothes, bound at the waist where a knife and short sword were fixed to his belt.

The only place Anna had ever seen such weapons was in a museum. Behind glass, they rested, old and still, as if their souls slept, dwindling almost to nothing, and existing only in a dream of a bygone era, when their honed edges meant life or death. But the array of weapons this man wore were not antiques. They were worn with a sense of purpose, and there was no doubt they were intended for use. There was something in the way this stranger stood, perhaps confidence, that suggested proficiency with these martial tools. Because of this, though the man had assumed a neutral stance, his weapons seemed alive with dangerous potential.

†

The appearance of the man did not increase or diminish Faedyn's apprehension, for the stranger's appearance was not altogether warlike or peaceful. Faedyn scrutinized him from head to toe, and though details could tell much in many circumstances, this man's story was still a mystery. In his eyes Faedyn saw a hardness, a battle-weary stare he'd not seen in a long time.

The stranger spoke in Vena, the common language among the elar, which had changed only a little since the most ancient times, and even less since the Dark Age. He used an elaran greeting, but not a very polite one. "Who are you and where are you going?"

Faedyn answered in kind, using a language that felt old and forced on his long-exiled tongue. "Such suspicion. Is that the way the elar of Farhalin greet strangers these days?"

"These days are full of trouble," the man said.

Faedyn glanced around. He could hear the faint creaking of hidden bows, strings pulled taught with the moment of judgment. "So it seems," he said.

The two men stood in motionless silence, testing the other's intent and resolve. It was the epitome of elaran behavior. Everything happened beneath the surface, in many subtle layers of context. On the surface, all was calm and silent, but for each of them a clear dialogue was taking place. Anna, Ken and Mouse waited in this cloud of increasing anxiety. Faedyn was as still as stone, his eyes fell into an almost unconcerned gaze. Ken slowly clenched his hands into fists. The tension of the moment was almost unbearable.

Finally, a faint smile broke across the stranger's lips. He made a subtle, soft whistle, and all around, more men emerged from the forest as silently and mysteriously as he had. They lowered fine, steel-tipped arrows as they came out from behind trees or from the brush, or from seemingly nowhere at all.

The man who had first appeared spoke again in Vena. "I am Lone, heir of Losin and Marah."

To follow etiquette, Faedyn would give his name now and their conversation could continue on more or less equal terms. "I am Faedyn ... of the Fairwood," he said. For Lone and the other elar, this was a strange reply, since the elar generally identified themselves through lineage rather than location, and since in Vena, *Harulin,* the Fairwood, wasn't so much a place as an idea. There was no single place known as the Fairwood.

Lone seemed satisfied though, at least for the time being. "We saw fire on the bluff last night. Was that you?"

"Yes," Faedyn said. "My companions are students of lore who seek refuge at the Shrine of Andurin."

As the conversation developed, the men surrounding them relaxed their guard, mirroring the disposition of their leader. This was a big relief for Anna, Ken, and Mouse, who couldn't understand a word of the conversation.

"Well, Faedyn of the Fairwood," Lone said, alluding with amusement to Faedyn's mysterious identity, "you are a strange sight in this cursed land." The word he used for "strange" had a hint of *foreign* and *human* in it. By their dress, it would be obvious they had come from Midgard. "You have a long journey ahead, and it appears you've come a long way already. Come with us and stay tonight in our home." Then his expression became grim and ominous. "For in this wood, the darkness carries mortal danger."

This speech raised many questions in Faedyn's mind, but he had a feeling they would be answered in time, so he asked only one. "Where is your home?"

Lone laughed. "We come from Hidden Glade, where Lord Soren will welcome you in our hall."

18

HIDDEN GLADE

The steady rhythm of walking put Anna's nerves more at ease. Faedyn and Lone led the way, with the rest of Lone's men spread out in a loose circle surrounding them, always half-hidden in the forest.

When they first appeared, Anna was sure these men had been ready to kill them. Now they seemed more relaxed, and Faedyn said they were going to be their guests. However, to say they had relaxed their guard entirely would be a gross over-statement. Their attention was directed outward now, with a vague apprehension at the dark and distant reaches of the wilderness. Anna had the sense they feared something out there. At least that was something she could understand, though it brought her no comfort.

Occasionally, she would catch a glimpse of ghostly stirring eyes as one of the elar peered at them through the woods. Those placid, haunting looks carried with them the enigma of an alien mind. It was a look that reminded Anna these men were not human. And yet, there was something about them, an odd familiarity that had been growing ever since Anna had met Faedyn. Perhaps it started even before then, when she saw the Malar assassin in the alleyway near her old apartment building. But she found it hard to believe that monster was related to the elar who accompanied them now. These people seemed so beautiful—sad perhaps in some deep way—but with a quality of beauty she had never seen before.

"Do you think they're friendly?" Ken said.

"I don't know." Anna looked to Mouse, whose silent judgment she had begun to count on. She could not catch her attention though. Mouse was gazing up at the trees as they walked, at the old gnarled branches that hung as still as statues while songbirds flittered here and there among them. She seemed to be in a dream. They all seemed to be in a dream.

The route they followed twisted and turned without end. Anna tried to keep track of the general direction they were traveling, but even that became impossible. The only thing clear was, step by step, they were moving into a forest that was older than anything they had seen, a truly primordial realm, where the trees were thick as houses, immense ancient things whose irregular trunks grew thick with shadows, in a light that was dim, even at noon. And from the lofts of their branches, great vines drifted down, and on their bark, creepers and mosses congregated, and around their huge bases grew plants like glenfern and maidenhair.

They had crossed into the Rimwood, Faedyn explained, which had protected Hidden Glade for thousands of years. It repelled enemies and invaders, the curious and the lost alike, for only the initiated could find a true path through. All others would be confounded. For them, every path led outward, and before they were even aware of it, every seemingly straight line curved away, redirecting all but those few whom the Rimwood recognized and allowed to pass. In this way, many wanderers and lost travelers who may have haphazardly stumbled on Hidden Glade, didn't, and were never the wiser for their missing it. And many who sought it, who plunged into the

Rimwood determined to find its center, were driven to madness in the attempt.

The men that accompanied them closed their ranks and led them through the Rimwood toward their home. As they progressed, some of the tension they carried eased. Of course, that was natural with homecomings, but not all of the tension dissipated. A portion of it seemed permanently fixed.

When they finally came upon Hidden Glade, it was sudden and startling. A large green clearing spread out before them. A gentle breeze played there, tickling the tops of soft grasses that covered the ground. The wind sounded like a song of whispers. And seedpods floated in the air, catching the light of the afternoon sun.

She couldn't explain it, but nothing Anna had seen thus far on this strange adventure had such an effect as this place. It seemed to exist in some higher plane of reality, where colors shimmered and shapes hummed. The sight of it took her breath away, which was an expression she never understood until the unexpected beauty of that moment.

All of the elar, including Faedyn, stopped and bowed deeply toward the center of the clearing. When they straightened up, they held their open hands together for a moment, as if in prayer. This was surely Hidden Glade, but there was no sign of any home or buildings. Anna heard faint voices, though, all around them. It was unmistakable, voices that carried in the air, somewhere between distant and near.

"Look," Ken said. "There, in the trees."

Anna followed the line of Ken's pointing finger. Around the perimeter of the glade, the forest grew thick. The trees were huge, ancient things, dense with foliage. Suddenly, among the branches of these trees, Anna saw people. At first, they seemed to be floating or perched on a slender limb. After a moment, however, Anna saw they were standing on a platform. Then, in the weird way that hidden patterns can be abruptly revealed to the senses, Anna saw now that high up in the trees were many similar platforms and catwalks, half visible through gaps in the thick wall of woods that ringed the glade. In at least one place, she saw what looked like the walls of an entire building nestled in the trees.

A horn blew, an eerie wail, like the distant cry of a wolf in the night. Mouse craned her neck, looking up and all around in the branches above them. Anna realized that although they hadn't noticed it a moment ago, above them, surrounding the clearing, stood a whole village of buildings, catwalks, and platforms built among the trunks and branches of this ancient wood.

Lone led the group up a narrow stairway that wound around the base of a massive tree. As they climbed higher, Anna flattened herself against the tree and gripped the bark with her fingers, but suprisingly, she didn't feel the quake in her knees she expected. And when they all stepped out onto a broad platform, some two stories up in the air, she didn't feel the rush of vertigo. She was aware of it slightly, but it remained in the margins of her consciousness, as if its impact was dulled in this place, the edges blunted. Neither did she feel any apprehension when she looked down the winding catwalks that led away from the platform. She could see more platforms and buildings scattered through the forest canopy. And there were more stairs rising to higher levels, far up in the trees, but somehow she did not fear this place. It was a strange thing for her to feel comfortable so high off the ground.

Perhaps she had overcome her fear, but she thought it more likely there was something reassuring here, for despite being built in the trees, the architecture was anything but crude or temporary. Everything had the same solid feel as the trees themselves, withstanding the passage of time for hundreds and hundreds of years.

The decks, buildings, stairs, and catwalks were made of many kinds of lustrous woods whose different natural colors were worked together to accentuate sinuous forms. In some places, such as the tops of railing posts and joints of supporting beams, fine-wrought metals ornamented the wood with intricate designs, twisting organic patterns that, despite an underlying symmetry, resembled the tangled branches of the forest itself.

Some other elar were on the platform to greet them, including several women. They spoke to Lone briefly and then stared at Anna with curiosity and suspicion. Anna felt small and uncomfortable under the unchecked gaze of these women, whose features were almost unbearably perfect. Anna tried to avoid their piercing eyes, shrinking back behind the bulk of Faedyn's body and trying to occupy herself with looking elsewhere.

At this level, a series of catwalks meandered all the way around the central glade, joining up many scattered platforms, most of which surrounded small domestic buildings. From the chimneys of a few of these houses thin lines of smoke billowed lazily up through the upper reaches of the canopy and into the open sky. On the far side of the glade, through a few layers of trees, Anna could see the facade of a much larger building with great doors ajar. Beyond was a gaping, dark interior.

They were led down a long catwalk, through a pair of sliding doors, and into a small room. At first glance, the interior seemed rather bare, but as with everything here, the details revealed a richness that was perceived almost subconsciously. The room was comfortable and inviting. The floor was covered with woven matting. In the middle of the room was a low table where they sat on embroidered cushions. A woman brought hot tea and a tray arrayed with simple foods. After a fleeting look, their hosts withdrew in silence, and their party was left alone.

Faedyn took a long appreciative sip of his tea.

"What are we doing here?" Anna said.

"We are being welcomed," Faedyn said. "In time, we'll be taken to see our host, Lord Soren, but first we must be given a chance to rest and be refreshed. Anything else would be rude."

Apparently, there was nothing to do but wait. Mouse gobbled down some small cakes, and Anna tried the tea. It was the same memorable brew Faedyn had served just a few days ago and a world away. Somehow, though, this tea seemed even better, and it quite refreshed her after the long day of walking.

"Is it safe here?" Ken said.

"We're as safe here as anywhere else," Faedyn said cryptically.

"How far is Andurin?"

"It's still a long journey from here."

Ken shifted his weight and fell silent.

"This place," Faedyn said, "has long been a sanctuary for the elar. Even the oldest among us has no memory of its beginnings. Time has stood still here, but now I sense the spirit of this place is troubled. A cloud of darkness hangs over it. Rest now, for I don't know what trials await us."

19

LORD SOREN

In time, Lone returned and led Faedyn and the group across various catwalks to the far side of the glade, where a great hall was held aloft by columns of living trees. The large doors were richly carved, inlaid with silver, and so well made that despite their size, they appeared to float on the hinges supporting them.

Inside was a large cathedral-like space. Afternoon sunlight streamed through clerestory windows in luminous diagonals, radiant with golden light. Deep shadows prevailed everywhere the light didn't strike, and it took a moment for Faedyn's eyes to adjust. The pillars of the hall were living trees growing up through the polished hardwood floors. Branches spread out and supported the lofty vaults of the ceiling. The trees and the architecture were in perfect accord, the rough forms of nature harmonized with the crisp lines of craft.

Beyond the rows of columns, in the side aisles of the hall stood many silent people. From the shadows at the far end of the hall emerged Lord Soren and Lady Nemona, their eyes gleaming and calm, like moonlight reflected on a still lake. Both had silvered hair. Nemona's was long, with several braids that fell around her like cascades of water. Her green robes trailed on the floor behind her, and the long sleeves fell loosely at her sides, covering all but the tips of her delicate hands.

Soren's head was crowned with a silver diadem, fixed in the center with an elara stone that glowed with a pale green light.

Faedyn bowed. Anna, Ken, and Mouse each made quick and clumsy attempts to do the same. The long silence that followed must have seemed unnatural to humans, but was the custom among these people. *Now,* Faedyn thought, *we will test the memory of Hidden Glade,* for he had been there before and stood before Lord Soren in the distant past. But that was another time. Faedyn had changed with age, battle, and the darkness that weighed heavy on his soul … while Soren had remained unchanged by the long years.

The lord of Hidden Glade spoke in Vena, his voice as clear and sonorous as the ringing of a prayer bell. He spoke deliberately and formally. "I am Soren, heir of Senith and Lyssa, and here is Lady Nemona, heir of Illyan and Nenova," he said. "You are welcome in the Hall of Hidden Glade, though of late there is little peace to be found in this place."

"I am Faedyn of the Fairwood," Faedyn said. "And these young humans are students of lore. We are on a pilgrimage to the Shrine of Andurin."

Lady Nemona spoke, "I thought the lore of the elar had all but faded from human memory."

"There are some," Faedyn said, "who carry on the traditions."

"It is a strange sight," Soren said. The Vena word he used for *strange* had a sense of delightful surprise. "And as such, we welcome it. The eldest girl has the look of the elar. Is her bloodline known?"

"No," Faedyn said quickly. It was a lie, but until he knew more, it seemed prudent to keep many things secret. "And she has only recently become aware of her ancestry." That much was true.

†

Though she couldn't follow it, Anna listened to the conversation with interest. It was marvelous to listen to. The unfamiliar words were like the unfolding of an incomprehensible dream, and yet, intuitively she seemed to have a feeling for them, and to grasp some distant margin of their meaning. She leaned over and whispered to Ken, "What language is that?"

Before Ken could answer, Soren caught her eye with a powerful gaze and spoke to her in perfect English. "It is Vena, my young friend, the language of the elar, and I'll warrant you'll soon understand it better than he does."

Soren continued his speech in English without missing a beat. "I will not deny I am happy to see you, for it is said 'a stranger from the forest brings a blessing from God.' But I wish you and your company had passed far from here. Farhalin is cursed, and Hidden Glade, once a haven, has become a prison for those of us left who dwell here."

"I confess," Faedyn said, "I have heard, in the whisperings of the forest, some evil infects this land." In the suggestive manner that is characteristic of the elar in formal situations, this was a clear request to hear the full tale to which now Lone and Soren had both eluded.

Soren's face became grave, and the people in the wings, listening, watching, fell into an even deeper silence. "A creature of darkness haunts these woods," Soren said, "terrible in form, insatiable in hunger. An awesome beast, with the strength of twenty men, unharmed by blade or arrow, a loathsome thing, twisted by an evil that grows to the south, deep in the Murkwood. This demon has plagued us now in every season.

"It began in the fall, under the auspices of violent storms. For weeks a gloom hung over the wet wood. The sky was gray and the ground damp. All but the evergreens were bare as bleached bone. The smell of leaf-rot filled the air. We first heard of the creature from wanderers and the elar in the Western Heartwood. It slaughtered them by one and twenty and dragged their corpses back to the Murkwood. All through the winter, death and fear spread through the forest like wildfire.

"Slowly, those who were left fled or sought refuge here in Hidden Glade, where the Rimwood has kept us safe from such evil for as long as any of us can remember. Here we live in the old way, like our ancestors did in the shadow-wake of the Dark Age. We are watchers. We live here, heartbroken, but in peace. One day, perhaps, the Lords of Light will come and take us to our heavenly home. But now, a beast from hell comes for us, and the Rimwood no longer repels it. Somehow the creature has found a way through.

"It comes from the dark wood, to this very clearing, appearing like a specter, part shadow, part form, to wreak havoc among us. Six were slain two weeks ago this night, all young and armed. Only one was found, torn limb from limb, his belly gored and eaten."

Now the subtle pall over this place, and the sense of evil Faedyn had sensed in the forest, came into focus. The elar who attended the council hung their heads. Whether for shame or grief, Faedyn couldn't say.

†

Ken found the whole story unsettling, and he suddenly wished he were back at St. Christopher's, sitting in calculus, well on his way to being a doctor or an engineer, or to some other respectable position. For a moment, he wished he had never heard of the Loremasters or the elar. Even more to the point, he wished he had never met Anna Karova. He didn't understand why Smith and Faedyn had gone through so much trouble for her. Was she really that important?

Smith called this world a sanctuary, but as Soren came to the end of his tale, Ken would have felt more comfortable in the worst neighborhoods of the city than he did in this place.

"For now, we are safe in the Glade," Soren said. "The creature comes only on the dark moon, when its powers are greatest. But it will return, and the forest outside the Rimwood is never safe after nightfall. No messenger we have sent to the outside has ever returned."

"You must stay here," Nemona said, in a voice so beautiful, so inviting, that Ken presently forgot all his objections.

"Don't risk continuing onward to Andurin," Soren said. "Please, stay with us."

Faedyn bowed. "For now, with deep gratitude, we accept your invitation."

Ken could stand the fact these elar were basically living in a giant treehouse, but what he couldn't stand was their politeness. *An invitation?* This place was periodically attacked by a monster that eats people. It wasn't an invitation at all. They were stuck here.

Distracted, Ken caught the hazel-gold eyes of a woman who watched from the wings. His thoughts were drowned, became a confused muddle. He couldn't take his eyes from her. *So beautiful!* And yet, he reminded himself that she was probably hundreds of years old.

A sharp jab from Anna's elbow jammed into Ken's ribs. "Ow," he said, the spell broken, and he was startled to notice everyone was bowing but him. He quickly bowed with rest of them.

Everything happened with a formality far greater than Smith had prepared him for. The subtleties of etiquette, the formal speeches, the precise and delicate gestures, all seemed beyond his grasp. All went beyond the present knowledge of the Loremasters. He felt hopelessly lost, swept up in a world at once far more real and more strange than anything he had imagined.

Soren and Nemona faded into the shadows once more and disappeared from the hall. The other elar began to leave. There were murmurings among them, and even some laughter, as if merriment might dispel the grim tale they were living. They all spoke Vena, though, and despite what little Smith had taught him, he couldn't understand a word of it.

"Ah, this is Shen," Lone said in English. A man approached them from the front of the hall, where a crowd still lingered. "He is the heir of Soren and Nemona."

Faedyn bowed.

"It is a pleasure to receive you," Shen said in English.

Shen was somewhat ostentatiously dressed compared to the other inhabitants of Hidden Glade. His robe was a purplish hue, unlike the grays and greens and browns that had filled the room, and its edges were richly embroidered with many colored threads. Around several of his fingers hung delicate, jeweled rings.

"Let us show you what comfort we have," Shen said. "There is time before dark to bathe in the Mahara, where the pains of enduring the long years are eased in a warmth from the belly of earth."

What? Ken was beginning to think there must be a translation gap between Vena and any human language. The elar spoke English flawlessly, and Smith had taught him about their gift for all languages. In fact, most elar spoke many human languages, ancient and modern, and spoke them all with a fluent command of vocabulary, syntax, and phonology. Yet, the manner of their speech conveyed something hesitating, something alien, as if they were always aware of a thousand inexpressible things, of the untranslatable, of the limits and inadequacies of their every word. And still, with every word, they seemed to mean more than they actually said.

20

A Much-Needed Bath

Ken followed the group as Shen led them from the hall. Outside, they descended a broad stair, winding around several large tree trunks to the ground. They followed a well-worn path through the trees, toward the banks of a steaming turquoise stream that wound through the woods. The river was about ten-feet wide and five-feet deep, crystal clear and fed by hot springs. Water spilled gently over rocky ledges in miniature waterfalls, swirling into deep steaming pools along the banks. The riverbed glittered with rounded stones scattered among ribbons of soft white sand.

As they approached, a woman emerged, naked, from the water. The sight arrested Ken's attention to such a degree that he suffered from a kind of tunnel vision, erasing all other details from the scene. He felt he shouldn't look, but wanted to, and couldn't help it in any case. The woman walked toward them without the slightest hint of shyness or embarrassment. Ken felt the flush in his cheeks spread throughout his body and a vague kind of terror came over him. He dared not look at Anna.

The woman said something to Faedyn in Vena, and Faedyn went with her to the edge of the river, where he undressed and followed her into the water. Ken noticed other people bathing in the river, men and women, soaking in hot pools, washing each other with a cheerfulness quite uncharacteristic of the elar, from what he had seen.

Some more women arrived, wearing robes and bearing armfuls of towels and stacks of clean clothes. The woman with the hazel-gold eyes that Ken had noticed earlier was among them. Finally, almost unintentionally, Ken glanced over at Anna. Her expression was unreadable.

Shen must have seen the hesitation in both their eyes. "Few humans have ever had the privilege to bathe here," he said. "Please, make yourself at home. There are other matters I must tend to." And he departed, leaving Ken alone with Anna, Mouse, and a dizzying group of elaran women.

Did they expect him to strip down in front of all these people?

The golden-eyed woman held out a stack of folded clothes for him. "I'm Alia," she said. "These are for you."

"Umm … thanks."

She looked at him with eyes like shimmering jewels. The thin robe she wore barely concealed the curves of her body. She seemed half curious and half repelled by the sight of him. "You are from Midgard," she said, "from Middle Earth."

"I uh … I guess so."

"Will you bathe with me?"

Under different circumstances, this was just the sort of situation Ken would have considered a dream come true. But now that it was coming true, he looked at Anna with unconcealed panic in his eyes. What were they going to do? But all Anna offered was "I won't look if you won't look."

"You better not," Ken said.

"Believe me," Anna said, "I've got no desire to see you naked."

His dream was becoming a nightmare.

"Well, will you?" Alia said, taking her robe from her shoulders and letting it fall to the grass at her feet.

Ken just stood there like a statue, too embarrassed to move.

"He's shy," Anna said.

Alia looked over at Anna and then at Ken, clearly not understanding, and just as clearly deciding she didn't care to. She shrugged her shoulders and joined a few others making their way down to the water. One of the women looked back at Anna. *"Mahara he, invul na,"* she said invitingly. Some of the women laughed, and Ken had the stinging thought they were laughing at him.

"Well?" Anna said.

"Well what?" Ken said.

"Turn around," she said. Ken looked at Mouse, as if she would help. Mouse just scrunched up her face and stuck out her tongue.

Finally, Ken turned around.

"And you'd better not peek."

"Don't worry," Ken said. "I don't want to see you naked either."

Within a few moments, Anna and Mouse were in the water and had gone behind some rocks. He looked at them all, feeling desperately alone, but he couldn't bring himself to take off his clothes. He was too shy to be naked in front of all those people. "C'mon," Anna seemed to say, her head just visible, but Ken couldn't hear her over the sound of the water.

"I'm going to go down stream a ways," Ken said, pointing. He didn't know if they could hear him. "Just down there, around the bend." He walked away from where everybody was bathing. There was a bend in the river, marked by some large boulders, and beyond there he should have some privacy.

.

21

Feast in the Hall

Anna adjusted quickly to her new clothes, once she had figured out the various ties that held them in place. Still, she found herself occasionally touching the soft, silken sleeve of her jacket with unconscious admiration. The swim had refreshed her. She felt a pang of hunger, though, as they stood at the edge of Hidden Glade and watched a parade of elar walk toward the center of the clearing. Anna couldn't see clearly through the tall grass and dimming light. Faedyn turned to her and whispered, "They're honoring the spirit of the Glade."

The sun had gone down, and the sky turned a deep blue to the east above the arc of the treetops. A song broke the silence, the voice so clear it took a moment for Anna to realize it wasn't some strange musical instrument. The people around her also began to sing. They had beautiful voices. It was a sad song, as far as Anna could tell, but with a sense of hard-won hope. Though she couldn't discern the words, she seemed to feel its meaning, as if it sprang from the depths of her soul, as if it expressed her innermost self even more clearly than she could. Tears welled up in her eyes. She tried to remember her mother's face, and unconsciously she put a hand to her chest, where the photo was tucked away in her new jacket.

Mouse held fast to her arm, and Anna could feel Ken at her other side, adjusting his clothes. She kept her eyes on the sky, as it turned the deepest blue. Then it seemed as if the stars were sung into existence before her eyes. When the heavens were filled, the song ended and the night was upon them. How quickly darkness fell here. A chorus of crickets rose up in the background.

She could see dim glowing orbs in the trees that marked the stairwells and catwalks of the village. And all around the glade, the people began to climb to their homes, a slow and solemn passage, spiraling upward into the trees, while the distant solitude of night reigned.

†

A contingent of warriors were stationed outside the open doors to the hall. Inside, globes of light hung in the high vaults and bathed the lofty space in a fiery, flickering yellow glow. Many people had already gathered and the hall was filling fast. They sat cross-legged on cushions along either side of long, low dining tables that had been set out for a meal.

Upon these tables, others were busy setting all manner of foods and great jugs of water and wine. They shuttled to and from side doors in the aisles bearing smoked meats and fresh bread, bowls of fruit and edible plants. The smell of strange spices filled the air like the sweeping vista of an alien landscape—foreign smells, unheard of smells, but smells that made their mouths water.

Lone led them all to the far end of the hall. They were given a place with a good view of Lord Soren and Lady Nemona, who sat at a smaller table on the dais at the head of the hall. Both nodded at their arrival.

Dinner followed. There was no lack of food, and they were encouraged to have their fill, though the elar themselves seemed to eat sparingly. After a while they felt deeply satisfied, and a warm glow filled their bodies from the weak rodeilberry wine the elar set their tables with.

More for amusement, it seemed, than from an interest in edification, a few of the elar had taken to teaching Anna and Ken some words in Vena. Among those elar was a man named Fyorin. *"Meahrl* is the word for this type of bread," he said.

"Merl," Anna said, breaking off a piece of the bread.

"No," Fyorin said, and he said again distinctly, "meahrl."

"Mearl," Anna tried again, but there was some sound they were making that she couldn't quite reproduce. Some of the elar laughed as she tried several more times.

"The elar can live on meahrl alone," Lone said.

"But who would want to?" Fyorin said, which got a good laugh from the others.

"How do you say thank you?" Anna said.

"We don't say that in Vena," one of the elar offered. "We say *'Ama'a tahma ea.'* Thanks be to the *ama,* the spirit."

Anna repeated the saying the best she could, "Ama'a tahma ea."

"Ama," the man said, trying at the same time to show her the shape of his mouth when he said it.

"Ama," Anna said, but she could see by the smiling faces she had gotten it wrong again.

"You try," they said to Ken, and when he tried, they laughed even harder. He tried several more times, setting the table to a roar with what was finally an almost ridiculous and hopeless effort.

It went on like this for some time. Anna's mind was like a sponge to the fluid stream of this language, which had flowed constantly around them all afternoon. How, she could not say, but already she seemed to have grasped the meaning of many words, and certain phrases were becoming familiar. Patterns and principles emerged almost spontaneously in her consciousness. Conversations that had somehow stayed in her mind, unintelligible to her through the day, and disparate voices in the background, all were coming back to her now with increasing clarity. The clouds of babble that represent an unknown language were breaking apart, revealing to her the structure of Vena like a multi-faceted jewel, taking in the light of the world and throwing off the most wonderful colors she had ever heard.

They learned many words through the course of the meal. And it was all in good fun, with the elar making them try again and again to pronounce words. But no matter how close they came, they were either still wrong in some subtle way, or the elar would not admit otherwise. It seemed at times they were playing a game to see how long they would labor at the attempt. Still though, it was all in good fun, until Anna heard something she didn't like.

As Ken tried again and again to say a word Fyorin had taught him, one of the elar made a remark in Vena to the others. Raven-haired Paetha had birdlike, predatory features and a haughty air. Earlier he had scoffed at teaching them any Vena. Now he said in Vena, "Human speech is always flawed, because their feeble minds can't comprehend the depth of language." Apparently, he thought they wouldn't understand his comment, but Anna understood his meaning well enough, and it wasn't in good fun.

Ken was still half laughing, but the elar grew silent around them as Anna stood up with a violent coordinated spasm of muscle. Her hands trembled. Her eyes grew dark. In her mind was a cacophony of static, and she could feel rage like the beating of a terrible drum in the distance. She took a breath, and everyone was amazed when she spoke, for she spoke all in Vena. She spit her words toward Paetha like venom. "Speech is flawed when you try to hide your meaning from those around you." Correct pronunciation or not, they all understood her and what she meant.

Looking from the elar to Anna, Ken was astonished, but still didn't understand a word that was said. Mouse tugged at the hem of Anna's jacket, a look of fear and worry upon her silent face. Faedyn said nothing, but watched all this with grave interest. The commotion had even caught the attention of Lord Soren and Lady Nemona.

"Of course, you are right," Fyorin said in English. "Please sit down. We would never mean to offend a guest. Isn't that right, Paetha?"

"Yes, I'm sorry," Paetha said with cool indifference.

Anna shrank from the eyes of Paetha, suddenly self-conscious of the disturbance she had caused. She looked down at Mouse, who urged her to sit. Then she looked to Faedyn. His face was blank, unreadable. A strange mixture of shame and pride came over her.

Her face steeled, she sunk back to the floor and sipped her wine. It had been rude, terribly rude, what Paetha had said behind their backs. But she wondered at her anger, her trembling rage. She had felt a surge of power, like when she had picked up a steel pipe and smashed that boy's skull, and it frightened her.

"What just happened," Ken said to her after a moment, and when the conversation around them had resumed.

"Nothing," Anna said. "He said something rude, that's all."

"You spoke in Vena."

"I did, didn't I?" Anna almost laughed. The implications of it hadn't really occurred to her until now, so seamlessly had an understanding of the language come to her.

Some music and dancing had started, and the elar seemed to love these things. They also loved stories, and as the night wore on, they began to tell them. Some of the story-tellers spoke in English for the benefit of their guests, and some chanted in Vena, long sad lyrics of love and violence.

Many stories were told, and although so much was still a mystery, Anna learned a lot about the history of this world. For example, humans still lived on Elara, even after the earth she knew and most of humanity had separated from it. These humans, the descendants of lost tribes, lived to the south, mostly in the kingdoms of Roethia and Drighton. In times gone by, these people still knew the elar well, but for a long time now, they have kept to themselves. Even here, the story-teller said, the two races have drifted apart and gone their own way in the world. Contact has dwindled ever since the time of the Elara-war, the *Marhea et'Elara*. There were many stories of that time.

Between tales, Faedyn stood, bowed to their hosts, and made as if to leave. He turned to Anna. "The elar can tell tales for hours," he said. "I need some fresh air. But stay and listen. I'll be outside with the watchmen." He left the hall to join the soldiers who stood guard, and Lone went with him. Anna, Ken, and Mouse remained until they could barely stay awake.

Finally, Fyorin led them off to homes high in the trees and deep in the dark wood. Standing on the adjacent platform, sleepy-eyed, Anna could see, through the trees and branches, light from the great hall where the old tales were still being told. Exhausted, she and Mouse retired to their small room and fell asleep together between a soft bed and a heavy blanket.

†

In her dreams, stories of a bygone age replayed themselves. Only three of the magic swords survived the Dark Age—Saraden, Elladen, and Rayaden. Their blades were milky white, a forging lost to an ancient past. It was Beyore who betrayed them all, a dark power revealed in him. The bane of the elar, they called him.

Saraden was captured by the enemy. Elladen was destroyed. Battles raged across Elara. All would have been lost but for Rayaden, whose power was like a grace upon them, even now. Elara would have fallen were it not for Elgard, Rayaden's wielder by birth, who gave it up to save it, and faced death without it at his side. A warrior called Miura took the sword and laid it to rest in some hidden hollow at the far reaches of the world.

They sang a song about Miura, this bearer of great burdens, for as the armies of darkness approached their woodland home, he left the woman he loved to make his fateful journey. She was Elgard's daughter, Yume. Later, she was captured by the Malar. On the eve of battle, when Elgard could not give them Rayaden as ransom, they killed her. When Miura returned, Yume, and all his people were dead. In her dream, Anna translated the end of the song for Ken and Mouse, moved by its tale of loss and woe.

†

> So that hero departed, delving deep into darkness,
> At once for love, and for revenge.
> He was never to return, to wood or mountain,
> Forever to wander, a restless spirit,

A ghost-battler, a demon-fighter,
A lonely warrior, lost between worlds.
And they say Yume's eyes, glowed like elara-stone,
And they say her skin, shone like starlight.
And the people pray to her, when passing
    woodland streams,
Where her sad spirit, is said to ever dwell.

22

WAITING FOR THE DARK

Days passed. The moon waned to a silvery crescent. The people of the Glade, in hushed voices, talked more about the beast. They said it would attack again when that crescent moon, which grew slimmer night by night, finally disappeared. So Hidden Glade gradually filled with an air of dreadful waiting.

Faedyn went with Lone and the other warriors out on their patrols beyond the Rimwood. The forest seemed deserted, quiet, and everywhere it spoke of the coming darkness. Frequently, Faedyn and Lone talked together in the evening, out on the edge of the glade, or on some high platform overlooking it.

Faedyn asked many questions about the beast. What did it look like? How big was it? How intelligent did it seem? From which direction did it come? What weapons had they tried against it and what effect, if any, did they have? The answers he got were vague and sometimes conflicting, but slowly he was beginning to understand this enemy.

Faedyn devised a plan, a kind of trap. It was dangerous, but it could work. To even have a chance, though, the first thing they needed was some exceptionally strong rope.

†

In those days, while the elar waited for the curse to fall upon them again, Anna continued her study of Vena. Fyorin had volunteered to continue teaching her, and they spent much of the day conversing in the ancient language. He was curious about Midgard and wanted to hear about the city. In return, she learned about Andurin, where the great Shrine was built on the side of a sheer cliff. And she heard of Torselend, deep in the White Mountains, and of the falcon riders of the wild North, and of Roethia and Drighton, where humans still lived under a long line of proud kings, and of the eastern coast, where merchant ships set sail on the high seas.

Anna retold all these things to Mouse, who would listen long into the night. They bathed in the river, and played a game the elar had that was almost identical to chess. Mouse seemed content here in Hidden Glade. She ran about, exploring the catwalks and trees like a creature of the forest. And the elar seemed to take a special delight in watching her. Fyorin explained that because they lived so long, children were a rarity among them.

At night, before sleep, when she felt afraid and alone, Anna would take out the picture of her mother and look at it. Her mom's smiling face reminded her of home, and she tried to remember what it felt like to be held safely in her arms, sheltered against a world of darkness. She tried to remember what it felt like to have those eyes look upon her with loving kindness, and she wept, quietly, unable to completely capture that feeling.

†

Ken was used to the busy pace of school, the city, and life as a Loremaster's apprentice. There was little for him to do here, and he soon found himself battling boredom more than anything else. Sure, the women were beautiful, but they were hopelessly out of his league and seemed to have little interest in talking to him. That left … let's see … absolutely nothing to do but wait for the monster to come and eat them. Not a pleasant way to spend one's time.

For two or three days he stewed, wandering about. He tried to strike up a few conversations, first with Faedyn, and then with Anna, but everybody seemed busy doing something. Finally, he decided he better practice his viewing skills. He still needed the practice, and within the void of viewing he would at least find some relief from himself.

He sat in his small room, high up in the trees. Before him, on the low table, he had put some paper and a pen he had brought with him from home. He stared at the pen for a moment. It was an ordinary rollerball pen with black ink. You could pick one up from any drug store in the city for a buck fifty. But here, in the middle of another world, it seemed quite extraordinary. The printing on its side now seemed mysterious and esoteric: *Uniball-Vision fine, Waterproof/Fade-proof.* It was like a spell, an incantation for writing.

The paper looked incredibly white, a uniform emptiness, a field of universal potential. Ken picked up the pen impulsively and deftly twirled it around his thumb in a habitual way. The Loremaster's science of viewing was a way to access information remotely, to see things from afar, to peer through time and space. It was essentially a systematic form of psychic vision. There was always some margin of error, particularly when working with the future, but the Loremasters had protocols that controlled for this, and their accuracy was remarkably high.

Unfortunately, Ken couldn't follow all those protocols in his current situation, but he would just have to do the best he could. Usually the Loremasters worked in conjunction, a few of them viewing the same target to verify results. Ken was just one lowly apprentice, but he had some consistent success with his viewing practice. Furthermore, typically the viewers weren't aware of what the target was. This was to minimize any unnecessary influence of the ego, reducing the chance that imagination or anticipation would influence the vision. Ken had nobody to feed him targets, so he would have to assign his own.

He had tried this a few times before, but he had no way to verify the results, and undoubtedly his choice of subjects had guaranteed his imagination caused a considerable amount of static. The same thing would happen now if he chose, for example, Alia as his target, the elar woman with the hazel-gold eyes. But it was a danger no matter who or what he chose as his target.

To start with, he wondered what Smith was up to at home in the Citadel. Twirling the pen one last time, he hovered the tip over the expanse of white paper. He activated a strict pattern of breathing to calm himself down and initiate proper brain activity. Then he cleared his mind and cued his target—*Smith.*

He began to look for the fleeting, ghostly images, often only simple shapes, that would take him further into the vision. Sometimes words would come to mind. Whatever came, he would write or sketch on the paper, and continue without analyzing or judging the data that accumulated. There was a sub-conscious feedback mechanism that would take him deeper into the vision and give him a clearer view. His mind would begin to resonate with the target. Ultimately it was possible to see the target with photographic clarity, to smell odors, to hear conversations, even to sense thoughts and emotions.

This time though, nothing came, at least nothing that clearly wasn't static. Various images and memories of Smith and the Citadel rushed in to fill the void, but Ken had trained enough to recognize these as products of his own immediate consciousness. This was the problem with knowing the target. He dropped the pen and sighed. Even with the static, he should have gotten something. It didn't make sense. Something always came, even if it was inaccurate. Then he remembered, of course, that their techniques did not allow them to view targets across the veil between worlds.

What could he target that was here in Elara? How about—*Andurin*. Perhaps he could find something out about their destination. If they ever got there, it might be useful. He readied himself to do another viewing.

It began with a few simple shapes, a horizontal curve, some vertical and diagonal lines. His hand worked quickly with the pen to record them. Then some words: valley, buildings, brown, gold, river, cliff. With the words, the shapes began to refine themselves into water and rock, hills and structures, long empty hallways. Soon he was seeing Andurin from a bird-like view. He looked down on a valley that twisted through towering cliffs. A river ran through the valley. Roaring surges of water cascaded over rocks and filled the air with a fine mist.

Ken dropped the pen, absorbed in the vision. He strained to see more, beyond the edges of his sight, but static was beginning to creep in, fanciful imaginings, anticipation and worries. There was something more though. For all its beauty, there was a sense of tension, even danger, that lurked behind those alabaster walls. But with these thoughts came the deluge of conscious static, all the unchecked thoughts that play in the mind came crashing in to obliterate his view.

Ken sighed. The work was exhausting, and he really had no way of knowing how accurate his view had been. There was no point in making a sketch. Who would he show it to? Instead, he would try one more target.

He took up the pen and went through his breathing routine once more. Then he cued his target—*the monster.*

After a few moments, he drew a circle, and then some vertical wavy lines. When the words came—*darkness, water, rotting, blood, bones, teeth*—it was important not to be caught up in them, not to judge them or become disturbed. He went further into the vision. A dark forest enveloped him, dense with the smell of decay, thick with moisture, trapped in an endless fog. Further, deep in a murky canyon, a dirty stream fell over a rock face, slick with oozing slime. The water poured into a black pool overhung with dead branches. Behind those falls was a hole in the rock, the dark entrance of a horrible cave.

As he drew near the cave, his fear overwhelmed him and he broke from the vision. Quickly he started to sketch what he had seen.

†

The moon was almost gone. The thinnest shard still hung in the evening sky, a light threatening to go out. When full darkness came the next day, the beast would come. The people of the Glade had grown grim with anticipation. Each visitation had ended in more deaths, and now the proud people looked frightened, haunted. The clar lived exceptionally long lives, but those lives could still be cut short by violence.

That night, Faedyn came to talk with Anna while Mouse was out exploring the far reaches of the catwalks. "Tomorrow night," Faedyn said, "We expect this beast to come."

Anna took a troubled breath. "What's going to happen?"

"You'll stay in your room, with the doors locked. I will stand watch with the other warriors."

Anna didn't speak, but the worry she felt was written plainly on her face, the fear that something might happen to Faedyn.

"Don't worry," Faedyn said. "I have a plan." He paused for a long moment. "But if things should go wrong, there's something I want you to have, a treasure from your ancestors." Faedyn took the Elara-stone from a deep pocket and held it up.

The jewel was fitted to a necklace that Faedyn put around Anna's neck. The green glow from the center of the stone intensified and spread evenly across its smooth surface.

"It's beautiful," Anna said.

"Keep it hidden beneath your clothes. Don't show it to anybody. If things go wrong though, you must find a way to Andurin and show it to Princess Arisu, high priestess of the Shrine. Trust no one else."

23

The Beast Attacks

Anna woke in the middle of the night, her heart beating hard against her chest. Under the blankets, her legs were damp and cold with sweat. She tried to remember the dream she had, but the darkness that filled the night seemed to cover everything, with no distinction between the outside world and the interior of her mind.

Without the help of her eyes, she slid out from under the covers, trying not to disturb Mouse from her sleep. In the dark, she fumbled for the latch that opened the locked door. Their room that night was high up in the trees, where Faedyn thought they would be safe, far from the glade itself, where the beast was expected to attack. Luckily the heights here still didn't bother her. Ken was sleeping in a room next door. They were supposed to stay inside until morning, but she just wanted to see if she could see anything.

Outside, with her eyes adjusted, by the pale-yellow globes that lit various platforms, Anna could see a ways through the moonless night. The trees were quiet. Below her, through the blackness and branches, she could make out several levels of platforms. But she could not see the hall or the glade itself. The platform where she stood was too far back and too high. She worried about Faedyn, somewhere down there, standing with the other warriors, and she felt drawn downward to see the glade and the night watch.

She clutched the Elara-stone pendant at her neck and glanced back at the little hut where Mouse still slept. She decided to go just far enough to see the glade, to make sure Faedyn was all right.

Barefoot, she sneaked downward on a path that led toward the glade. It was the deep of night. The other dwellings were silent and darkened, their platforms abandoned. As she descended, the air became heavy with moisture.

Lower down, she could see through the trees to the first level of walkways that ringed the glade. There were a number of guards who stood in the luminescence of pale lanterns. She didn't recognize Faedyn among them, so she crept still further, down another level toward the glade, until she was right above those guards.

Now she could look down on the clearing, where another group of warriors stood in a circle, each facing outward to keep watch in every direction. Anna crouched down in the darkness. The men held spears and wore pieces of leather armor. She saw Faedyn among them. She recognized his short white hair and his broad back.

Anna lay down, her head at the edge of the platform, unable to return to the safety of her room. She had to see what was out there. As she watched, a ground fog rolled in from the south, a greenish mist that curled around the ankles of the watchmen. And from the forest floor, a sickly stench rose up, like stagnant, fetid water.

The men below whispered to each other and seemed more alert, watching the edges of the forest, which had been lit all around with lanterns. On the platforms, the guards drew arrows and nocked them to the taught strings of their bows.

†

At the edge of the forest, in the darkness that spread between two lanterns, Faedyn's keen eyes saw something. A hulking mass crouched between the shadows and the trees. The red glow of the creature's eyes watched them in silence.

"It's here," Lone said. "The beast."

"I see it," Faedyn said, his voice hushed. "Spread out. Get on either side of it."

The warriors spread out along the edges of the clearing and began moving toward the beast.

Suddenly the creature bounded into the open. In the darkness, shadow still covered much of its form, but clearly the monster was huge. Even on all fours it was almost as tall as a man, and when it stood up, looking about with hungry eyes at the men who stood guard, it must have been ten or twelve feet.

It was a true monster, a creature spawned from dark powers in the dank holes of the earth, a perversion of nature, bulging with muscle beneath a hard mottled hide. Bared teeth were sharpened to razored points, and from its open mouth, hot breath bellowed out loudly in visible puffs of steamy vapor.

The creature dropped back to all fours, snarling in an almost human-like expression of malice. This was no mere animal. A terrifying consciousness lingered behind those red eyes, a twisted being, tormented by hate.

Faedyn's plan suddenly seemed like so much folly. What ropes would hold such a creature? Still, if they could immobilize it, perhaps they would have a chance to cut into it cleanly. But they had to lure it into the snare they had set.

The archers on the platform above let loose a volley of arrows that whistled through the air and stuck into the creature. It cast off most of the arrows with an irritated shake of its body. They seemed to do little more than anger it. Its grotesque head panned up to look at the platforms above, where the archers stood.

"Over here," Faedyn shouted. The creature looked his way. He had to lure it forward.

A warrior had worked his way around the edge of the clearing to flank the creature. Without warning he charged in, aiming to hack at the monster's neck with his sword.

"Wait!" Faedyn shouted, trying to stop him.

The creature reacted with terrifying speed, its massive bulk moving in a single twitch of sudden violence, biting the man as he came, shaking his body and slamming it to the ground, a heap of bloody death. It clawed at the remains, and then bit off the man's head and shoulder and ate it, bones and all.

Some of the others almost rushed in for revenge, but Lone shouted at them, "Hold your positions!"

Faedyn moved forward, brandishing a spear. The monster charged, stopping just short of Faedyn's spearpoint, then reared up to its full height. Faedyn took a chance and drove his spear upward into the creature's ribs. It bit in, but not deep enough. The creature's massive arm swung down onto Faedyn's spearshaft, breaking it in two, and then arced up to catch Faedyn in a blow that hurtled him backward through the air.

He landed with a thud on the hard ground, disoriented and twisting from pain. He turned on the ground, shook his head, and looked as the beast dropped down to all fours and approached him, its jaws gaping, wet with blood and saliva.

Faedyn didn't move. He clutched at his battered ribs. *Just a little closer,* he thought. The monster approached, a few steps further, the hunger of blood-lust in its eyes. *Just a couple more steps ...*

Then Faedyn shouted, "Now!"

On the platform above, one of the guards cut a rope that released a massive boulder they had hefted high in the trees. There was a hiss in the branches overhead, and a thick rope, half buried, sprang up from the ground. A snare looped around the creature's arm as it stood on all fours, cinched tight, and jerked the monster off its footing, dragging it quickly across the open ground, then yanking its massive body up into the air.

The monster howled in pain as its shoulder separated and the soft tissue began to tear.

The archers launched a new volley of arrows into the dangling beast. The creature thrashed about in captivity, clawing at its arm, enraged and roaring. It twisted and bounced around in the air, straining the muscles and tendons of its shoulder, but the rope held. Suddenly the creature turned its head and bit into its own arm, gnawing and tearing visciously, until the weight of its body ripped arm from torso, and the monster fell to the earth.

Even so wounded, the creature was dangerous. It was up from the ground in a second. The warriors backed off, but the beast lumbered into the woods, disappearing in the darkness.

†

Anna had watched, terrified as the battle unfolded. She was frozen, stuck to the platform. Her fear of heights had returned with the appcarance of the creature, and she lay there unable to move until it had lumbered off into the night. Not that she could have done anything to help, but nevertheless, she could not move, and had watched both awe-stricken and horrified.

Faedyn had been knocked through the air by a blow that should have killed anyone. He still lay there on the ground, clutching his ribs. Now that Anna could move, she sprang to her feet and rushed down to the clearing. Guards looked at her strangely as she passed.

Faedyn looked in pain as she arrived at his side. "What are you doing here?" he said.

"I'm sorry. I was worried about you."

"I'm fine," Faedyn said. "Help me up." Anna put her arm around him and helped him to his feet. He groaned as he straightened his battered body.

"You killed it," Anna said.

"Not likely. Now let's get you back to your room. You should be looking after Mouse and Ken, not an old man like me."

24

THE MONSTER'S CAVE

There was a great commotion at dawn. A gathering was called in the great hall, where Lord Soren praised Faedyn and the warriors for their success. All the people were there. Faedyn sighed, impatient to speak. "The creature is not dead," he said. "Such a monster does not die so easily. We must track it to its lair and destroy it while we can, while it's still wounded and vulnerable."

"Lord Soren," Lone said. "Faedyn and I should go alone. Any more will only slow us down."

Soren looked to Faedyn.

Faedyn nodded. "We can leave as soon as possible."

"Very well," Soren said. "But you should have a sword, Faedyn of the Fairwood." He signaled an attendant who brought a sword from the wings. "I give you Vanar," Soren said, "a weapon forged by the fathers of Hidden Glade."

Faedyn accepted the sword into both his hands. He stepped back and bowed deeply. "I have heard of Vanar," he said. "You honor me with such a fine gift."

Outside, Faedyn and Lone armed themselves for the journey. They would travel light and move swiftly. Faedyn fixed Vanar at his side. They took some water and food. The crowd from the hall had poured out after them. The people stood around in the glade, and gazed down from the walkways above.

Anna, Mouse, and Ken were there at Faedyn's side as he readied to leave. Ken was looking up at the monster's huge arm still hanging from the tree. A certain sense of awe and dread came across in his expression.

Anna stepped forward. She put her hand on Faedyn's sleeve and stopped him for a moment. "Why do you have do this?" she said. "Why do you have to go?"

"Because it must be done," Faedyn said.

"Be careful," Anna said. "I don't know what I would do if anything happened to you."

Ken looked from the monster's dead arm to Faedyn. "Yeah," he said. "Be careful."

Faedyn smiled. "Don't worry."

"Hey," Ken said, "take this." He dug into his pockets and pulled out a piece of paper, twice folded. He unfolded it and showed it to Faedyn. "It's a drawing of the creature's lair—from a viewing I did. It might be helpful."

Faedyn took the paper. "Thanks, Ken."

"Let's go," Lone said, and the two men walked away, without looking back, and disappeared silently into the forest.

†

In previous attacks, the creature had left no sign of its passing through the Rimwood and the surrounding forests. Now, bleeding and wounded, its stealth had crumbled, as if a spell had broken. The creature had crashed desperately through the woods. Heavy footprints were still fresh in the damp earth. Saplings had been bent over and branches broken. And the beast's blood stained the leaves and ground. It was a trail that took none of the subtle skills of tracking to follow.

Faedyn and Lone followed the track south through the old forest beyond the Rimwood. The trail of blood diminished, but still the creature had left an unmistakable path of tracks and broken branches. As the morning passed into afternoon, they pressed on. They did not stop to rest or eat, but ate what food and drink they had on the move.

The woods grew gloomier as they went. Less and less sunlight filtered through the dense canopy. The ground became muddy and the foggy air grew thick, infused with the odor of rotting vegetation. The trees here were different, twisting and drooping, with great tentacles of exposed roots tangled together across the forest floor. Even at midday, it seemed almost like night, and the sounds of animals echoed eerily through the darkness. Unseen frogs croaked, and cawing crows passed overhead with a flurry of flapping wings.

"We have entered the Murkwood," Lone said.

"The creature's lair must be here somewhere."

The path led them into a swamp. Knee deep water slowed their progress, and they struggled to determine the creature's course. Here and there they found a bent or broken branch to go on. That was all. Yet Faedyn led them onward, following his instincts, and the general direction the beast had taken.

On the far side of the swamp, they came to a place where a small stream flowed from a narrow valley. A little ways on, the valley became nothing more than a rocky fissure in the earth, where darkness dwelled deeper still.

"This is it," Faedyn said, though there was no sign of the creature, or any other beast.

"Are you sure?" Lone said.

"Look at this picture," Faedyn said, drawing from his pocket the paper Ken had given him. He unfolded it and showed it to Lone. "Ken drew this from a vision he had."

Lone looked from the picture to the entrance of the narrow valley. The similarities were readily apparent. Ken's picture, scribbled in black ink, showed a rocky canyon identical to the one before them. "He is a seer?"

"In a manner of speaking," Faedyn said. He folded the paper, returned it to his pocket, and drew Vanar from its sheath, the metal gleaming, even here. He took the first steps up, following the rocky edges of the stream. Lone followed, drawing his sword. They proceeded cautiously up the slope. The walls grew steeper until they gave way to cliffs that stretched some twenty to thirty feet overhead.

The narrow canyon twisted and turned, obliterating any view of where they had come from. The rock walls were covered with wet slime, black fungus, and creeping vines. Faedyn's heart beat faster. There, in a niche in the rock was the first sign of the beast. A skull was set there, the bone yellowed and smeared with mud. As they continued, they saw more skulls lodged into cracks in the cliff walls and set on ledges. No doubt these were promises of the doom that awaited those who continued onward. Faedyn felt his old anger awaken, the rage of his past. But he stopped the flow of that feeling, even as it tried to rise within him. He couldn't let blind rage take over.

Above them, the roots of the Murkwood overhung the edges of the canyon walls, as if they threatened to form a roof over the narrow passageway, sealing them in this damp tomb with so many other unfortunate dead.

Faedyn knew the depths of evil, the depravities it sank to. Age-old memories of war would not let him forget. The distant horrors and the heartache still clung to the surface of his soul like the ever-fresh droplets of a bloody dew. His great loss still hurt him, even more now that he had returned to Elara. That was why he had to destroy this monster. It was as much for himself as it was for the sake of their journey or the people of Hidden Glade. And he wondered now, in the gloom of this place, was it just a selfish hate that drove him onward? Had the darkness that touched him simply returned to renew his bloodlust?

They came at last to the end of the canyon, walled in on three sides. Ahead, the stream poured over the blackened cliff into a dark pool, a slowly churning morass of foul water. A three-foot lizard slid into the pool and dissapeared into the depths.

"It's a dead end," Lone said. They stopped at the banks of the pool and looked for some sign of the beast.

"There," Faedyn said, "do you see it?"

"Where?"

"Behind the falls, a cave."

Lone saw where Faedyn pointed, and without further discussion they took their first cautious steps into the pool. They waded around the perimeter and edged behind the rushing water and the noise of the falls. Inside the cave, the water was still knee deep. Lone carefully removed two torches from his pack and lit them, handing one to Faedyn.

Swords and torches held high, they waded back into the darkness of the cave. Droplets of water fell from overhead like an irregular, sickly rain. The flames of their torches flickered and sputtered. The passage went back some ways, ever darker. The water depth rose until they waded up to their waists, and then higher.

The water was up to their chests when the precariously burning torches revealed this passageway also came to a dead end.

"This can't be right," Lone said, waving his torch back toward the entrance, his eyes nervous.

"Here, take this," Faedyn said, handing Lone his torch.

Lone held the two torches up in one hand, their flames and smoke licking the low ceiling.

Faedyn waded forward in the pale-yellow glow, shadows moving across the walls of the cavern as the flames jumped. He reached out with his free hand and felt the rough wall, sliding it down below the water line. Beneath the surface, he continued to grope until he came to a place where the wall gave way. He reached further in, dipping his whole shoulder into the water, and with his foot felt for the bottom until he was sure. Yes, beneath the surface was a wide tunnel that continued onward. The insides were smooth, worn by the passage of water and time. A man could easily swim in, but he had no idea how far the tunnel was submerged.

"There's a tunnel," Faedyn said. "Wait here. I'm going to see where it leads." He didn't wait for an answer. He sheathed Vanar and took a deep breath. As he sank beneath the water he could hear Lone protesting, but Faedyn followed his instinct, and the sense that the creature was nearby.

Underwater, Faedyn kicked downward into the tunnel and pulled through the water with his hands. He swam into utter darkness. For some ways he went, conscious of his heartbeats, and of every muscle contraction needed to move him forward. But long before he ran out of breath, he saw a faint light and the tunnel opened up. He rose to find the surface. Still holding his breath, he allowed the top of his head and his eyes to emerge from the water.

A large cave opened up before him. Scant light filtered down from overhead, where a hole in the high ceiling opened up to a murky sky. Water dripped down with the light and fell upon a heap of bones and corpses.

He should have gone back for Lone, but something drove him forward alone. In one smooth motion, he rose from the water, drew Vanar, and stepped up into the cave, dripping wet and ready for battle. The heavy air reeked of death, and the smell of the beast lingered nearby.

Faedyn gripped Vanar, ready for anything, and his eyes darted around to the dark corners that lay everywhere beyond his vision.

He had taken only a few cautious steps when the beast exploded out of the darkness with a roar, swinging its one arm like a huge, claw-tipped club overhead. Faedyn dodged the blow, turned and swung Vanar's keen edge into the creature's neck.

The blade cleaved deeply, and the beast careened forward, out of control. It flailed its arm wildly, blinded by rage and madness. Faedyn stood back, looking for an opportunity to strike again. Finally, though, the creature's wounds and exhaustion took their toll. The beast collapsed face down near the wall. It convulsed once, and then managed to turn itself over on its back. It lay there, exhausted of strength, blood flowing from the new wound.

Faedyn stood above the wreckage and looked down at the creature. For a moment, rage and anger seemed to leave its body. A natural clarity returned to the creature's eyes, only to see its own doom. Faedyn hesitated with Vanar held above his head. But the evil that dominated the creature had not left entirely, and even this could be a trick.

Vanar came down, cutting again into the creature's thick neck. Blood sprayed across Faedyn's face, and he cut again until the beast's great head separated from its body.

Silence returned. Faedyn stood in horrible triumph. His own exhaustion came over him, and his ribs ached. Evil always left its mark, and it felt as if that darkness in the creature's eyes had left an impression on Faedyn's already tainted soul.

He heard Lone's voice behind him. "Faedyn? Are you all right?"

Faedyn turned and nodded. "It's over," he said. But he knew it wasn't over. A greater battle was just beginning. He did not fully grasp it, but he knew the curse of this creature was only a symptom of a greater evil spreading across the three earths. Not since the Dark Age had such monsters roamed the world.

25

The Return of Heroes

The night was long and dark. Anna stayed out late with Mouse, waiting on the platform for Faedyn's return. When the night dragged on and they did not show, she worried almost to the point of despair. Again and again, she tried to reassure herself. "They must have camped overnight on their way back," she said, because she couldn't bear the thought of losing Faedyn. She had come to trust him, to admire him, and in this strange place, to rely on him more than any other man she had ever known.

Ken stood with them for a while on their vigil, and for once he seemed to understand. He looked at Anna and recognized her concern. He saw the surface of her fear, her naked loneliness, and tried to comfort her. In the glow of the lamplight, under a starry sky, he spoke with a sincerity seldom managed by boys his age. It was a sincerity marked not so much by the words, but by the feeling of sympathy behind them. "Don't worry, Anna," he said. "He'll be all right."

Mouse finally had to insist they go up to their room. "They must have camped out," Anna said again. But she could only half convince herself. She lay awake much of the night, clutching the gemstone that Faedyn had given her. A sickly feeling came over her as she remembered long nights like this when her mother was in the hospital. Anna never knew if she would be there in the morning, and eventually, she wasn't. She had to go on alone. She had never wanted to be alone, and now she was afraid that Faedyn would leave her too, that he would disappear into an unseen death.

Mouse drifted in and out of sleep by Anna's side, curled up in a ball one moment, then stirring to put an arm around her the next. Anna took comfort in Mouse's presence, drifting off herself sometime long after midnight. But her dreams were grotesque and troubling, keeping her in a fitful state, even in sleep.

Dawn brought an end to the suffering of Anna's night. She mustered a renewed sense of hope, and by midmorning, Faedyn and Lone returned. Anna rushed out to meet them, and they were welcomed by the rejoicing of the whole community. Lord Soren and Lady Nemona came out to greet them as heroes, and a ceremony was held to give thanks to the spirit of the forest. That evening another great feast was prepared, a celebration to mark the end of this dark time.

Over and over, Faedyn and Lone were asked to tell their story. Faedyn didn't seem to enjoy telling stories. All he would say of what happened was that they found the beast, and that Vanar, Lord Soren's gift, had served him well. Lord Soren invited them to stay on in Hidden Glade, but Faedyn said they must move on. "We set out for Andurin," he said. "And I fear we are long overdue."

The people became very curious about Faedyn. Where did this warrior come from? Who was he that he should shoulder their burden and destroy the creature that had so recently haunted them? They were less willing now to accept such a vague origin as the Fairwood. So, with good nature and admiration, they questioned him.

"Where are you really from?"

"How long were you in Midgard?"

"What were you doing there?"

"How old are you?"

"Did you fight in the Elara-war?"

"Whose line are you descended from?"

"You look familiar. Should we know who you are?"

Anna was ever by Faedyn's side, almost clinging to him, and she watched all this. She could see Faedyn was holding something back. She watched as he skillfully avoided their questions, redirecting the conversation. There was something he didn't want to tell them, some secret about his past. The subtleties of Faedyn's face had somehow opened up to her, and she could see the inner conflict stirred by their questions. He wasn't trying to deceive, but there was something in his past that pained him, something he'd rather forget, and he didn't want to open that door to others. Somehow seeing this made Anna feel even closer to him, and she wanted to comfort him.

Lone did what he could to shield Faedyn from questions. Mostly the people wanted to hear about the creature, and Lone would oblige, retracing their steps through the Murkwood, the dark pool, the cave, the underwater tunnel, and how he found Faedyn standing over the dead beast. Storytellers among them began to spin their own versions for the entertainment of the crowd, and they wove the threads into older stories, myths, and legends from times gone by.

When he could, when the attention had turned to these tales, Faedyn made his exit. He turned to Anna before leaving. "Enjoy the party," he said. "But don't stay up too late. Tomorrow we leave for Andurin." Then he sneaked out of the celebration with what seemed a great weight still hanging on his head.

Anna didn't stay long. With Faedyn gone, her interest in the party was gone, as well. Mouse and Ken were content at their table, watching the entertainment, but she couldn't stop wondering about Faedyn. What still troubled him now that the monster was dead and they could go on to Andurin? What was he hiding? She left the hall just in time to spot Faedyn climbing a stairway up to the higher levels, and she followed him.

She climbed after him, up through the ancient trees, gnarled with memories that twisted back through the ages. Making no attempt at secrecy, she simply followed him upward. If Faedyn knew she was there, which seemed likely, he didn't turn, stop, or slow his ascent. Nor did he rush, but climbed steadily upward to the highest levels.

Near the top of the canopy, the branches and leaves opened up to a clear night sky. Emerging from the thick woods below was like surfacing from the depths of an ocean into a surprisingly airy world that stretched outward forever. The star-filled sky evoked a sense of boundless space and time. There, Anna caught up with Faedyn on the highest platform, lit by starlight, staring up at those distant suns in the black of night.

As Anna approached, Faedyn spoke, his eyes still fixed upward. "I lived in the city for so long I almost forgot the grandeur of the night sky." In this way he greeted her, and confirmed what she suspected, that he had known she was following him all along and simply chose this moment to meet. He had a way of lending weight to a moment like this, of making each and every encounter reverberate with a deep significance, impossible to grasp in its totality. Perhaps that comes from such long life.

Anna looked up at the stars. They were scattered across the heavens like silver dust, twinkling in multitudes far greater than she had ever known. The black space between the brighter stars she knew was filled with many smaller, dimmer stars she had never seen before. In parts of the sky, these faint stars were clustered together in dense gatherings of ethereal light. There were dim milky patches too, that spoke of stars in even greater numbers, and heavenly lights too distant to discern from the earth, even out to the ends of the universe.

"I've lived in the city my whole life," Anna said. "I never knew you could see so many stars."

"The light from these stars takes thousands of years to reach us," Faedyn said. "In a couple thousand years, I wonder who will be here to see them."

"Will you live that long, Faedyn?"

Faedyn seemed to think about this as he stared up at the stars. "Not likely. I've already lived many long years."

Silence passed between them. The stars held fast, a testament to an unspoken history.

"There's something I need to tell you," Faedyn said. "I've debated when, and even if I should, for it could place burdens on you that you may not want."

"What is it?"

"Remember when I spoke of your ancestors?"

"You said you knew my father."

"Yes, the father of your bloodline. Well, you must know … you are a descendent of Lord Elgard, the last wielder of Rayaden."

"I know that story," Anna said with some excitement. "Rayaden is the magic sword Miura hid before he disappeared from Elara. His girlfriend, Yume, was killed by the Malar."

Faedyn nodded and looked off into the distance. "That's right. And that's why the Malar are after you. The Loremasters were right to think you have something they want. But it's not a gift for viewing they seek. They have witches who are adept enough at that."

"Then what is it?"

"You are an heir to Rayaden. Through you its power could be restored. The Malar would do anything to either possess or destroy that power. Rayaden will respond only to a descendent of Elgard's line. I thought the line had died out … until I met you."

Somehow it all made sense to Anna. Rather than feel surprise, she felt at ease. She felt comforted even, by this figure of the past, Lord Elgard … her father. It was as if some hidden piece of herself had come into focus. But something still bothered her. There was still something Faedyn was holding back. "Faedyn, how do you know all this? How do you know for certain I am Elgard's descendent?"

Faedyn seemed to weigh his answer for a moment. "As I said, I knew Lord Elgard. That gem you wear belonged to his daughter, Yume. You've noticed how it glows. It only does that for the heirs of Elgard's bloodline." He was looking at her now, with the deepest longing of memory written upon his face.

And then it came to Anna. She understood. She knew what Faedyn's secret was. "You're Miura, aren't you?"

Faedyn's long silence spoke a deeper truth than any words could. He looked away from Anna and stared off into the night. Finally, he looked back. "I *was* Miura. That was a long time ago. I've been afraid of that secret ever since we crossed over into Elara."

"But you're a hero," Anna said, amazed that Faedyn was afraid of anything.

"What do you know about heroes?" Faedyn said.

"Not much, I guess."

"Well, I'm no hero. Anyway, it would be best if we kept this secret for now. Can you do that?"

Anna nodded.

"Now get some sleep," Faedyn said. He nodded downward toward the hall where the celebration was still going strong. "They think this darkness has passed, but I fear it is only beginning."

26

Namh's Dream

The stars shone brightly over Andurin, and that dust of the heavens cast a pale light in the darkness. The bare granite peaks that surrounded the valley framed the sky with silver and shadow. The sound of the river and the great falls rushed and roared in the night. And on the valley floor, trees whispered and wild deer moved upon moonlit meadows.

High above the valley floor, the great Shrine perched on a sloping ledge in an otherwise sheer cliff wall. Its buildings were quiet in the deep of night, when even the elar rest. In her chamber, Namh of Aamu slept beneath woolen blankets and a quilt of torha-down. Even in summer the air could be cool at this hour, and the wind that sometimes blew down the valley swirled in her open window, rustling various papers that were pinned down by stacks of books on her desk.

Her dream took her out across the landscape of Elara, her beloved home, as if the great falcons of the wild North bore her on their wings. She flew where she willed, ranging far on the wide earth. Above her, streaks of meteors punctuated the steadfast stars, and wisps of cloud passed by at the edge of space. Below her, the features of the world—its winding rivers, old forests, green hills and jagged peaks—were illuminated as if by ethereal light, for even in the night they were revealed to her vision.

Such a beautiful world! It filled her with the kind of love that can sustain one through the long years. She drifted on like this for some time, until she noticed a strange darkness in the south. At first it was only something in the corner of her eye, a speck in her vision that was more a feeling of doubt than anything particular, a curious tiny dread that drew her attention. But as she gazed southward, that feeling grew into a darkness greater than the dark of night, like a storm cloud, billowing up on the far horizon.

At the sight of that black cloud, Namh's chest grew tight. Yet she flew south, at first slowly, drawn by its mystery, and then ever more quickly until she was rushing toward it. And though there ever seemed to be some distant darkness even greater, she came at last upon an enormous black cloud of smoke rising from the earth. Below her, a city burned, its timber buildings engulfed in merciless flames and its stone castle and walls crumbled in ruin.

Suddenly she felt a familiar presence, and a dear voice entered her dream. "Namh, awake and come to me."

Princess Arisu!

Namh awoke at once, leaving the vision of her dream for the quiet of her room and the stillness of the Shrine. She rose from bed and dressed quickly, fastening her white robe at the shoulders and fixing her long hair back with a golden clasp.

Princess Arisu didn't always heed the conventional rhythms of the day and night. She watched near and far, following subtle paths of thoughts and dreams across the world and beyond. That was her way, but the princess had not visited Namh's dreams in a long time, and her call seemed urgent. So, with the still-fresh image of that burning city in her mind, Namh hurried off.

The Shrine of Andurin was a large complex of interconnected buildings, with halls, libraries, temples, baths, and living quarters. A veritable maze of corridors existed between any two places, but Namh knew them all, even in the dark. Her love for this place had kept her here for the last five hundred years of her still youthful life, long after she had ceased to be a regular student.

She had become a servant of the Shrine, and was chosen to be an attendant and apprentice to the princess. There were many lofty hierarchies that stood above Namh at the Shrine, great teachers of various arts, representatives of the lordly houses, and dedicated servants much older than Namh was. But Princess Arisu stood apart from them. Arisu was the keeper of the Shrine, oldest and wisest of all the elar.

Back toward the cliff wall, the oldest parts of the Shrine contained the entrances to caves, corridors, and rooms that had been carved out of the solid rock. There she found Arisu in her familiar place, a large chamber of finished stone, an ancient hall extending back into the mountain.

During the day, the hall was lit by skyward-angled clerestory windows, reaching out to the cliff face. Along the sides of the chamber were wooden pilasters that rose almost to the ceiling before merging into the smooth, stone walls. These wooden sentinels held small lanterns that cast just enough light to see by at night. The alcove where the princess sat was in shadow, but a moonbeam shone through a clerestory window, falling upon a strand of her white hair and a fold in her robes where they billowed out on the thick carpet spread beneath her.

Namh approached and bowed. "I'm here, Princess."

Arisu's voice did not seem old on the surface, but there was something in it, some overtones that spoke of many long years lived. "Tell me about your dream, Namh."

"My dream?"

"Yes. You saw something."

Namh recalled flying over Elara, and the black smoke to the south. "I saw a city in flames."

"Helmas Calador, the capital of Roetheia. That was the city in your dream."

Namh wondered at the thought of it. "The kingdom of the humans? Destroyed? Was it a true dream, then?"

"Perhaps," Arisu said sadly, "but it is a dream of the future, and the future is not fixed. Relations between Roethia and the kingdom of Drighton, far to the south, have long been strained. There are thoughts and rumors of war among them."

"Humans are always thinking of war. I wonder sometimes if the world wouldn't be better off without them."

Arisu was silent for a moment. Namh couldn't see her face in the shadows. "Take care in your own thoughts, Namh. Think back to your dream. Was there anything else?"

Namh shut her eyes and tried to recall the images, and even more the feeling of her dream. "There was something else," she said slowly, still searching her mind to find expression for it. "Beyond the black smoke, there was a greater darkness, more felt than seen, a foreboding dread on the distant horizon."

"Yes," Arisu said. "The influence of evil is growing throughout the three earths. A new prince of the Malar is rising to power. The Elyx-ular have opened new pathways between the worlds, and the dark mages have taken the first steps to uncovering the ancient secrets of the Crypt. I fear a war is coming that will engulf us all."

"What of the great houses, the lords of Elara? Can they not rally to defend us?"

"In time they must be summoned. But I fear their strength has waned. Many of our people grow complacent, hiding in their distant homes, forgetting the threat of their enemy. They wait for the Lords of Light to come and take them away, but they forget their charge while they are here, to be stewards of this earth. There will be much debate among them about the need for action."

"What hope is there, then? Our race dwindles even to this day, and if the Malar return again to Elara …"

"There is always hope, Namh. Our hope now lies in Rayaden, the lost sword of Elgard's bloodline. I cannot say how—such things are not visible to me—but a true wielder of Rayaden can lead us through the coming darkness."

"But Rayaden is lost, and the line of Elgard is dead."

"Even now, hope comes to us. Soon you will understand."

Namh tried to see Arisu's face in the shadow of the alcove, but couldn't. It was strange to see her so shrouded in darkness, and Namh was uneasy about all that she had seen and heard. She bowed, and made to leave, but Arisu stopped her mid-turn. "Namh?" she said, a sudden tenderness in her voice, a motherly care that made Namh love her all the more.

"Yes?"

"Much may be asked of you in the coming days."

Namh knew this was a question she had to answer. "Princess Arisu," she said, "I will do whatever you ask."

"Good," Arisu said. "That's good." But there was something in her voice that Namh had never heard before, something grave and troubling.

27

The Path to Andurin

They set out from Hidden Glade early in the morning. Glimmering droplets of dew still clung to every surface of the forest, and the first beams of sunlight cut through the shadows that still lingered beneath the canopy. The whole of Hidden Glade, it seemed, was there in the clearing and on the platforms to bid them farewell. Lord Soren made a short speech, which aside from sounding very formal, made no sense to Ken, since it was all in Vena. Ken just bowed when everyone else did, looked for that golden-eyed goddess in the crowd, and then filed into line for their walk through the Rimwood.

Faedyn, Ken had discovered, wasn't fond of a lot of discussion while walking. He particularly wasn't fond of talking about how far things were or how long things would take. Presumably he knew these things, but all Ken got were vague redirecting answers when he asked. He finally figured out it would take about a month to reach the Shrine.

"I'm sure Faedyn could travel faster if it weren't for us," Anna said.

"Really?" Ken said. "I could travel faster if I had the Land Rover."

Anna laughed. "But where are you going to fill up on gas?"

They journeyed northwest through the forest, making camp well before sundown on that first day. Faedyn lit a fire and went off into the woods to find food for supper. They had brought food with them this time, but they would add to it whatever they could gather or hunt along the way.

Ken dropped his pack and sank to the ground, his back against a broad tree. A month of this, he thought, of walking all day and sleeping on the ground under an open sky. He was already dreaming of his comfy little hut in Hidden Glade, and taking a warm bath in the river with Alia. He took a deep breath and sighed. That would have never happened, not the way he imagined it, anyway.

The sun fell as they ate their dinner around the fire. Afterward, they drank tea as the stars came out beyond the treetops. "It's so peaceful here," Anna said.

"Peace," Faedyn said, as if turning the idea around in his head. "Sometimes I wonder if we have ever really known such a thing. There is always a war somewhere, always hatred and malice in people's hearts. What real peace can be found on earth?"

A silence fell over the camp with Faedyn's words. Neither Anna nor Ken knew what to say. "I'm sorry," Faedyn said. "I didn't mean to dampen your spirits." He smiled and looked up toward the distant, unchanging stars. "For the moment, peace is indeed upon us. Have some more tea."

Eventually, Ken made his bed by the fire, near Anna and Mouse. All afternoon as they walked, he had been thinking. If Anna really was the one the Loremasters were looking for, then she probably had an incredible natural gift for viewing. Maybe he should be doing more to teach her. Besides, he was desperate to have something to talk to her about.

"If you want," Ken said, "I could teach you how to do viewing. It's not that hard, just takes practice."

"What kinds of things can you see?" Anna said.

"You can see the future," he said, trying to get her excited. It worked on him, after all, when Smith told him he'd be able to see the future. He'd pictured winning the lottery, but it turns out it doesn't exactly work that way. First, it takes a group of Loremasters to achieve any sort of real accuracy. Secondly, random things are more difficult to see. And finally, Smith would kill him if he tried to use viewing like that.

"I'm not sure I want to see the future," Anna said.

"You can see the past too, distant places, all kinds of things."

"The past might be nice to see, I guess. But wouldn't your master, Mr. Smith, disapprove of you disclosing your secrets."

"They're not secrets. He's going to teach you anyway when we get back, and you become an apprentice yourself."

"But I'm not sure I want to join your little club … or go back for that matter. I like it here."

"What?"

"I like it here."

"You're crazy."

"Maybe," Anna said. "Anyway, what good does it do you? Look at you. You can see the future, but you still don't have a car."

Ken laughed. She was right. They had abandoned the poor Land Rover in the middle of nowhere, and now he spent every day walking more than he ever cared to. "But it does all kinds of good. If what you see is accurate, anyway. That's how the Loremasters have become so powerful. That's how Faedyn and Lone knew where to find that monster. I saw it. I drew them a picture."

"I'm sure Faedyn would have found it anyway."

"Yeah, right. I forgot you have a crush on him."

"What!" Anna said, sitting up straight.

"See what I mean. Must be right, eh Mouse?"

Mouse just cocked her head and stuck out her tongue at him. "Oh whatever," Anna said. "I'm going to sleep."

†

The next day, they moved on, and after a week of daily travel they emerged from the dense forest. They pressed on under a wide blue sky streaked with high clouds. The landscape continued to change. The hills flattened out into low undulations that stretched out to the horizon. They walked through high grasses and golden fields as herds of deer and elk stood in the distance like aimless, wandering armies. Once they even walked quietly right through the middle of a herd, while the animals grazed and walked around them.

Anna looked happy under that sky and among those grasses in the grayish-green clothes she wore now. The waves of her hair were pulled back and almost shimmered in the sunlight.

"Did you grow up in the city?" Ken asked as they walked. He didn't really know what to say to Anna, but whether from loneliness, homesickness, or something else, on these long days of walking he felt a constant desire to talk to her.

Anna seemed confused for a moment. "Pretty much," she said. "My mom and I used to go to the beach sometimes before she died. How about you?"

"I was born in the city. But I've been going to boarding school since I was nine."

"Did you like it?"

"It was okay. More fun than home, I guess. And that's where Smith found me."

Anna slowed for a moment, as if her thoughts were bleeding energy from her legs. She looked at Ken with a sudden interest. "What are your parents like?" she said.

Ken slowed too, taking time to consider the question. He was trying to think of the right word, trying to articulate the feeling he had when Anna mentioned his parents. "Distant," he said, finally.

The days were long, providing time for meandering conversations as they walked and while resting in camp each evening. During this time, Ken and Anna truly became friends. A new feeling grew between them, born out of the deep, natural sympathy of one human being for another. With Mouse, they walked on together, following the sun as it set in the west each evening, not knowing what lay beyond that strange horizon.

†

These were the happiest days Anna could remember since before her mom had gotten sick. Every day she awoke to a clear sky and a beautiful sunrise. Her feet walked upon the ancient earth. They crossed a wide landscape, so different from the city where she grew up. She felt a connection to the distant past, and to the future. A sense of unbroken continuity came over her. She felt her thoughts reach out to touch the wind and the grass and the animals all at once.

She told Ken about the place where she had lived in the city, about her school and the people there. It all seemed so far removed, so unreal to her here. One night, she even showed him the picture of her mother. She still carried it close to her breast, deep within the folds of her clothes. He had looked at it with some interest, remarking how kind her mother looked. Anna looked at the picture for a long, quiet moment before putting it away again. Although she was content to have everything else from her old life fade away, she always sought those strands of memory that remained of her mother. When she found them, when she could hear the sound of her mother's voice, or feel the comfort of her touch, a bittersweet ache swelled in her heart, a hollow hurt that seemed would never leave her.

Still, there was no doubt she had found some happiness here. It was so beautiful, and she was delighted to find she could learn the language. And now that she knew something about the father of her elaran bloodline, she felt she was on a path she had to follow. She felt like there was a place where she belonged. She only worried that somehow she would let Faedyn down, that everyone would discover she was actually useless, after all.

There was something else, as well though, far below the surface during those days of travel. The world lay open before her with a more peaceful clarity than she had ever known before. She was filled with hope, but there was still a fear inside her, a doubt and a darkness that wouldn't let go.

†

Mouse slept curled up in a little ball next to Anna's side and dreamt of days far back in her own brief history. She had always been certain there was a monster in the closet of her bedroom. She knew it, without a doubt, from as far back as she could remember.

When she went to sleep, she had to make sure the closet door was securely closed, so the monster couldn't get out. But with the door closed, she had to endure her own imagined image of the thing lurking in the corner of the closet, waiting silently to get her should the opportunity arise. It was a horrible thought to have while she lay in her bed, the sheets pulled up to her chin—a hideous monster crouching in the darkness, patient as a shadow where no light shines.

How could she ever sleep? She would have to stay awake, watching. For if she watched, perhaps the door would never open. She could hear traffic and people in the street below her window, but they wouldn't save her. The father was back from wherever he went, and she could hear him and the mother arguing out in the living room of the shabby apartment. They wouldn't save her, either.

The arguing of the parents turned to shouting, and then to yelling and screaming. That was the way it went. It always started with arguing, but it never ended there. No, they couldn't help her. Nobody could help her. She was all alone, and the monster was always waiting.

A stack of shelves stood against the wall beyond the foot of her bed. On those shelves she had placed her little treasures, her most prized possessions. Most of it was junk she found around the apartment, little shiny things, colorful pictures, bits of metal and glass. But she had a few toys, too. Her favorite was a barbie doll the mother had given her for Christmas last year. The little doll sat upright on the edge of the shelf, looking out, looking beautiful, looking hopeful for a bright and happy future.

The mother's screaming suddenly stopped as a loud thud shook the wall in Mouse's room and rattled everything on her shelf. The little doll toppled off the edge and fell to the floor. The father was still yelling. There was a scuffle and another thud. Then the apartment door opened and slammed shut. After that, silence.

Mouse lay awake in her bedroom. The monster waited in the closet. She could hear the mother crying for a while, but didn't dare go out there. After a while, the parents' bedroom door slammed shut. There was nobody to help her, nobody to comfort her or tell her that things would be okay.

The father was still gone the next day, and the mother was freaking out about something. She was tearing the apartment apart, looking for something. She became increasingly agitated, dumping drawers on the floor and rummaging through every corner and cupboard, scattering piles of unopened mail, dirty clothes, unwashed dishes, making a horrible racket.

In her room, Mouse crouched on the floor, trying to ignore the noise. She held her little doll and rocked back and forth on her heels. When the mother had exhausted her search of the apartment, she burst into Mouse's room and towered over Mouse's head. "I had a yellow box," she said. "It was hidden in the bureau. Where is it?"

Mouse clutched her doll and silently looked up at the mother.

The mother seemed to shake with fury. "Where is it?" she screamed.

Mouse didn't speak.

The mother began to search her room. "Stupid, useless girl," she muttered, "can't even answer a simple question." She tore the sheets off the bed, emptied the dresser and kicked the clothes around the room. Then she looked over Mouse's shelves, and with angry, frustrated sweeps of her hand sent all of Mouse's treasures crashing to the floor.

Mouse rocked back and forth.

"Where is it?" the mother yelled. She picked Mouse up by the shoulders and shook her.

Mouse just hung there, limp as a doll, and didn't respond.

"God damn it, say something!"

Mouse didn't say anything.

"Why don't you say something?" the mother screamed. Then she set Mouse down and slapped her across the face hard enough to knock her over. "You're going to be punished," she said, "because you're a bad girl. You're a wicked little girl who needs to be punished."

The mother grabbed Mouse by the wrist and dragged her across the floor toward the closet. As soon as Mouse crossed the threshold of the closet door she began to scream, a high-pitched wail of terror.

The mother pushed her into the corner and released her. Mouse couldn't move, though. She just screamed and screamed.

"Shut up!" The mother yelled and slammed the closet door.

Mouse stopped screaming as soon as the door shut. She heard the latch click, then footsteps, then her bedroom door closing. A few moments later she heard the apartment door open and shut.

Then silence again. She was alone in the dark. But she knew she wouldn't be alone in that closet forever. When night fell, the monster would come for her.

Hours passed. Only the slightest bit of light came into the closet through the crack at the bottom of the door. In the dim glow she could make out the walls of her prison. And from the fading light she understood the passage of time, the coming of night, and the approach of her doom.

She had tried more screaming. She had tried pushing the door. But nothing worked. Nobody came. She sat by the door hugging her knees, stared at the corner where the monster would come, and cried softly in the waning light. With each passing moment, she became more and more afraid, until darkness was almost complete and she knew it was time. The monster had come.

It reached out for her, but somehow it couldn't touch her. Something had happened. Someone else was there with her, protecting her. She saw a beautiful woman with long white hair and a pale-blue gown embroidered with gold. A radiant light surrounded her. "Do not be afraid," the woman said. Mouse felt immediately comforted, and the monster vanished.

"There was a monster," Mouse said.

"It cannot reach you now. You are safe," the woman said. "I will stay with you."

"Who are you?" Mouse said.

"I am Arisu," the woman said.

After that, Mouse slept in the peace of an embrace gentler and more loving than any she had ever known.

28

Shrine of Andurin

"We're getting closer," Faedyn said, as he walked along-side Anna, Ken, and Mouse.

Anna looked up at him and smiled. She was eager to see the Shrine of Andurin, for she had come to understand the deep significance the Shrine had for the elar.

"I sure hope so," Ken said. "I haven't been walking all this time for my health, you know."

Faedyn laughed.

The landscape had begun to change again. They started to climb into the foothills of mountains. They passed through stands of tall pines and green meadows where clear brooks bubbled, fed by the snows of still far-off peaks.

Two days more of walking, and then they climbed steeply upward. The air grew thinner, and the pine trees were fewer, stunted by altitude, clinging to bits of dirt and bare rock. They followed what appeared to be a well-worn path, until at last, just past mid-day, a grand vista left no doubt they had arrived.

"Behold," Faedyn said, "Andurin."

A thousand feet below them spread a broad green valley. For three or four miles the Andu river wound through the middle of the valley, fed by many smaller streams. The river was shallow and peaceful on the valley floor, but it came into and departed the valley through steeply gorged canyons that turned its waters white with rapids. All around, the valley floor was surrounded by bold granite peaks. They stood near the top of one of the smallest of those peaks and looked upon a landscape of such grandeur that it filled each of them with new-felt awe. Here were the signs of untold eons, a history of the earth that stood quite apart from the history of people. It was a piece of the world that seemed to have endured from the beginning.

Looking out across the valley, they could see thin water-falls that fell, cascading like veils from the high cliffs, spreading out in mist-like clouds as they plunged to the valley floor. Somewhere here was the Shrine of Andurin. Anna searched but could not find it. "Where is the Shrine?" she said.

"You cannot see it from here," Faedyn explained. "It's on the far side, further up the valley. We'll camp in sight of it tonight, by the river on the valley floor. You'll see. At first light tomorrow, we will make our climb."

They descended on a steeply-sloping path down to the valley floor. For a long time, they traveled along massive granite formations and along the edges of steep cliffs. Anna found that here, as in Hidden Glade, the dizzying heights did not affect her. She felt unafraid and sure of her feet as they descended. Feeling the end of their trip approaching, they walked with renewed vigor. Soon enough, they reached the bottom and entered into the trees at the base of the high peaks.

From there, they followed the path up the valley. They crossed the river by way of an ancient stone bridge, its sides covered in bright green mosses, and its top worn smooth by many years of use.

There was no mistaking the moment when the Shrine came into view. The setting sun left that side of the valley in shadow, but its white buildings were clearly visible, stacked up high on an imposing cliff wall. The ledge it perched on slanted downward offering only a hint at how it might be reached. The buildings seemed to grow out of the rock, blending seamlessly with the jagged, uneven ledge and the sheer cliff face. From such a distance, the Shrine resembled an immense formation of white crystals. A sense of its scale was difficult to grasp, but Anna could tell it was big. Many windows overlooked the valley, but she could see no people, and the place had a sense of stillness that matched the great walls of rock surrounding it.

"How did they build that?" Ken said.

Faedyn laughed. "Very carefully."

Anna was nervous and excited. She was anxious to see the Shrine. Faedyn had told her about a great library there, the largest in all of Elara. But she also knew things would change. Faedyn had fallen into an ever more pensive mood toward the end of their journey. She was sure that somehow the truth of Faedyn's identity was what bothered him. Miura was a hero of the Elara-war, but it pained him to be reminded of those days. It was a burden for him, as if he still carried the weight of Rayaden on his back.

That night, Anna found a moment to speak to him alone. She stole away from Ken and Mouse to find Faedyn a little way from their camp, looking up at the stars. He looked down at Anna as she came up beside him.

Anna met his gaze, wondering what it must be like to have lived for so long. She wondered about the mysteries of his past. Where did he hide Rayaden? Only he knew. And what happened after he disappeared from Elara so long ago? The stories said he traveled to the dark lands, to Maleistria, to avenge the death of Yume and the destruction of his people.

"You must miss Yume," Anna said. She was aware of how limited her experience must be compared to Faedyn's, but she knew loss. And she knew what it was like to miss someone you love.

Faedyn's expression did not change. His eyes were like hardened steel in the silvery light. He looked away, up toward the stars once again. A stoic sigh escaped his lips.

For a while, the silence of the night passed between them, a silence filled with the chirping of crickets, the gentle flow of the river, and the soft breeze that blew through the trees. Anna was happy to just stand beside him. There was a great comfort in it, a safety she felt in his presence. "What will happen when we reach the Shrine?" she said.

"There is a woman there named Arisu. She is one of the elders and the keeper of the Shrine. I have heard her voice calling to me, even from Midgard."

"Why was she calling you?"

"I have only guesses, but there is more to you being here than what the Loremasters know. You are a descendant of Elgard. The stone around your neck is proof of it." He paused in thought. "There is a purpose to you being here, Anna, and you must know that whatever that purpose is, it could be dangerous. People may ask things of you. I may ask things of you. But you alone must decide your path."

"I know," Anna said. She looked up at the stars, and in that moment felt the weight of the unknown upon her, the uncertainty of the future, and the fear of such heavy decisions.

†

At first light, before the sun broke above the peaks of the eastern wall, they set off. The Shrine was so high on the cliff Anna wasn't sure how they would reach it. The path they took led up out of the valley and began to climb steeply. For a while the Shrine was out of view, and the path turned into a series of switchbacks leading ever upward.

As the sun rose, they looked down on the river from high above the valley floor. Along the rocky path were curious stacks of stones that marked the way, and which stood as another testament to the stillness of the mountains.

Anna marveled at the heights, but her fear did not grip her as it might. She walked upward resolutely, following Faedyn's footsteps. With her eyes fixed on the ground in front of her, she was startled when she lifted her head and saw other people coming down the path.

Two elar, a man and woman, dressed in brown traveling clothes, descended the path ahead. They paused briefly when they saw the party and bowed in greeting. Faedyn bowed, and the strangers passed by in silence. Only the slightest change in their expression betrayed their surprise at seeing Anna, Ken, and Mouse. Anna watched as they continued down the mountain. The woman looked back once and caught Anna's eye briefly, with a curious, almost suspicious look on her face.

Further on, they came to a point where the switchbacks ended, and they traversed the side of the mountain for a long way. At last, the view opened up and they could see the Shrine again. Although still some distance away, they could see now the massive size of the buildings. They stood almost level with the Shrine at a point that overlooked the whole valley. A pale blue flag was posted here by more stacks of rocks. The fabric unfurled in the slightest breeze, its edges frayed and weathered.

The road to the Shrine was clearly visible now, marked at regular intervals by a series of the same weather-worn flags.

The path curved downward a way to their left and then snaked upward along a ledge in the cliff wall.

"We're almost there," Ken said. A twinge of anxious fear ran through Anna. Although this was the sanctuary they sought, where the Malar would not find her, she knew that within these walls she would find more than a simple refuge. There was peace in this place. She could sense that, but she felt the stillness of the mountain like the quiet before a storm. In the distance, thunder rolled ominously on a dark horizon. The earth itself was pregnant with the promise of troubled times. How could she tell Ken, who had endured so much in the belief that she would be safe here? He still thought they could wait out the danger, but she knew already in her heart she could not hide from her enemies forever. It was a foolish dream to think this place would be the end of her journey. It was only the beginning.

The way became ever more refined as they continued. The edges of the path were lined with carefully laid stone, and steps were finely cut into the rock where the way was steep. They went down for a while and then began to climb again toward the Shrine's entrance. As they ascended this final length, the buildings of the Shrine loomed against a clear blue sky.

At the top, they were met by a woman in white. A golden circlet adorned her forehead. She stood tall and stately, her long, ash-blond hair shifting in the breeze. Gold ornaments adorned her ears and braced her close-fitting gown at her hips. Anna had never felt so intimidated by the presence of another woman. She was overwhelmingly beautiful, and stood with a sense of total self-possession and awareness. Her eyes fell on Faedyn as she spoke in slow and formal Vena. "Welcome travelers. I am Namh of Aamu, servant of the Shrine of Andurin and attendant to Princess Arisu. The princess has been expecting you."

Faedyn bowed slightly. "Call me Faedyn," he said simply and in English. The woman's lips pressed together in an expression that could have been disappointment, as Faedyn continued to introduce the members of their party.

Namh didn't look at Anna, Ken, or Mouse as they were introduced. When Faedyn had finished, she spoke again in formal Vena. "Please, come with me. We have rooms prepared for you."

They admired the spectacular views as they walked, following Namh around a terrace that overlooked the valley. At the far end of the terrace, they entered the labyrinthine interior of the Shrine.

They passed few other people in the hallways, and those they encountered looked at them with great curiosity. Anna imagined humans were rarely, if ever, seen at Andurin. Namh brought them to a suite of rooms that overlooked the valley. Several attendants brought tea and food.

When they were left alone, Faedyn began to pace the room.

"Can you tell me more about this princess?" Ken said.

"She's one of the elders" Faedyn said, "and the keeper of the Shrine." Faedyn paused at the window and looked out over the valley, but he was obviously distracted from the view. "I should tell you, Ken, there's more to this than you know."

"More to what?"

"To our presence here. I have kept my true identity secret from you, and from the Loremasters for all these long years."

"A secret? Who are you, then?"

Faedyn paused. "I am ... Miura, heir of Mara and Yenifar."

"Miura?" Ken said. "Like in the story? The one who hid the sword?"

"Yes," Faedyn said. "And there's more. Anna is the heir of Elgard. She is a true wielder of Rayaden. That's why the Malar sought her out on Midgard."

"I thought it was because of the prophesy," Ken said.

Faedyn's ears perked up. "What prophesy?"

Ken became suddenly shy and quiet, as if he realized he said something he shouldn't have.

"Go on, Ken," Faedyn said. "What prophesy?"

"The Loremasters have an old prophesy, that a human girl with elaran blood will come among them. She will be the key to the future of humanity. Through her, they will see through the gaps between worlds, and guide mankind to its ultimate destiny." Ken looked to Anna. "It's you," Ken said. "They think you're the one they've been looking for."

Anna looked to Faedyn.

"We have kept too many secrets," Faedyn said.

29

KAI AND SULKI

Nightfall came, and from the balcony of his high tower, Kai looked out over the city of Maleistria. A multitude of lights, lanterns, and fires spread out below him in the streets and buildings. All the way to the walls of the city they spread, where the lights of the city guard and the massive fires that marked Maleistria's great gate shone in the darkness.

Soon ... very soon, this city would be his. The witches of the Elyx-ular held the real power behind the emperor's throne, and soon they would put him on it. Sulki had promised him that. They will unite all of Maleistria and the three worlds under a single rule. They will bring a new glorious, golden age to the earth.

There was but one danger that lurked in all his visions of the future. Of all things, it was a human girl, a bastard child from an ancient bloodline of the elar. As unlikely as it was, she could have the power to wield Rayaden, if it ever was found. That girl was a small, annoying itch he wished he could scratch, a troublesome thing he wished he could blot out of existence.

Behind him, the lights of his private chamber burned. From within, Sulki came out into the night air. Sulki, who had raised him from birth, who had taught him how to see far and future things, and how to control people with a word, and how to kill them with a sword. She was his mentor and advisor. She was a mother, a sister, and a lover. Oh, beautiful Sulki. Her footsteps were soft on the smooth stone. Her lithe body was undaunted by the chill in the air. The black dress she wore, silver-clasped at her breast and hip, left most of her exposed, and her pale skin seemed aglow in the darkness. Moonlight glimmered off the silver that ringed her arms and dangled from her ears, and from the diadem that crowned her forehead. She shone like moonlight reflected in the clouds. Gossamer grey silk hung about her hips like mist and blew like wisps of smoke from her silver armlets. Her long, raven-black hair came to life in a breeze that blew across the parapet.

She stood close to Kai.

Kai inhaled, smelling her sweet fragrance.

Sulki's body pressed toward him. "One of the assassins has returned from Midgard," she said. "All the girls have been eliminated, except one, who disappeared from the city before they could kill her."

Kai sighed, annoyed that this matter could not be altogether closed, worried that the girl would still haunt his dreams. "What was the name of the girl who escaped? Do they know her name?"

"Anna Karova. But she is a human being. What harm can she do to us? Even if she could wield Rayaden, that sword is lost forever."

Kai tried to forget about the human girl, that annoying little itch. There were so many other things, more immediate things to think about ... like the emperor, Drakhil, and his sons, Malfot, Nykhil, and Durok. How he grew tired of those names. "All of this waiting makes me impatient," he said.

Sulki looked out over the city. "All that we have seen and planned must happen in time. Your life has been a testament to patience. But you will not have to wait much longer."

Kai thought about his dealings with the court today, how the self-serving sons of the emperor quarreled over kingdoms, slaves, and the never-ending wars in the Outlands. "They call me a freak," Kai said.

Sulki laughed. "They resent that we made you our representative at court. They are jealous of the power of the Elyxular. They fear you, and they are right to do so."

"They have no vision for the world," Kai said. "All they care about is their wealth, and their petty notions of power."

Sulki smiled. "True power is the power to remake the world. The emperor has long been nothing more than a symbol. Soon, very soon, he will be dead."

"Why don't we take care of them all at once, the emperor, and his sons?"

"With Drakhil out of the way, the princes will fight among themselves, blaming one another for their father's death. Each will seek the throne at all costs, and the city will be thrown into chaos. You, Prince Kai, will be our savior."

Kai turned to Sulki as her arm caressed his neck. Her face was filled with a radiant hope, an unspeakable beauty. Her red lips parted slightly with the inspiration of her breath. His hands touched her cool skin, felt the concave curves of her waist, and her moonlit eyes dimmed in his shadow as they came together for a kiss.

30

Princess Arisu

When the princess called for them, Namh led the group through a labyrinth of corridors. Mouse walked quickly to keep up with the others. She understood fear, and she saw clearly that Anna was afraid. Mouse tried to stay close to her as they walked, to give her some sense of reassurance, but Anna seemed wholly distracted by whatever lay ahead.

Mouse felt a kind of comfort walking amidst her friends. She could hide safely in the middle of them as they towered around her. She shrank down further as they walked, lightened her step, and wondered, as she often did, if she could hide forever.

Namh led them back toward the rock face upon which the Shrine was built. There was something about the name *Arisu*, that stirred some memory in Mouse. She couldn't quite place it. Perhaps it was from one of the stories Anna had told her. Perhaps Faedyn had mentioned her sometime before. The memory was close to her, but she could not reach it.

They came at last to a great arched doorway, where massive wooden doors hung in a passage carved out of the rock. All around the arch, the doorway was framed by intricate ornamental carvings of geometric and plantlike patterns. Here and there, the faces of stone animals seemed to gaze out like curious guards keeping a silent watch.

Namh pushed the doors open. It made no sound and seemed almost effortless. They entered a large hall made of stone and ancient timber. Sunlight shone in through clerestory windows above them, and overhead a few tiny birds flittered in and out of the radiant beams.

Following Namh, they walked to the center of the hall. At first the others blocked Mouse's view, but as they stopped, she peeked around Ken's back.

Princess Arisu sat perfectly still on a thick, brightly woven carpet covering a raised platform at the head of the hall. She wore pale blue robes, tied and adorned with gold brocade and embroidery. The robes spread out around her, concealing her legs entirely. Her white hair cascaded down from an intricate arrangement at the crown of her head. Her skin seemed to glow in the sunlight. Delicate hands were folded in her lap.

Arisu's eyes were pale almost to the point of being white. They did not seem to focus as they entered, but held a fixed, soft gaze that reached out to the ends of the earth, and to the far reaches of time and space. Mouse had never known such beauty as she beheld in Arisu's face, which long years had not touched with wrinkles or lines, but only with an ever-increasing benevolence and grace. Mouse remembered her immediately from her dream. How could she forget the angel that saved her?

†

Faedyn looked at Arisu. She sat with a stillness like that of the ages long passed. Her pale blue gown fell to the floor and billowed around her like mist. The tresses of her white hair adorned her face, which even to Faedyn seemed an extraordinary confluence of the beauty of youth and the wisdom of many long years. Her pale grey eyes gazed through them, fixed and unmoving.

Faedyn bowed deeply and the others followed. The weight of decisions made and deeds done long ago were heavy upon him as he straightened himself and stood with formal attention.

Mouse scurried out from behind them and made as if to run toward Arisu. Anna quickly grabbed her, and held her gently. The little girl was easily subdued. She stood quietly, but there was a curious expression on her face. She seemed to almost pant with excitement. There was a look of rapt joy on her usually sullen face that made her seem almost a different person. Her eyes remained fixed on the princess.

Arisu smiled, a subtle expression touched by amusement, happiness, and loving benevolence. At first, she seemed to smile at Mouse, but somehow it was clearly meant for them all. Arisu's smile spoke to each of them, like words with many layers of meaning.

Although Faedyn knew her pale eyes were blind, he felt they saw through everything. They saw the soul in a way that seeing eyes were blind to. Those eyes knew and understood the core of a person's being. And their desires, fears, thoughts, and dreams were all transparent to them. The effect, to Faedyn, was both comforting and disconcerting. Arisu, more than anyone, could see who he really was, where he had been, and the darkness and depravity to which he had once fallen.

†

The eyes of Princess Arisu terrified Anna. They seemed to see right through her, and she feared what they would find. There was a joy in Mouse that Anna had never seen, and didn't understand. Anna held her like a shield and awaited whatever fate would bring.

"Welcome to Andurin," Arisu said. "You have travelled far from your home, and at last, Miura of Arran has returned from exile."

"Princess Arisu," Faedyn said. "I heard you from afar, and this girl, Anna—"

"Yes," Arisu said. "I know. But your journey from Midgard took longer than I had foreseen."

"A darkness infects the forests to the east," Faedyn said.

"The influence of evil spreads to every corner of the three earths. It clouds my vision and is an invisible poison to everything is touches. Even here we are not safe from it."

Anna thought about the dreams that plagued her nights, in which a dark presence drew near to her, a palpable evil, indescribable upon waking.

"There is always hope, Anna," Arisu said, as if she had been reading her mind. "But the sanctuary you seek cannot be found here. War is coming, a war for the fate of the earth. There will be no safe place under heaven."

"The Malar have found a way to Midgard," Faedyn said.

"Agents of the Malar are abroad even here in Elara."

"We should never have left the city," Ken said.

"You would all be dead now had you stayed," Arisu said.

There was silence in the hall for a moment. Arisu sat motionless. Her eyes seemed to gaze out to the ends of earth. "A new prince is rising to power in Maleistria," she said. "Kai is his name. The mages of the Crypt have begun to explore forbidden secrets. Under Kai's rule, they will unearth things that should never have been made. He will seek to unite all of

Maleistria under his rule. And then he will turn to Elara and Midgard."

"To what end?" Faedyn said.

"To destroy them, to bring down the veil between worlds and fulfill the rebellion of Saziel, to wipe out human beings and create a single earth under his dominion."

"Then the fate of the earth itself is at stake. How can we stop him?"

"Rayaden must be recovered. Its power fades as long as it lies hidden. That is why you are here, to find Rayaden. For in it lies the hope of Elara and Midgard. The elar grow distant from one another, and complacent in their ways. Their distrust of humanity deepens with the passing of years. Only a wielder of Rayaden can stop Kai from destroying the three earths. You, Anna, are the last heir of Elgard's bloodline. Only you can take up the hidden blade that holds our hope."

Namh stirred from her quiet stance, a look of incredulity on her face. She seemed about to speak, but an almost imperceptible gesture from the princess warned her to remain silent.

Anna stood motionless, unable to speak. She looked away from Arisu's terrible eyes.

"It will not be easy," Faedyn said, as much to Anna as to Arisu. "I did not hide Rayaden with the idea that I would ever have to get it back. It would be another long journey, a dangerous one, and one that in the end may prove impossible."

Anna remained still, her head hung down, lost in thoughts of the city, and the billions of people in the world she had come from. Could it be that they would all perish in a coming war they knew nothing about? Could it be that hope to avoid such a future rested within her? It was too much. She thought about her mother, and the father figure she had found in her elaran blood.

Faedyn put his hand on Anna's shoulder. "Consider your path well, Anna. There will be no turning back once you have chosen. There may yet be other ways to avoid the ends that Arisu has foreseen."

"It's okay," Anna said. "I don't know if I can do what you're asking, but if Faedyn will lead us, I'll follow."

"Anna," Ken said. "We don't even know if what she's saying is true. The Loremasters have never seen the future she describes."

"No end is certain, Master Ken," Arisu said, "but the vision of your order is limited by the separation between worlds. They cannot see what lies beyond Midgard."

"It's okay, Ken," Anna said. "You don't have to go. Who can say what will happen in the future, anyway? Our actions decide what will really happen. All my life I have wanted a father, and now it seems one is calling out to me. I can't explain it, but here in Elara, I have felt a kind of belonging that I never felt in the city. I ... I have to go."

"Rest among us here for a while," Arisu said. "There is still some time to prepare for the journey. But whatever is to be done, must be done, for I tell you the world is changing, and what we do will decide the changes to come."

31

A City in Darkness

Having retired early, Ken sat in his room, leaving the others to discuss plans for yet another journey. He tried to do some viewing, but it was impossible. His mind was too excited, too active and agitated. Faedyn had tricked them. He had lied to Smith about what he knew. He knew from the beginning Anna was a descendent of Elgard. He didn't bring her here for her safety at all. He and Arisu had their own agenda.

The question was, what was he going to do about it? Anna was determined to go on with Faedyn, to recover Rayaden … and then what? Smith had been certain Anna was the one, the key to the future of the Loremasters and their endeavor to understand the destiny of mankind. But Anna wasn't interested in joining them. Perhaps they had contacted her too soon. Maybe everything was thrown off by the influence of the Malar. Or it could all be part of the prophesy in some convoluted way he could scarcely fathom. Arisu had said their vision was limited by the separation between worlds, and he knew that was true. How much could that affect their predictions if the Malar had begun to change the unfolding of events on other worlds?

It was all so confusing, and the thoughts ran around and around in his head all evening. He analyzed various possibilities until he exhausted himself, only to find that he had gotten nowhere, or right back where he began. He couldn't force Anna to stay at Andurin. She had to be free to do what she wanted. And in that case, he would have to go with her. Smith had told him that he was to watch after her, no matter what.

But what if what Arisu said was true, that a war was coming that would affect all three earths? The Loremasters would have to be warned. He would have to go back to tell them. What if they were wrong about Anna all along? What if all their predictions were wrong? If they were warned now, perhaps they could do something to help mankind.

On the other hand ... he shook his head for a moment to think how many hands he must have by now. His head was going in circles. But seriously, he couldn't just abandon Anna. Could he? Maybe he would have to.

It was getting late. The murmur of talk in the next room died down, and he figured the others had gone off to bed. A cool breeze blew in his open window, an air so crisp, fresh, and clear that it seemed to be composed of entirely different elements than the air in the city. Even at the top of the Citadel, the air had never seemed that clean.

Ken inhaled deeply and sighed. His mind was still too jumbled up to sleep, but he shut the window against the cool night air and lay down on the bed anyway. Perhaps his brain would work better in a horizontal position. He would go through everything again, trying to take everything into account, examining each detail to see if he had missed anything, weighing the pros and cons.

Despite himself, it wasn't long before he fell fast asleep.

†

Ken inhaled sharply through his nose as if it were his first breath, and he seemed to awaken, eyes opening wide. The room was dark, but he knew right away where he was. He was quite clearly in his own bedroom high atop the Citadel. The familiar, subtle hum of the skyscraper was all around him. He sat up in the darkness.

Everything in his room appeared exactly as he had left it, but something was wrong. He couldn't tell what it was at first, but there was something not quite right. A dim glow of light came through the windows, but it wasn't the light of the city. It was too still, and seemed to come more from above than below, casting shadows about the room at odd angles he had never seen before.

Aside from the distant drone of the building's circulation systems, it was so silent. Ken pushed aside the covers of his bed and stood up. The lush silk carpet felt incredibly soft under his bare feet. He walked over to look out the floor-to-ceiling windows spread across one wall of his modest room, and there he saw something so strange, so totally foreign he couldn't even comprehend it at first.

The city was dark. The lights had all gone out, and the buildings and boulevards lay in heaps of shadow. Where millions of electric lights once flickered, flowed, and buzzed ceaselessly, like a rolling sea of glittering jewels stretching out to every horizon, now there was nothing. The buildings looked like hollow shells, devoid of life. The streets and distant highways were like rivers of darkness.

A silvery glow radiated through the window from a waxing, gibbous moon that hung brightly above the dark city. And millions of twinkling stars shone, never before visible when so much artificial light had blazed beneath the heavens.

There was a disturbing stillness to the landscape. No endless stream of cars moved, no airplanes flew, no radio-towers blinked. And yet, looking closer, Ken noticed small signs of movement and light. But these signs were, if anything, even more disturbing than the stillness and the dark.

Fires burned here and there, far below, billowing black smoke into the night air. Furtive shapes that could have been people skittered now and then across moonlit streets or in and out of the firelight. Somehow, the way they moved worried him, as if they moved out of fear. And there was something more, something he couldn't see, but which seemed to lurk in the shadows of the buildings below. Unseen, it evoked a silent terror within him.

Suddenly Ken noticed a presence in the room with him. It didn't startle or scare him, but he turned around simply knowing someone was there. When he turned, he saw Princess Arisu standing in the room with him. Although the room was dark, he could see her clearly, every detail of her face, every golden thread of her elaborate gown. "Princess Arisu," he said. He was confused to see her, but somehow simply accepted her presence without question. He looked out the window at the darkness of the city and then back to the princess. "What the hell is this?"

"This is a dream," Arisu said, her voice calm and soothing.

"Have you conjured up this vision to frighten me?"

"No, Master Ken. This is *your* dream. I have simply come here to help you through it. We hide ourselves from some dreams, you know, for they are too terrible to contemplate. The subconscious knows, and we turn away from what we might not want to see."

"Is this the future?"

"Yes. But as you know, the future is not fixed and all ends cannot be seen."

Ken looked down at the city once more and again sensed some hidden menace, some horror that went beyond mere darkness. Then, behind a crumbled ruin of a building, he thought he saw a giant, hulking form move deeper into the shadows. "My God, Arisu," he said. "What's down there?"

"War. A war is down there, Master Ken. And the servants of Prince Kai, who bring this war upon us."

"I have to go look," Ken said.

"I will be here, watching over you," Arisu said. "But be warned. Although this dream cannot physically harm you, there are things down there that even in a dream could leave a lasting mark on your psyche."

As he walked from his room and through the corridors of the Citadel, he called out for Smith, but there was no answer. Somehow, the building still had some power, because the air was going and the elevator doors sprang open when he came to them.

He pressed the button for the ground floor. The doors slid closed and he began his long descent. It seemed strange to him that the elevator was working. The lights were on and everything worked normally. He stared at the closed doors as he fell to the earth, wondering what he would find on the other side.

The lobby of Parkview Tower was dark. A spillage of electric light radiated out from the elevator. Ken walked across the empty floor and opened the front door. A hot wind blew through the streets. The moon was high overhead, but in the city, it seemed a strange, alien light to see by.

Garbage littered the curbside. Debris and wrecked cars were strewn about the street. At the end of the block a fire faded in a metal trash can. Directly across from the front of Parkview Tower, on a bench by the stone wall that bordered the park, he saw the shape of a person in silhouette, slumped over on his side like somebody sleeping.

Ken crossed the street, marveling at what he could see of the buildings up and down the block. Some of them were completely destroyed. Huge piles of rubble lay at their doorsteps. The windows were blown out, and inside all you could see was the blackness of empty space.

A hat covered the man's face. Ken approached and tried to get his attention. "Hey … hey, Mister." The man didn't answer, and Ken guessed why even before he put a hand on the man's shoulder. There was something about the stillness of the man's body.

Ken reached out, touching the lifelessness of dead flesh, and without thinking he brushed the hat aside. The man's face was a ghastly mess, shocking to behold. The eyes were sunken in, the face shriveled and lips drawn back to reveal rotting gums. It wasn't until then that the smell hit him. He gagged once and nearly vomited as he retreated back across the road and up a side street away from the park.

It was the same everywhere. Litter and rubble were scattered across the sidewalks and spilled into the streets. Abandoned cars, some overturned, others wrecked or burned out, blocked most of the roadways. Bodies lay rotting wherever they had fallen. And there was a new smell to the city, a smell of death, backed up sewage, and unchecked decay.

Ahead, Ken saw a man emerge from the shadows and run through the moonlight across the street, dodging motionless cars as he went.

"Hey," Ken shouted. The man turned and held a rifle up momentarily, but he didn't see Ken and kept running.

Quietly, Ken backed into the shadows against the buildings and continued slowly forward. Even though the night air seemed calm, his heart began to speed up. His breath stopped and started intermittently in a kind of anxious stutter.

Suddenly, a bright shard of fire rocketed through the air into a second story window in the building next to Ken. The deafening blast of an explosion knocked him to the ground. Bits of brick and glass rained down in a strange silence.

As he looked up, a woman ran out the front door of the building, eyes wide with panic. She tried to yell something, but before any sound came from her mouth, her body was torn apart in a hail of bullets. The muzzle flashes of automatic gunfire could be seen on the far side of the street. More guns returned fire from the smoking building above.

Ken was suddenly in the middle of a battle. The silence of the dark city was replaced with a cacophony of gunfire and shouting. Ken scuttled backward on his belly, sticking close in the shadows by the edge of the building. Once he was a little farther back, he got up and ran. He rounded a corner and raced down another street, away from the battle.

Just as the gunfire was beginning to fade in the distance and Ken was beginning to catch his breath, a man came running toward him out of the darkness ahead. He had a rifle too. Ken froze.

The man shouted at him as he approached. "Giant! A Giant is coming! Run!" The man ran right past Ken and didn't look back. There had been a look of fear on his grizzled face.

"Giant?" Ken looked down the empty street. It was dark, and the gunfire of the battle suddenly stopped, leaving an eerie quiet.

Ken walked forward a little further and stood in the middle of the street. A growing, rhythmic sound interrupted the silence, a sound like giant footsteps. Closer and closer those footsteps came, louder and louder.

Looking down the dark street, Ken remembered peering down on the city and sensing some horrible menace that lurked in the apocalyptic night. He stood still, paralyzed with dread.

The anticipation grew almost unbearable as the thundering footsteps grew louder. Then the thing came into view from a cross street, smashing the side of a building as it rounded the corner, sending an avalanche of brick and stone and noise cascading into the street below.

An angry colossus in black silhouette. Was it a monster? Was it some kind of war machine? Ken couldn't tell. It crushed a car flat under its giant foot, and its head, twelve stories up, slowly turned. The unfeeling orb of a single, red, cyclopean eye gazed down the street toward Ken.

In a moment, Ken knew without a doubt the thing had seen him, and that it had no mercy. Looking into that eye, Ken found a well-spring of horror, as if in this moment before his life was stamped out, it embodied the destruction of civilization … and the end of all mankind.

From this nightmare, he suddenly seemed to wake again. He was back in his room in the Citadel, high above the city. Arisu was there with him, her presence now a welcome comfort. She seemed to understand his thoughts intuitively and communicated to him without speaking. She stood motionless, her pale eyes gazing ever outward.

"This is the future, Master Ken. This is the war Prince Kai is bringing to Midgard. Nothing that any one person can do alone will stop it. I will do what I can to warn your people, but only a wielder of Rayaden can prevent the total destruction of our worlds. This I have seen. Anna is the last of Elgard's line, but she will need help, your help, if she is to return with the hope that Rayaden holds for us."

Ken suddenly awoke yet again, only this time for real, back in Andurin. His clothes were damp with a chilling sweat that covered his body. Arisu's voice echoed in his head. "Anna will need your help." And yet, that soothing voice came from the midst of a horrible vision.

32

Quest for Rayaden

Anna and Mouse joined Faedyn for breakfast. Anna had tried to rouse Ken with a knock on his door, but he grumbled something about sleep and refused to get up. So they sat without him, enjoying their meal and the view, as the sun climbed slowly above the eastern wall of the valley and cast its radiant beams like a blessing upon the day.

Anna was troubled, though. She didn't know if she could believe she was the hope for stopping the destruction of three worlds. How could she do that? It made no sense. She could believe she was a descendent of Elgard and that somehow, she was meant to find Rayaden. The stone hanging from her neck was enough to convince her of that.

Elgard, though long dead, was the only real father she had ever known. She felt he was calling out to her across the ages. Perhaps it was a foolish thought, a childish conceit others might laugh at. Nevertheless, it was enough for her. She wanted nothing more than to respond to that voice, and to make her father proud.

She was determined to go through with this journey, wherever it would lead her. But what about Mouse? She was still so young. Surely, she should stay behind. Ken would have to make his own decision, but Anna had to admit she hoped he would go. He was a link back to the city and the other world she came from. She had gotten used to traveling with him, and annoying as he was, she had begun to like him—just a little.

As they drank their tea, there was a knock at the door. The door opened and Princess Arisu entered, Namh at her side. Despite Arisu's blindness, she walked gracefully, with no help or hesitation. She seemed completely aware of her surroundings. "The night was filled with terrible visions," Arisu said, "There is now no doubt of the coming war. We must find Rayaden, and quickly. Anna, are you still willing to go on this journey?"

There was something about the way the princess spoke that frightened Anna, as if she were aware of unspeakable consequences involved in every decision. Anna nodded her head, though. "I'll do whatever I can."

"I will send Namh with you. She has some knowledge of ancient arts that may assist you."

Faedyn nodded. Namh's face was set in a duty-bound resolution.

Arisu said, "Perhaps Mouse will agree to stay and help me while Namh is away. I will need a new assistant."

Anna worried Mouse would refuse, but she was wrong. Mouse was drawn to the princess. Instead of insisting on going, Mouse looked to Anna only for permission to remain at Andurin. *I'm sorry,* she seemed to say, *will you be all right if I stay?*

Anna nodded. "I'll be fine. Faedyn will take care of me."

"So much depends on your success," Arisu said.

Ken's door opened abruptly, and a sleepy-looking Ken with mussed-up hair walked into the room. "All right, all right," he said. "I'm going too."

Anna couldn't help but smile.

"I can't just trust Faedyn to look after you. Who knows what could happen?"

"We'll need to leave soon," Faedyn said. "Before the deep snows cover the passes over the White Mountains."

Arisu nodded. "We will talk further, Faedyn, but in the meantime, Namh will make any arrangements you need."

"I'll just have to know where we're going," Namh said.

"South from here," Faedyn said, "following a path into Roethia is the easiest way. From there, west into the mountains, first to Torselend, then over the pass and across the wastelands to the western coast. Hidden on the shores of the ocean lie the ruins of an ancient elaran city, Alha'na, whose wreckage has survived since the Great War. That's where I left Rayaden, and where no doubt it remains."

"How can you be sure it's still there?" Ken said.

Faedyn almost laughed. "Because it's guarded by one of the wyrmarath."

"The what?" Anna said.

"A dragon," Namh said, as if suddenly aware their quest was doomed.

"Oh great," Ken said.

"Really?" Anna said. "A dragon?"

"That's what you would call him, I suppose," Faedyn said. "His name is Yagul, and he will not want to part with Rayaden."

"I thought all the dragons had left the earth a long time ago," Namh said, "moved on to other worlds."

Arisu nodded in understanding, as if finally working out a problem she had long puzzled over. "Yagul, it is said, was always stubborn, even for his kind."

"Greedy too," Faedyn said. "He would probably sleep in that city, guarding his horde until the end of time, if he could. In any case, he won't be happy to see us."

33

The Seal of Malhak

In Maleistria, the Elyx-ular have existed for millennia. The members of the order have always been women, witches who have served as seers and advisors to the emperor, as well as to nobles, warlords, and tribal leaders. Their ability as seers led to a natural alliance with the mages of the Crypt, who were ever seeking to preserve the knowledge and treasures of their ancestors, and to understand their long-buried secrets.

Kai was born into the Elyx-ular, the product of genetic manipulation and careful control of Maleistrian bloodlines. He was a descendent of Lord Saziel, and his real mother was a witch named Skorra, a woman rumored to have been a mistress of the emperor. Skorra died in childbirth, and Kai was raised in the Elyx-ular, the only son of all those women. And he was raised by them with a secret purpose for which he was bred, to take the throne of Maleistria and reunite the three earths, to usher in that age of glory Lord Saziel had promised them long years ago.

As he often did, Kai dreamt of the Crypt, its massive ziggurat looming over the palace like a psychic magnet. He heard a kind of terrifying hum that came from within. Its secret depths, sealed and dark, called out to him.

He awoke suddenly, his heart pounding. His room was dark. The hour was early, still in the deepest, quietest time of night. Some hint of moonlight shone in from the balcony.

The image of the Crypt still vivid in his mind, Kai slipped from his bed and crossed the cool, stone floor to the balcony. He could see the Crypt's ziggurat from there. Its massive shape was like an anchor of darkness in a city where so much was lit by lamp and flame. The fortress-like building was constructed of enormous blocks, fit together with the finest seams, but was otherwise unadorned.

From this angle, Kai could see the bridge that connected the palace to the state entrance on the upper levels of the ziggurat. The main entrance was on the other side at the apex of a great stair. As big as the ziggurat was, the majority of the Crypt was underground. Its many deep levels were sealed off to any passage in … or out.

Kai grabbed his belt, threw a cloak about him and left his chamber. The halls of the palace were quiet, and they flickered in the orange firelight of dim lanterns fixed to the walls. He descended the tower, and passed into the main palace building. Even the guards who stood watch barely took notice of him. They were used to Lord Kai's strange behavior, to his midnight jaunts about the palace grounds.

Soon he found himself crossing the bridge to the entrance of the Crypt. Guards stepped forward to block him, but when they saw his face, they saluted and made way.

There were grand halls in the upper levels of the ziggurat. This was the realm of the mages, for the Crypt was theirs. It was their treasure, and their responsibility. They had a kind of university here for their ranks, and many of them never left the Crypt, once they came here. They lived a sort of cloistered existence within these walls. They were scientists, some of them, and engineers, philosophers, and bureaucrats.

The base levels of the ziggurat contained food storage, armories, dungeons, and slave holds. It was a central part of Maleistrian civic life. Kai descended past all this via an enormous staircase at the heart of the building, a stair that connected the upper levels to the subterranean realm.

In the first of these lower levels the mages had their workrooms and laboratories. Here they tinkered with certain books and artifacts containing bits of knowledge and technology whose understanding had been lost since the Great War. Kai visited occasionally to monitor their progress for the Elyxular. Currently, they were working on a program to turn human slaves into berserkers for the wars in the Outlands. The court laughed at such ideas, but Kai had seen some promising results from the combination of drugs and psychological conditioning they were using.

Although the mages worked through the night, Kai descended past these levels also, to the massive chamber that lay below. At the entrance, the guards bowed and stepped aside for him to enter. Inside was an enormous rectangular hall, a place where few people ever went, but which Kai had seen countless times in his dreams. In the feeble, flickering torchlight he saw the huge stone doors that locked off the vast, deep levels of the Crypt. Those doors stood a hundred feet high and fifty across, and on them was the Great Seal of Malhak, the first emperor to rule Maleistria.

Kai approached with a reverence born out of those strange dreams, and the knowledge that these doors had never been opened. The real purpose of the Crypt lay below them, where the powers of the Great War were locked away. The weapons inside had once brought the world to the brink of utter destruction. The Crypt had been built to store these secrets and keep them locked away, forever.

Kai put his hand on one of the great doors and listened for any sound, any sign of what lay beyond, in the dark, secret depths of the Crypt. All he really heard was the silence of stone. But in his mind, he still heard the whisper-sound of his dream. Then he heard footsteps behind him, and the voice of Tyral, Archmage of the Crypt. "Lord Kai?"

"Yes, Tyral." Kai spoke without turning, still looking up at the Great Seal.

"My lord, I was told you were here. Is there anything I can do for you?"

"No, Tyral."

"My lord ... it's late, and we should not be here."

"Why, Tyral? Why shouldn't we be here?"

"My lord, you know as well as I what lies behind those doors."

"No Tyral, I don't. None of us really knows any longer what's behind these doors. Perhaps the old giants are dead."

"My lord ... please. These speculations are pointless. Let us retire for the night."

Kai sighed deeply and turned to face Tyral. "It is late, isn't it?"

"Yes, my lord," Tyral said.

"I'm sorry to have woken you."

"Not at all, my lord. But let us retire now."

Kai nodded his cheerful agreement. He must let Tyral believe that his visit here was nothing but a whim, a late-night fancy, a dream.

34

Lives of the Elar

During the day, Anna, Mouse, and Ken were left to themselves to explore the Shrine. They wandered about, marveling at the art and architecture, and admiring the scenic vistas overlooking the valley. They turned heads wherever they went, and took a secret pleasure in surprising such seemingly unflappable people.

They saw the great hall at the heart of the Shrine, where cloistered servants kept a vigil, praying both day and night. They saw workshops and galleries, kitchens and storehouses, courtyards and common rooms, where the day-to-day business of the Shrine took place. There was a bath house too—everything one could need or want. The place as a whole seemed to have the atmosphere of a monastery or an old university, but it was only half full. Many places were abandoned, unused, or suffering from neglect, and it was clear there was a time when many more people would have lived here.

When they finally found the library, Anna eagerly led Mouse and Ken inside. Having spent many hours in the stacks of the city's public library, she felt instantly at home. The main part of the Shrine's library was one great room. Two stories of bookcases lined the walls and windows offered spectacular views. Heavy wooden tables were arranged symmetrically in the center of the space. Spiral staircases led to a second level balcony that surrounded the perimeter. Coming off the main room, doorways led to ancillary rooms and passageways.

The old wooden shelves housed all manner of books. Most were large, leather-bound volumes, the spines imprinted with gold and silver Vena script, which Anna was beginning to be able to decipher. She would have been content to simply wander there for hours, but a librarian approached them almost immediately upon entering. "You must be the visitors from Midgard," she said in English.

"I guess there's no hiding it," Anna said. For a tight-lipped people, word sure got around quickly. She wondered how much most of them knew.

"I'm Tara," the librarian said. "Is there anything I can help you find in our library?"

"Do you have anything in English?" Ken said.

"We have Shakespeare," she said quite proudly, "and translations of various religious texts. We also have some thirteenth century chronicles. They're all very rare."

"Sounds intriguing, but I'll take a rain-check."

"A rain-check?"

"Yeah. You know, like a ticket for later if the game's rained out."

Tara looked confused.

Mouse shook her head in embarrassment.

"Well, it was nice meeting you," Ken said. "I'll catch up with you two later."

Tara still looked confused as she watched Ken go. She looked out the window for a moment, as if to see if it was raining, then turned her attention to Anna and Mouse. "How can I help you?" Although her beautiful features where typical of the elar, something about Tara's perky demeanor seemed unusual, almost youthful, and Anna realized she still knew so little about the culture of the elar.

"I'd like to improve my skills in reading Vena," Anna said. "And learn more about this world and your people. Are there any books about the culture of the elar?"

Tara seemed confused again. Her face, so expressive, pouted as she thought.

Anna tried to explain in Vena.

At last Tara's face lit up with understanding, and she went on in Vena. "The elar don't write many books about such things. We all live our culture, and have little interest in reading about it in books. But I think we have just the thing—a book written by a human, actually. He was a visitor here a long time ago, a scholar from the kingdom of Drighton, far to the south. He wrote a book called *The Secret Lives of the Elar.*" She almost giggled then. "I don't think our lives are so secret," she said, as if she couldn't help sharing this comment. "Anyway, it's an obscure little volume, but he had it translated into Vena and presented our library with a copy. Come, I'll show you."

Tara walked with the confidence of someone who knew every book in the large library, its exact location, and its contents. They passed through a large wooden door into a smaller side room filled with books, and through another door into yet another room with even more books. Anna and Mouse followed, their heads craning around to take in each new room and the multitude of old books.

They went through room after room, each lit by a single window, the only break in the continuous shelves that ran around the walls. Each room had a reading table in the center of the floor, surrounded by chairs. Finally, Tara stopped in a tiny room that seemed as far from the main hall of the library as one could get. She stood on a stool, and on her tiptoes reached for a slender volume bound in modest green leather. "Here we are," she said, pulling the book from the shelf and setting it on the table.

Anna opened to the title page and translated the Vena script: "*The Secret Lives of the Elar,* by Sigbert Oswen of Moordown, South Drighton."

Tara looked back the way they had come and then turned to Anna. She hesitated to speak for a moment. "Can I ask you a question?" she said quietly, practically whispering.

"Of course," Anna said.

"How old are you?" Suddenly, Tara herself seemed very young.

"Sixteen," Anna said.

Tara's eyes widened. "So young," she said. "And already a scholar."

Anna laughed. "I'm not really a scholar. I just like books. How old are you?"

"One hundred twenty-eight," Tara said. "For us that's still quite young. I've been a librarian for only ninety-three years."

They were silent for a moment.

"I guess we're both young in our way," Anna said.

Tara smiled. Then, as if remembering her duties, she bowed briefly. "I'm sorry," she said. "I'll leave you to your reading. Please let me know if there's anything else I can find for you." Then she headed back toward the main hall of the library.

Mouse sat down first, eager to look at the book. It was a bit of a laborious process at first, as Anna refined her understanding of Vena script, but soon the words were making sense to her. Then, as she understood them, she would translate as best she could and read them aloud in English, so Mouse could understand.

Anna started at the beginning of the book, but soon was skimming and skipping around, looking for concise information on the most pertinent topics. The book was conveniently broken down into chapters, the first paragraphs of which usually contained a summary of the most vital information. Reading on after that generally revealed only greater details and wordy observations, commentaries, and speculations by the author. Anna read.

†

Concerning the elar: The elar of the forests and mountains are still courageous and fair. Since ancient times, when their great cities gleamed in glory, their numbers have ever dwindled, their powers faded, and they have sought refuge in the old places of the earth, and made their homes there. But the nobility of their character has never diminished. They have endured through millennia, steadfast in their ways, while mankind has all but forgotten their lasting struggle.

Physiognomy: For the most part, the elar do not look much different from human beings. They are generally tall in stature, youthful looking, yet wise, with fine facial features and ears that are ever so slightly pointed at their tops. This look may be considered elaran, but their most distinguishing characteristic may be, in fact, only their unearthly beauty, their grace and elegance, and a vague sense that their gestures and expressions are not human. The elar live a very long time, some of them well over two thousand years and throughout their lives, even into what would be considered old age, they remain youthful, swift, strong, and disciplined.

Social Structure: Elaran lore says that long ago, the Lords of Light brought the elar to the earth from the heavens. They made the elar stewards of the earth, and charged them to care for it, until the Lords of Light return and take them to their home in the stars. Since the fall of their cities and the end of the Age of Darkness, the elar have lived in hiding, shrouded by mist and mystery, never forsaking their charge, nor their ultimate destiny. The loose hierarchical structure of elaran society is based on age and wisdom as much as lineage. They have no written or formal laws, although councils have the power to pass judgment. Order is maintained through self-discipline, an emphasis on social conformity, and an ethic that stresses the nobility of service and self-sacrifice. Some elaran groups are semi-nomadic, while many others still build great halls in secret forest groves and hidden mountain valleys.

The Arts: The elar have an extremely refined sense of aesthetics that has evolved out of their long history, traditions, and lifespans. They cultivate many arts, beginning their education with the literary, musical, and martial arts, and continuing on to learn many others. If one of them shows promise in a particular field, they might endeavor to study under a master of the art. The elaran aesthetic is austere, deceptively simple even at its most decorative, and possesses a subtlety derived from nature rather than artifice. The objects they make tend to grow even more beautiful with age, and a common theme is the beauty and sadness of fleeting things. Their craftsmanship is without equal, and once known, it is never difficult to discern objects of elaran origin.

Language: The elar have an almost supernatural gift for languages and most know many, both of elaran and human origin. Due to cultural factors and their long lifespans, their own languages have changed at a much slower rate than human languages. Many elements from the most ancient elaran language are still recognizable in Vena, their most common speech, with the greatest changes having occurred during the turmoil of the dark times.

Religion: So much of elaran tradition, like polished wood, is layered with many shades and meanings. The religion of the elar, if it may be called that, is no different. The elar are deeply spiritual, and yet there is no organized religion among them. What might be called their religion is a loose, nameless collection of stories, beliefs, and practices that are simply and plainly an integral part of their way of life. They believe above all else in an ineffable, transcendent being, from which everything comes and is sustained, and of which everything is a part. Beyond this, the elar have an understanding that there are many planes and realms of existence, in which many strange and conscious beings dwell. Accordingly, they have many beliefs and practices regarding spirits, deities, and unseen forces both good and evil, but there have been many misconceptions regarding these beliefs. The Vena word *ama*, for example, has sometimes been translated as 'deity' or 'god' but is probably more profitably rendered as 'spirit-force' or 'spirit-nature' because the elar seem to accept every little thing, as well as the totality of the world as permeated by the *ama*. They have many sacred places in the depths of the forests and mountains, and wherever they have traveled. Often, they have built a small shrine there, dedicated to the *ama* of that place. The elar sing songs of sadness and love, meditate deeply, venerate their ancestors, and they pray, to God, to the *ama*, to great spirits, and to the Lords of Light. To outsiders their religious beliefs may seem full of paradoxes, ambiguity, and contradictions, but to one of the elar, needless to say, it all makes perfect sense.

Saziel's Rebellion: In ancient times, before the Dark Age and the Age of Water, the elar and the tribes of humanity dwelled closely together on the earth. In that time, the elar kept constant contact with the fledgling race of mankind, and spread much of their knowledge to them. When love saw fit to bind them together, there were times when the two races even intermarried. For a long time, it seemed things were destined to continue like this. But as humans spread across the earth and their number grew ever greater, many of the elar longed to return to their Golden Age, when their civilization was at its height and mankind was yet a dream, an unheard-of future. A lord of the elar named Saziel thought this way. He believed the elar should rule the earth. Instead, they passed on their secret knowledge, and diluted their noble race with the blood and offspring of human beings. Humanity was like a plague upon the planet, he said, an infestation that needed to be controlled or wiped out. Many of the elar followed Saziel, but they say his soul was twisted by a dark power and all who followed him were also corrupted. These rebels founded their own kingdom, and made their homes in darkness and shadow. They took human slaves to satisfy their lusts, and from the good creatures of the earth, they created monsters and abominations. They waged a terrible war against the elar and humans alike. The great elaran cities were utterly destroyed, human civilization was cast into ruin, and the world was plunged into the darkest age that ever was.

Three Earths: The elar say that the great war Saziel unleashed brought about a time so violent and horrible that the conscious reality of the world was broken. gradually, three distinct earths coalesced from the fragments of the ancient time and were girdled by distinct spheres of consciousness. These worlds, they say, like all worlds, are

divided by the thinnest of veils, and in some way, are forever connected.

†

Anna looked out the window at the setting sun. Mouse had
fallen asleep at the table while she read. She closed the book.

The sun had just started to set. As the light dimmed to
dusk, the room seemed to shrink. She had a strange feeling, a
whisper of the future she was tumbling into. She couldn't quite
hear it clearly, she couldn't quite see it, but it frightened her.

Three worlds hung in the balance. A war was coming that
could destroy them all, and she was somehow at the center of
it. She wanted to be strong, to help Faedyn and Princess Arisu,
but she felt powerless. She had never been able to change anything. Her mom had wasted away before her eyes. Nothing she
could do would stop her suffering. Nothing could ease her
pain. And in the end, Anna could do nothing but watch her
die, just hold her hand as she slipped away. Nothing could stop
it—no act, no promise, no hope, no prayer, no amount of
effort, no outpouring of love, nothing—nothing could stop
death from coming.

She sniffled and wiped away a tear that had welled up in
the corner of her eye. The others would be wondering where
they were. She put her hand on Mouse's shoulder. "Wake up,
Mouse," she said. "It's time to go."

35

Faedyn and Arisu

Anna, Ken, and Mouse had already retired for the night when Namh came to summon Faedyn to Arisu's private chamber. Faedyn had expected this meeting would come, and he went immediately.

The corridors of Andurin were quiet, and dimly lit at night. Namh walked a pace ahead of Faedyn, without saying a word. Faedyn watched the fall of her bare shoulders as she walked. She was quite beautiful, and she seemed at home here, but she carried some hidden tension around him, a silent distrust. No doubt it was because he had lived in exile for so long.

When they arrived at the door to Arisu's chambers, Namh stopped. She turned to Faedyn, her voice hushed. "I trust the princess," she said, "and the truth of her vision." Her tone was cold, but personal, with a confidence that acknowledged they now had a mutual purpose. "But are you sure about this girl? Even if we manage to recover Rayaden, do you really think she can learn to wield it?"

"She is a descendent of Elgard," Faedyn said, as if that should suffice, "and the blood of the elar has awoken within her."

"You know what I mean," Namh said.

Indeed, Faedyn knew exactly what she meant. "Human beings have some strength of their own, Namh. It's true their lives are short and fleeting, but don't underestimate their potential."

Namh looked away. Her lips pressed together in an odd, unreadable expression. "The princess is waiting for you," she said, and knocked at the door.

†

Arisu stood at the open window, as if looking out over all of Elara, and perhaps over Midgard and Maleistria as well, across the veil between worlds. She turned as Faedyn closed the door and stepped toward the center of the room. Once again, it was clear her blindness was no impediment to her vision. Faedyn sensed that she saw him, not with her vacant, white eyes, but with the space that surrounded them, with the very medium of reality in which they existed. And with this vision she saw him through and through. His own doubts, his own fears, the darkness in his past, and his suffering were laid bare to her.

"Good Faedyn," she said, "your path has been a long and painful one."

Faedyn felt as if she spoke directly to his heart. He could not help but make some confession of the evil he still felt lodged there. "For long years," he said. "I dwelled in Maleistria, in that realm of darkness and despair. I waged many vengeful wars there, rampaging among my enemies, killing thousands with wanton abandon." His hands began to shake, and his voice broke with an impossible collision of sadness, guilt, and anger. "I filled myself with hate, Arisu, and a darkness that still grips me in the depths of my soul."

She came close to him, and put her soft hand on the side of his face. The great surge of emotion seemed to fall out of him. The shaking of his body stilled, and the ease of his breath returned. Arisu's hand moved softly down his cheek. Faedyn closed his eyes in the ecstasy of a peace he had long forgotten. Arisu's body moved closer to embrace him, conveying a comfort far beyond words. Her cheek brushed his, and her lips, close to his ear, spoke softly to him. "Your sins are already forgiven," she said. "But you must forgive yourself. Until then, you will never believe it."

Her voice was filled with a depth of understanding and authority he had never experienced before. He simply nodded his head as she released him.

"Come and sit," Arisu said. "There is much to talk about."

†

They talked until late in the night. Arisu questioned him about Midgard and the Loremasters. What were their goals, she wanted to know, and what ambitions did they have? Also, what political, scientific, and psychic powers did they possess? And what did Faedyn think of them? Could they be relied upon as an ally if it came to war?

Faedyn spoke frankly about the things he knew. The Loremasters had grown very secretive over the years, and had amassed great political and technological powers. The development of their viewing methods had increased not only their accuracy, but the scope of their visions. They continued in their purpose to divine the progress and destiny of mankind. They could be very manipulative when it came to the course of human events, but as far as he could tell, they always had the best interests of humanity in mind, and for that reason he believed they would be a friend in any war against the Malar.

Arisu told Faedyn about events in Elara since the end of the Elara-war. For the most part, there had been peace for many years. But the great houses of the elar were diminished from the war, and through the years they had dwindled still further. Many of the old lines had died out. Few were left to remember the terrible threat the Malar represent, and fewer still placed any faith in the deeper ways of the ancient arts. The distances between their hidden homes seemed to grow greater and greater. Communications between their enclaves trickled and slowed almost to the point of stopping. Many of the elar had begun to isolate themselves. Their people turned inward, and in many ways had forsaken their connection to the world at large. Some hid their complacency in a fervent show of their religion. Others clung to the false peace of luxury. When they met, it was often to squabble over trivial affairs. It would be difficult to rouse them into any united course of action.

The remaining tribes of humanity had prospered in Elara, but the elar had less and less contact with them, preferring to live apart, in secret, and at a distance from human affairs. Aside from small conflicts, for a time the humans had been blessed with some peace, but hidden tensions grew again between their greatest kingdoms. Namh had a dream that Roethia's capital burned, and there were rumors of trouble on their border with the neighboring kingdom of Drighton.

Finally, she came to the topic it all led up to. "This young girl," Arisu said, "Anna Karova, is heir to a special gift that goes back to the Golden Age of our ancestors. And now I believe so much may rest on one who can wield Rayaden. That she is a human will put doubt into the minds of many of our people. What can you tell me about her?"

"She never knew her father," Faedyn said. "And her mother died recently."

Arisu nodded her head slowly, as if carefully considering these things.

"The Malar must know of her existence. Their assassins were in the city where she lived, and I'm convinced they were looking for her. I ran into two of them. They had murdered at least one other girl who bore the blood of elar. The Loremasters found Anna before the assassins could get to her. They had their own reasons, a prophesy they have about such a girl."

"A prophesy?"

"Yes, that a high-born girl would come among them to complete their vision, to fulfill their understanding of human destiny."

Arisu seemed to stare off into an unimaginable distance. "What is she like?"

"Strong-willed, with some natural courage in her. She learns quickly. And yet there is some part of her that seems unsure of herself, that is filled with doubt."

"You don't think we are making a mistake?"

Faedyn thought for a moment, surprised to hear such hesitation when earlier Arisu had been so sure of what needed to be done. "No," Faedyn said. "Clearly she is the last of Elgard's line. But more than that, from the moment I saw her, I have felt the call of destiny. I did not return to Elara for nothing. Seeing her changed everything for me. Even when I heard your voice, I resisted, but when I saw Anna, I knew I had to return."

Arisu nodded in understanding. But there was something that still troubled her. Faedyn could see it plainly, something that troubled her vision of the future.

"What is it?" Faedyn said.

"Her dreams are hidden from me. I cannot see them. She seems capable and willing, but I am blind to her inner life."

"What does it mean?"

"I don't know. But it worries me. Dark powers can shield such things from my sight. They can give false visions too. Have you noticed anything peculiar about her behavior?"

"No," Faedyn said.

"Does she complain of headaches or ailments?"

"No."

Arisu sighed. "You must watch her closely on your journey," she said, "and protect her with your life. There will be many dangers, even before you reach your goal. The influence of evil is spreading across all three earths. It is still mostly hidden, perhaps, like a poison in the soil that cannot be seen, or a snake in the grass when farmers go out to their fields. But in the end, evil always reveals its true face."

36

WAY OF THE SWORD

The morning sun beamed into the hall where Arisu sat with regal poise. Some of her hair was elaborately pinned with golden ornaments, while long strands hung to their full length around her. Next to her, something lay covered with a large, green cloth embroidered with silver. Mouse stood now at Arisu's side, as her assistant, while Anna, Ken, Faedyn, and Namh stood before them.

"Tomorrow you will leave on your journey," Arisu said. "You have come a long way already, and deserve more rest, but there is little time to spare. By now you know the path you travel will be dangerous. Yet you go with the hope that your actions may help us all in the coming darkness. Go then, with my blessing."

"Thank you, Princess," Faedyn said, speaking for them all. Anna felt excited, anxious, and tired. She had awoken again from a nightmare in the night. The dark shape that haunted her took many forms and could emerge from the context of many varied dreams, but she always knew the moment of its arrival from the horrible feeling that came over her. Sometimes it was accompanied by a terrible noise, or an awful stench. Sometimes it came as a shadow, other times as some strange and alien form. In some ways she had grown used to these dreams and they bothered her less, but they still left her with a sense of dread that lingered through the day.

Arisu continued, her speech formal and somewhat cere-monial. "To aid you in the task ahead, I present you with these gifts." With a sweep of her hand, she unveiled the bundle beside her. On the rich green cloth lay two swords in their scabbards, the pommels and guards elegantly wrought from silver metal, inlaid with sinuous designs in reddish-brown. The handles were wrapped tight with fine leather. Next to them was a white staff topped with a slender, cage-like ellipti-cal ornament.

"To you, Anna and Ken, I present these swords," Arisu said, "They come from the Shrine of Karan, far to the north, forged by the hands of our finest smiths, before the time of the Elara-war. They will serve you well."

Arisu and Mouse seemed to share a psychic connection. Without a word, Arisu appeared to guide Mouse, even answer-ing her unspoken questions about which sword to present first and to whom. Accordingly, Mouse picked up one of the swords and presented it to Ken, who bowed deeply before tak-ing it. "Thank you, Princess," he said.

Then Arisu's full attention fell on Anna. Faedyn nudged her and she bowed timidly. Mouse smiled as she handed Anna the other sword. It was lighter than she expected, and the craftsmanship had a tangible beauty. But still, there was some-thing about its heft that unnerved her. It reminded her of when she had held a steel pipe in her hands and crushed the skull of that boy in the alley behind her old building. It reminded her of that feeling of uncontrollable rage, of forget-ting herself in the fury of violence, and it frightened her.

"Thank you," Anna said, her voice quiet.

"Namh, I give you the Lamp of Lunara, a rare artifact of the Golden Age. I have taught you its power, and I pray its light may dispel the darkness of your journey."

Namh bowed, thanking the princess, and took the white staff Mouse held out to her.

"And dear Faedyn, I have nothing to give you which you do not have already. Go, therefore, with my heart, and the knowledge that once again your selfless sacrifice will serve our people."

Faedyn bowed. "Princess Arisu, you have given me the greatest gift then, and a chance to find my redemption. What more could one ask for?"

†

Later, Faedyn showed Anna and Ken how to attach their swords to the belts of their travelling clothes. He took them alone to the north wing of the Shrine, which was entirely abandoned and in disrepair. They kicked up many years worth of dust as they walked through the long corridors. There was such a deep quiet at this end of the Shrine that their echoing footsteps seemed to awaken the very walls of the building. He led them to a large empty room with a wide and well-worn floor.

The room was somewhat dark. Anna and Ken stood in the doorway together, while Faedyn strode across the darkness and pulled aside huge tapestries that covered the windows along the far wall.

Daylight burst into the sleepy space. Some tiny birds that had nested in the high rafters were startled into the air and flittered back and forth, chirping in the sudden light.

The room appeared to be a practice hall for martial arts. There were racks along the walls that held various weapons, practice swords, gloves, fencing masks, and different types of armor. All of it was covered with thick dust.

Faedyn blew the dust off a heavy leather jacket. "It looks like martial arts isn't studied as much as it used to be," he said. "But if you are to be a wielder of Rayaden, Anna, you must begin to learn the art of sword."

Anna nodded weakly and swallowed, even though her mouth was dry.

"And if you are to protect her, Ken, you should learn as well."

"Right," Ken said, deftly drawing the sword Arisu had given him.

Faedyn laughed. "Young human males are always so eager to die," he said. "It never changes."

"But I already know how to use a sword," Ken said.

"Is that so?" Faedyn said.

"Sure do," Ken said and made a flourish with the sword.

"Good, we'll start with you then. But we'll begin with practice swords."

Ken sheathed his sword and, following Faedyn's lead, removed it from his belt. Faedyn tossed him a practice sword and Ken caught it out of the air by the handle. He let the blade swing down and then up over his head in a ready stance.

"Are you sure you know what you're doing?" Anna said.

"Just watch," Ken said.

"We'll begin slowly," Faedyn said.

Anna backed up toward the racks of armor on the wall. She was worried about Ken. Did he really know how to use a sword? Where did he learn?

Faedyn swung his sword at Ken slowly. Ken easily parried the blow and moved to counterstrike. Faedyn dodged Ken's blade, and they went back and forth like this for a while. As they continued, however, Ken seemed to move faster and faster while Faedyn actually seemed to slow down, his moves careful and precise. Once or twice, Ken got inside Faedyn's guard and touched him with his practice blade.

Ken was breathing hard, but he seemed pleased with himself. "See," he said. "I told you."

"You do seem to know a thing or two," Faedyn said casually as they continued.

"Five years of fencing at Saint Christopher's," Ken said between breaths. "And two years of kendo with Amano Sensei. I know some judo too." He seemed quite proud of himself.

"That's good," Faedyn said, effortlessly moving inside Ken's guard, disarming him, and sweeping his legs. Ken flew into the air and fell hard to the floor. Faedyn held the tip of his blade to Ken's throat as he lay helpless and in pain on the ground. "Then you know how to fall," he said. "But don't mistake kindness for weakness. It's different when lives are at stake."

Ken nodded silently, looking sufficiently humbled as he lay there on the hard floor, his eagerness to fight somewhat tempered.

"Now it's your turn," Faedyn said, turning to Anna.

Anna took another step back, looking at Ken as he got up from the floor. "I don't think I can do that," she said. "Maybe this was a bad idea."

"Don't worry," Faedyn said. "Everybody needs something different at the beginning. Let's just start with getting comfortable handling the sword. I will be teaching principles of armed and unarmed combat simultaneously. We'll start very slowly, and continue each day as we journey south. Don't worry," Faedyn said. "Trust me."

Anna looked into Faedyn's eyes, and again found there the reassurance and strength that she needed. "Okay," she said. "What do I do?"

†

Faedyn continued to teach them until noon, when they broke for lunch. Aside from Faedyn effortlessly dumping Ken onto the floor whenever he got too excited, they practiced very slowly. Nevertheless, it was hard work, and they were both tired and hungry by the time they finished.

"I do feel a little more comfortable with this thing," Anna said as she took up the sword Arisu had given her. She was surprised how Faedyn's simple exercises had changed the feeling she had when she held it.

"It's only a place to start," Faedyn said. "There's so much more I need to teach you, and even what I know is little compared to some."

After lunch, Anna looked for Mouse but she was nowhere to be found. Mouse was used to being on her own and was already making a home of the Shrine. She had probably made a nest in some long-forgotten room near Arisu's chambers. But it made Anna sad. She hadn't had time to think much about leaving Mouse behind. She had gotten used to having her close by, and once again it seemed all Anna's plans for the future, however modest, were crumbling before the demands of an uncooperative present.

Anna had wanted to take care of Mouse, but the truth is that Mouse had taken care of her. Now they would be parting ways, and Anna couldn't help but worry about where the path she was on might lead.

The afternoon was spent packing for the road and gathering provisions from the storehouses. Namh was very helpful in getting anything Faedyn said they needed, and by evening they were ready. The sun dropped over the horizon. Slowly the sky darkened and the stars shone ever more brightly. Mouse had returned, but she seemed distant, and Anna already knew she would sleep little that night.

37

LONG LIVE THE EMPEROR

The banquet hall of the Emperor's Palace was full of people. Socialites, merchants, and military men with enough influence or wealth to attend such dinners filled the furthest reaches of the great room. Ahead of them were nobles and courtesans, mages of the Crypt, and some witches of the Elyxular. Kai sat in silence, observing the orderly proceedings, taking note of the chaos lurking beneath the farce of such civilities.

The princes sat at the high table, drunk on their power and full of themselves. Malfot was a fat slob, his corpulent body draped in the gaudiest of clothes, his sausage fingers shining with jeweled rings. Nykhil was a short weasel of a creature, nervous and beady eyed. He was a schemer and a liar. Durok had his father's good looks, and he was strong, a master with a blade. But he was cruel and sadistic in ways that even Maleistrians found distasteful. Rumor had it he was impotent, and this fact had driven him to such excess. The world would be better off without them.

Emperor Drakhil sat at the center of the high table, splendidly arrayed in red and gold robes. Mora, his long-time companion, sat at his side, adorned with jewels. Drakhil laughed at something as servants filled his cup with wine and replenished his plate with meat. A poison taster stood close at hand, testing everything that came the emperor's way. A poison taster would be able to detect the presence of any potential poison, even those with no taste or smell, an impressive ability developed over ages of war and political assassination. *Of course,* Kai thought, *a poison taster would make an excellent assassin.*

Two members of the Black Guard stood nearby, assigned as the emperor's personal security. They were watching after him day and night. Kai almost laughed aloud when he thought of that. The Black Guard were followers of the Cult of Saziel. They had their own agenda as well, and they were more closely aligned with the Elyx-ular than they were with the emperor and the royal family. The Elyx-ular may even use Black Guard assassins to do away with the emperor. That could be them standing there. Kai did laugh aloud now.

His neighbor at the table, Lord Sorrich, a military advisor to the emperor, took notice. "Something amuses you, Lord Kai?"

"Ah, yes, Lord Sorrich. But it's a private affair, and likely wouldn't amuse you, anyhow."

Sulki thought it best if he didn't know the details of the plan. Perhaps she was right, but curiosity was a bitch. So was waiting.

And so was boredom. After a while, Kai yawned. He longed for this affair to be over. He longed for Sulki. The very thought of it stimulated his attention. Where was she? She had been conspicuously absent the last few days.

Emperor Drakhil rose to address the crowd. *Ah, finally,* Kai thought. But it wasn't over yet. Drakhil usually left these banquets early, after muttering some stately nonsense Kai had long ceased to listen to. Mora would quietly follow him some time after that. Then at last, after a polite interval, Kai could make his escape. Presently, the emperor made his exit, followed by the Black Guard and a small entourage of attendants.

After about twenty minutes, Mora left, and Kai prepared to make his departure as well. Often the real partying would start now, but he had no desire to watch those princes make even greater fools of themselves. But just as he was making his way toward a back exit, a commotion erupted at a door by the head table—one of Mora's servant girls in violent hysterics. The princes rose from their seats. Then someone shouted, "The emperor is dead. Emperor Drakhil is dead!"

The room erupted in chaos. Everyone rose from their table, gasping and shouting. So many confused, disbelieving, happy, sad, angry, terrified people. They began to move, pushing each other, toward the high table and toward every exit of the room. It was madness, and it was glorious.

Kai peered over the teeming throng as courtiers jostled him. The princes fled the hall while more Black Guard soldiers flooded into the room. Kai pushed and kicked his way to the door at the back. "Excuse me," *umph.* "Pardon me," *whack! Thud,* "Oh I'm terribly sorry, Madam."

Outside the hall, the frightened people hurried home while the curious and the scheming rushed toward the emperor's apartments. Kai took the long way, hoping it would be quicker. When he arrived, however, he still found a crowd of people blocking the way.

"Make way for Lord Kai," he shouted, announcing himself with imperial grandeur. And it worked. The crowd slowly parted, and the Black Guard soldiers guarding the entrance to the emperor's apartments stood aside for him.

The apartments had a series of rooms leading inward to the emperor's most private chamber. In the outermost room, a number of high-ranking nobles and advisors conferred with each other in grave, somber tones.

Kai continued inward. The place had the hushed but busy atmosphere of a crime scene. He had been to a number of them as a representative of the Elyx-ular. Witches were often requested as seers in such matters, but mages were sent to investigate the physical evidence.

This one was a gruesome scene. There was nothing subtle about the work that was done. The assassins wanted to make it very clear the emperor had been brutally murdered. In the third ante room, three of the emperor's attendants lay dead, their throats slit and bled out on the fine carpet. What a pity. Another was in the first ante room. And in the emperor's chamber, Drakhil lay dead in all his finery. Mora mourned over his body, and the three princes stood nearby trying to fig-ure out how to take advantage of the situation.

The two Black Guard soldiers who were guarding the emperor also lay dead near the door. Both had been stabbed in the heart, one also bore a ghastly wound on the shoulder. Blood was spattered everywhere.

Archmage Tyral had arrived with several of his advisors. "How?" he said. "How could this have been done in such silence? How did the killers escape?" He and his assistants scurried about the room, examining everything.

"And who is responsible?" Prince Nykhil said, clearly eying his two brothers.

"Perhaps it's you, Nykhil," Durok said.

"Me?" Nykhil said. "Malfot is eldest. He stands to be emperor."

"Where are the emperor's final statements? I demand to see them," Durok said.

Nykhil laughed, "Why? Do you expect them to name you emperor? Pity there would be no future heirs."

"We'll sort this out," Malfot said. "And if either of you is involved, whatever you hope to gain, you will get death instead."

From an inconspicuous place on the perimeter of the room, Kai observed the madness of the scene with quiet satisfaction. *The emperor is dead,* he thought. *Long live the emperor.*

38

The Journey South

They left before sunrise. Faedyn woke Anna in the darkness, and she dressed quickly. Their presence at the Shrine had already brought enough attention. Arisu wanted them to depart as quietly as possible. In time, she would have to inform the great houses of their mission, but until then their purpose would remain secret.

Anna wrapped her traveling coat tightly around her as they stood outside in the cool night air. Her pack felt heavy on her back, loaded with food and supplies. Overhead, the stars still shone brightly, while unseen beyond the peaks of the valley, an orange glow rose to the east, a slow explosion of light that brought the coming day.

Faedyn was stoic and resolute as always. He already looked out along their path down to the valley. Namh looked uneasy. She had donned a grey, hooded cloak over her traveling clothes, and carried the white staff Arisu had called the Lamp of Lunara. The top of her ash-blond hair was braided, and the rest fell long and free behind her. The Shrine had been her home for many long years, and now she was leaving. Ken stood beside her, looking still half sleep. He shuffled his feet, squinted one of his eyes, and yawned.

Arisu stood before them with Mouse at her side. "You go with my blessing," the princess said. "The path is clear to you. Travel well, and may the ama protect you on your journey."

Mouse met with Anna's eyes and spoke in the silence that Anna had learned to interpret. *I'll be fine,* she said, *but I miss you already. Be careful and come back safely.* Then she added, *and watch after Ken.*

Anna's smile was bitter-sweet. Mouse ran forward and hugged her. A tear rolled down Mouse's cheek when she looked up. Anna had never seen her cry before.

Anna couldn't cry. Instead, she steeled her face. "I'm not good at goodbyes," she said to Mouse. "So just … take of care of yourself, okay."

Mouse embraced her one last time, and they set off along the path they had ascended, down into the valley. From there, they would journey south toward the kingdom of Roethia.

Namh led them by a different pathway out of the valley, and they met up with the river again downstream, beyond the rapids. They would follow the Andu southeast for several days, toward the inland Sea of Ourth, then turn south through the foothills of the White Mountains. Eventually, they would meet up with the Brea, a river that passed through the kingdom of Roethia on its long path to the ocean.

Entering Roethia briefly, they would load up on fresh food and supplies before making for the pass at Torselend and the wastelands beyond. Yagul's lair, Faedyn told them, lay on the distant shores of Elara, where earth, water, wind, and fire met. There they would find Rayaden, in the ruins of a city that had somehow survived the separation of worlds, a fossil of the ancient earth.

†

By the morning of the fourteenth day, it seemed they had been travelling much longer. They had grown used to the loads they carried, to smaller meals, fewer luxuries, long days of walking, and sleeping on the hard ground beneath an open sky. They had grown used to the quiet of the foothills, to the wide landscape dotted with granite boulders and clumps of trees. And for the most part, they had also grown used to living in the company of each other. As the newest member of their party, Namh remained aloof, often walking ahead or behind, and rarely sharing the thoughts her pensive silence shielded. In camp, she would talk with Faedyn if necessary, but she never said a word to Anna or Ken.

Anna woke just before sunrise, as usual. The sky grew light and the stars were fading in the west. She suspected Faedyn and Namh were already awake, but she heard nothing. It was a cool morning, and the now smoldering coals from the fire no longer threw off any significant heat. Sometime in the night, she had snuggled against Ken's back to keep warm.

Ken had talked her to sleep that night, enumerating the various adventures he had gotten into at St. Christopher's. It was so like a boy to brag about mischief, but they laughed, and she liked his stories. Now, as she lay with her body pressed against his in the dawning light, she wanted this moment, between the world of her sleep and the day ahead, to last just a little longer. She would never admit to him, of course, that it was anything other than staying warm, but it felt good to be so close to him. There was a kind of physical comfort in his presence that intensified with every square inch of her body that wrapped against his. She felt at home in Elara, but still, she was so glad Ken was there with her.

Anna reached her hand up and put it on Ken's shoulder. She squeezed gently to wake him. "Ken," she whispered.

He did not move.

Anna squeezed a little harder, and whispered again, "Ken, it's time to get up."

Ken moved slightly, adjusting his body against hers in his sleep. He made a sound, something between a sigh of pleasure, a groan of pain, and the *mmm* you make when something tastes good. But he didn't open his eyes, and after a moment he appeared to fall completely asleep again.

Anna sighed. He could still be totally annoying, even while asleep. Suddenly she sensed a footstep on the ground next to her. She turned, and looked up to see Faedyn standing above her in the morning light.

"I'll wake him up," Faedyn said.

†

Ken drifted deeper into sleep. He had awoken to the sound of Anna's voice whispering softly in his ear. Her warm body was pressed against his. She was saying something about getting up, but that was crazy. Who would want to get up now? He wanted only to rest, and enjoy the feeling of this moment.

Unfortunately, the next thing he felt was something very sharp jabbing into his stomach. His whole body convulsed in pain. It felt as if every nerve in his body lit up at once, waking him instantly. He jerked forward into a half sitting position where his neck came to rest on the razor-sharp edge of Faedyn's sword. If the twitch of his muscles had carried him just a little further, he would have cut his own throat.

"Hey," Ken said, trying not to move too quickly. "What was that for?"

"Time for practice," Faedyn said, removing the sword from Ken's neck.

Ken checked his neck for blood. "Are you crazy?"

"No," Faedyn said. "Now get up."

Faedyn had been training them every day, but this was taking things a bit far. Just after waking, before he would allow them to eat any breakfast, they practiced. And they practiced again in the evening, after they were exhausted from a day of walking. Every day he seemed to go a step further with each of them, pushing them to their physical and psychological limits. Either he really thought they might need to defend themselves in very short order, or he was just trying to piss him off.

Ken grabbed his sword and rose from his bed, scowling. He wasn't going to let Faedyn get the better of him.

Faedyn attacked without warning or formality, swinging his sword in a wide arc.

Ken stumbled backward out of the way, drawing his sword and holding it out in front of him, both shield-like and threatening. He had learned better than to attack Faedyn haphazardly.

Faedyn beat aside his blade and came at him again. Ken did his best to avoid the attack, but he felt himself getting caught behind, and before he knew it, he was backing up, swinging his sword wildly in desperation. Faedyn was relentless this morning, his movements smooth and precise, dispassionate and deadly.

Anna and Namh looked on. "Keep moving," Anna said, trying to help, but Faedyn promptly knocked Ken down. He didn't even know how it had happened. Faedyn pinned Ken's sword to the ground under foot and swung Vanar downward. The tip of the Faedyn's blade stopped an inch from Ken's eye.

It took a moment, but Ken finally started to breathe again, and Faedyn let him up.

"You did well," Faedyn said.

"Yeah, right," Ken said.

Namh continued to watch, but looked disinterested as always.

"Let's practice a few basics," Faedyn said, "and then it's your turn Anna."

They did some basic movements, strikes, blocks, and evasions. Then Ken and Anna practiced them slowly against each other. Ken marveled at how quickly Anna had improved. She was athletic, and moved with an ease and grace that Ken admired. And despite her modesty, she had a natural talent for swordplay. She was always eager to practice now and had started to challenge Ken when they worked together.

But Faedyn was in a harsh mood that morning. "Enough," he said after only a short time. Then he attacked Anna without warning.

"Aaah!" Anna retreated desperately.

Faedyn continued with the same kind of relentless attack he had used on Ken.

Anna scrambled to stay out of the way. At first, she was still smiling, trusting Faedyn and rising to the challenge, but Faedyn pressed without mercy. Ken could see Anna getting frustrated, then scared, and then angry, the emotions stacking one upon another.

"Cut it out," Ken said. But Faedyn didn't stop. He kept attacking Anna, pressing in on her, foiling every movement she made, taking advantage of every opening.

In that moment, it seemed their practice had turned to cruelty. Faedyn was deliberately trying to frustrate her. Ken felt stuck, not knowing if he should do something, and then not knowing what that something would be. He looked on, increasingly uncomfortable, as Anna scrambled around erratically, desperate to avoid Faedyn's attacks. The grace of her movement completely vanished. Her hair became a tangled mess covering her face, and she began to make sounds like the growling of a cornered animal.

Suddenly, her eyes blazed, and she just seemed to explode in a wild, shrieking fury that took everyone by surprise. She lashed out at Faedyn, swinging her sword in an uncontrolled frenzy of genuine violence. Faedyn stepped back, careful not to hurt her with his own blade. Anna came at him with a murderous rage, swinging her sword again and again and screaming at the top of her lungs.

She was completely out of control, but in a few moments, meeting no resistance from Faedyn, she seemed to exhaust herself. She collapsed to a heap on the ground, breathing heavily, seemingly unaware of everything around her. Slowly, her rage subsided. She lifted her head, clearly confused. Her eyes softened, and she seemed to struggle to understand what had happened. She looked up at Faedyn, then dropped her sword, scrambled up from the ground, and ran off.

Ken ran after her.

She didn't go far. Out of sight from the others, behind some bushes and trees, she had collapsed to the ground, crying. Her head buried in her arms, her whole body convulsed as she sobbed.

Ken approached slowly. "It's just me," he said. He squatted down and reached out to put a hand on her shoulder. Her heavy sobs subsided. She sniffled and shuddered. "It's okay," Ken said. "He was asking for it."

Evidently, this was not the right thing to say. She buried her head deeper into her arms and renewed her sobbing convulsions.

Ken sat down on the ground next to her and put his hand on her back, trying to comfort her. He dared not say anything else.

Soon she calmed down again, enough to speak through huffing breaths. "I didn't know what I was doing, Ken ... I lost control ... I tried to hurt him, Ken ... I really tried to hurt him."

"He's okay," Ken said. "Nothing happened. Everything's okay."

Faedyn appeared behind him. "Ken's right," he said. "Everything is okay. I'm fine."

Ken gave Faedyn an angry look. The whole thing was his fault. But there was something in his voice that seemed to calm Anna. Faedyn's words seemed to comfort her in a way that his couldn't.

"It's okay," Faedyn said again. "Are you hurt?"

Anna sniffled and sat up. "No," she said.

"Then stand up," he said softly.

Anna stood up, and when she did, she grabbed onto Faedyn, hugging him with the same intensity with which she had just tried to kill him. "I'm sorry," she said. "I'm so sorry. I tried to hurt you."

Faedyn put his arms around her. "It's okay," he said. "I'm sorry to put you through that. I had to know how you would react under real stress. I had to know your limits."

"You wanted that to happen?"

"I didn't know exactly what you would do."

Anna released her grip on Faedyn and looked down at the ground, ashamed. "Sometimes," she said, "when I get angry, I just lose control. I just go crazy and I don't even know what I'm doing."

Faedyn nodded. "There are ways to control it," he said. He reached out and wiped the tears from the corners of Anna's eyes. "C'mon," he said. "Let's go eat breakfast. We still have a long day ahead of us."

†

It was a hard day. Faedyn led them onward, continuing south toward Roethia. The terrain was easy going, considering what he knew about the path ahead, but a silence had fallen over the group after the excitement of the morning. There was a weariness in their step that hadn't been there since they left Andurin.

Anna felt ashamed by what had happened. Faedyn could see that clearly enough. And Ken was still mad at him for pushing her so far. Namh had kept her thoughts to herself these past two weeks. She seemed even more quiet now. The hardship of the journey had suddenly hit them all.

Faedyn steeled himself against all doubt and walked on, occasionally glancing back to make sure the others were still following. There would be a setback in Anna's training, of course, but it was a necessary setback. She would have to learn to control that rage, just as he had. He understood the violence of rage. He could help her overcome it, but because he understood, it also troubled him. Where did such anger come from? How deep did it dwell? Anna still struggled with the loss of her mother. Perhaps her own helplessness in the face of death was at the root of her anger.

They broke for a quick lunch. Everyone ate silently, and Faedyn pressed them to finish so they could start again. He didn't want them to rest too long today. Idleness and time for thinking could be bad with morale so low.

Afterward, as they marched onward, Namh set a pace with Faedyn. For a while, she walked beside him quietly, until Faedyn had grown used to her being there. Then she spoke. "I know she's a descendent of Elgard, but perhaps it's useless to teach humans art," she said. "Everything they touch is corrupted."

Faedyn sighed. "Have we been any better?" He thought of his own failings, his own rage and anger. "It was our conflict that brought the ancients to ruin. You can't blame humanity for everything. We brought our own darkness to the world."

39

Rest at Haigar

Travel was easier along the east bank of the Brea, but there were certainly days when walking seemed difficult for Anna. The beauty of the landscape faded. The hope that in Rayaden she would find herself, her past and her future, all passed away. Instead, she turned inward with a kind of dumb despair.

Still a teenager, she found herself longing for the child-like comfort of her youth. She missed the days when no demands were placed on her, when her mom would take her for picnics in the park, and when she understood who she was and what she was supposed to do because it was all so simple.

She missed Mouse, and although she talked to Ken more, it wasn't the same as having another girl to talk to. Namh wouldn't really speak to her, which made matters worse. She missed other human beings, hot baths, and a roof over her head. She even missed the city, and she certainly missed eating at Alberici's Pizzeria.

On the worst of these days, sometimes there was nothing left but to put one sore foot in front of the other. On the best of them, there was just a vague feeling she was headed in the right direction.

For several days after her blow up, she refused to practice with a sword. The incident had brought back the memory of the boy from BS-Click, and she couldn't stop thinking about it.

She had done it to save Mouse and she didn't question that part, but she couldn't help but wonder if it made her a bad person. In a way, it wasn't so much what she had done that bothered her, but how she had done it, in a fit of fury, rage, and hate. In that moment, she had lost herself to something horrible, some dark, intangible force. She had gone out of control, and if she could attack Faedyn like that, who knows what she might do if it happened again.

But in the end, what good would inheriting a magic sword be if she didn't know how to use it. So she began to practice again. And though they continued with many of the same drills, Faedyn's focus now was on her frame of mind, teaching her to avoid frustration and to stay calm, no matter what happened.

There were other things to help pass the time, as well. Soon they would enter Roethia, and the people there didn't speak Vena, or English for that matter. They spoke Coram, which in one form or another was common among humans throughout Elara. Namh spoke it fluently, and with the elaran ability to learn languages, it was no problem for Anna to pick it up. Faedyn knew an old version, but he quickly updated his knowledge. Things were more difficult for Ken, of course. But he was getting better, and it was always entertaining to hear him stumble over words and sentences.

†

"Look," Ken said, running a few steps toward the river and pointing across. There was a man on the far bank, fishing. He was dressed in ragged clothes and wore a wide brimmed hat.

"He's human," Anna said. "We must be in Roethia."

"Stop gawking," Faedyn said. "There's a whole town ahead. Besides, we should be keeping a low profile."

254 | Matthew Lowes

"Why?" Ken said.

"Because many Roethians don't trust us," Namh said. "The elar have kept to themselves for a long time now."

The man across the river waved.

Anna waved back, and they walked on. The path soon became more like a road. "Haigar is the northernmost Roethian settlement of any significant size," Faedyn said.

Soon they saw crops growing on the surrounding hillsides and the wooden cottages of farmers dotted the green landscape, east and west of the river. Peaked roofs pointed skyward and smoke billowed gently from stone chimneys as evening came on.

When Haigar came into view on the far bank of the Brea, they saw tightly clustered buildings with timber frames and stone facings. A modest wall enclosed the town and a bridge spanned the river at the east gate. At the northern edge of town stood a tall watchtower, where a contingent of the Roethian army would be permanently stationed.

"Cover your weapons," Faedyn said. "When we reach town, stay close together. We'll find a place to stay where we can rest and resupply for the journey onward. I don't want to stay here longer than necessary. Our business lies to the west, far from the borders of Roethia."

†

The bridge was busy with pedestrian traffic and Haigar's eastern gate was wide open. Sleepy guards stood nearby, leaning on spears. It was the last day of market, when farmers, craftsmen, and traders from nearby villages came to buy and sell. The guards took little notice of their arrival, but a few villagers looked them twice over. With their strange clothes and travelling packs, perhaps they appeared to be traders, but a discerning eye might wonder where exactly they were from.

Anna had to remind herself that although the difference between elar and human was clear to her, it would not be to other humans. Namh had wrapped her grey cloak around her. With her hood up, she walked much more wearily than Anna knew she was. She gripped her white staff as if to support herself, and a hint of fear troubled her usually steady eyes.

Anna looked up at her as they followed Faedyn down the crowded cobblestone street. Farmers were securing their loads on carts for the journey home, fisherman were discounting the last of the day's catch, and traders were trying to make their final deals before the day's end. "Are you all right, Namh?" Anna said.

Namh looked down at Anna. She had barely said a word to her the whole journey so far. She looked at Anna and almost laughed. "I've never been around so many humans before," she said.

"This is nothing," Anna said. "You should see the city where I come from."

"No thanks," Namh said. "The smell here is bad enough."

There was indeed a peculiar smell to the place, an unfortunate amalgam of scents. There were cut flowers, spices, and fresh foods in the market, but there was also the smell of animals, unwashed citizens, raw sewage, and ripe decay. After so many days in the fresh air, it seemed overwhelming. "Yeah," Anna said, "about that I'm inclined to agree with you."

They continued on past the market, before turning down one of the narrow streets that crisscrossed the old town in a maze of crooked angles and odd intersections. Here the buildings appeared even more ancient. The stone that filled the walls between the timber skeletons of these old buildings had in places been repaired with field stone, or with clay bricks, or rudimentary cement, so a mosaic of weathered materials lined the streets.

Faedyn stopped. Above them, a sign hung by rusted chains from a wooden arm attached to the frame of a two-story building. The sign's red paint was cracked, chipped, and worn dull by the years. There was a stylized picture of a griffin and some words in Coram that Anna couldn't make out.

"It's an inn," Faedyn said.

"Looks more like a barn," Ken said.

"We should be careful about where we stay," Faedyn said. "You and Namh wait here. Anna and I will go in and check it out."

†

Faedyn opened the heavy wooden door, which creaked on its rusty hinges.

The darkness of the interior nearly blinded them, and it took a moment for Anna to make sense of the space. But some light filtered through the filthy, clouded windows at the front of the inn, and the innkeeper was in the process of lighting oil lanterns to illuminate the house against the coming night.

The ground floor of the inn looked more like a tavern than a lodging house. A large room was filled with heavy wooden tables, worn and ale stained, edges smoothed by many years of resting hands, leaning forearms, and kicked up boots. The dull floorboards creaked underfoot and the timber overhead, already dark, was nearly blackened from the smoke of oil lanterns and candles.

There were only two people sitting at all those tables, two men sitting alone, getting an early start on a night of drinking. They didn't even look up when Faedyn and Anna walked in.

The innkeeper lit the last of the lamps and stepped behind the bar. Faedyn crossed the room. Anna stayed close by. The innkeeper looked them over. He was a rather short man, but a thick grey beard distinguished his face. The top of his head was bald, but the grey hair around the sides was long. He narrowed his eyes as they approached the bar. "What can I do for you?" he said in Coram.

"Lodging," Faedyn said, matching his accent. "Two nights, for myself, my daughter here, and two other traders from Gurunfel."

The innkeeper didn't answer immediately, but looked at Faedyn closely, a question perhaps on the edge of his mind. But whether it was a conscious or unconscious suspicion, Anna couldn't tell. Either way, the moment passed. "Market time is busy," he said. "I have only one room, but for twenty a night you're welcome to it."

"That'll be fine. We're used to sleeping in camps, anyway." Faedyn produced a bag of Roethian coin to pay the innkeeper. "Anna, go fetch the others."

Anna hurried out to get Ken and Namh, who were still waiting in the street outside.

A door at the side of the tavern led to a steep wooden staircase. The innkeeper, lantern in hand, led them up the rickety stairs to the second floor. "My name's Baldis," he said. "Just let me know if there's anything you need." They walked down a narrow hall, permanently askew from the settling of the old building.

Baldis showed them to a small, dusty room overlooking the street below. Only dusk-light filtered in the dirty windows. After lighting a lantern for them, he retreated to the door. He seemed to take a long look at Namh, whose face was still hidden behind her hooded cloak. "We'll serve dinner in an hour," he said. "You can take it here or downstairs. I'll have my boy bring you fresh water." With that, he left them.

They unburdened themselves and each found a place to rest—on the bed, in the chair by the window, or leaning against a pack on the floor. Fatigue and the strangeness of new surroundings left them in silence, and the lamplit room seemed terribly enclosed after so many nights of sleeping under an open sky.

Shortly, a rap at the door roused them from their rest. Anna rose from where she lay sprawled on the floor to answer it. A boy stood in the doorway, tall, dark-haired, wide-eyed, and beautiful! He carried a huge jug sloshing with water, his muscles rippling with the weight of it. Anna's eyes met his across the doorway, and she was lost for a moment in his youthful humanity.

"I'm Brega," he said.

"Hi." She still stood in the doorway. She couldn't think of what else to say. Brega adjusted his grip on the heavy jug of water. "Oh, sorry," Anna said, realizing she was blocking the way. She stepped aside. "Come in, come in."

Brega made his way across the floor, the water sloshing, and set the jug on a heavy table in the corner. He glanced at the others where they sat resting. Ken eyed him suspiciously. Faedyn rose from his chair at the window, thanked him, and gave him a Roethian coin.

"Thank you, sir," Brega said. He looked at Anna, "Let me know if you need anything."

He stood at the door for a moment before leaving. There was a curious expression on his face as he looked again from Faedyn to Namh and back to Anna. Then he left them alone again.

40

Soldiers of Roethia

Through the thin floor of the room, Anna listened to a steady stream of customers arriving at the tavern below. Darkness had fallen outside, and Faedyn sat at the table making a list by the lamplight. There was loud talk and laughing downstairs—then music, as well. Namh had lit another lantern and was reading from a book she always carried with her. The sound of merriment grew louder.

"Can we go down there?" Anna said. "We need to eat, and I want to see the people."

"We can eat here," Faedyn said. "We're not from here, Anna, and I don't want to attract attention. I'm beginning to think we should have avoided this place entirely."

"Why?" Ken said.

"Because the people are restless. I can feel it. Namh feels it too. They go about their daily business, but something is unsettled in them, just below the surface."

"They're human beings," Anna said. "Perhaps you've just forgotten what we're like."

Faedyn smiled. "Perhaps."

"Besides, somebody has to go down there and ask them to send food up. Ken and I will go. We've been deprived of human company for so long. Don't worry. We'll blend in well enough."

"Ah, the life of an exile," Faedyn said. "But Ken can barely speak a word of Coram."

"I'll do all the talking," Anna said.

"I'm a mute," Ken said, drawing a zipper line across his mouth. "And I'm starving. And I'm dying to get out of this room."

Anna flashed Ken a smile. Then she looked to Faedyn and spoke in Vena so Ken wouldn't understand. "It'll be good for him," she said. "He'll finally have to keep his mouth shut."

Faedyn laughed. "Okay," he said. "But be careful, and don't attract attention to yourselves."

†

The noise grew louder as Anna and Ken descended the narrow, lantern-lit stair. They opened the door to the tavern at the landing. The room was full of people, mostly men, but women and children too. Every table was full and many more people were standing, everyone talking and laughing. They drank mugs of ale, broke hearty loaves of bread, and slurped up bowls of stew. A man played fiddle in front of the now dark windows. Nobody seemed to take any notice of their arrival.

"Looks like a party," Ken said, practically shouting above the noise.

"Hey, there's Brega," Anna said, pointing across the room to where Brega was pouring pints from a giant barrel behind the bar. She started toward him, moving through the crowd.

"Wait," Ken said, moving after her.

Anna turned back for a moment to be sure Ken was following. "Remember to stay quiet," she said.

Ken scratched his tousled hair. "Yeah, right," he said, and furrowed his brow the way he always did when he was irritated.

"Hey," Brega shouted above the crowd as they approached. He smiled and waved them over.

"Good evening," Anna said in flawless Coram.

"How is your room?" Brega said, handing out two pints and taking some coin in return.

"Very comfortable," Anna said.

Brega kept busy while they talked, occasionally breaking off to exchange some words with another customer. "Good," he said. "My father will be happy."

Anna nodded. "We … uh …" but Brega's attention was drawn away for a moment.

"What's your name?" he said, turning back to Anna and Ken.

"Oh, sorry, I'm Anna, and this is Ken." Brega wiped his hand on the soiled apron he was wearing and shook both their hands. Ken just nodded, smiled, and pretended he understood every word they were saying. "Ken doesn't talk much," Anna said.

Brega looked at Ken and just nodded, accepting this fact without question. "Where are you from?" he said.

Anna felt a momentary panic. What would she say? She couldn't tell him the truth. "We're … traders," she said. "We came from …" What was it that Faedyn had said? "Gurunfel."

"Where?"

But just then a man next to them yelled something, laughed, tipped, and suddenly careened off his stool, crashing to the ground in a chaotic heap. Anna jumped back into Ken, who caught her and then stepped between her and the man, who was now picking himself up off the floor. The man was still laughing. His friend shook his head and helped him up. "Pardon him," he said. They headed for the door.

"Sorry," Brega said. "It's the last night of Market." He gestured to the now vacant stools. "Sit down, sit down." He put a plate of bread and cheese in front of them. "Eat something." He poured two mugs of amber ale and plopped them down on the bar in front of them. "On the house," he said. "I'll be right back. I have to clear some tables."

"Did you order more food?" Ken said when he was gone.

"I didn't get the chance. He said he'd be right back, though. We may as well eat something while we wait."

They ate and people-watched, waiting for Brega to return, who seemed to keep getting sidetracked.

†

A commotion at the front door suddenly drew the crowd's attention. The people surged backward a little and hushed to a sober murmuring.

Anna and Ken stood up on the horizontal supports of their stools to see what was going on. Five men stood by the door wearing bright steel helmets and white surcoats over chain mail. The surcoats bore the royal eagle crest of Roethia in blue. They had swords and knives at their sides. "Soldiers," Ken said.

The crowd slowly parted, making a space in the center of the room. One of the soldiers wore a more elaborate uniform than the others. He had a long, pale green cape and fancy leather gauntlets. The sides of his helmet were carved with ornamental wings. This man removed his helmet, handed it to one of the others and addressed the crowd.

"I'm Captain Raeic. We have just arrived from the capitol with urgent orders to secure the town and recruit new soldiers for the army. I'm sure you've all heard of the trouble on the southern border. Well, it's getting worse, and many are predicting a war with Drighton. Therefore, by order of the king, all able-bodied men between the ages of sixteen and forty are to report to the hall at North Tower tomorrow by noon. They are being inducted into the Roethian Army. Violators and those harboring them will be subject to the full authority of the king's law."

There was a sudden, angry shout from someone in the crowd and a drunken man burst out, charging at Captain Raeic. He was yelling something incoherent as he threw a punch toward Raeic's head. The captain dodged the punch and the man fell forward wrapping his arms around Raeic's waist. Raeic shrugged him off as two of the other soldiers pulled the drunken man to the ground, beat him into silence and dragged him from the tavern.

The captain continued as if nothing had happened. "Lastly, there have been reports that foreign spies and agitators are at large in Roethia. The safety and stability of our lands is at stake. Report all suspicious persons to the authorities."

Captain Raeic and the other soldiers marched out. The room burst into a roar of suddenly very sober discussion, and Anna explained the situation to Ken.

"Let's go," Ken said, stepping off his stool.

"Where?" Anna said.

"Back to the room," Ken said, taking hold of Anna's hand and leading her through the crowd.

Anna held tight to Ken's hand as he made a way for them. She looked back once and saw Brega across the room. Their eyes met for a moment. Then Ken led her into the stairwell and they headed up the narrow stairs together.

41

An Unfortunate Situation

Ken and Anna rushed into the room without the food they had been sent to get. Ken closed the door and made a point to latch it. Faedyn and Namh looked up from the small table where they were talking, instantly aware that something had happened.

"What's wrong?" Faedyn said.

"There were soldiers downstairs," Ken said. "They just arrived from the capital. The king of Roethia is conscripting all able-bodied men into the army."

"When?" Faedyn said.

"They have to report to North Tower tomorrow by noon."

"What's the big deal?" Anna said.

"Don't you get it?" Ken said. "They'll force me to join up if we stay here. Faedyn too."

Outside their window they heard a growing din of noise, the rattle of horse-tack, the creak of carriages, and the loud footsteps of many boots marching in unison.

"What's that?" Anna said.

Faedyn looked out the window at the street below. "More soldiers," he said. By lamplight and torches, a small army marched through the streets toward North Tower. Curious onlookers peered down from the windows above, and crowds emerged from the doorways to watch. Some people waved to the passing troops, welcoming them to town. A soldier on horseback shouted out greetings. But somehow it seemed as if the town was suddenly under siege.

Ken, Anna, and Namh crowded around the window with Faedyn to watch.

"In my dream," Namh said to Faedyn, as if picking up the thread of an earlier conversation, "I saw a Roethian city in flames."

"We may need to leave earlier than planned," Faedyn said.

"That's not all," Ken said. "The captain said they were on the lookout for spies and foreigners."

Suddenly there was a knock at the door. They all turned their heads toward the sound. The door was closed and latched. Someone knocked again.

"We're trapped," Anna whispered.

Faedyn reached for his sword and stepped quietly toward the door. The others followed suit. Namh gripped her staff in both hands, and Ken and Anna nervously picked up their swords.

"Who is it?" Faedyn said.

"It's Baldis," the old innkeeper's voice could be heard clearly through the door. Faedyn motioned the others to move off to the side, where anyone who entered wouldn't immediately see them.

"What do you want?" Faedyn said.

"I have your supper."

Faedyn carefully unlatched the door. He opened it only a crack and peered out. The others watched. Ken gripped the handle of his sword tightly, hoping there would be no reason to use it. Then, still hidden by the door, Faedyn leaned his sword up against the wall and motioned for the others to hide their weapons.

"Baldis," Faedyn said with a friendly smile, "please come in." He opened the door wide and the innkeeper entered carrying a large wooden tray of food.

Baldis waddled over to the table and set the tray down.

"Thank you so much," Namh said, clearly trying to be friendly.

"Yes, thank you," Anna chimed in.

"You were awful cautious about opening the door," Baldis said as he arranged the food on the table. "You needn't be afraid of criminals here."

"I apologize," Faedyn said. He laughed then. "We're not used to town. With all the commotion outside we got a little nervous."

Baldis turned around and his gaze went straight to Faedyn's sword by the door.

There was a moment when everyone in the room seemed to exchange glances, waiting for something unsaid to be said. Faedyn had placed himself between Baldis and the door.

It was a tense moment. Did Baldis know they weren't Roethian? Would he report them to the authorities? Or maybe he already had.

Finally, Baldis broke the uncomfortable silence. "You don't have to lie to me," he said. "I know who you are."

"What do you mean?" Faedyn said cautiously.

"I know you are elar. But trust me, I want to help you."

Faedyn scrutinized the old man. Was he telling the truth or was this a ploy to stall them until the authorities arrived? "Ken, check the hall and close the door," Faedyn said.

Ken poked his head out into the hallway. All was quiet. He closed the door and latched it.

"He is telling the truth," Namh said. "He does mean to help us." Baldis looked at Namh, a wonder-filled look on his face.

"Why would we need your help?" Faedyn said to Baldis.

"You may have seen the soldiers outside," Baldis said. "They have secured all the town gates. Tomorrow, you and the boy will either be conscripted into the Roethian army or arrested as spies. There have been rumors the elar are advising the kingdom of Drighton."

"We need to leave town," Faedyn said. "Can you help us do that?"

"The western gate is still manned by the local guard. A nephew of mine is in charge of the watch tonight. I can arrange safe passage for you."

Faedyn considered this for a moment. "How do you know we're not spies from Drighton? Aren't you afraid of betraying your people?"

"Most of the people these days don't trust the elar. They think they're working with the king of Drighton against us. That may or may not be true, but I know the elar as good people, and I don't think spies would travel in a group. My father, may he rest in peace, was once injured from a fall in the mountains. He was saved by the elar. He would have died then, had they not found him and nursed him back to health. I grew up hearing stories of that time, of the beautiful people, and the wondrous things he saw when he lived among them. So you see, I am a simple man, Mister Faedyn. My family has always held the elar in high regard, and I only wish to repay the kindness that was shown to my father. Lord help me if you are spies, but somehow I don't think so."

"Very well," Faedyn said. "We thank you for any help you can give us, and I can assure you we're not spies, so your conscience can rest easy. We come from the north, and are on a journey that will benefit all the people of Elara."

"There may be soldiers patrolling the streets all night, but from the rooftops, I think you can make it almost all the way to the western gate unseen."

"Our journey is long," Faedyn said, "and we had hoped to resupply here."

"I'll send my boy, Brega, with a load of provisions to meet you beyond the western gate. Please stay here while the arrangements are made. I promise you'll be safe."

42

THE DEATH OF PRINCES

The chaos and instability following Emperor Drakhil's death were just as Sulki had predicted. A torch had been set in the Maleistrian court. Now Kai stood back to watch it burn. Tyral and his mages could come to no conclusion regarding the emperor's death. Each prince had troops and assassins loyal to them, and warlords of the Outlands were known to have spies in the realm. But the mages could not figure out how the assassination had been carried out. Kai had, of course, offered to assist them, but the visions of the witch-seers were cloudy and vague, suggesting if anything that one of the emperor's sons was behind it.

Malfot threw a tantrum before the nobles, demanding to be declared emperor, but there were endless legal arguments. A number of nobles, and most notably Princes Nykhil and Durok, made injunctions against it, calling for an independent investigation to oversee the mages and their handling of the matter. Several lawyers handling these cases were assassinated themselves, and it wasn't long before Malfot was found dead, his fat body hunched over a full table in his private chamber, his face fallen in a plate of food.

The mages said it could have been a heart attack, an unfortunate thing, but not related to these recent assassinations. They were merely trying to calm the masses, because of course

Malfot's poison taster was nowhere to be found. Durok and Nykhil blamed each other openly, but each was secretly glad Malfot was out of the way.

Kai took a drink of wine and admired Sulki as she reclined in his bed chamber. Loyal soldiers of the Black Guard were stationed outside, a new precaution that seemed prudent in these troubled times. "Ah, Sulki, how do you do it?"

She smiled. "I visit their dreams," she said. "And there I plant wicked seeds that take root in the darkest regions of the mind."

"Let me guess. It was Nykhil who killed Malfot. It has his touch."

Sulki laughed. "He thinks he will be emperor."

"But who killed Emperor Drakhil?"

"The Black Guard, of course. What other assassins have we ever used?"

"But the guards were killed."

"Yes, and who would ever suspect them now?"

Of course, Kai thought. They sacrificed themselves for the perfect murder.

"I brought you something," Sulki said.

Kai looked at the long box on the table, smooth heesha-wood, inlaid with silver.

"Open it."

Kai unlatched the box, and lifted the lid. There lay Saraden, the last of the magic swords, that like Rayaden, had survived since the Golden Age. Sulki had shown it to him once before, when he was young.

"This, as you know, is the greatest treasure of Elyx-ular," Sulki said. She stood behind him, naked, her arms around his shoulders as he gazed at Saraden. "And you, my lovely prince, are our greatest achievement. You are a true son of Saziel, descended from his bloodline. In you is the blood of our emperors, and also the blood of Gairen, last wielder of Saraden."

"How can that be?"

"How else? One of our witches seduced him on the eve of the battle in which he died."

Kai lifted the sword and held it in his hands. He felt a surge of power, of strength and resolve. The ancient sword felt good in his hands. It felt right, somehow … perfect.

"You are already a great swordsman. With this sword you will become invincible."

Kai drew the sword a few inches from its sheath and gazed at the white metal of its blade. He took a deep breath, then pushed the sword back and set it down. "Sulki?"

"Yes."

"I've been having a dream."

"About the Crypt?"

"Yes. It's like a voice is calling out to me. I see the Great Seal, and I want to open it."

Sulki held him. "The mages believe the Crypt holds our past, but in fact it holds our future. Its secrets, its knowledge, and its power are your destiny."

There was a sudden knock at the door. Kai grabbed Saraden and went to answer it. Sulki backed into the darkness, disappearing in the shadows.

"What is it?" Kai said through the door. "Why do you bother me?

"My lord, Prince Nykhil is dead." It was Thei, captain of his loyal Black Guard.

Kai threw open the door. "When?"

"Not more than a few hours ago, my lord. His servants just discovered him. The mages are on their way from the Crypt now."

Kai's eyes grew wide with excitement. "Fly, my friend. Send word to your soldiers to arrest Prince Durok now. Charge him with the death of his brothers, and the emperor as well. He will be the final proof of their utter corruption. I shall be close behind you."

Kai glanced back into his chamber, but did not see Sulki. Then he threw a cape about his shoulders, stepped out into the hall and closed the door behind him.

He walked confidently through the palace halls. The people looked to him with some glimmer of hope in their eyes. Yes, they thought, there is someone who knows what he is doing, someone who can restore order and dignity to this world. A crowd of people gathered outside Nykhil's chambers, but Kai walked past them.

He saw ahead a contingent of his Black Guard soldiers knocking and shouting at Prince Durok's door. "Break it down," Kai shouted. "The empire will not stand for this blatant disregard for authority."

The soldiers broke in the door and quickly searched Durok's chambers. The bodies of two slave girls lay in pools of their own blood. Their fatal wounds were recent, but there was no sign of Durok. "My lord, he's not here," Thei said.

"Look here," Kai said, pulling aside a thick tapestry and revealing a secret passage. "He's escaped."

"Seal the palace," Thei said to the other soldiers. "And send word to close the city gates."

Kai sighed. "He will be long gone by now. Perhaps he is less of a fool than his brothers."

43

A Narrow Escape

Namh and Ken kept a nervous watch at the window as the night wore on. The wait seemed long, and they ate little of the food they had hungered for. Roethian troops continued to march into the city, and regular patrols had already started. Unfortunately, with so many soldiers moving about, it was impossible to predict when and where they might be.

Faedyn paced the room with uncharacteristic impatience. At one point, he reclined on one of the beds. He shut his eyes as if to rest, but he was up again within minutes, clearly agitated by the situation. "It's funny," Faedyn said. "For hundreds of years I lived in exile, and now I have no patience."

Anna sat on the floor, her back leaning against the wall and her arms wrapped around her folded knees. After so many days of travelling, they had fallen into trouble without warning. All because of politics—because of a war they had nothing to do with.

She reached into the folds of her worn and dirty travel clothes. The photo of her mom was safe, buttoned into a deep pocket that pressed against her left breast. Her finger brushed the wrinkled photographic paper as she tried to recall the image from memory.

The difficulty lay in separating that singular image from the myriad nebulous memories and feelings she had when she thought about her mom. After all, she had looked different in Anna's earliest memories, and she had certainly looked different after cancer had taken its toll.

It wasn't so much that she couldn't remember how she looked, for there was, she supposed, always some sense of that, however vague. But she wanted to really *see* her, not in the general way memory allowed, but really see her. She wanted to look into her eyes and see the light in them. She wanted to observe all the various expressions the day brought to her—so many beautiful changes she hadn't appreciated at the time.

Anna took the photograph out of her pocket. Of course it couldn't satisfy the longing she felt, but at least she could grasp it, and she could see her mom as she had looked in one particular, happy moment.

"What time is it?" Faedyn said, stopping to stare at the door.

"Surely past midnight," Namh said. "But there are still soldiers in the streets below, as if they can't wait for their petty war."

"You talk as if the elar never had any wars," Ken said. "But I know that's not true."

"Quiet," Faedyn said, thinking he heard the sound of someone approaching. But the hall was silent.

Anna wondered if her mother had ever known anything about their family history. Her mom had worked hard her whole life and had never expected anything other than what came to her. She had never grown bitter, even when she was dying and couldn't afford to pay her medical bills. Anna just wished she could go back now and tell her about Elara and Lord Elgard, and about Rayaden, and the noble inheritance of their family.

Somehow, because all these things were tied together in her mind by a web of longing and hope, she vaguely imagined Lord Elgard and her mom falling in love and living together. And she imagined somehow that Lord Elgard really was her father and they could all live happily ever after.

Suddenly someone knocked at the door. Everyone stiffened to attention. Anna stuffed the picture back in her pocket, snug against her breast, near to her heart.

†

Faedyn answered the door.

Baldis did not enter. "Quickly," he said. "I've sent Brega to meet you with your supplies beyond the west gate. You must go now before the changing of the guard."

He led them down the hall and up another flight of stairs to the garret. Anna and Ken followed closely behind Faedyn and Namh.

In the garret, Baldis and his family had a modest home. He took them to a small bedroom in the back, and they huddled in, cramped in the tight space.

"Here," Baldis said, opening the shutters on the window. "Brega has snuck out of this window many times. Follow the roofline to the east-west road, and then head toward the west gate. You can go as far as Miller Street. Brega says the wall in the alley there is covered with vines and easy to climb down."

"Thank you," Faedyn said.

"Hurry."

Faedyn stepped out onto the roof and into the night. Namh followed and Ken quickly after her. When it was her turn, Anna ducked her head through the window and stepped out without hesitation.

The resolution in her step didn't last, though. In the moment she set both feet upon the roof and stood up, a paralytic fear gripped her. The sloping surface was unstable and clearly not meant to be walked on. The moon cast just enough light to see the edge and the fall beyond it. The alley was black with night and she could not see the street below.

She began to shake and gripped the window sill even tighter. Ken saw the fear in her eyes. "Faedyn," he whispered ahead. "Wait."

Faedyn and Namh looked back to see Anna trembling at the window sill, her legs shaking uncontrollably. She tried to breathe, great gasping breaths that did little to calm her.

Faedyn knew right away what the problem was, but Namh looked confused. "What's wrong with her?" she said.

"She's afraid of heights," Ken said.

Namh looked past Ken at Anna with impatience. "Afraid of heights?" she said, as if that were the most ridiculous thing in the world. "Why didn't you say something before?"

"Because I thought I was over it," Anna said, for a moment more pissed off than afraid.

Ken touched Anna's arm. "You can do it, Anna," he said.

Anna's arm relaxed a little under Ken's touch. She was able to take a deep, slow breath.

Ken nodded his head with encouragement. Behind him, Namh and Faedyn were waiting, still as gargoyles perched on the rooftop. She thought of something Faedyn had said during one of their many sword lessons. "You must stay completely calm," he said, "even in the midst of your greatest fear."

Anna released her grip on the window sill and put her weight on her feet again, balancing precariously on the sloping roof. She took a step, and then another one.

Ken held out his hand for support, but she was more afraid to lean on it than not to. Slowly they began to move along the rooftop.

They didn't get far before Faedyn held up his hand, signaling them to get down and be quiet. In the street below, they heard two soldiers on patrol. The light of the lanterns cast a flickering halo of light that lit up the alleyway as they walked.

Anna, Ken, Namh, and Faedyn crouched silently on the rooftop and watched until the glow of their lanterns dimmed down another alleyway.

Anna tried to think about only two things as they moved on—slow, calm breathing and solid foot placement with every step. But the light of the passing patrol below had reminded her just how high up they were. Now only darkness was beyond that edge again, and she could feel the fear creeping back into her.

With a single stray bad thought, her concentration was thrown. Her breathing became shallow, and her legs began to shake again. It was a slight quiver at first, but it seemed to increase with each step she took.

Perhaps foolishly, Anna didn't stop. She took step after shaking step on a dwindling supply of oxygen. Partly, it just didn't occur to her to stop, but behind that was another fear. At that moment, she was more afraid of holding everyone up than she was of falling.

A cool night breeze picked up and blew through Anna's hair. For a moment she felt unbearably exposed, and then she seemed to leave her body entirely. Her leg jerked with the next step. Her foot slipped, and she fell, sliding toward the darkness. There was a moment in which she tried to grab hold of the edge, then a glimpse of the crescent moon, high in the sky, bright, and completely indifferent.

†

"Anna!" Ken said, reaching out as she fell. He took a step, about to jump after her.

Namh held the boy back. She was amazed how the foolishness of humans could multiply. They rarely seemed to think before doing anything. She held Ken by the collar until the impulse to jump left him.

They looked down to see Anna sprawled on the street below. Still on her back, she waved to them, signaling she was okay. She looked shaken though, and maybe injured.

"You two continue on," Namh said. "We'll meet you at the west gate."

Before either of them could argue, she slid over the edge, nimble as a cat, held herself by one hand for a moment, and then dropped to the street below. She and Anna would have a better chance of sneaking through the streets alone. Faedyn wouldn't like it, of course, but he was smart enough to see what was best.

Anna tried to stand up, but collapsed back to the ground in pain. "I'm sorry," she said, as Namh crouched beside her.

"Never mind that," Namh said. "How is your ankle?" She nodded toward Anna's right ankle.

Anna tried to move her ankle, as if just noticing she was injured. She winced in pain. "It hurts."

There were limits to what she could do, but Namh had some knowledge of magic. Arisu had taught her the basics of the ancient arts, as she knew them anyway, through what knowledge had survived the ages. Now she had to put the art of healing into practice, fast. Another patrol could come around at any time.

"Relax," Namh said, taking Anna's ankle and rotating it a little. Anna twitched in pain. The ankle was badly sprained.

Namh held Anna's ankle firmly. Her hands seemed to melt onto Anna's flesh as she tried to erase the separation that existed between them. She muttered a few words in the ancient language, and through the words breathed the clarity of her intention. That breath passed through her hands into Anna's ankle. She felt too much doubt, too unsure of what she was doing. But in the back of her mind, she trusted Anna's ankle was listening. "Try it now."

Anna moved her ankle around a bit, apparently without any severe pain. "What did you do?" she said.

"I fixed it. Now let's go. See if you can stand on it."

Anna got to her feet. Her ankle looked weak, but at least she could stand on it. Namh could see the silhouettes of Faedyn and Ken above, still watching them. She waved them on. Anna waved too. But they stayed there watching until Namh led Anna, limping a little, down a small alleyway and out of sight.

Namh's night-vision was doubtless better than Anna's, and the girl seemed shaken by her fall. She took Anna by the hand and led her down the dark alleyway. She attuned her ears to the way ahead, listening for any sound of footfall.

Namh took them on a circuitous route toward the west gate, along the smallest, quietest, and incidentally the dirtiest paths through town. The narrow lanes reeked of human refuse, and their feet splashed in muddy puddles.

The trip was going well, until the back door of a pub opened ahead, and a soldier walked right out into the alleyway in front of them.

Namh and Anna stopped mid-step, hoping the night was enough to hide them.

The soldier belched loudly and without looking around went about his business of pissing in the street.

When he finished and turned to go back inside, he saw Namh and Anna standing in the shadows. He furrowed his brow, clearly drunk, and confused by their silent presence.

"Hey, who is that?"

Namh didn't answer. Anna stayed behind her.

"I say, who's there? Don't you know there's a curfew?"

Namh turned to whisper to Anna, "Stay here." Then she walked out of the shadows.

The soldier's eyes grew big and he almost staggered with surprise at the sight of her. Few human women could compare with Namh's beauty, and those who could were not frequently encountered by soldiers of the Roethian army, certainly not in the back alleys of provincial towns.

"I'm sorry, miss," the man stammered, clearly unable to wrap his mind around Namh, or fit her into his limited and currently alcohol-infused worldview. "I didn't realize ... I mean where were you going? If you don't mind me asking ..." He straightened his clothes nervously and adjusted the sword that hung from his belt.

Namh just smiled. She walked toward him, fixing his eyes with a charming, seductive gaze. Her movement was calm and graceful, without fear, and without any sign of threat. She walked right up to him, so close that her body brushed against his.

The man was sort of paralyzed by her actions and probably wondering if he had simply drunk too much. Namh put her hands on the man's waist. She fingered his belt, and stroked the hilt of his sword. That was probably going too far, but by this time she was enjoying herself. She had complete control of the situation.

Namh looked into the man's eyes and smiled. For a moment, she almost felt sorry for him. And then, without warning, and without the expression on her face or the calm ease of her body changing, she thrust her knee into his groin.

The blow was not hard enough to cause any real damage, but it was hard enough and sudden enough to make the soldier forget all about Namh. He didn't even know what had happened. His whole body just doubled over.

Namh caught his shoulders gently in her hands, turned him, and eased him down to the ground with a kind of benevolent reassurance. The man groaned, but slowly, under Namh's touch, his whole body began to relax. She laid his head softly on the ground by her foot. She crouched down next to him, put one hand on his chest, passed the other over his face, and said softly, "sweet dreams."

He was smiling, and fast asleep.

Namh motioned for Anna to come and follow her.

"Is he asleep?" Anna said as she came over.

"A deep sleep."

"He could warn the others tomorrow. They might come looking for us."

"Not likely. I'll wager he'll never tell a living soul about what happened. By the time he wakes up, he won't even be sure it did happen. Now let's go."

†

They rushed down several more alleyways, and turned several corners, hoping not to run into any more trouble. Anna's ankle ached, but it was so much better than it had been. Her thoughts raced around without resting. She was still embarrassed by the fall, and she wondered about Namh. Just what was she capable of? How had she fixed her ankle, and how did she put that man to sleep? Was it magic?

At one point, Namh paused, and Anna thought she might be lost, but they turned one more corner and there ahead they could see the alley open onto the wide east-west road. As they approached, two people emerged from the dark doorway of a shuttered building. Anna stopped, her breath suspended in a limbo of dread.

To her relief, Faedyn and Ken stepped into the moonlight. "What took you so long?" Faedyn said "I was starting to get worried."

"Anna, are you all right?" Ken said.

"I'm okay," Anna said, but she certainly didn't want to discuss it. "Hadn't we better get going?"

"The west gate is only a block from here," Faedyn said.

After peeking around the corner in both directions, Faedyn declared the way clear. "Don't run," he said. "Everybody stick together and walk toward the gate."

Anna was so nervous when they hit the open street that she didn't notice when Ken took her hand. She just clung to it as they walked, an odd party at a quiet hour of a crazy night.

The great wooden gate was closed, and two guards stood at its sides, lit by torches fixed to the watch-towers. It seemed unlikely they would open it for them, in which case this whole escapade would have been pointless.

The guards took a step forward as they approached, brandishing their spears. "State your business," one of them said. "You are out past curfew."

"We're friends of Mister Baldis," Faedyn said.

The guard was unimpressed.

"We're on our way home to Gurunfel," Faedyn said. "My youngest has fallen sick. Please let us pass."

"Nobody is allowed to pass after curfew," the other guard said.

Perhaps the guard had changed already, Anna thought, and they had missed their chance to escape. She clung tightly to Ken's hand.

Just then, an officer emerged from the guard tower, a big barrel-chested man with a huge bushy mustache. "Open the gate," he bellowed.

"But, sir—"

"I said open the gate, you idiot. These people have leave to pass."

The guards opened the heavy gate, allowing them to walk out into the darkness beyond the city wall.

The officer followed them.

"Thank you," Faedyn said.

The big man shrugged. "My uncle said you're good people. No sense you getting caught up in all this trouble."

Faedyn nodded. "We are in his debt, and yours."

"Brega is waiting for you down the road with your equipment and supplies."

Without further word, they followed Faedyn into the night.

They found Brega waiting in the dark, a hundred yards beyond the west gate. He signaled with a chirping whistle as they approached. A donkey cart was there, loaded up with their equipment and supplies.

Brega stood there smiling as they donned their gear. "Father says you can take the cart, if you want it," he said.

"We'll travel faster without it," Faedyn said, "but thank your father for us. You have both been a great help."

Brega nodded, and watched Anna finish adjusting her pack. "Travel well," he said. "And good luck to all of you."

"What about you?" Anna said. "What will you do tomorrow?"

"I'll join the army," Brega said, "and become a soldier of Roethia." There was neither pride nor fear in his voice.

"Be careful," Anna said, "and take good care of yourself."

Brega laughed. "I always do."

"Farewell," Faedyn said.

Anna lingered for a moment.

"C'mon, Anna," Ken said.

"I thought he was mute," Brega said.

"Hardly," Anna said.

For a moment they stood in silence. "Well …" Brega said, "so long."

"Maybe we'll meet again sometime."

Brega nodded. Their eyes met for one last moment. Anna smiled and waved briefly, then turned and hurried along, limping on her sore ankle to catch up with the others.

44

Into the White Mountains

Faedyn followed the road westward for several hours, passing quietly through the darkness without any source of light. He drove them onward, hoping to get as far from Haigar and the Roethian army as possible. Anna's ankle was clearly still bothering her. Now was not the time to rest though, and she seemed to manage well enough.

They spoke little in the quiet dark that night. Each kept their own thoughts, and listened to their own footsteps on the rough road. They were on their way again after too short a rest. Anna and Ken were nearly falling asleep as they walked, stumbling along to keep up.

Their sojourn had been risky though, however brief, and Faedyn was glad to be moving on. It would be too easy to forget the importance of their purpose. He felt the weight of his duty to push them onward to their goal. They had yet to pass over the mountains and cross the wastelands to reach the western coast.

Rayaden awaited them, and he felt in his heart, more than ever, that destiny had brought them all to this place. A war was coming, a greater war than the one Roethia feared. And he knew somehow, as Arisu had, that Anna had some part to play in it.

They left the road a few hours before dawn, and walked across wide fields of open country to camp among the hills. Faedyn stayed awake while the others slept. The sun rose, a huge, fiery orange ball that exploded on the eastern horizon, and new light was cast on the long day ahead of them.

†

The weeks that followed were difficult for Anna. Although the days were filled with little more danger than the possibility of reinjuring her almost completely healed ankle, there were times when she felt she didn't want to go on. She worried about Brega, and wondered how he was faring as a soldier. She wished they had been able to stay longer in Haigar. And she doubted everything—most of all, herself.

When the group was spread out, as they crossed open ground, winding their way through the foothills of the White Mountains, occasionally she found a chance to speak with Faedyn alone.

"Your ankle seems better," Faedyn said. "But something else is bothering you."

"I … I'm scared, that's all." Admitting this to Faedyn wasn't quite as hard as admitting it to herself, but she certainly wouldn't have told Ken or Namh.

"What are you afraid of?"

"I'm afraid all this is meaningless, that even if we succeed, it will never change anything. I'm afraid that I'm not the person you want me to be. Even if we do find Rayaden, and even if we don't die in the process, how will I ever have enough skill to use it?"

Faedyn simply nodded and put his arm around Anna as they walked. He did not dismiss or belittle Anna's fears, and this simple acknowledgement went a long way toward setting

Anna more at ease. If what she was feeling didn't mean she was crazy, if Faedyn was there with her, then maybe she could handle it.

"Are you afraid of anything, Faedyn?"

Faedyn was silent for a moment. He seemed to sigh mid-stride. "I'm afraid of my past," he said, "that nothing can make up for some of the things I've done."

Anna thought about the boy she killed, and she felt she knew exactly what Faedyn meant.

"And I'd be lying if I said I wasn't afraid of Yagul." Faedyn smiled, "I barely escaped with my life last time we met."

"I guess we all fear something, huh?"

"It's difficult not to. But a wise man once said that to set aside one's fears is to take a step toward the truth."

"Why is that?"

"Because fear can mislead you, and in the end, it doesn't change the path you're on."

Anna thought about this as they walked. They saw smoke on the southern horizon, a Roethian settlement most likely. Faedyn had steered far clear of such places ever since they left Haigar.

"I'll tell you what," Faedyn said. "Let's agree to set aside our fears together, as much as we can."

Anna looked up at Faedyn and smiled. "Okay." And in that moment, she felt she could do anything as long as Faedyn was with her.

†

The White Mountains grew ever larger in the distance each day they walked, a jagged line of grey whose white tips disappeared into the sky on a hazy day. As they climbed up into the wooded foothills, those formidable peaks seemed an impossible wall of unscalable rock.

But like many things seen at a distance, the sight was deceiving. There were ways up into the White Mountains and even ways to cross them, if one dared. Few did, however, for west of them lay a vast wasteland, a desert that stretched almost to the coast, and there were few profitable ventures that would lead one there.

From the foothills, they came to a glacial valley that stretched up to the craggy peaks above. Anna and Ken were constantly straining their necks to look upward at the imposing height of the mountains ahead. Faedyn and Namh led them onward, steadfastly walking on the rough, untrodden terrain. The sides of the valley were steep and the U-shaped floor upon which they climbed was strewn with a virtual river of loose rock. Carried down by long receded ice, these rocks ranged in size from small stones to behemoth boulders, as big as houses. The surface of these relics was grown over with bright green and orange lichens.

"Isn't there a road to Torselend?" Ken said, his legs sore and his brain tired from hours of strategic foot placement.

"You don't like this road?" Faedyn said.

"Even the Land Rover couldn't make it up here."

Faedyn laughed. "Get used to it. Torselend lies high on the base of the mountain. We won't be there for another two days, and from there it will be a steep climb to the pass."

"Will we have a chance to rest in Torselend?" Anna said.

"The elar of these mountains are industrious folk, but they are not without civilities. We should have a soft bed and good food before we face the mountain pass."

But that was not to be. Despite their hopes for a soft bed, a hot bath, and a good meal, they would find no rest in Torselend.

45

Torselend

Like Hidden Glade and the Shrine of Andurin, the history of Torselend goes far back into the dawning of Elara. With their ancient cities destroyed in the Great War, the elar were scattered in the upheavals of the Dark Age. The world broke apart, and when the dust settled on Elara, people gathered here and there to rebuild what was left of their civilization.

Thus they came to Torselend, where they mined the mountain for its riches, and for the raw materials to recover some semblance of what they had lost. They dug deep into the earth, to bring out precious metals and exquisite gemstones. And artisans began to work their trades again, gradually reinventing the craftwork of their ancestors.

This hidden enclave prospered, not swelling in numbers as human settlements did when riches were discovered, but increasing in wealth and culture. They traded with settlements across Elara—in the wild northlands, the eastern shores, and the southern forests—everywhere the elar had made their hidden homes. For many years they traded with the human kingdoms as well. Torselend gems were especially prized by the merchant princes of Padjia.

They built their great halls and their homes into the mountainside, carving elaborate rooms out of the solid rock. They filled them with rich tapestries and ornamental furniture studded with jewels. But they were not made soft by their luxury. They found peace in their work, in the hard rock of the earth, and in the appreciation of their crafts.

†

Having camped near the top of the valley that night, Anna woke with the others early the next day to continue their ascent.

"Seems like we've climbed a mountain already," Ken said, "and we're not even to the bottom yet."

Beyond the valley they reached a place where among the scattered scree, solid rock jutted out of the earth and reached skyward.

Faedyn found what he was looking for there—a narrow path cut into the rock, leading south along the base of the mountain. The path was hidden from any casual observation from below, but once found it was clearly a deliberate construction, a narrow road along the mountainside. Not the kind of highway Ken was looking for, but a road nonetheless.

They followed the road southward, winding their way along the base of the mountains for an entire day. Anna could feel her breath straining a little as the air thinned, and it was cooler here than it had been in the valley below. The drop in temperature didn't seem to affect Faedyn or Namh, but when they stopped to camp that night among the barren rocks, Anna shivered in the cold. They had a meager supper, and Faedyn promised they would reach Torselend by evening the next day. Anna huddled close to Ken, shamelessly pressed against him, seeking his warmth throughout the cold, starry night.

She was glad to be moving again in the morning, but the path they followed became treacherously steep in the afternoon. Whereas before, the narrow trail ran along the base of the mountain, now there were places where it cut into the mountain itself, and the ground dropped away below. As these drops grew steeper and higher Anna's nerves began to get the best of her. Soon they were making their way on a slippery, rocky path that couldn't have been more than a yard across, a hundred feet up on an almost vertical cliff wall. Above them, the rock face reached up as far as the eye could see. It would be dizzying even for someone who wasn't afraid of heights.

Anna hugged the cliff face, using every available handhold for extra stability. She kept breathing, and placed one foot in front of the other, trying to put her fear aside. Because really, she knew she had excellent balance, and she would have had no trouble running down this path if it were only a little closer to the ground.

She was sorry to be slowing the group down, but she wasn't going to make the same mistake she made on the rooftop in Haigar. A sprained ankle was lucky in that case, but here a fall would be fatal.

Every now and then, when she thought she couldn't take it anymore, or when her foot seemed stuck, unwilling to take the next step, Faedyn would be there. He was keeping an eye on her. And all he had to do was smile, touch her shoulder, or ask how she was doing, and somehow, she was able to go on. "We're almost there, Anna. Just a little further."

It was strange though. She had wondered about her fear of heights since Haigar, because she really thought she was over it until she stepped onto that roof. It hadn't bothered her high in the trees of Hidden Glade, or on the high cliffs in the Valley of Andurin. Perhaps there was something about those places, where the elar lived, a kind of magic, or spirit that dwelled there, that made her feel safe. But here, close to Torselend, she felt her old fear stronger than ever.

†

The sun had set below the peaks when they came to Torselend. Because of the mountains, a long extended twilight lasted well after sunset, before the sky would truly grow dark. For although the sun had dropped below the mountains, it had not yet reached the western horizon beyond.

Faedyn paused momentarily. He thought it was only a little further. But the last time he came this way, he had passed through in the middle of the night. He had sneaked past the halls of Torselend without stopping and headed straight for the pass.

There was something that bothered Faedyn as he led Anna, Ken, and Namh ever closer to this next stop on their journey. Try as he might, he could not figure out what it was. The feeling was too vague. It was as if he were missing something, or had forgotten something, or that something was simply out of place.

Nevertheless, he led them onward. The precarious path they followed was cut high on the steep mountainside as they approached. They could not see Torselend from any distance. It was carefully hidden. At last, the mountain curved inward, and a final turn revealed the hanging valley where Torselend had been built.

The small valley was surrounded by steep mountain faces. At the back of the valley, Torselend's great hall was carved into the rock where the rising sun would shine through its clerestory windows. A wide, stone staircase led up to its darkened entrance, and flanking the doorway were huge monolithic columns.

Around the sides of the valley, more buildings were carved into the rock, and up to several stories of darkened windows could be seen. Inside would be the dwelling places of the elar who lived here, as well as their storehouses, forges, workshops, and the entrances to the mines that fueled their prosperity.

A mountain stream flowed through the valley and cascaded over the edge in a waterfall. Faedyn stood with Anna, Ken, and Namh for a moment on a broad ledge overlooking the valley. Torselend was an impressive and beautiful sight. Doubtless they all were anticipating the reception they would receive.

Faedyn's sense that something was wrong grew clearer though, for there was no sign of anyone in the whole valley. All those windows and doorways were dark. There was no movement. Not a single person could be seen. There was no smoke from a fire, no clamor of the anvil, no sign of activity anywhere. And nobody had been there to greet them, not a single warrior guarded the valley, something Faedyn had expected.

A lonely wind blew down from the mountain and whistled through that place. It was a hollow, empty sound that made Faedyn uneasy.

"Something is wrong," Faedyn said.

Namh quickly surveyed the entire valley. "Where is everyone?"

"Maybe they're all inside," Anna said.

"I don't think so," Faedyn said.

Namh looked up at the dusky sky. "It's going to be dark soon. We should find out if it's going to be safe to stay here."

Ken scratched his head. "It looks deserted."

"Let's check it out," Faedyn said. "Everybody stay together. And be on your guard. I don't like the look of this."

They descended a well-worn stair that wound down into the valley. Despite the strange circumstance, Anna walked easier now that she was away from the cliff that dropped off behind them. It was Faedyn who was on edge now. He tuned his senses, smelling the air, and listening to any far-off sound the wind brought with it.

†

To Ken, Torselend looked like the deserted ruins of some ancient civilization. But the eerie quiet of the valley was at odds with the knowledge that somebody was supposed to be living there—and was supposed to feed him some dinner. And who knows when he would get that bath now.

"Hello?" Faedyn called out in Vena as he approached the nearest building. Ken watched as Faedyn stepped up into the doorway. Namh was right on Faedyn's heels, her white staff, the Lamp of Lunara, in hand. He and Anna followed a few steps behind.

They crowded into the small, empty foyer. The walls were bare rock, gold-illumed in the waning light. They searched an adjoining room and a room at the top of a flight of stairs. All were empty, and dust blew through them as if nobody had lived there for some time.

Namh gazed off at an empty wall as if listening for something beyond it. "Something terrible has happened here," she said. "I can feel it. It's like … like the whispers of ghosts."

"It's like everybody just vanished," Anna said.

"C'mon," Ken said, "An entire town doesn't just disappear without a reason."

Faedyn turned to head out. "But what is that reason? That's what troubles me."

They went into several other buildings, making a quick search of them. They found a few things seemingly left behind, some books, stoneware, wooden tools, and furniture, but everything of any real value was gone, as was every living soul who might have occupied those rooms in recent history.

"Perhaps they moved someplace else," Ken said, trying to come up with a rational explanation that didn't make him more nervous than he already was.

"Not likely," Namh said. "There is a sacred shrine here the elar would never abandon. The people of the White Mountains have been living here for thousands of years."

"Thieves then? Bandits?"

"Then what happened to the people?"

With more time, Ken could do a viewing and maybe find out something about what happened, but there wasn't time. And to be honest, his current mental state wasn't conducive to viewing. An anxious mind couldn't see past its own anxiety.

"Come," Faedyn said. "Let's check the Great Hall. I would rather make for the pass in the dark than stay here if there's any danger."

†

Namh feared what they might find in the great hall. She suspected the elar of Torselend were dead. Why or how or when she couldn't tell, but they had met some grim end. She felt it in her bones, a disturbing pang of ghostly whispers.

They stood on the wide, stone steps, looking up at the dark entrance of the great hall. The monolithic facade loomed tall overhead.

Their footsteps seemed loud as they climbed slowly to the entrance. Namh walked side by side with Faedyn. She looked to be sure Anna and Ken were close behind them.

Night was falling outside. The first stars began to shine behind high, wispy clouds. Standing on the portico and looking into the great hall was like gazing into the depths of an immense cave. Scant light filtered in from the dark-quick sky. No torches lit the interior. No globes of light illuminated its high vaults. The portico seemed, with all its grandeur, an entryway into a tomb. And as Namh remembered the deep mines below, she wondered if it was.

Crossing the threshold, Namh whispered a prayer to the spirit of the mountain, a prayer of protection, and held the Lamp of Lunara aloft, willing it to light. The oblong cage at the tip of her staff began to glow with a cool white light from within. She had not practiced this in some time, and it was a bit of a strain to maintain the light or to make it any brighter. Thus, at the moment, the legendary lamp wasn't much brighter than a dim torch.

Namh held the staff aloft. The light it cast reached only so far, a dim sphere, beyond which was still complete darkness. They couldn't see the lofty vaults, and what little they could see—a patch of the intricate mosaic floor, the shoulders of massive columns—made the umbrae of the shadows seem even greater.

They stepped forward cautiously. The hall appeared empty. Their footsteps echoed in the cavernous space.

"There's nothing here," Ken whispered. "Let's go."

But Faedyn walked a little further, leading them on. His eyes narrowed. Deep shadows played across his face. He listened intently, and seemed to sniff at the air. He felt it too, Namh thought, a strange presence that was too quiet and odd to be sure of. But if Faedyn felt it too …

Then, from the darkness beyond a row of columns to her right, Namh heard something. A scrape and a clicking sound. Faedyn's head snapped in that direction. Namh took a few steps toward the columns and held out her staff to illuminate the aisle beyond.

There was a shape at the edge of the lamplight. At first, she couldn't tell what she was looking at, but suddenly it moved and two glowing eyes appeared in the inky dark.

Startled, Namh stepped back and thrust her staff out, throwing light onto a terrifying sight.

The creature's body was covered with dark scales that seemed to puff out as it stood up from a crouch. It was the size of a man and vaguely shaped like one, but there the similarities ended. The plate-like scales on the top of its head folded back. The oblong pupils of its yellow eyes narrowed, deep within the wrinkled folds of ridged eye-sockets. A vicious mouth opened to reveal crooked rows of razor-like teeth.

All this in the briefest of moments. *Thip.* She heard a sound in the air and felt a painful sting in her abdomen. She cried out, stumbling backward.

"Namh!" Faedyn said, drawing his sword and stepping in front of her. But the creature retreated into the dark.

Namh looked down. A quill-like dart was stuck in her belly, and she could feel the tingling spread of poison radiating out from the point of impact. The dart tore at her flesh when she pulled it out. She threw it on the ground and covered the wound with her hand.

They heard the shuffling sounds of movement in the darkness all around them, and the guttural clicking sound of some utterly alien language echoed in Namh's ears.

Ken and Anna stood back-to-back and drew their swords.

"Go," Faedyn said. "Let's get out of here!"

But even as they started for the exit, their escape was blocked. A teeming horde of the creatures surrounded them, just beyond the reach of Namh's lamplight, which still shone dimly.

Darts hissed through the air, and Faedyn, Anna, and Ken were each hit several times. Namh's thoughts grew heavy.

Ken and Anna toppled over from the poison first, sinking to the ground and falling limp against each other. Faedyn blinked his eyes and brandished his sword. *Thip ... thip.* Another dart hit Namh in the small of the back, and several more hit Faedyn.

Namh fell. She felt her limbs stiffening and couldn't move them. She saw Faedyn, sword in hand, protecting Anna and Ken, who lay sprawled unconscious or dead on the floor. More darts flew out of the darkness at him. One thwacked into the side of his neck. He staggered and fell to one knee, stabilizing himself with his sword, swaying unnaturally. Namh's vision blurred. Then the Lamp of Lunara flickered ... and went out.

46

RULER OF MALEISTRIA

Kai stood in front of the empty throne of the emperor. Before him, filling the throne room, a full court waited, including a host of lords and nobles, most of whom had already accepted the practical application of his rule. In the time since Nykhil's death and Durok's flight from the city, Kai had taken on more and more of the executive responsibilities of running the city and the empire. After all, the Black Guard was at his command, and soon everyone else would be, as well. Why shouldn't they be? He was their natural leader.

Those who didn't respect him, clearly feared him now. That's why he made a point of having elite Black Guard soldiers visible from every point in the room.

"Hail, Lord Kai," a resounding chorus of voices greeted him.

Kai bowed, a grand gesture, and held up his hand in welcome. There was some cheering and chatter that followed. He was adorned in the finest clothes, custom made and carefully designed to display his authority and rise to power. They were not mere courtly clothes, made for gaudy banquets and debauchery. Instead, they showed a certain warlike spirit.

When the crowd had quieted, he spoke, assuming his full authority in the tenor of his voice. "My good friends," he said.

A deep silence fell over the room in anticipation of what Kai would say.

"As many of you know, my mother was Skorra, and in my veins is Emperor Drakhil's blood."

Kai paused dramatically to let this point sink in, clearly setting himself up as the legitimate heir to the emperor's throne.

"But I tell you, the age of the emperors is over." There was a murmur in the crowd. "From the beginning, the reign of the emperors has been marked by fear—fear of the past, fear of knowledge, and fear of our destiny. We have become no better than our brethren on Elara, hiding in their mountains and forests, forgetting their sacred duty as stewards of the earth.

"The Lords of Light put us on this planet for a purpose. That is what Lord Saziel fought for in the Great War. He is the true living father of our people, and his blood flows in my veins. And so, I declare myself prince, and ruler of Maleistria."

"Hail, Prince Kai!" Their voices resounded like beautiful thunder.

Kai drew Saraden from its sheath and held it high above his head. "Behold, Saraden, last blade of Alania, the sword of our ancestors. This is the beginning of our destiny. I will fulfill the promise of the Great War. There will be a new Earth, reborn from the ashes of the old. There will be a return to the glory of the world that was at the dawn of our history, a return to the world that is our birth-right. And our reign shall endure until the ends of the earth."

The crowd was stirred to a war-like frenzy. "Hail, Prince Kai. Hail, Ruler of Maleistria," they cheered. Kai listened to them, and smiled. He caught a glimpse of Sulki in the back of the throne room, watching, smiling. The whole scene was perfect—beautiful!

At last, he returned Saraden to its sheath, quieted the crowd, and sat solemnly on the great throne. He put his hands on his thighs, held his head high and his back straight, looking down upon the court. "And so," he said, as if making another proclamation, "without further delay, let us hear the day's reports."

One by one the people stepped before him, bowed deeply, hailed him as prince and ruler, and read their reports on everything from food production to the wars in the Outlands.

"Is there no news of Durok," Kai asked at last, "our royal brother in exile?"

"No, Prince Kai. There has been no word of him."

Kai sighed. It vexed him that Durok had managed to disappear so well. If he just knew where Durok was, he might manage to have him quietly killed. Perhaps the exiled son of a dead emperor was no longer a threat, but Kai would rather be sure of such matters. "Certainly," Kai said. "He still has spies within the city that inform him. Let it be known that he is outcast, a murderer and a traitor, stripped of his titles and sentenced to death if he returns to the city."

47

A Dark Prison

Anna's consciousness rose out of a black pit of nothingness. She awoke slowly. At first, she just had some vague sense of being, and then of breathing. Who she was came next, but nothing yet about what had happened. She was lying on something very hard, but she couldn't move her body. Her eyelids fluttered and opened.

It was dark. Somewhere the glow of torchlight flickered. She closed her eyes again.

A moment later, when she opened them a second time, a face hovered above her. It was a man's face, a human, but somebody she had never seen before. The details were difficult to make out. One whole side of the face was in shadow and the other side only dimly lit by the torchlight.

He had a bushy black beard and waves of thick black hair that hung about his face. His eyes were deepset between a furrowed brow and high, pronounced cheekbones. There was an urgent intensity to his look. And yet, for a moment, he smiled down at her.

She still couldn't move her limbs. She tried to say something, but her voice got stuck somewhere between her brain and her mouth.

"You'll be all right," the man said in Coram. "The effect will wear off soon."

What had happened vaguely came back to her, and a wave of fear accompanied the memories. She tried to say something again, tried to ask about Ken and Faedyn and Namh. It came out as a kind of mumbled moan.

"Don't worry," The man said. "Your friends will be okay. We're all okay … for now." His face receded into the darkness.

When Anna started to move, and tried to push herself upright with her arms, the man returned. He put his arm around her back and helped her sit up. He leaned her against a rocky wall so she could rest.

"Thank you," Anna said, speaking Coram.

The man sat nearby, and finally Anna was able to look around. They were in an underground chamber of some sort. All around was darkness and rock. The floor and the walls had been roughly cut, but were fashioned into the semblance of a small room.

On one side of the room, a wall of iron bars sealed them in. Beyond the bars, a larger room was adorned with crude furnishings. A single torch burned there, fitted into an iron fixture mounted on the wall.

Ken, Faedyn, and Namh were unconscious and lying on the ground nearby.

"They're all right," the man said. "The poison isn't fatal. It only induces sleep and paralysis. They each got hit a couple of times, but they'll be awake soon enough."

Anna touched her arm where the poison barb had pierced her. It was still sore, and her joints ached. She bent her knees, trying to loosen them up. "We're in prison?"

The man scratched at his dark beard. "A dungeon of sorts. I'm Baron."

"Anna."

"Where did they catch you?"

"We were in Torselend."

"You still are. Under it, anyway. The mountains here are riddled with mines and tunnels."

The others stirred—eyes blinking, struggling to move. "Take your time," Baron said to them. "There's no place to go."

†

"Where are we?" Faedyn said when they had all sufficiently restored themselves. They conversed in Coram, as it was the only language Baron spoke.

"Imprisoned in the mines below Torselend," Baron said.

Namh looked at Baron suspiciously. Her ice-blue eyes were piercing, even in the dim light. "What are you doing here in Torselend?"

"You mean aside from rotting in this cell? I'm a miner. I came into these mountains from Roethia to seek my fortune. There are jewels here you know, and gold."

"So you're a thief," Namh said.

"Listen, lady, or whatever you call yourself. The elar don't own these mountains, and they don't own the riches of the earth, either."

"But these are our mines," Namh said, "and our home above us."

"Take it easy," Ken said in English, clearly catching enough of the conversation to understand Namh's anger. "I'm sure he's not responsible for what happened to your people."

Baron clawed at his beard, puzzled by Ken's words, then went on in Coram. "Look, I was brought here, same as you, captured by those … those monsters out there. I've been in this damn cell for two months. What do I know about Torselend or your blasted mines?"

"Enough," Faedyn said, somehow managing to calm everyone down with a word, and bring them all back to the dangerous predicament they were in.

Faedyn stood up. He walked over to examine the bars that sealed them in. They were heavily bolted into the rock, the door secured with a formidable lock. Their weapons and gear were piled on a wooden table pushed against the wall on the far side of the room. He could think of no immediate way to reach them. There were two doorways out of that larger room. Both were just dark cutouts in the rock, leading to some other room or passageway.

Faedyn turned back to his fellow prisoners. "What can you tell us, Baron? What are those creatures that captured us? I have never seen anything like them."

"I don't know," Baron said. Then he turned his head to look at the wall, a pained expression on his face, reluctant to say more.

Faedyn was patient though. He waited quietly and it wasn't long before the need for company won out, and Baron began to talk.

"I came up to the mountains a year ago with a partner. We'd worked all kinds of schemes to make money, and when we heard tell of the gold and jewels to be found, we decided to have a go at it. We slaved away for six months in Roethian mining camps south of here. Then we decided to do a little prospecting on our own. We found a cavern and went deep into it." He paused and sighed, as if to collect his thoughts.

Baron looked again at the wall. "We saw strange things in that cavern. Visions … ghost worlds. I wondered if we were going mad, but we found jewels—oh, did we find jewels—and so we went further. But we went too far. My partner … he fell when a natural bridge collapsed behind me. He was swallowed up by the earth—gone in an instant. I couldn't go back, so I pressed on, wondering if I'd ever find my way out alive. I stumbled into this mine by chance.

"Those creatures … I don't know what they are. They were everywhere in the main shaft, a whole army of them. I managed to stay hidden for a few days, and I watched them. They were moving things, treasure mostly, but they weren't moving it out of the mines, they were moving it into the mines. It didn't make any sense. But I didn't care. I got what I could and tried to escape.

"They shot me with their poison barbs, same as you. When they first brought me here, there was another prisoner. One of the elar from Torselend. He said the creatures had come out of a natural cavern that connected with the mine. A doorway to another world. He said it shouldn't have been there. Said it was the end of the world. He went on about the Lords of Light, rambling like a madman, same as I'm doing now. Said there was a battle in the mines. With … the *skrati,* yes, that's what he called them."

"Skrati," Faedyn said. "That's an old word, a kind of demon that lives in the earth. Baron, what happened to the people of Torselend?"

"The battle was lost," Baron said. "The skrati killed them, every one of them, and dragged them down some hell hole deep in the mine."

Faedyn sighed and Namh bowed her head—to think of all those people lost.

"We have to get out of here," Anna said.

Baron huffed with an amusement clearly born of desperation. "You and me both, kid."

48

Demons of the Earth

Three of the skrati emerged from one of the dark doorways in the larger room beyond their cell. It was difficult to tell whether they had been there all along, watching them, or whether they had just arrived from elsewhere in the mines.

Namh watched them closely. Many strange beasts inhabited the world, possessing various degrees of intelligence, but nowhere in the great library at Andurin was there a description or picture that matched these creatures. She wondered if they really were demons.

The three skrati regarded their prisoners and spoke to each other in a bizarre language of clicking and breathy sucking sounds. Namh noticed the spiny barbs that jutted out from their forearms, just like the ones they had been shot with. It must be some natural predatory or defensive mechanism. For clothing they wore only leather belts, fairly crafted, from which hung pouches. Namh noticed some keys hanging from one of their belts.

The largest of the creatures examined the gear piled on the table in disarray. He pulled Namh's staff from among the packs and swords. The creature handled it deftly. One of the others said something. The skrati that held Namh's staff looked from the staff to Namh. He said something to her in his strange language.

Namh didn't answer.

The skrati tossed the staff back on the table and ruffled his scales, clearly irritated. He sucked and clicked at the others and stormed out. One of the others followed, leaving the skrati with the keys to keep guard. That was a mistake, Namh thought. The creature crouched down by the far wall and remained perfectly still.

Anna came over to stand by Namh. Despite herself, Namh was beginning to like the girl. She did have some elaran blood, after all.

"Where do you think they come from?" Anna said, her Coram wonderfully fluent.

"They are not from Elara, or from any of the earths we know of," Namh said. "Legends say that humans were not the only fledgling race to take root in the old earth. Perhaps they drifted into their own world too far back in the earth's history for even the elar to remember. Or perhaps they are from another world, altogether."

"But why would they be here?"

"Every world has cracks and seams in the constructs that define their boundaries. In troubled times, these places can become unstable. Arisu warned of this. There must be a rift in the boundary of Elara here. Perhaps these creatures stumbled into the mine from a cave in their own world."

Ken spoke up in halting Coram. "How are we … get out?"

"Be patient," Faedyn said.

"Yeah," Baron said. "You may be done for, anyway."

"Baron," Namh said, still at the bars studying their guard. "Have you deciphered any of their language?"

"Are you kidding me? Just the sound of it is enough to drive you insane."

"Do you have any plan to escape?"

"I was just getting around to that when they threw you in here. Lucky me, I stuck around."

"Well?"

"Look, they're obviously keeping me alive for a reason. We could stage a fight. One of you could threaten to kill me. When they step in to stop it, we'll jump them."

Namh laughed. "That won't work."

"Why not?"

"Because they've already decided to kill you tonight."

"What? How come they've kept me alive until now, then?"

"Because they like fresh meat," Namh said. She looked over her shoulder at Baron. "Of course, there's no accounting for taste."

Baron scowled. "Well, do you have a better plan?"

Namh smiled. She clicked and sucked in her breath loudly in an exact imitation of the alien language.

The guard stirred from his stone-like vigil. His scales perked up. He rose from his crouch and took a hesitant step toward the cell.

Namh clicked several times and exhaled. The guard crossed the room toward Namh. It was working.

The skrati guard said something. Namh mirrored it back to him perfectly. She moved her arms in a way that approximated his body movement. *Just a little closer.*

The guard stepped forward again. She would have no time to be subtle about this. But they were already locked up, so what did she have to lose?

One more step and … now! Namh shot her long leg out between the bars and hooked the back of the skrati's leg, then grabbed his throat between her thumb and fingertips. Her quick, decisive movements took the guard's balance. He toppled to the ground in front of Namh, his arms flailing up as he fell. Namh grabbed a spine that protruded from his arm, pulled it out, rotated her hand, and jabbed it into the soft flesh of the creature's armpit.

It took only a second, and Namh was crouched by the fallen guard, one hand softly covering his eyes, the other gently resting on his chest. She had a sweet, motherly look on her face. "Good night," she whispered, and the guard was out cold.

Before anyone could say anything, she had taken the key, applied it to the lock, and opened the door. She turned around and gestured to the open door. Anna smiled at her. Baron looked terrified.

"You could decipher that language?" Faedyn said, obviously impressed.

"Only a little," Namh said. "Hardly matters though. If you say it in the right way, some creatures will do almost anything."

Faedyn raised his eyebrows.

Namh shrugged. "I was a little wild in my youth," she said. "We're just lucky these skrati are as predictable as most men. Now let's get out of here."

They exited the cell and gathered up their gear, as quickly and quietly as they could. Baron grabbed the torch and stood impatiently by the door.

†

They went out the side door in single file, Baron leading the way through the cramped, narrow passageway, the ceiling just overhead. Faedyn followed, sword drawn and ready. They traveled quickly, shuffling down a maze of corridors. Baron paused at each intersection to make a quick calculation about which way to go next.

"I hope you know where you're going," Faedyn said.

Presently, their course brought them to a wide gallery with a high ceiling. Openings were cut through the rock wall, overlooking the grandeur of the main shaft below. The mine was lit by what seemed like thousands of torches. The shaft burrowed horizontally into the mountain, an immense, subterranean space, carved out of the rock over many long years. Its sheer size was difficult to encompass with the eye. On the far side, terraced levels were cut into the rock. In various places could be seen swathes of darkness suggesting the entrances to deeper shafts and tunnels.

Such an incredible sight might have lifted their spirits were it not for the skrati horde who swarmed about the shaft like an angry nest of ants. Anna could see how the people of Torselend would have been overwhelmed by the sheer number of them. They appeared a busy lot, parading in and out of subtunnels, and exploring the new land they had conquered.

"We'll never make it to the exit that way," Baron said. "We'll have to find another way out."

Suddenly a skrati climbed up from below and appeared in one of the openings. He shrieked in surprise and clicked frantically before Faedyn swung his sword up, cutting him across the torso and knocking him backward.

Hundreds of skrati heads looked in their direction, and a cacophony of clicking and slurping echoed through the mine. Some had spears, some had elaran swords stolen from Torselend, and all had poisonous spines jutting from their forearms. They started moving toward them en masse.

"Um … we have a problem," Ken said, drawing his sword.

"Run, you idiot," Namh said. "Everybody run!"

"This way," Baron yelled. "Follow me."

Another skrati leapt through the opening and charged at Anna. Ken jumped between them and stabbed the creature with his sword. It made a horrible screech and was still screaming when Ken kicked it backward off the point of his blade.

They ran, following Baron, flying down another wide corridor at full tilt. They came to a room where the carved floor of the mine had collapsed into a natural cavern. The hole was a dark, black opening, like a yawning mouth ten feet across. The bottom sloped steeply downward and was littered with rubble and rock. Baron leapt in.

The rest of them followed, scrambling downward as fast as they could in almost complete darkness. The sounds of the skrati giving chase began to fade away behind them.

Some twenty feet down, the passage narrowed and then opened up into a small room where Baron stopped. The air was moist here, and Anna felt a cool draft rising from the depths of the cavern. Small stalactites reached downward from the ceiling, and the floor was rough and wildly uneven.

"We should keep going," Faedyn said.

"There's time to rest," Baron said. "The skrati won't come down this tunnel. I hid out here for a week before I got captured trying to get out through the main shaft."

They stood there in the light of Baron's fading torch. Anna listened intently for any sign those creatures were coming in after them, but nothing came down the tunnel. Baron was right.

"What keeps them from coming down here?" Anna said.

"I don't know," Baron said. "Maybe something down here they don't like." The torch dimmed.

Baron crouched down, set the torch aside to burn out, and lit a battered oil lantern he found in the pile of gear he had stashed earlier. The latern lit, he carefully adjusted it to a dim glow.

Faedyn gestured to a hole at the far side of the room, "What's down there?"

"I didn't go further, for fear of getting lost again, or worse." He continued to gather a few other things from his gear—an oil flask, a few torches, rope, and three pitons. "Looks like now we don't have a choice."

49

The Oshii

They descended into another tunnel that continued downward. One at a time they made the steep descent into the passageway below. From there, they began to travel downward, hopeful of finding some alternate route to the surface.

With his lantern, Baron led the way, followed by Faedyn, Anna, then Ken, and Namh in the rear. They made slow progress at first. Having found their way into a natural cave system, the floor of the sloping tunnel was rough, uneven, and often muddy. In places, the walls closed in, forcing them to turn sideways to slide down and through. In other places, where the ceiling dipped low, they had to crawl on all fours to continue.

In no time at all, Anna was muddy and scraped up from head to toe. Ken had cracked his head half a dozen times on the jagged rocks of the ceiling, grunting and cursing each time.

After about an hour they descended into a large, long cavernous room that extended horizontally for further than the lanternlight revealed. Large stalactites hung from the high ceiling and massive stalagmites grew up from the floor. In some places, the formations had grown together, creating huge columns in the lofty, cathedral-like space.

Baron held the lantern aloft and they admired the grandeur of the natural cavern, studying the many side passages branching off from it. They looked for any sign of a way to the surface. Suddenly Baron jumped back a step, the lantern wavering wildly in the darkness.

"What's wrong?" Faedyn said.

"There ... there was somebody there," Baron said.

"Where?"

Baron stepped forward again, holding the lantern high. Above them, on the side wall was a sort of balcony. A number of passages opened onto it like so many windows with a view into darkness.

They followed Baron's searching gaze, until they all saw what Baron had seen—a pale, grey, humanoid creature about half the size of a man. It was naked, hairless, and sexless. For its slight frame, the head was disproportionately large and dominated by two huge, completely black eyes. It stood as still as the rocks surrounding it, a stillness that made it seem unreal.

Namh gasped, an expression filled with wonder, reverence, and awe.

Baron recoiled in horror, holding his lantern out as if it could ward off evil. "Somebody give me a weapon," he said.

"Shhh," Namh said. "You'll scare it away."

"There," Ken said, trying to use his Coram and pointing to another place high on the ledge.

"There's one there, too," Anna said. "What are they?"

"Oshii," Namh said.

"What?"

"The grey dwarves," Faedyn said.

Namh bowed toward the creatures, who still showed no sign of moving. "They are tunnelers, living in the space between worlds. They have not been seen in Elara since the boundaries of the three earths coalesced into separate spheres."

More and more of the Oshii appeared on the high ledges and alcoves of the cavernous gallery.

"They are only watching," Faedyn said. "We should keep moving. Perhaps one of these passageways leads to the surface."

Still and silent, the black eyes of the Oshii watched their nervous passage.

"Ahh!" Ken shouted, suddenly stopping dead in his tracks. Anna turned to see him stark white and staring at one of Oshii standing only a few feet away. Everyone stopped.

"It just … appeared there," Ken said, reverting to English. "He … he just walked right out of the rock." Ken stared into the creature's black eyes.

"Don't look at them for too long," Namh said, close behind him. "They will steal your mind."

Ken broke his gaze. "I can see why the skrati wouldn't come down here."

Anna was not afraid, though. She felt no threat from these mysterious beings. She felt certain they meant them no harm. But why did they show themselves? There must be a reason. What was it? She gazed into the black eyes of the Oshii, looking for an answer.

As she looked, the creature seemed to sway a little. They all seemed to be swaying, almost imperceptibly. Their black eyes were like windows into the vastness of space, a deep void in which all things were possible. Suddenly, she could hear them.

She could hear their voices in her head, speaking in unison, a kind of whispering, picture language of the mind.

"Anna, are you all right?" Namh said. Her voice seemed distant.

"I can hear them," Anna said. "They're speaking to me."

Namh put a concerned hand on her shoulder and looked from Anna to the Oshii.

"It's okay, Namh. They want to help us."

"What are they saying?" Faedyn said. Anna could hear the concern in his voice as well, but it too seemed distant. The whispers of the Oshii's telepathic messages were almost overwhelming. Yet she had a sense they were shielding her from the immense depths of their consciousness. How else could they make contact on a level she could understand, and that would not drive her mad? For even the slightest glimpse of the conscious minds beyond those whispers was an awesome, almost rapturous experience. She could lose herself so easily.

"Anna," Faedyn said loudly, the concern in his voice was suddenly desperate, but so far away. She had collapsed into his arms. Funny, she had not realized it. His arms felt strong and she was comforted. "Anna!"

She had to speak now. "Faedyn ... I'm all right." Her own voice seemed as distant and monotonous as the others, who had gathered around her.

Anna listened to the whispers of the Oshii and spoke. "The boundaries of this world have grown too thin here. Rifts have begun to open up into other worlds. It was not meant to be. The skrati are not meant to be here. These Oshii ... they are here to fix things, to make it right."

"What about us?" Ken said, trying again to keep up in Coram. "They want to help?"

"We must keep to our path, for many things yet to unfold will depend upon it. There is a way out, but we must go deeper to find it. There is a passage under the mountains. They have prepared the way, and have fashioned a boat for us."

"A boat?" Baron said. "That doesn't make any sense. We don't want to go deeper. We want to go up. Can't they show us a way to the surface?"

"That is not possible. They are going to collapse the mine and the caverns overhead. The skrati must not be allowed to stay here, for the sake of their world, as well as this one."

The Oshii were beginning to leave now, fading into the shadows and the rocks. Anna felt their voices receding. Their parting thoughts seemed more like a prayer than a goodbye, and then they were gone.

Anna woke as if from a hypnotic trance, her body still limp in Faedyn's arms. The faces of her friends looked down on her, the lanternlight flickering across their faces.

"I'm okay," she said.

Faedyn helped her to stand.

"I'm all right," she said. "But we should go now. Give me the lantern. I know the way."

"This is crazy," Baron said. "What if they're lying to us? What if they mean to lead us astray, to die beneath this cursed mountain?"

"What choice do we have?" Faedyn said. "Any tunnel we take may lead to our deaths."

50

A Long Descent

Anna led the way onward, at first with a certain hesitation, but gradually with a growing confidence that she really did know where she was going. Near the end of the great gallery, she found an inconspicuous tunnel through a crack in the rock, just wide enough for them to fit through.

"There are so many other tunnels," Baron said. "The bigger ones might be more likely to have an exit."

"Are you sure this is the right way?" Faedyn said.

Anna nodded, and stepped downward into the sloping, narrow tunnel. Faedyn followed, then Ken and Namh. Reluctantly, Baron came in after them.

The tunnel widened slightly a little way in, then angled steeply downward. Soon they were practically stacked up on top of each other, as they climbed downward using ledges and handholds to support their descent. The passage wound down like a wayward staircase, twisting and turning ever deeper into the earth.

At one point, they had to pound in a piton and fix a rope to navigate a long vertical drop. Later, they stopped so Baron could adjust the wick on the lantern and refill it with oil. Occasionally, other passages led off horizontally, or downward in other directions. But at each place, Anna seemed to know without thinking which way to go. It was as if the Oshii had implanted a map in her mind. She could not access the map consciously, and yet it showed her the way.

As the hours passed, though, a growing nervous tension began to build. For they all knew that with each step downward, they traveled further from the surface, from the light of the open sky, from fresh air, and from any hope of making it out alive. In such a place, doubt creeps in through every pore. What if Anna was wrong? What if Baron had been right? With each step they came closer to their doom, if doom is what awaited them. Surely there was no returning along the path they had come.

Even Anna was afraid they might never find their way out, and yet she had to lead them on. She believed what the Oshii had told her, and she just held onto that belief. She just held on and kept going.

†

Ken felt like they were approaching the center of the earth. That was far from the truth, of course, but they were deep enough that he had spent the last several hours seriously thinking he may die here. It was a sobering thought, and not one he enjoyed contemplating. There were still a lot of things he would like to do in life. He certainly never thought he would die in a dirty hole on another world trying to find a magic sword that could save the earth. It would be funny were he not so obviously in that hole, and so far beneath the surface that it was difficult to imagine finding a way out.

Finally, they reached the bottom of their descent, and as they emerged into a cavernous room, Ken saw something that made even this miserable fate seem bearable. The long ovoid room they entered was made entirely of white crystal. Huge translucent boulders carpeted the uneven floor. Giant shards transected the space, lattice-like, in various directions. Massive crystals grew from the walls and the ceiling all around them. They were inside an enormous geode.

The sight was so unexpected and beautiful, an almost impossible natural creation, that for a moment Ken forgot about death. For a moment, he forgot himself entirely. Awe swept over him. His head slowly panned, mindless, jaw agape. The others were equally amazed, and for almost a minute they simply stood there silently, in admiration of such beauty, and of the beauty of a life that could reveal such wonders.

They moved slowly through the crystal room, as if they had disturbed a secret the earth had kept hidden for millennia. They had to climb over and around crystals that would have been difficult to imagine without seeing them. Ken felt as if he were in a land of giants, or that he had been miniaturized by some wizard's spell, or some mad scientist's machine.

When they reached the other side, the room narrowed to a small exit, which they crawled through. There, an even greater wonder was revealed to them, something beyond Ken's wildest thoughts about the inner realms of the earth.

51

BERSERKERS

Kai's dreams about the dark depths of the Crypt intensified. He saw the Great Seal broken before him. The doors of the crypt opened, a yawning blackness beyond, from which voices whispered. Sometimes he would awaken in the middle of the night from these dreams and, as before, he would descend into the Crypt to stand before the Great Seal. He wondered at the marvels that must lie beyond it.

Sometimes Tyral would accompany him, but the mage said nothing now. He would only watch in silent worry. Kai asked questions about what lay beyond, but Tyral answered vaguely, insisting they really didn't know much, only that the first emperors had locked monsters within the Crypt, and that it must never be opened.

"They know more than that," Sulki told him later. "The mages know more than anyone about what lies beyond the Great Seal. Their ancestors, on the old earth, could harness vast energies, and they understood the power to control the forces of life itself. With this power, they fashioned giant warriors to fight for Saziel in the Great War. These are the monsters Tyral fears to speak of. With each evolution, they became more powerful, until a single warrior could raze an entire city to the ground. Those giants roamed the land, holy warriors, spreading fire and destruction, until the world broke apart in the chaos, and the three earths were drowned in water. They were born in the vaults of the Crypt, and some of the giants are entombed there, still alive, but asleep for millennia."

Kai nodded, and for the first time he understood his vision. Those holy warriors, those spirits of the earth must be awakened to fulfill the promise of the Great War. A new earth can only be born from the ashes of the old. There must be a cleansing fire, and a single earth restored to the natural harmony that existed when the world was young.

All in due time, he thought, quelling the rise of his impatience as he descended to the lower levels of the Crypt. There were other matters to attend to at the moment. Tyral had informed him that they had achieved success in making berserker troops from the fittest of their human slaves. "With this development," Tyral assured him, "we have created a new use for humanity. I have prepared a demonstration."

Kai replied, "We have always had difficulty getting humans to fight for us. They are weak, and if left unbroken, they have too many of their own ideas."

"I assure you, Prince Kai, these humans, if you can still call them that, do not care who they fight for, and we have been able to enhance their strength considerably."

They stood at the edge of a big stone pit, rectangular in shape, such as one might use to house wild animals. The walls were deep enough to prevent any escape. Inside were three Maleistrians. At one end of the pit was a wide steel door, sealed shut at the moment, but which could be raised to release the berserkers.

One of Tyral's assistants approached. "The serum has been administered, sir, and they are beginning to show signs of the reaction."

"Good," Tyral said. "You see, Prince Kai, the serum excites their nervous system into a state of almost uncontrollable frenzy."

Kai nodded his head, gesturing to the Maleistrians in the pit. "Who are these men?"

"They are criminals, deserters from the wars in the Outlands. They have already been sentenced to death."

"Arm them," Kai said.

"Excuse me?"

"Give them swords."

"Yes, I uh … guards, throw your swords into the pit." The guards nearby reluctantly drew their swords and tossed them into the pit. The men inside took them and looked up at Prince Kai.

"Fight hard," Kai said. "If you survive, I will free you."

The men gripped their swords with renewed vigor. They spread out and tried to stand ready, bracing themselves with what courage they had.

"Proceed with the demonstration," Kai said.

"Open the gate," Tyral shouted to his assistant.

The assistant threw a lever and the gate slid upward rapidly. The holding pen inside was dark.

Suddenly, three huge human males came charging out of the darkness, screaming wildly, their eyes crazed, their faces contorted in preternatural rage. They were naked and unarmed, but their teeth and nails had been filed into sharp points. Spells had been written on their bodies with black warpaint.

They moved with such swiftness, and such unpremeditated, fearless abandon, that the Maleistrians in the pit faltered back for a moment, their swords wavering.

In an instant, the berserkers were upon them. Two of the men were overwhelmed. The berserkers swept aside their swords, and leapt onto the men in a violent frenzy, bringing them to the ground, clawing at them and taking horrendous bites of flesh from their throats.

The third man managed to swing his sword as one of the berserkers rushed in, but he only caught a hand, severing it at the wrist. The berserker couldn't have cared less. He clobbered the man in the face with the stump of his arm, blinding him with streams of blood, and bit into him as if he would eat his very bones.

One of the other berserkers picked up the mangled corpse he had created and threw it against the wall, screaming in anger. He looked about for a brief second, and then attacked another berserker, tearing him apart. He roared, his face covered in blood. Then the last berserker charged in, a sword now in his remaining hand, and with a swift stroke, beheaded him.

With nothing left in the pit to kill, the last berserker looked up at Kai, the guards, and other observers. He had only one hand, so he dropped the sword and began clawing his way up the wall, grunting and panting.

"Don't worry," Tyral said nervously, "we are completely safe."

The guards moved toward the edge of the pit jabbing their spears down at the creature. The berserker grabbed one of the spears and fell backward pulling a guard into the pit. He killed the guard almost instantly.

By then, men had come with bows, and fired at least ten arrows into the monster. Still, he only died after he ran, screaming, head first into the wall so hard that it crushed his skull.

Kai and the others looked down on the bloody mess that remained in the pit. A hushed silence came over them.

Kai's expression had not changed at all. "Interesting," he said.

"You see," Tyral said nervously, "they go crazy with blood-lust. They will kill anything in their path. On the open field they would eventually exhaust themselves. Then, if still alive, they fall into a soporific state in which they are easily managed."

"I see," Kai said, nodding his head rather frankly.

Just then a soldier of the Black Guard shouldered his way through the crowd of mages. "Prince Kai?"

"Excuse me a moment," Kai said, and stepped aside to hear the man in private.

"My Lord, we thought you should know right away. Some of our spies have returned from the Outlands. They say Durok is raising an army there, rallying local warlords to his cause. They say he means to challenge your rule, my lord, and he will soon be ready to march on Maleistria."

Kai was angry, but it was not unexpected. "Send word to our distant armies to return home. We shall face Durok here, where our victory will be remembered forever." He turned back toward the pit. "Tyral," he said, "make me a legion of these monsters."

52

THE UNDERGROUND LAKE

Even Faedyn marveled at what they found, as they emerged into a cavern so vast they seemed to be outside, in a starless, pitch-black night. The lantern only revealed a seemingly endless darkness beyond the range of its light, but the quality of the air gave Faedyn the impression the cavern was truly immense. And at the bottom of a sloping rock field, they discovered the shores of a huge, subterranean lake. A boat was resting among the rocks at the edge of the water, just as the Oshii had said.

The boat was a large canoe-like vessel, similar to those used by the elar of the lakelands in the North. The skin was made of thick chula bark and its prow was ornamented with the head of a bird, ornately carved from whitewood. There were five seats inside. Some paddles, blankets, torches, and provisions had been left for them.

"This is a good sign," Faedyn said. "And lucky too, since we didn't resupply in Torselend. The Oshii have been true to their word. We may yet find a way out of here, but we'll need our strength. Let's eat and rest a while before crossing the water."

They prepared a light meal, huddled together around Baron's lantern. As they tended to their stomachs and their sore legs, an odd sense of everyday routine pervaded in this extraordinary place. Faedyn was glad for the break in the tension. Who knows what this next leg of the journey would hold for them, or if they would find a way out on the other side of the water, but for now, the group could rest, concerned more with the necessities of life than the inevitability of death.

Bellies full and wrapped in blankets, the others dozed off for a while as Faedyn stood vigil. Upon waking, they had another small meal.

Baron ate quickly and ravenously. "You know, I really have to thank you people," his mouth still full and chewing, "for breaking me out of there. I owe you one."

"It was in our best interests," Namh said.

"You're a difficult one to get along with, aren't you?" Baron said.

"What Namh meant," Anna said, "is that you don't owe us anything."

Faedyn smiled. "Come, let's ready the boat."

As they gathered their things and stowed them in the boat, the lantern began to dim. Baron adjusted the wick, filled it with lamp oil, but still it began to sputter. "Damn it!" he said, frustrated by his inability to get it going again, then increasingly worried. "Without this, all we have is a handful of torches and who knows if they will last." Finally, he grew desperate. "Come on ... come on!"

Without a word, Namh lit the Lamp of Lunara, its cool white light a stark contrast to the flickering amber glow of the failing lantern.

Baron stopped fiddling with the lantern and looked up at the illuminated end of Namh's staff, dumbfounded. "What the ... why ... why didn't you do that before?"

"And waste all your fine lamp oil?" Namh said. "Besides, it's not without effort."

"All right," Faedyn said. "Everyone into the boat."

†

As she stood at the shoreline, Anna could see the rocky bottom with crystal clarity. At the edges of the light, however, the surface of the water looked black, dark, and undisturbed. Some part of Anna wished they could leave it that way. Something about the lake frightened her, the stillness perhaps, and a sense of its awful depth.

Namh was already on board. Ken and Barron boarded and each took a seat in the middle of the boat. Anna took a breath, carefully stepped in, and joined Namh near the bow, where she could guide them according to the subconscious map the Oshii had implanted in her mind. Faedyn pushed them off, and jumped in at the stern.

They paddled out onto the dark water, without knowing how far it was to the other side. Namh held her light high over the bow, but Anna could only see so far. For a long time, all she saw was water in every direction, still as black glass. And all she heard were the ripples of the bow-wave and the rhythmic dipping of the paddles.

For a long time, they passed over the lake. Anna tired of looking out on a changeless view. For all they could see, the entire universe could be composed of nothing but water and darkness. So when Anna saw something out of the corner of her eye, she thought at first it was a trick of the mind.

There had been a flicker of blue light somewhere in the darkness beneath the surface of the water. Surely her mind was beginning to play tricks on her. But there it was again. It was a shimmering blue shape gliding through the darkness for a fleeting moment. Then it disappeared.

"Did you see that, Namh?"

"What?"

"There was something in the water."

"Where?"

Anna pointed, and they both scanned the water off the starboard side. Another shimmering thing appeared beneath the surface—a long, smooth shape that cruised around in a circle, shook briefly, and shot off into the dark. "There, did you see that?" Anna said.

"Yes."

"What was it?"

"I don't know."

Faedyn called up from the stern. "What's wrong?"

"There was something in the water," Namh said.

Ken looked back at Faedyn, but Faedyn didn't say anything, and they kept paddling.

Anna and Namh saw more and more lights and shapes in the water. Ken, Baron, and Faedyn saw them too, staring into the depths as they paddled.

Then, to the amazement of all, an impossible ambient light cast dim rays from overhead, as if light from a distant sun filtered down through so much water. And they began to see strange lights in the air, as well, floating and swimming around in the distance, shimmering silvery quick things, and great ponderous grey things. But all the while, they still floated on the stillness of the lake.

Anna clutched the bow and looked out with equal amounts of fear and awe at those strange sights above and below the surface of the water. Ghostly jellyfishes drifted by in the half-light, and strange tentacled creatures, hulking things, shuggled expectantly in the dark depths, barely visible. "Namh, what's happening?"

Namh's eyes were wide, and she looked up at the distant dim light of an alien sun. "It's the light of another world … beneath the waves of an ocean. This whole region is unstable. The boundary of our world has worn thin here."

"Keep paddling!" Faedyn shouted, startling Ken and Baron out of the paralyzed bewonderment that they had fallen into. Half in fear and half in duty they dipped their paddles into the black water once again.

Anna looked down. She tried to follow the movements of something huge and tentacled in the deep. It seemed to see their boat, and perhaps taking it for a morsel of food, began to ascend from the darkness toward them. Her voice shook when she tried to speak. "Faedyn, something's coming."

Everyone looked down and saw the creature rise. It seemed slow at first, because of the distance and its great size. But soon they saw a writhing leviathan swimming toward them, growing larger and larger. There was no time to do anything. Even if they paddled with all their might, they would never escape. Even if they dove overboard, it wouldn't change anything. They simply watched in horror, waiting for the end.

When the moment came, the colossal tentacles spread apart and a giant mouth opened to engulf the entire boat and them along with it. But the creature passed through them like a ghost. They went into the dark cavern of that gaping maw, through the very belly of the beast, and survived.

The monster arced overhead, big as a whale. It coiled its tentacles briefly, as if in confusion, the massive bulk of its flesh shimmering in the pale blue light, and then shot off again, back toward the deep.

It was a long strange trip across the water. All of them must have, at some point, been shaken to the core, and had some doubt or question about the nature of the reality in which they lived. But slowly, the window into that underwater world slid shut, and they were once again alone in a dark, cavernous void beneath the mountain. Beyond the glow from Namh's lamp, the total absence of light once again reigned, and there was no movement except their slow and steady paddling.

They finished the crossing in silence, for what more could be said of the things they had seen. At last, they came to the far side of the huge lake. Again, Anna knew intuitively where they needed to go, and she guided them ashore.

†

They disembarked and unloaded their gear onto the rocky ground at the edge of the water.

Faedyn dug into his bag. "We'll rest here and then continue. Drink as much you can and fill everything that can hold water," he said. "From here on, conserve every drop. If we have passed under the mountains, as the Oshii said, a desert wasteland awaits us on the surface."

They filled every container they had, and thus burdened, after a long rest, began their ascent. Anna found the passage she was looking for nearby, and they started a slow upward climb. The way up was not nearly as steep as the way down had been. The passages they followed angled upward gradually, and so it was a long way until they found the surface.

At last, they came to a large room where the air was drier and warmer. As they continued around a gentle curve in the tall chamber, they saw some natural light on the rocks. Finally, sunlight shone directly into the cave, almost blinding them with brightness. They stopped for a moment to allow their eyes to adjust, and all breathed a sigh of relief.

53

The Wastelands

A broad flat plain stretched to the horizon below. Along the base of the mountains, the plain was sage colored, but in the distance, it turned to a dull khaki. As far as the eye could see, there was no sign of water in the wide expanse. Surely some small streams must run down from the mountains, but they would dry up in the searing heat of the desert flatlands.

They had emerged by an outcropping of rock at the base of the mountains. When Anna looked back at the cave, she saw only an unassuming hole in the rock. Certainly, it betrayed nothing of the vast caverns below.

Faedyn dropped his pack to the ground. "We'll rest here today, and try our hand at some hunting. There should be some wild game at these higher altitudes."

"Shouldn't we press on while there's light?" Ken said.

"You can't travel the desert by day," Faedyn said. "The heat is unbearable. We'll travel by night until we reach the coastal range."

"How far is it?" Anna said.

"It could take a week to cross the desert. There should be a string of spring-fed oases just past the half-way point. If we're lucky, we'll find one."

"And if we're not lucky?"

Faedyn didn't answer. He just looked out over the seemingly endless sands.

"I am forever in your debt," Baron said. "A debt that one day I hope to repay, but I can go no further with you. I must return to Roethia. I'm afraid my family must think I'm dead by now."

"Take some food," Faedyn said. "You can see the way to the pass from here. It should still be clear for some time. With any luck, you will be home before winter settles in."

Baron accepted some food, said his goodbyes awkwardly, and started walking off. He turned back for a moment and said, "Farewell, and good luck to you all, wherever you're going." Then he turned and headed up toward the pass.

†

Their hunt was successful, and they feasted on fresh meat that afternoon. Then they slept for a while in the shade of the rocks, weary and sore from their journey under the mountain.

A gentle hand woke Anna at sunset. It was Faedyn. He looked down on her and smiled. "Time to go."

Anna stretched and looked up at the wide sky ahead of them. There was still a thin glow on the western horizon, and above, the stars were out in a sky that faded from dark blue to black.

They ate again before heading down into the desert below. A gibbous moon rose to light their way, hanging high and bright above the mountaintops.

Anna trudged along in the line, soldier-like and half asleep. The night air was quite cool, and she wished she had another jacket to put on.

The hours passed strangely at night. There was little to mark the passage of time or the change of scenery. Anna's whole world was on the ground just ahead of her feet.

As the night wore on, the ground leveled off and became sandy. The brush that grew on the mountainside thinned, until only a sparse scrub remained. Walking became difficult on the soft ground and every couple of hours they stopped to rest, take a little water, and empty their shoes of sand.

When dawn came, they were far from the mountains and surrounded by desert. Nothing lived there, save the thorny, scraggly bushes that could somehow survive the long droughts between occasional rainfalls, and the flies whose ceaseless buzzing started just after dawn.

The ground was parched, dry as old bones weathered by the sun, and the air itself was desiccated. Once the sun was up, it didn't take long for the heat to rise.

With their blankets, they fashioned lean-tos to shade them from the harsh sun, but nothing could shade them from the merciless heat. And nothing could protect them from the marauding hordes of flies trying steal the moisture from their skin, their mouths, and their eyes.

Nevertheless, Anna fell upon the hard ground, tried to cover her face from the flies and was soon asleep.

†

Anna woke to the searing heat of late afternoon. She squinted her eyes in the brightness. The ground shimmered in the distance.

Ken swatted at the flies that buzzed around his head. "It's so damn hot," he said.

Faedyn sat upright with his eyes closed, indifferent to the flies that crawled across his face. "Keep your mouth closed and breathe through your nose," he said. "You'll lose less water."

Ken was right, though. Anna couldn't believe the intensity of the heat. It felt like they were on the surface of an alien planet, unsuitable to human life. Her head ached, and it was difficult to think straight.

They waited, longing for the sun to go down, watching as it dropped toward the west. When it finally did, exploding, huge and red on the horizon before dipping out of sight, they took down their lean-tos and packed their gear. They ate what food they could, drank some water, and began another night of walking.

There was a kind of relentless horror to the trek that left them with no relief, no respite, no real rest. By day, there was unbearable heat, fitful sleep, and swarms of flies. By night, there was the cold and endless walking on the barren ground, when all one really wanted was to lie down and rest. And always, there was thirst. Faedyn rationed their water carefully. Their mouths were so dry, they could barely eat, and whatever they drank never really satisfied.

For three nights and three days they traveled like this, in an almost endless, weary silence. At dawn on the fourth day, Faedyn announced their water supply was running low. "We must find an oasis by dawn tomorrow, or we'll be in trouble. There should be one nearby."

54

For Want of Water

Their water was almost gone when they huddled under the lean-tos that morning with the hope of getting a little sleep. They would have enough to last another night of walking perhaps. After that, without finding water, they would die. They all knew it.

Anna drank a little from her canteen. The water was warm, but as it slid past her cracked lips and into her mouth, it felt like the essence of life itself. *Water.* She kept repeating the thought in her mind, as if by thinking she could produce more of it.

Only a few days ago, they had been in a boat on the underground lake. How she wanted to dive into that lake now and drink from it with abandon. All that water, and all they had wanted at the time was to see the sun. Now they hid from the sun, and there wasn't a drop of water to be found.

When this thought occurred to her, Anna started to laugh, softly at first, but then louder and louder as if the laughter built on the sound itself. Soon she was laughing loudly, and by then she wasn't even sure what she was laughing at, only that it was ever so funny.

Ken looked at her, stonefaced and worried. But it only made her laugh more.

Faedyn came over and put a hand on her shoulder. She stopped laughing almost immediately. Something about Faedyn's touch. "Anna," Faedyn said. "Are you all right?"

Anna blinked her eyes, trying to remember what had been so funny. It worried her that she couldn't remember. They were all so tired and thirsty. "I'm okay," she said.

"Drink a little more water," Faedyn said, "and try to get some rest."

Anna laid her head down on her pack, closed her eyes, and listened to her labored breath. Inhale … exhale. Eventually those breaths would just stop. She wondered what it was like to die of thirst.

†

Anna dreamt. She was in the old apartment she lived in with her mom. It was so much nicer than the dive she had lived in by herself. And there were many wonderful things there that brought back good memories. Bright colorful pictures she drew in art class were tacked to the refrigerator with magnets shaped like little fruits. Afghans her mother crocheted were folded over the back of the couch.

On the coffee table was a photo album with pictures from their last trip to the beach. Her mom had taught her how to body surf in the salty waves. She was afraid at first, but then it had been so much fun. She remembered the feel of her mother's arms grabbing her and holding her close, just as a giant wave came crashing into them. Her mom smiled down at her. Her wet face beaming with happiness, her eyes sparkling like the water in the afternoon sun. Anna remembered the tangled tresses of her long wet hair, and the feel of her body pressed against hers, soft, and slick as a seal's in her tight swimsuit.

The sun was shining in through the window in the kitchen. It was such a pretty light. She had just poured a huge glass of water and she drank it all in one go, chugging down the clear liquid and relishing every wet, delicious drop of it. It tasted so good, and was so satisfying. She took a deep, healthy breath and exhaled every troubled worry from her mind.

Her mom wasn't home from work yet, and Anna would sit on the floor and read to pass the time. She looked forward to her mom getting home. They would make dinner together and then play a game. Boggle was her favorite. She could still recall the noise of shaking those crazy cubes, and the sound of their pens, writing furiously as sand poured through the hourglass.

Her mom arrived home as usual, a little after six, but right away Anna knew something was wrong. She was quiet all through dinner, and so Anna was quiet too, picking at her food with her fork.

"Aren't you going to eat any more?" Mom said.

"I'm not hungry," Anna said.

"Me too." Mom cleared the table. Usually that was Anna's job, but her mom did it with such authority that Anna just stayed at the table, sitting silently.

Her mom emptied the dirty dishes into the sink without washing them. Finally, she turned around with a look on her face Anna had never seen before, a look so charged with emotion, so filled with loving anguish, that Anna nearly started crying before a word was said.

"Anna, we have to talk."

They sat on the couch together, and somehow, even without knowing, Anna felt what was coming. She looked down at her mother's hands as they held hers.

Her mom took a deep breath. "I went to the doctor today," she said.

Anna was silent, her own small hands rested in her mom's.

"They said I'm sick, honey."

"What's wrong?" Anna said without lifting her head, her voice weak.

Her mom struggled to speak. "They say … they say it's cancer."

†

Ken drifted in and out of sleep that day. His breath was shallow, and he slumped under the shade of the blankets, half conscious. He could feel his own body beginning to break down, and he worried about Anna. She slept so deeply today that it frightened him. So he sat near her head, waved the flies away from her face, and made sure she kept breathing.

Faedyn and Namh slept on and off through the heat of the day. Faedyn went out into the hot sun three times, each time jogging off in a different direction. The last time, Ken watched him in half-dazed disbelief. A while later he returned again.

"Anything," Namh said.

"Nothing," Faedyn said.

Ken drifted off to sleep again. There had to be something he could do. There had to be some way to find water. There had to be, because soon they would die without it.

55

BATTLE FOR MALEISTRIA

Prince Kai, ruler of Maleistria, sat on his throne. The throne-room was empty, except for the Black Guard stationed at the doors. His heart seemed heavy, and his thoughts deep, unwordable.

He recalled making love to Sulki in the night. Such passion, such sensuous, unadulterated pleasure. Their entanglement, their movement, their desire, was the genesis of a new world.

They stood on the balcony afterward, satiated, the sweat on their bodies drying in the cool air. The lights of the city were numerous and bright. The fires at the gate had been stoked. The city's forges burned around the clock and there was ceaseless activity. Everywhere the people were preparing for war. Even beyond the walls of the city, the fires of camps could be seen for miles, of warlords and tribes who had answered his call or the threat of his sword.

There, in the Crypt, Tyral's work continued. He had emptied the slave-pits of strong males and conditioned them for the berserkergang. They built solid-walled cages onto wagons, with which the berserkers could be positioned and deployed. And for each unit, they had trained handlers from among the ranks of apprentice mages.

His spies sent word that Durok had managed, in a short time, to assemble a massive army, capable of matching his forces. Durok claimed to be the rightful emperor of Maleistria and promised to reward those who followed him with all the spoils of war: land, wealth, titles, and slaves.

The nobles of the city, and the captains of Kai's armies rallied around him. They were ready for battle. This was a world of almost endless warfare, but not in many long years had open war been fought so close to the city.

Kai looked off to where the sea crashed against the rocky shores. Only there could he rest his eyes on a darkness that stretched as far as his eye could see. *Peace,* he thought. That was why they must fight this war, and the war to come. It was only the beginning, but he would make such a beginning as would be remembered until the end of days. He would not risk a siege. He would fight Durok's army on the open field, outside the city walls.

A messenger of the Black Guard entered the throne room and bowed before him. "My lord, Durok's army approaches."

"Send word to my captains. Move our forces outside the wall. Leave only some archers on the battlements, and a small contingent of the Black Guard inside the city."

"Yes, Prince Kai."

"And fetch my armor."

†

Kai stood on the battlements in all his war-gear, surveying his lines of infantry, twenty thousand strong. Archers had been placed on the flanks and between the battle groups. Behind his rear battle group, in front of the gate, a wedge of berserker wagons had been wheeled into place. Their handlers were posted nearby, armed with the potent serum, and pre-pared to turn them loose if needed.

The field was hemmed in on the sides, by the sea on the one hand, and by rugged hills on the other. Durok would be forced to face them head on.

By late afternoon, Kai watched Durok's army moving into position. They were roughly matched, his scouts estimating at least twenty thousand infantry men, plus archers and some cavalry, but every one of them was a battle-hardened soldier, veterans of wars in the Outlands. Durok's men were drawn together from different armies, though, and perhaps not well organized. That had yet to be seen, but many of the troops in his own rear battle groups, however well trained, would be seeing their first large battle.

Durok would be eager for bloodshed, and would not likely wait for morning to attack. Kai descended from the battle-ments and rode his black horse to the front to make a showing for his men.

Storm clouds rolled in from a darkened sea. Kai drew Saraden and held the sword high above his head, in sight of all. Lightning flashed, and Prince Kai shouted above the rolling thunder. "People of Maleistria, the power of your ancestors is with you!" A roar rose among the crowd from his elite troops. "Fight for them, for this land, and for this earth that is your home." Another roar was raised from the ranks, even louder than before.

Kai pulled on the reins of his horse, who reared up against a flash of lightning. "Your destiny is at hand!" And the roar of thunder and twenty thousand men was heard.

Kai rode up and down the ranks, Saraden held high, bol-stering the spirit of his army. Lightning flashed again, thunder rolled, and it started to rain. But the valiant soldiers of Maleistria paid it no mind. They were ready, and eager for war.

In the depths of the palace, Sulki sat, muttering and chanting in a cataleptic trance. Her eyes rolled back. Her teeth chattered. She saw the umbra of the outer darkness roll in like an inky shadow. She reached out, casting fear and doubt into the hearts and minds of Durok's army.

Kai rode to the rear, dismounted, and climbed to the battlements once more, ready to orchestrate the battle. "Spread word among the men," he said to the first of his messengers. "They are to draw no quarter, take no captives, show no mercy for this petty band of brigands who would defy us."

They waited, grim faced in the rain, until the time came, and the enemy started to advance. They came slowly at first, shouting their war cries, rattling their spears and shields.

As Durok's troops came into range, Maleistria's archers fired the first volleys into their midst. Arrows darkened the sky, carving their arcs, messengers of doom. Many enemy soldiers fell, but still they came, a relentless mob, hell-bent on war.

A distant wailing horn sounded in the growing darkness, and the vanguard of Durok's troops charged.

The deep, bellowing horns of Maleistria sounded in reply, and Kai's elite soldiers ran to meet them head on. The two armies clashed in a thunderous collision in the middle of the field.

Durok's cavalry charged their left flank, but were repelled by arrows and spearmen who held their ground. The horses were in a panic, and they retreated in disarray, right into the advancing enemy infantry.

The fighting became fierce. There were several more charges by enemy formations, and the two armies pressed against each other in a gruesome melee of death and carnage. From the battlements on the city wall, Kai watched, and listened to the distant rattle of wood and steel, to the screams of the wounded, and to the roll of thunder.

"Send word to the mages below. Ready the berserkers."

Archers, out of arrows, joined the fray, killing with short swords or whatever other weapons they could find. At the center of the field, fresh soldiers were forced to fight on the bodies of the fallen. Those that weren't dead already were trampled and suffocated. In places the armies fought atop heaps of bodies, yet they could not break through the lines of Durok's army.

The head handler signaled to Kai from below. The berserkers were ready, foaming at the mouth, shaking with rage in their dark cages. Kai raised his hand, looked out on the battlefield, and lowered it, releasing the terror they had created.

Those mutant men, naked, painted with spells, and armed with heavy maces, were set loose. They tore through the field with a savagery impossible to describe, killing anything and everyone in their path. They smashed through the line, dying without care, killing without thought, and charged on in their murderous rage, into the remaining ranks of the enemy lines, and into the dark distance.

56

Arrows in the Sand

Anna blinked open her sticky eyes, looked out, and thought Ken had finally lost his mind. Evening was approaching, but the temperature hadn't dropped yet, and Ken was sitting out in the sun, cross-legged, doodling in the sand with his finger.

Anna's next thought was perhaps she had lost her own mind. She blinked her eyes, but he was still out there. "Ken," she called out to him, her voice hoarse and weak. "What are you doing?"

He didn't reply, just kept doodling in the sand.

Faedyn stepped into view, peering into the lean-to from outside. "He's looking for water."

"Are you sure?"

"In his mind. He's looking for water in his mind."

Perhaps she really *had* lost it. Anna crawled out from under the lean-to and pulled herself to her feet. She took a few steps toward Ken. Faedyn followed her.

"I don't know why I didn't think of this before," Ken said, as excited as one could be under the circumstances. "There's definitely water out there. I saw it." He had drawn wavy lines in the sand, and written words like water, pool, wet, muddy.

Suddenly Anna got it. He was doing his little viewing trick. "Where, Ken, where is the water?"

Ken looked discouraged. "Well, I don't know exactly."

"I'm not sure that helps then."

"What we need is a direction," Ken said.

"Distance is also important," Faedyn said. "If the water is much more than a day's walk, we'll be dead before we get there."

"Okay, I have an idea," Ken said. "I'm going to make three independent observations of the target, focusing on the closest source of water. For each viewing I'll draw an arrow in the sand. But I don't want one viewing to influence the next so I'm going to close my eyes. Before each one I want you to turn me around so I don't know which way I'm facing. Just make sure I'm in front of a clean patch of sand."

It sounded crazy. "Will that work?" Anna said.

"I don't know," Ken said. "But the way I figure it, we don't have much to lose."

"Try it," Faedyn said.

Ken closed his eyes. Anna took him by the shoulders and spun him around a few times. He staggered a little, until it was quite clear he had no idea which way he was facing. With his eyes tightly shut, he dropped to his knees in the sand and was still for almost a minute. Then he reached out and drew an arrow in the sand, pointing off in a slight angle from the direction they had been going.

Anna helped Ken to his feet again, his eyes still tightly shut, and spun him around a second time. Ken knelt down, concentrated for what seemed like a long time, and then drew another arrow in the sand. The arrow pointed off wildly in another direction, perpendicular to their line of travel. Anna made a silent face at Faedyn.

"Now the third one," Faedyn said.

One last time, Anna helped Ken up and spun him around. This time, as he knelt in the sand, Ken drew an arrow that pointed in exactly the same direction as the first arrow.

Finally, Ken opened his eyes to examine the arrows. "The last one is the same as the first," Anna said.

"That's a good sign," Ken said. "I would do more, but unfortunately the longer I do this the more inaccurate my observations are likely to become."

"It's good," Faedyn said. "We'll try that direction. The moon will be almost full tonight, so we'll have a good chance of spotting vegetation, rocky outcroppings, or any other possible sign of water."

Ken dug into his pocket. "We'll need to follow that direction as precisely as possible." He pulled out a small foldable compass, and opening it, dropped to his knees again by the first arrow. He put the compass in the sand and turned it. "If we just follow this bearing, we'll know we're on course."

"Did you carry that all the way from the city?"

"Yeah," Ken said, half laughing at the absurdity of it. "I threw it in my pack before we left. I totally forgot about it until today, but I guess it was a good idea after all."

†

When the moon rose, they set off again following Ken's compass bearing. Traveling at a pace half of what they had managed on previous nights, they staggered forward, exhausted and dehydrated. They drug their feet in the sand, too weary to pick them up. Once, Anna fell to the ground. She didn't know if she had tripped or fallen asleep. Namh was behind her, and helped her to her feet, mumbling something she didn't understand.

Periodically, Ken stopped to check his compass, and with her head down or looking for signs of water, Anna occasionally walked right into him. They spoke little or not at all. They all knew what shape they were in, and what their chances were if they didn't find water. Faedyn kept reminding them to keep an eye out.

Sometime in the night, they drank the last of their water. It wasn't much. Anna opened her mouth and inverted her canteen above it, waiting for one final drop that never came. She prayed silently, because it was all that was left to do and it helped to keep her mind from worse thoughts. *Please God, let us find water.* Then she put one foot in front of the other, walking on, into the seemingly endless night.

When the glow of dawn appeared in the east, it had a look of doom. As tired as she was and without water, Anna dreaded the rising of the sun. She dreaded the day, and the merciless heat, and wondered how much longer they could survive.

The light drifted upward in the sky. The stars faded, and the sun began to climb. Ken trudged on, urging them forward, eager to find the water of his vision, and for a while they walked on into the morning. But it was no use. It was already beginning to get hot.

"We'll camp here," Faedyn said.

Ken stopped, turned. "It can't be much farther. Just a little farther and maybe we'll find it."

"We can't keep going in this heat," Faedyn said. "We'll rest here until sunset and then try again."

They struggled to erect the lean-tos, and then crawled under them and collapsed.

†

Everyone except Ken fell fast asleep. Although Ken was exhausted, and his thoughts addled by dehydration, he couldn't sleep. He kept looking at his compass, and out across the sand and rock.

He couldn't help feeling that he had let everyone down, that if they died here, he was responsible. They had followed his heading, but found no water. He looked at Anna where she lay sleeping. It must be just a little further. It had to be. He had to find it.

Ken crawled out from underneath the lean-to, and stood up in the bright, mid-morning sun. He consulted his compass, summoned all of his strength, and walked off.

He took nothing with him. If he didn't find the water soon, he wouldn't need anything, anyway. The truth is, he wasn't thinking too clearly, and somewhere in the back of his mind he knew that this could be the last mistake he would ever make. But it just had to be there. It had to.

The hot sun beat down on him. He could hear his shallow breathing as if each breath were a monumental effort. He shuffled onward, body bent, eyes narrowed in the blinding light.

He had walked for no more than an hour when he came to some low-lying rocks. Crawling up onto them, he discovered a narrow canyon that cut into the earth, invisible from any distance. And as he peered down into that canyon, he saw life. In the shadows of the canyon walls were green plants and small trees, and birds flittered here and there among the rocks. And below that, at the very bottom of the canyon was water, a beautiful pool of blue water.

He was too exhausted and hot to do anything but smile, and he almost laughed a little. It was just like his vision. The pool was a long way down though, and it would take time to find a route. He thought of the others back at camp. If he slipped and fell on the way down, they might all perish. Every cell in his body cried out for water, but he took a breath and turned back, determined to share that drink with Anna, Faedyn, and Namh.

The others were still asleep when he pulled the roofs of the lean-tos aside. They hadn't even noticed he was gone. They looked at him as if he were crazy, as if the sun had cooked his brains. "Water," he said. "Water!"

They looked at him silently, blinking their eyes, and with the kind of patience one bestows upon a child. *How sad,* their silent faces seemed to say. *Yes, we need water. Now lie down like a good boy so we can get some rest.*

"No," Ken said. "I found water. I found it! Get up."

They clearly didn't know what to think. Of course, it would be nice if that were true. They wanted to believe it. But that was impossible. How could he have found water when they had all just been sleeping there? *He must have had a dream. Poor boy can't tell the difference anymore.*

"Get up, I tell you," Ken said. "I found water. I went off while you were sleeping. It's not far. Get up."

They began to move at last. "Are you sure?" Faedyn said.

"Yes, I'm sure. Believe me."

They packed everything quickly and Ken led them off, again following his footsteps. The others trudged on behind him. "You're positive you found water?" Namh said.

"Yes, I'm sure. It's not far." He was so happy the heat barely seemed to touch him. Only in the last ten minutes of walking did he begin to wonder. Did he really find water? Perhaps he had just imagined it, a mirage in the sand. Maybe he really was leading everyone to their deaths.

But at last, they came to the rocks he had seen, and there was the canyon, just as he remembered it. To his great relief, the others saw it too. They looked down at the green foliage, the birds, and the beautiful pool of water and rejoiced.

They quickly found a way down. The temperature dropped as soon as they got below the lip of the canyon. They descended a shady, rocky slope along the wall of the canyon. Ken could feel moisture in the air and breathed deeply. How incredible that such a drastic change could exist, that so much life, so much water and cool air could exist in the furnace of the desert above.

When they reached the bottom, they lowered their heads to the pool and drank. They laughed, relaxed, and drank as much as they could.

†

For two days they stayed at the oasis, recovering their strength. They napped in the cool shade, swam in the pool, and washed their clothes. Anna spent hours watching the tiny white butterflies that gathered on the rocks by the water, and the birds that flittered about in the trees. They ate fresh meat from a three-foot water lizard Faedyn caught. And they slept through the night, out under the stars that twinkled high above the edge of the little canyon.

They were happy just to be alive, and the place seemed like paradise. Nobody mentioned how Ken had wandered off into the desert alone. It had been a foolish thing to do, but they were all too pleased with the result to say anything.

They could not stay forever, though. Their need for water had been satisfied, and their want of rest had been granted.

They had been granted some moments of real peace, a deep happiness born out of simple things—to drink water, to eat food, to rest in comfort, and to be among friends.

Nevertheless, the great purpose of their journey was now close at hand. They would have water enough to reach the coastal range. And there they would find the ruins of Alha'na.

When she slept now, Anna dreamed of Rayaden, that ancient sword of the elar. She saw Lord Elgard, his face handsome and dignified, reaching out across time, holding out the sword for her to take. He said, "It belongs to you now, my daughter. You must discover its secrets and fulfill your destiny."

57

THE COASTAL RANGE

The air was cooler, and water and wild animals were abundant in coastal range, desolate as it was. Grass and scattered oaks grew on the hills. Streams trickled through the valleys. Herds of deer roamed the landscape, and hawks swooped overhead.

To the west, a single dark mountain loomed above the hills. The distant summit of its broad conical mass was enveloped in a wispy haze.

"There," Faedyn said, pointing. "That's Yagul's mountain."

In the morning, the mountain was shrouded in mist, veiled in a white fog that faded into the western sky. As the day wore on, the mountain revealed more and more of itself, until it stood dark and imposing against the sunset. They camped in sight of it in the afternoon. At that hour it was a grey, mono-lithic mass that dominated the horizon, rising above all the surrounding hills.

Faedyn insisted Anna and Namh rest, while he and Ken went hunting for deer. He was unusually adamant, and Anna thought Faedyn must want to talk with Ken alone. As childish as it was, she was jealous. She felt close to Faedyn, and she wanted to be the one to go hunting with him. It irritated her that she and Namh were left at the camp.

Namh sat by the fire they had started and began to comb out her long hair. Ever since their escape from Haigar, Anna had admired Namh. She could be cold, and even abrasive, but she had a good heart. It only took falling off a roof and spraining her ankle to realize it, but she was strong, smart, and beautiful too.

She went over and sat by Namh. "Doesn't it bother you that they left us here at camp?" Anna said.

"No" Namh said. "I've had enough walking for today. Of course, I don't really care for hunting either. Do you like to hunt?"

Anna thought about it. "Not really. I always feel bad for the animal."

"Then relax," Namh said. "If you want, I'll get those snarls out of your hair."

Anna sat, looking west toward the great mountain, while Namh worked her long fingers through her tangled hair. It seemed to soothe every ache and pain she felt in her body, and to ease every tension in her mind and spirit. Her mom used to comb her hair like this, and when she did, Anna felt she could tell her anything. She could speak the things that troubled her, whatever they were, all the things that were otherwise so hard to say.

Anna spoke, her voice soft and thoughtful, as she gazed off at the distant mountain. "I killed someone once, in the city."

Namh listened, and continued to comb through Anna's hair.

"He was going to hurt Mouse," Anna said. "I was so mad, so angry. I hit him in the head with a pipe and he died."

Namh said, "Sometimes we wish things hadn't happened the way they did. Not because we were bad people, even when we're less than perfect, but because now we have to live with what happened."

"What bothers me the most is I wanted to kill him. It just pushed me over the edge. In that moment, I lost myself in anger. He had to be stopped. I know that, and I could do it again if I had to, if there was no other option. But maybe there was some other way. I don't know ... but I know I don't ever want to feel like that again."

"There is always a chance to find forgiveness. But we cannot live in the past."

"Do you forgive me?"

"Of course I do, Anna. You were brave to protect your friend."

She smiled. "Thank you, Namh."

†

Faedyn and Ken walked across a shallow, grassy vale. Their bows were strung and held lightly in hand.

"Ken," Faedyn said. "You've proven quite resourceful on this journey. You're not bad with a sword, and you've become quite good with a bow as well."

"Thank you," Ken said, feeling fairly proud of himself.

"Do you believe in the future, Ken?"

"What do you mean?"

"A war is coming, not just between Roethia and Drighton, but a war for the earth itself, for all three earths."

"Yes, I know," Ken said. "I saw all that in a dream when we were in Andurin."

"Then you know what is at stake."

Ken nodded. They crossed a small stream at the bottom of the vale. They continued to talk as they walked on, conscious of each other, and listening, but looking ahead at the open terrain.

"Anna is special," Faedyn said. "Your master, Smith, knew that. Didn't he? But it's more than just her psychic potential. As a wielder of Rayaden, she is heir to a power that goes back to the old earth, and to the dawn of our people. That power can turn the tide of the future."

"What do you want me to do?" Ken said.

"Just be ready. We must do whatever is necessary to protect Anna and bring back Rayaden. And if anything happens to me and Namh, you must get her safely back to Andurin."

"I'll be ready," Ken said.

As they climbed the far side of the vale, two deer appeared ahead, eating grass. "You take the shot," Faedyn said.

Ken nocked his arrow and pulled his bowstring, pushing the bow forward. For a moment the whole world seemed taut, and then he let his arrow fly.

†

They ate well that night, and relaxed afterward, sitting around the fire. The logs they threw on were consumed in flame, and the fire crackled and popped. Showers of sparks drifted upward in the night. Crickets chirped loudly in the grass beyond the firelight.

Faedyn spoke. "When we find Yagul's lair, we'll try to take Rayaden without a fight, but that may not be possible."

All were silent, watching the orange flames flicker upward, feeling the press of the heat on their skin.

"Yagul is a dangerous creature," Faedyn continued. "He is not a dumb brute. He is highly intelligent, and his natural weapons are formidable. But like any creature, he has his weaknesses."

58

Duel of Princes

After the berserkers had broken through the line, Kai's rear-guard troops surged through, sending the rest of Durok's army into disarray. The fighting continued, but it wasn't long before the enemy faltered.

Kai sent cavalry groups into the scattered enemy with devastating effect, and soon the battle was won, the enemy routed. The few berserkers who remained alive had collapsed in utter exhaustion and fell into a vegetative state among the heaps of dead.

His soldiers gave chase through the night, and the following days, slaughtering everyone they came upon. But it was a captain, returning late with his troops from the hinterlands, who finally caught up with Durok. He was captured alive, delivered to the Black Guard, and brought before Prince Kai in his throne room.

A multitude had gathered around the edges of the room to see Kai's judgment dispatched, to witness the end of a dynasty. Kai sat slouched on his throne, as if merely to look upon Durok alive was a great disappointment to him.

Tyral was at Kai's side to read a list of crimes. "You are a murderer and a traitor to Maleistria. You masterminded the assassinations of Emperor Drakhil and of your brothers, Princes Malfot and Nykhil. You raised a foreign army and attacked the city of our ancestors. You have lost in battle, and yet still you refuse to acknowledge Prince Kai as our rightful ruler. How do you answer?"

Durok spat at Kai's feet, and said nothing.

Thei and his Black Guard soldiers began to draw their swords, but Kai raised his hand to stop them, a calm, dispassionate look on his face. A murmur spread through the crowd. "He is entitled to his opinion," Kai said, and there were a few hesitant laughs among the people.

Good, Kai thought. It was not enough to kill Durok. He must make an example of the fallen prince. He must leave no doubt about the authority of his rule.

"Give Durok a sword," Kai said. "Perhaps he can speak better with a blade than his mouth."

Thei stepped forward to protect him. "My lord?"

"You heard me," Kai said. "Give him your sword."

Thei drew his sword, and with great hesitance, stepped forward slowly to obey Kai's command.

A murmur of confusion rose up in the room, and Durok looked confused most of all, as Thei approached him, offering the sword.

Kai threw off his heavy cape. "Let him test his fate against my sword," Kai said. "It's the least I can do for a former prince of Maleistria, however fallen from grace."

Thei backed away quickly after handing Durok his sword, and the collective murmur rose up again as the crowd took a few steps back.

Kai stood, breathing softly, taking in everything, Saraden still in its sheath at his side.

Durok tightened the grip on his sword, his body tensed. His face flushed, growing with anger, conflicted between the sense that this chance was an insult, and a determination to take every advantage of it to kill Kai.

Suddenly Durok sprang forward with a shout, swinging his sword overhead.

Kai showed no sign of concern. He turned out of the way of Durok's sword at the last moment, and passed Durok so closely that he rolled off his shoulders. Durok turned to face him again.

As the two parted, Kai's hand found the hilt of his sword, and Saraden made a beautiful, almost musical sound as the white blade sprang from its sheath. Kai stood still then, Saraden raised in his right hand, his left hand still at his side, his eyes downcast and calm.

Durok attacked again with a flurry of multiple sword strokes. Kai moved smoothly, perfectly coordinated with the attacks, glancing Durok's blows off his sword. He was playing with him, feeling Durok's sword, his arm, the movement of his whole body, his anger, and his twisted soul, all through Saraden's blade.

Finally, Kai deflected one last blow, stepped to the side and arced Saraden overhead. Durok raised his sword in a desperate block, but Saraden cut straight through it, cleaving down the center of Durok's face and body.

Durok fell among the pieces of his sword, his life's blood spilt on the floor of Maleistria's throne room. Kai stood over him. The room was silent, the crowd in awe.

Then Thei shouted, "Hail, Prince Kai!"

And the crowd followed, shouting in concert, "Hail, Prince Kai!" They were happy to live under the rule of such greatness.

59

The Ruins of Alha'na

Anna felt apprehensive as they made their approach on the eastern slope of the mountain. Faedyn stopped them at a large overhanging boulder. There was a small hollow underneath, and there they carefully stashed the bulk of their equipment, taking with them only their weapons, the clothes on their backs, and a small supply of water and rations.

The grasses of the coastal range gave way to a desolation of black rock, huge boulders, and ancient lava fields. This charred, burnt wasteland spread far and wide, all around the mountain's base. It was as barren and inhospitable as the surface of the moon, and the crumbly black masses of dried lava were a nightmare to navigate. Progress was slow. The sharp, uneven ground was painful to walk on, and Anna was accumulating innumerable scrapes and bruises on her legs.

Slowly the massive volcano got closer, towering above them, an imposing sight. The ground began to slope upward. Anna saw no sign of the old city. No ruins, no sign of human or elar, could be seen in the scorched vista before them.

"Everything is burnt up," Ken said. "Is that because of the dragon?"

"No," Faedyn said. "That's from the volcanic eruption in ancient times."

"How do you know the city will still be there as it was when you left it?" Anna said.

"Because Yagul rules over this mountain, and he does not like change."

It took them the better part of a day to cross the lava fields. When evening came, they stopped to rest among the bare rock of the mountainside.

The sun set, and a breeze blew in from the coast, chilling Anna to the bone. They huddled together that night for warmth, pulling their cloaks about them and staring up at the night sky, at the cold and distant stars, as if it held some promise of a future for them.

Anna struggled to find a comfortable position to sleep among the hard rocks, but the effort was futile. The mountain would not accommodate her, and she shivered through much of the night.

†

Dawn found them in a thick fog. It was impossible to see very far. The rocks at a distance seemed ghostlike, and beyond these apparitions was a uniform shroud of pale white.

Nevertheless, Faedyn led them onward. They traversed the mountainside, moving slowly toward the southwest slope.

As the morning wore on, the fog broke in places, offering temporary vistas of scree and talus. The fog banks drifted, great clouds that touched the mountain, and moved ponderously, like the ghosts of giants that once walked the earth.

They paused at the edge of a ridgeline. Haunted by cloud banks, the sight of a solitary ruin revealed itself. The walls of some ancient building, still standing, stood half buried in the mountainside.

"Look," Anna said, pointing.

As she spoke, the fog thinned to unveil the remains of Alha'na, elaran city of the Golden Age, vestiges of its magnificent buildings still standing in long-cooled lava fields. Through a momentary break in the clouds, the deep blue sea glimmered in the distance.

"Ah," Faedyn said. "I never thought I would see this sight again. It's exactly as I remember it. The bulk of the city is already buried between here and the sea. But what is left is full of splendor, even in ruin."

They walked in among the ruined buildings, which lay scattered oddly on the side of the mountain, half covered in mist. An eerie stillness pervaded amongst those ancient walls and toppled columns, all worn and pitted from the passage of so long a time.

"How did these ruins survive?" Ken said.

"By chance, I suppose," Faedyn said. "Most of the old cities were destroyed in the Great War. Those that were left were lost in the Dark Age, or sunk beneath the waves when the world changed. Perhaps these ruins were spared as a reminder of all that has been lost. Now Yagul's presence protects what's left of them."

They listened to Faedyn as they walked among the ruins. A kind of reverence came over them, as if walking through a graveyard. Faedyn led them upward, toward the facade of a great hall that stood half buried in the earth. The megalithic columns of that building bore witness to the glory of the Golden Age, and remained like sentinels, looking out over the edge of the world.

At last, they climbed up a wide, crumbling staircase and stood at the entrance to a great temple hall of Alha'na. Namh lit the Lamp of Lunara. Once they penetrated the dark depths of the mountain, it would be the only source of light they carried.

Walking under the portico that stood at the entrance of the ruined hall was an act of faith for Anna. It was a faith in everything her mother had ever told her—that we are all meant for a great purpose, and one has to follow their heart to find it. If we just did that, a single person could make a difference in the world. It was a faith in everything that happened and all the people she had met to bring her to this place. It was a faith in being a part of something far greater than herself. And finally, it was a faith in her companions, her friends, in Faedyn, Ken, and Namh, and in Arisu and Mouse back in Andurin.

The fog of morning had burned off by now, and the light of the early afternoon sun shone in the great temple doorway, illuminating some of the interior. The stone halls they had seen in Andurin and Torselend seemed now but poor imitations of what lay before them, both in beauty and in grandeur.

The vaults seemed impossibly high, and the rows of stone columns dwarfed them as they stood near the entrance. Four rows of these columns extended inward down the length of the hall, farther than any light would allow them to see. It seemed the darkness of an entire night could be contained within.

The Lamp of Lunara cast a cool light to see by as they moved farther back into the great hall. They huddled together in that light, and proceeded cautiously. The back of the hall was collapsed in ruin, its ancient walls and vaults crumbled into rubble that scattered across the once smooth floor. There was an enormous crack in the still-standing wall nearby.

Anna broke out in a full-body sweat. The heat rose as they continued, and steam vented from the rubble at the end of the hall.

Faedyn led them, through the crack in the wall, into a round, cavernous passage, an ancient lava tube that led deeper into the mountain. Anna wiped the sweat from her face, half crouched in the dim light. With each step, she felt more and more like an unwelcome guest. Perhaps it was her imagination, but she thought she could feel Yagul's presence in that place, an ancient vigilance, watching their every move.

Farther on, the tunnel intersected with the interiors of other small buildings that had been buried, as if the geometric lines of the city and the chaos of nature were at war with one another.

At last, they saw a dim orange light at what appeared to be an end to the tunnel.

"Quietly," Faedyn said.

The smell of sulfur and noxious fumes filled the air. Waves of fear and tension coursed through Anna's body as she willed herself to keep walking. The heat was almost unbearable, as if she were stepping toward the gates of hell itself.

60

The Seal is Broken

"Please … Prince Kai," Tyral said, bowing his head in a final effort. "These doors must never be opened."

They were gathered in the Crypt, beneath the ziggurat, in the huge room where the great stone doors shut off the lower levels, locked since the first emperors ruled Maleistria. The Great Seal of Malhak was carved into the stone where the two massive doors joined together.

Kai had brought an assembly of people to witness this historic moment. Thei and a contingent of his finest Black Guard soldiers stood ready. His advisors and the high-ranking nobles huddled nervously, unwilling to even whisper their fears. He caught a glimpse of Sulki, standing in the shadows, moving among the crowd. She had a subtle smile on her beautiful lips, and her eyes were filled with desire, with eager anticipation.

Tyral stood with four other arch-mages before the great stone doors. The four had already agreed to share their secret and open the Crypt. They had been convinced, in various ways, of the great destiny Kai preached, but Tyral had some lasting reservation.

Kai put his hand to Tyral's cheek. "Tyral," he said lovingly. "You have done such good work. And I want you to go on doing your work." Tyral shrank from the threat of Kai's loving hand. "Behind these doors, Tyral, is knowledge beyond your wildest dreams."

"My … my lord," Tyral said, begging to be heard. "The mages were forbidden to ever open these doors."

"And yet the secret of the seal that binds them lies within you. That alone is proof enough that it was meant to be broken." Kai turned to the crowd that had gathered. "Open the Crypt," he said for everyone to hear.

Tyral's face contorted in an almost physical pain. He bowed, shaking, his will broken before the crowd, and joined the other mages in front of the doors. The enormous Great Seal was high above them, far beyond reach. The seam where the two doors joined together was so perfect that even the thinnest of materials could not fit between them.

"There is another seal," Tyral said, "a secret seal that only the ancient lineages of the mages and their combined knowledge can reveal."

Then, in turn, each mage spoke part of an incantation in an ancient tongue from the Dark Age. It was strange to hear, the words of a language not spoken lightly, or often, and which took its toll on those who spoke it. Many in the crowd shrank from the the sounds they uttered.

At the end of this speech, a smaller seal appeared in the rock before of the five mages. Five circles were worked into the design of the smaller seal, equally spaced around the perimeter. The one at the top lay across the seam between the two doors.

The five mages huddled together around the seal. The vast hall echoed for a moment with the sound of the crowd shuffling backward, their conscious thoughts overwhelmed by fear of the unknown.

The four mages with Tyral each placed their left hand on one of the small circles on the seal, leaving only Tyral to place his hand on the top circle, across the seam between the two doors.

Tyral looked back at Kai for a moment. Kai's eyes were wide with anticipation. Then Tyral placed his left hand on the last circle, and the design of the seal began to glow with a strange red light. Tyral raised his right hand and, summoning his strength, cried out, *"Ahsh K'ahr Agnax'e!"*

The glow of the hidden seal ran up and down the entire seam between the two doors and spread across the Great Seal of Malhak, high above them. Then it faded quickly and disappeared.

A sound—a dreadful, deafening crack—broke the silence, as if the earth had split to its very core. The seam between the two colossal doors broke open from the very bottom to the very top.

All who looked on watched in fearful awe. Slowly, the doors began to open inward. A stale, howling wind blew out from within. It made a distant moaning sound and smelled of the ground and the deep.

The doors opened wide. All was darkness within, a yawning void that seemed to spread outward to devour them. The mages shuffled backward, trembling with the fear of what they had done. Tyral, at last, sank to his knees, unable to move further.

Kai put his hand momentarily on Tyral's shoulder, and then walked into the abysmal dark.

61

LAIR OF THE DRAGON

The tunnel opened up into a huge chamber, an ancient rotunda capped with a glittering dome, far overhead. Standing on the ruins of a balcony, they looked down to behold an awesome, terrifying sight.

Yagul slept upon heaps of ancient treasure, his huge leathery wings folded over the bulk of his black body like a shroud. His neck and tail wrapped close to his body, and his hideous head rested on piles of gold. Protruding from beneath his massive jaw, was the hilt of a sword.

"Rayaden," Anna whispered. There were other swords in that treasure-filled room, elegant weapons, all forged in the Golden Age, but she recognized Rayaden at once from her dream, and her eyes were drawn to it.

Faedyn held his finger silently to his lips. Namh dimmed the Lamp of Lunara. The far side of the chamber was crumbled in ruin, and the floor gave way to a deep crevasse from which a dim orange light illuminated the chamber. But dark shadows lurked everywhere, and where the walls had collapsed there were other tunnels that Yagul might use to come and go from his lair.

Ken drew an arrow from his quiver, but Faedyn held out a hand signaling him to stop. "All of you, hide here," he whispered. "And wait. Don't attack unless I signal."

Anna, Ken, and Namh hid themselves behind columns that encircled the rotunda, while Faedyn walked quietly down the stairs to the floor below, his sword sheathed, his hands empty.

"He's crazy," Ken whispered, as they watched from their hiding place. The dragon was so still he seemed almost dead, but even in that state, Yagul was terrifying. And to think that such a monster possessed an alien intelligence, impossible to fathom.

†

Faedyn descended the steps and stood before Yagul. He appeared asleep. Dragons could sleep for centuries, but you could never be sure. They can wake in an instant, as well as feign sleep better than any creature alive.

Faedyn took note of everything around him. A large shield lay on the floor nearby. The column behind him would make good cover. A tunnel to his left might be a good escape route. He caught a glimpse of Namh on the balcony above, waiting for him to take action.

Yagul did appear to be sleeping. Faedyn couldn't even tell if he was breathing. But the heat, the dim light, and the fumes in that room made it hard to be sure of anything. Rayaden was right there, within his grasp. For a moment he regretted ever leaving it here. Of course, the idea was to make it hard for anybody to take it, but now that it was him, he wished he had made it easier. He wondered if he could dislodge Rayaden from beneath Yagul without waking him. It was a dangerous gamble, but if they could get away while Yagul slept—

A deep booming voice suddenly broke the silence and filled the room. "I knew you were bad the last time we crossed paths, Miura, but I did not know you were a thief."

Yagul's eyes opened, but he didn't move at all. His jagged teeth stayed clamped together and his head remained resting on Rayaden. His voice emanated from a separate hidden organ the wyrmarath used for speech. It was disconcerting to hear such a seemingly disembodied voice.

Faedyn took a breath and stepped back. He bowed slightly. "I'm honored you remember me, Great Yagul." This was mostly politeness. Faedyn was not at all surprised that Yagul remembered, for his kind were famous for their acute memory. But there was also some strategy in Faedyn's words, for although dragons could be considered immoral, they were not without honor, and Yagul in particular was susceptible to flattery.

Yagul stirred, his muscles rippling, and shrugged the great shoulders of his wings. It was unsettling to see such a large creature move with total lack of effort. "Of course I remember you. You gave me my most treasured possession." Yagul moved his head, nudging Rayaden farther under him. Then he made a kind of laughing noise. "But you were a better man then than you are now, weren't you?"

Faedyn ignored Yagul's taunts. "If you remember so well, Yagul, then you will also remember the deal we struck."

"What deal?"

"That you would give up Rayaden if I came to retrieve it."

"I would never make such an agreement," Yagul said, his tail twitching.

"But you did. In your lust to possess it, you would have agreed to almost anything."

"Go home Miura … wherever your home is. Rayaden is mine."

"It belongs only to one who can wield it, Yagul, and such a person has been found. Now more than ever, its power is needed, for this world is in grave danger."

Yagul's whole body shook and moved. His angry head lifted. His voice bellowed. "What do I care for this world? Or for any world that is not my own."

Faedyn took another step back. "But you live here, and all your treasure is here. Please, for the good of the earth, give up Rayaden and we will leave you in peace."

Yagul opened his terrible mouth, yawn-like, and stretched his wings, filling the room with them and casting a dark shadow over Faedyn. "I see through you, elar," he said. "Who are you to speak of doing good? I see the hateful wars you have fought, the thousands you have killed." He laughed. "Yes, I see the poison in your heart, Miura. You should never have returned here."

Talking with Yagul, Faedyn had the strange sense he was communicating with only a small part of Yagul's mind, a part that deigned to interact with the beings of this world. Beyond was an alien consciousness, a vast intelligence that regarded him like an insect, but which was impossible to fathom or reason with.

Faedyn felt the part of Yagul that was willing to talk to him suddenly disappear. The dragon stood up, menacing, and his body swelled with breath.

At the last moment, Faedyn dove behind a nearby column. From Yagul's mouth came a torrent of fire. The surge of heat alone burned Faedyn's skin, and left him staggering in pain on the ground, half pressed against the column for cover. He prayed the others would wait for his signal. A dragon could only breathe so much fire before his glands were empty and would need time to refill. If he could deplete that fuel temporarily, they would have an opportunity to attack.

Faedyn reached for the broad shield that lay close by and drew Vanar from its sheath. He stepped into the open to face Yagul, the room around him smoking and charred, dark as night.

Yagul swelled again and unleashed another stream of fire from his mouth. Faedyn crouched behind the shield and braced himself. The fire struck like the blast of a burning wind, nearly knocking him over. The flames licked around the edges of the shield, burning his ankles, searing his sides. But the blast was somewhat less than the last one, and after a moment it flickered out.

"Now!" Faedyn yelled, casting aside the scorched shield.

†

Anna ran out from where they were hidden, her sword already drawn. "I have to get down there," she said, sprinting for the stairs.

"Anna, wait," Ken said, stepping out onto the open balcony and pulling his bow-string taught. He let fly his first arrow, which stuck into the creature's neck with absolutely no effect. The second missed entirely. He had to focus.

Faedyn had somehow charged past Yagul's head and thrust Vanar up into his underbelly, piercing a soft spot in the pit of his wing.

Yagul twisted his head around, his mouth wide, and snapped Faedyn up in his jaws. Yagul bit down, shook his head, then swung his powerful neck and threw Faedyn through the air. Faedyn's limp body flew twenty feet, impacted against the balcony on the far side of room, and fell to the ground with a deathly thump.

Anna screamed.

Yagul puffed up for a moment in angry, righteous triumph. Then Ken's third arrow pierced his left eye and stuck there. Yagul roared in pain.

Anna started toward Faedyn, but something stopped her. She saw Rayaden, lying there under Yagul amongst the piles of gold and silver.

At that moment, Namh raised her staff, shouting as she did, *"Lunara laina antar oen!"* The Lamp of Lunara lit up, casting out a white beam of light, bright as the essence of stars, blinding to behold. The beam of light fell on Yagul's head and he writhed and railed in pain, roaring with madness.

Anna saw her moment, dropped the sword she carried and ran, across piles of heaped gold, right under Yagul's belly. She grabbed Rayaden from amongst the ancient treasure, and scrambled on to the far side of the room.

Yagul stretched out the arm of his wing blindly and smashed it down on the balcony near Ken. Part of the balcony collapsed, crashing down to the floor below. Ken fell with it and disappeared into a pile of rubble and clouds of dust.

The Lamp of Lunara suddenly went out, and Namh collapsed to the floor in exhaustion.

Yagul staggered forward, disoriented. He half collapsed for a moment, his huge wings awkward and useless. Then he drew himself up and turned toward Anna.

Anna trembled to look at him, an arrow stuck in his eye and bleeding from a gaping wound in his side. She stumbled back a step, but behind her now was the deep crevasse, and far below, a river of molten magma. She could feel the furnace of heat on her back. Her knees shook as she neared the edge.

Yagul fixed one eye on her and snarled, filled with menacing, violent intent.

Anna took hold of Rayaden's hilt, and her breath returned to her. She inhaled deeply, and as she exhaled, she drew Rayaden from its sheath. The metal of its blade was a milky white, silent as a whisper, and light as a feather. She gripped the sword with both hands and held it out in front of her, the sword of her ancestors, the sword of her father. An inexplicable calm came over her, and she felt no fear in that terrible moment.

Yagul's body swelled. The power of his breath had returned to him. His mouth opened, and he unleashed a blast of fire, a cascade of flames that poured out of him.

Anna stood fast, and the flames bent away from Rayaden's white blade. A storm of fire roared all around her, and yet that blaze of malice could not touch her. The flames were foiled, as if by an invisible shield, and she remained unharmed in the midst of that conflagration.

Then the fire went out. Yagul's breath was spent again, and he roared with rage when he saw Anna still standing. The mighty dragon stepped forward, closing the distance.

Anna's heels were backed up to the edge of the crevasse, but she did not falter. Yagul lunged at her, his mouth open to snap her up in his deadly jaws.

Anna saw the whole situation with perfect clarity. She stepped aside as Yagul's jaws snapped shut, and arced the blade of Rayaden down. The edge cut effortlessly, and the sword went clean through the dragon's neck.

Yagul's head dropped into the crevasse, and his body, mindless, lumbered forward and fell in after it. Moments later, head and body tumbled into the bubbling magma, far below.

62

PAST AND FUTURE

Anna returned Rayaden to its sheath. The room seemed silent again, and dark, as dust from the battle settled.

Namh had recovered enough to stand, and she descended from the balcony to look for Ken in the rubble below. He must have been knocked unconscious when he fell. Namh moved some rocks to free him. Although he was battered, dazed, and confused, Namh managed to get him to his feet.

But where was Faedyn? Anna suddenly remembered, and saw him still lying on the floor where Yagul had thrown him. She ran to him and knelt at his side. His eyes were closed and his body was still, covered in blood from where Yagul's teeth had torn into his flesh.

"Faedyn?" Anna said. "Faedyn?" She touched his shoulder, and put her head to his bloody chest. His body moved ever so slightly. "Faedyn?"

Faedyn's eyes opened, cloudy and unfocused.

"Faedyn. It's Anna."

Faedyn smiled slightly, but his face contorted in a spasm of pain.

"You're going to be all right," Anna said. "We're going to get you out of here."

Faedyn turned his head to look up at Anna. His eyes cleared for a moment. Anna's chest convulsed with fear and agony, for in Faedyn's eyes she saw a familiar look, a look of resignation, a look of acceptance, a look of death. *I'm not going anywhere*, he seemed to say. *I'm going to die here.* He coughed. Blood trickled from the corner of his mouth. His skin was sweaty and pale.

Anna wept, for the thought of losing Faedyn now seemed unbearable. And those tears carried with them the pain and grief that the death of her mom had left her with, and the sadness that all such loss leaves with the living. She cried for that boy from BS-Click and for Yagul too. She couldn't help herself. She just couldn't bear any more death.

"You're going to be all right," she said through her tears. "You're going to be fine." But she didn't believe it. There was no way she could look at Faedyn, at the wreck that was left of his body, and believe it.

"Anna," Faedyn said, managing to quiet her as he always did. He moved his hand to touch her knee. "Anna, look at me."

Anna looked at Faedyn. She took his hand in hers, that hand that was so strong, and felt the weakness of his grip.

"It's okay, Anna. Everything is going to be fine. Do you hear me?"

Anna nodded her head slowly, sniffling. "Yes," she said.

"Do you have Rayaden?" Faedyn said.

Anna wiped tears from her face. "Yes."

"Show it to me."

Anna held up Rayaden so he could see, but he looked past the ancient sword, keeping his eyes fixed on Anna's face. "Good," he said.

His face briefly contorted again in pain. His breathing was so slow now, and he struggled to speak. "Anna ... there is always hope. Remember that." His eyes glazed over, and he seemed to stare past her, into a great distance. "At last, I have found peace," he said. "At last … I'm going home." Then he breathed his last breath, and died.

Anna remained, kneeling at Faedyn's side, his hand still in hers. Namh put her hand on one of Anna's shoulders. Ken put his hand on the other. For a moment, they all looked down in silence at Faedyn's lifeless body.

The earth started to shake while they stood there, the ground trembling beneath them.

"We must go," Namh said.

The ground shook again, and small bits of the balcony and ceiling crumbled off and fell to the ground around them. "What's happening?" Ken said.

"The volcano is waking up," Namh said. "For ages, Yagul's presence held the forces of nature in check here, but his time is over. Nothing can hold back the tides of the earth any longer."

There was another tremor, and a single, large chunk of the dome came crashing down in the center of the room.

"We must leave now while we have the chance," Namh said.

"What about Faedyn?" Anna said.

"His body must remain here," Namh said.

Anna and Ken looked at Faedyn's body.

"There is no better resting place for him," Namh said, "than here in the halls of our forefathers."

They said their goodbyes to the age-old warrior. He had become a friend, a mentor, and a hero in their eyes. With his passing, the last threads of a bygone era had come to an end. An unfound future lay before them.

The earth shook again, and the air filled with a roaring sound, a sound of doom that drowned all their fleeting thoughts. Bits of the balcony and high domed ceiling crumbled and fell around them. The magma deep in the crevasse began to bubble up, releasing clouds of noxious gas.

"We must go now!" Namh yelled above the raucous din of an angry earth. They fled from that place, over unstable ground, through shifting passageways and sulfurous clouds of steam and smoke, running for their lives as the ruins of the city and its ancient treasure were buried with Faedyn behind them.

When they reached the surface, they continued down the mountain and out onto the dried lava fields as quickly as they could. They carried on in silence. All through the night they made their way across the sharp, treacherous fields of ancient rock, while in the dark behind them the bright orange of fresh lava began to flow from vents on the mountainside.

At dawn they stood on the hills beyond and looked back. A large plume of smoke and steam poured out of the mountain.

"What now?" Ken said.

"We must return to Andurin," Namh said. "The great houses must be convinced to join together against the threat of war. And we must hope this ancient sword, Rayaden, can somehow save us from destruction."

Suddenly, as they watched, the top of the mountain exploded and blew off toward the sea. Massive heaps of rock and lava were cast out in the blast, and a great cloud of smoke and ash poured upward. A deafening sound overtook them, a sound that shook the earth to its core and a shockwave that nearly knocked them to the ground.

As the noise faded to a constant, distant roar, Anna and Ken joined hands, and they all stood there for a long while. Silent and awestruck, they watched the eruption, a sight so beautiful and terrifying that it seemed to echo both the creation and the destruction of the world. The beginning and the end passed before them.

Anna held Rayaden at her side. How could it save them? How could she wield such a power? How could she bear such a huge responsibility? The last remains of the elar's Golden Age were swept away, blown apart, buried by the earth, or melted down and cast into the sea. Would the cities of Midgard meet the same fate? Could humanity, in the end, just die out?

There was still so much uncertainty, but something had awakened inside her. She felt a new strength and a nascent awareness take hold of her. It felt as if she stood at the edge of a vast new world, and was not afraid.

Anna had a sense she had seen all this before, the three of them, standing on the hillside, watching Yagul's mountain erupt in the distance. Somehow, even in the wake of Faedyn's death, she had finally found hope. She had finally found the path she was meant to follow.

About the Author

Matthew Lowes is the author of numerous stories, books, and games. His post-apocalyptic novella, *The End of All Things*, was published by ShadowSpinners Press, and his science-fiction horror story, *A Darkquick Sky*, was featured in the ShadowSpinners Anthology. He has written a series of spiritual non-fiction books, a beginner-to-intermediate chess book, and a number of games, including the *Dungeon Solitaire* fantasy tarot card game. The *Three Earths* trilogy is his first major work of fantasy fiction.

Three
Earths:
Book
2

Dark Mage of
Midgard

Matthew Lowes

Thank you for reading!

The next book in
The Three Earths Trilogy is
Dark Mage of Midgard

Coming in 2026
from
Empty Press

matthewlowes.com